P9-BII-684

MIDDLE AGES AND RENAISSANCE

CULTURAL EVENTS ARTISTS AND WRITERS	DATES	POLITICAL WORLD EVENTS
	500	Charlemagne crowned Emperor (800)
	1000	Norman invasion of England (1066)
	1100	First Crusade (1096–1099)
Gothic cathedrals begun (St. Denis, Paris, 1144) (Chartres, 1145)	1150	
	1200	Magna Carta signed by King John (1215)
	1250	Marco Polo leaves for Cathay (1271)
Dante's *Divine Comedy* (1307)	1300	Hundred Years' War begins (1337)
Chaucer's *Canterbury Tales* (1386)	1350	
	1400	Battle of Agincourt (1415)
Gutenburg Bible (1456)	1450	Fall of Constantinople (1453)
Michelangelo (1475–1564)		Columbus discovers America (1492)
Raphael (1483–1520)		Henry VIII King of England (1509)
St. Peter's begun in Rome (1506)	1500	Martin Luther's 95 theses (1517)
		Council of Trent (1545–1563)
	1550	Spanish Armada defeated (1588)

BAROQUE

CULTURAL EVENTS ARTISTS AND WRITERS	DATES	POLITICAL WORLD EVENTS
El Greco (1541–1614)	1600	Jamestown settled (1607)
William Shakespeare (1564–1616)		Thirty Years' War begins (1618)
Cervantes, part I of *Don Quixote* (1605)		Mayflower Compact (1620)
Rembrandt van Rijn (1606–1669)		Louis XIV King of France (1643)
Taj Mahal begun (1630)		
Giovanni Lorenzo Bernini's *St. Theresa in Ecstasy* (1644)		
Samuel Pepys' *Diary* (1660)	1650	Restoration of Charles II in England (1660)
John Milton's *Paradise Lost* (1667)		Peter the Great, Czar of Russia (1682)
Sir Christopher Wren begins St. Paul's Cathedral (1675)		Salem witchcraft trials (1692)
Sir Isaac Newton's *Principia Mathematica* (1687)		
Pompeii rediscovered (1748)	1700	War of the Spanish Succession begins (1702)
Jonathan Swift's *Gulliver's Travels* (1726)		Louis XV King of France (1715)
		Age of Enlightened Despots (1740–1796)

CLASSICAL

CULTURAL EVENTS ARTISTS AND WRITERS	DATES	POLITICAL WORLD EVENTS
Voltaire's *Candide* (1759)	1750	Seven Years' War (in America, French and Indian War) begins (1756)
Immanuel Kant's *Critique of Pure Reason* (1781)		
Thomas Malthus's *Essay on Population* (1798)		Beginnings of the factory system and Industrial Revolution (ca. 1770)
		American Declaration of Independence (1776)
		French Revolution begins (1789)
Goethe's *Faust*, Part I (1808)	1800	Louisiana Purchase (1803)
Jane Austen's *Pride and Prejudice* (1813)		Battle of Waterloo (1815)

ROMANTIC

CULTURAL EVENTS ARTISTS AND WRITERS	DATES	POLITICAL WORLD EVENTS
Goya's *Witches' Sabbath* (1815)		Monroe Doctrine (1823)
Shelley's *Prometheus Unbound* (1820)	1825	Erie Canal opened (1825)
Victor Hugo's *Hernani* (1830)		July Revolution in France (1830)
Alexander Dumas' *Count of Monte Cristo* (1845)		Queen Victoria's reign begins (1837)
Karl Marx's *Communist Manifesto* (1848)		California Gold Rush (1848)

Music Appreciation

Second Edition

Music Appreciation

Second Edition

Robert Hickok

*Brooklyn College
of the City University of New York*

 Addison-Wesley Publishing Company, Inc.

Reading, Massachusetts · Menlo Park, California · London · Amsterdam · Don Mills, Ontario · Sydney

Cover photograph: the Ames-Totenberg Stradivarius, courtesy of J. Bradley Taylor, Inc., Boston. One of 12 crafted in 1734 by Antonio Stradivari at the age of 90.

Title page photograph: Ludovisi Triptych, 460 B.C., Thermes Museum, Rome.

Second printing, July 1975

Copyright © 1975, 1971 by Addison-Wesley Publishing Company, Inc. Philippines copyright 1975, 1971 by Addison-Wesley Publishing Company, Inc.

All rights reserved. No part of this publication may be reproduced, stored in a retrieval system, or transmitted, in any form or by any means, electronic, mechanical, photocopying, recording, or otherwise, without the prior written permission of the publisher. Printed in the United States of America. Published simultaneously in Canada. Library of Congress Catalog Card No. 74–20492.

ISBN 0-201-02925-1
ABCDEFGHIJ-RN-798765

For Paul and Laura

Preface

Music Appreciation is designed for introductory music courses at the college level. The book has been structured to be used in either a one-semester course or a course covering the entire academic year.

Part I deals with the materials of music on successively higher levels of consideration. Beginning with the characteristics of the individual musical sound, the book progresses through a discussion of how tones are combined to create musical elements—such as harmony and melody—and culminates in an examination of the materials on the still higher level of musical texture and form. This section concludes with a survey of individual instruments, including the voice, and explores combinations of instruments from the smallest to the largest, the symphony orchestra.

Using the material of Part I as a foundation, Parts II through VIII examine in chronological order the various stylistic periods, beginning with music before 1600 and proceeding through the Baroque period, the Classical period, the Romantic era, the nineteenth century, and ending with the music of our own time. A special chapter is devoted to music in the United States and includes jazz and popular music.

Each part begins with a chapter on the arts, philosophy, and politics of the period under consideration. Subsequent chapters deal with the general stylistic characteristics of the music of the period, with specific works and biographical material on the most important composers. Each chapter is followed by a summary and a list of suggested supplementary listenings. A general reading list as well as a comprehensive glossary are given at the back of the book.

A major emphasis of the book is on listening. Music examples represent both the best work of each composer and specific forms or styles. For example, Bach's Fugue in G Minor was selected to illustrate fugal procedure, Handel's *Messiah* illustrates the oratorio, Mozart's Symphony No. 40 in G Minor is an example of the Classical symphony, and Haydn's

Nelson Mass illustrates the application of classical forms to choral music. Chamber music, orchestral literature, and choral music are all well represented.

Music notation is used as an aid in the listening process. It is not expected that most students will be able to "read" as a musician reads, but that he will "follow" it, using the notation to keep his place in the flow of music and matching the music with the written description.

The detailed descriptions themselves are intended as guides in the listening process. Their usefulness is predicated on their combination with the listening experience as well as guidance, explanation, and demonstration on the part of the instructor. Divorced from the listening experience, such descriptions have little if any value. But when the analysis of a significant piece of music is combined with guided listening, the connection between the musical experience and the awareness of the principles upon which the music is based is meaningful and enjoyable for the student on both the intellectual and emotional levels.

This new edition of the book includes expanded coverage of such material as nationalism, romantic opera, impressionism, and jazz and rock. A new feature of the book is a chapter on ethnic music, which has been added to Part I. A new introductory section has been provided, and books on ethnic music, jazz, and rock have been added to the Suggested Reading list.

The content of the book provides comprehensive coverage of the subject matter. At the same time, the book's organization affords considerable flexibility for the instructor in his choice of materials. The book can be used *selectively* by the instructor, who is free to choose the kind of material that suits his specific objectives and the length of time at his disposal. Supplementary materials include a student workbook and record package.

This book is the result of almost twenty years of experience teaching introductory courses on the campus of a large college. During those years I have learned that most students enjoy learning about something their instructor thinks is vital and to which he is dedicated. It is for such students and such instructors that this book is written.

I have been assisted by many people in the preparation of the book. I am grateful to John Hochmann for his contribution to the introductory chapters for Parts II through VIII. The assistance of Bruce Macomber and Bonney McDowell in helping to prepare the material was invaluable.

New York
January 1975

R. H.

Contents

Drawing by Bob Essman

part I   Fundamentals

Throughout history, philosophers, scientists, novelists, and poets have grappled with the mystery of music's meaning. Five hundred and fifty years before the birth of Christ, the Greek philosopher Pythagoras concluded that music must be regarded as one facet of the universal harmony that also finds expression in arithmetic and astronomy. Centuries

Musical Sound

later, Johannes Kepler, a German astronomer, correlated the musical intervals with the movements of the planets and with astrology. Music, in Schopenhauer's philosophy, existed as the purest incarnation of "absolute will." Perhaps, as one scholar has said, it is the infinite quality of music that both tempts and simultaneously defies definition.

In current dictionaries, music is usually defined without reference to nonmusical, philosophical constructs. We no longer find music described as the expression of an innately harmonious universe or as a reflection of divine order. In place of these older, more poetic definitions, contemporary music theorists generally describe music as sound organized in time or as time defined by the sound that fills it.

The Talmud says that "if you want to understand the invisible, look carefully at the visible." Musicologists attempt to "look carefully" by studying the elements of music and the ways in which music is perceived.

To discuss a particular composition, it is necessary first to have some familiarity with the special vocabulary of music. This vocabulary is, in fact, a shortcut and convenience for anyone involved with composition, performance, or informed listening. It allows musicians simply to refer to "the tonic" rather than stumble over a description such as "the key note in which most of the piece is written." Similarly, the term *appoggiatura* is far easier to talk about than an imprecise reference such as "the note that seems to lean so heavily on the one following."

One common source of resistance to any sort of musical analysis is the mistaken fear that a composition reduced to its formal structural elements will somehow be divested of its unique mystery. Actually, the reverse is true. The more one knows about a composition, the easier it is to become totally immersed in the musical experience. It is unfamiliarity, not understanding, that raises a barrier to complete enjoyment.

Another nearly universal impediment to full musical participation results, ironically enough, from the sheer overabundance of sound all around us. We dress in the morning to the latest popular tunes, drive to work while songs pour from the car radio, then enter an office building piped with Muzak intended to soothe our frayed nerves. Yet, as the sounds swirl about, we do not ever truly hear them. Our inattention becomes a habit.

We can learn to listen more attentively only as we gain the tools of musical awareness. The danger is not that knowledge will somehow detract from our innate delight in sound. It is far more likely that a musical spirit, nourished with some degree of technical knowledge, will only be that much closer to Friedrich Nietzsche's evaluation that "without music, life would be a mistake."

The production of sound requires the vibration of a *sounding body*. A sounding body may be the string on a violin, the column of air in a wind instrument, or the skin over the head of a drum. When the sounding body is displaced from its original position, it tends to return to normal. Vibrations occur that set the surrounding air in motion and produce sound.

All sounds, however, are not *musical*. Many, such as the whistling of wind through the trees or the screeching of rubber tires against the pavement, are simply noises. Unlike these, the sounds of music are not random, but are highly organized. They are characterized by (1) pitch, (2) duration, (3) intensity, and (4) color, or timbre.

Pitch

If we were to pluck one of the strings on a violin, we would see it quiver, then gradually return to rest. If we could watch it in slow motion, we would observe a regular pattern of evenly timed *vibrations*. The vibrations can be pictured as follows, where *A* and *B* are fixed ends of the string and *C* is the point at which it is plucked:

Example 1.1

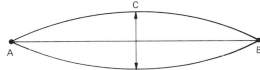

The frequency, or number of vibrations per second, determines the *pitch*, or highness or lowness of the sound or tone produced. Any particular pitch will have a steady, constant frequency. A faster frequency will produce a higher pitch; a slower frequency, a lower pitch.

The frequency of vibrations can be increased by decreasing the length of the sounding body. If the distance between *A* and *B* on the violin string in Example 1.1 is shortened while the same degree of tension is maintained, the vibrations will occur more rapidly and the sound will have a higher pitch. The relationship of size to sound can be seen among the instruments of the orchestra. Many instruments, such as the violin and the cello, look very much alike except for their size. Because its sounding body is longer, the cello emits a lower sound than the violin.

Pitch Notation

Throughout history man has devised a number of methods of writing, or *notating*, music. The Greeks notated music by means of letters, and the Chinese derived pitch symbols from literary script. But regardless of these early beginnings, our modern system of notation did not reach its present form until the seventeenth century. Musical notation as we know it today is not totally precise, but it does have the advantage of being serviceable.

The pitch of a sound is indicated by the position of a symbol (♩) called a *note* on a graphlike structure called a *staff*, consisting of five lines and four spaces.

Example 1.2

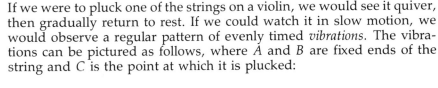

The nine lines and spaces of the staff represent specific notes and are named for the first seven letters of the alphabet: A, B, C, D, E, F, G. The location of each note is determined by a *clef sign* at the beginning of the staff. The *G, or treble, clef* (𝄞), and the *F, or bass, clef* (𝄢) are the most commonly used in our notation system, but are by no means the only ones available.

The G clef, which locates the note G, is placed around the second line of the staff. Therefore, counting up and down from G, the other lines and spaces of the staff are designated as follows:

Example 1.3

The F clef, which locates the note F, is placed around the fourth line of the staff. Therefore, the notes of the F clef are as follows:

Example 1.4

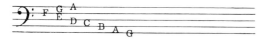

When a pitch is too high or too low to be notated on the lines or spaces of the staff, ledger lines are added above or below the staff. The notes A and C above the treble staff would be shown in this manner:

Example 1.5

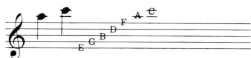

The treble and bass staffs meet at a point called middle c. This note, which is equally distant from each staff, is written by adding a single ledger line to either staff:

Example 1.6

When used in combination, the treble and bass clefs are capable of indicating a wide range of pitches.

Example 1.7

Together they are used for music written for the piano, for example. Ordinarily, the notes written in the bass clef are played by the left hand and the notes in the treble clef by the right. In instrumental music the treble clef is used for the violin, the flute, and other instruments that play in the higher ranges. Music for instruments that sound in the lower ranges, such as the tuba or double bass, is written in the bass clef.

However, some instruments are neither high nor low in range, but somewhere in between. For these middle-ranged instruments, a third clef is sometimes used. Known as the *C clef* (), it is located in various positions on the staff to designate middle c. Prior to 1750 it was used in as many as five different positions. Today, however, it is generally placed either on the third line, in which case it is called the *alto clef*, or on the fourth line, in which case it is called the *tenor clef*.

Example 1.8

The alto clef is used for the viola, and the tenor clef is often used for the cello and bassoon.

The reason for changing clefs is to avoid the use of ledger lines. For example, the following passage would require ledger lines from either the treble or bass clefs, but it can be completely contained on the lines of the alto clef:

Example 1.9

Pitch Names

Because the first seven letters of the alphabet are used to designate more than seven notes, each letter refers to more than one note. The letter C may refer to any one of seven notes on the piano keyboard. It is therefore often useful to employ a lettering system that distinguishes each note from the others. The following example shows the most common way of representing each note:

Example 1.10

Notice that middle c is written with a small c. The C above it is written as c^1, and the one below it as capital C_1. If we were to go to the next higher C in the treble staff, we would represent it as c^2, and the C above that as c^3. The C below middle c in the bass staff would be written C_1 and the next lower would be C_2. Thus the system could be extended to designate any note.

Intervals

The pitch relationship between any two notes is called an *interval*. The concept of a musical interval can best be understood in terms of the *octave.* Named for the Latin *octo,* meaning "eight," *octave* designates the interval between one note and the next higher or lower note having the same letter. Thus the distance from c to c^1 is an octave. Other intervals are also expressed numerically: the interval of a third, a fifth, etc.

The octave is the basic unit for measuring segments of musical space. Each note's octave sounds like a duplication of the original, except at a higher or lower pitch. This phenomenon, *octave quality,* occurs because the octave above any given note has exactly twice the frequency of that note. The note a^1, for example, has a frequency of 440 vibrations per second. Its octave has a frequency of 880 vibrations per second.

The piano keyboard encompasses seven octaves plus two additional notes. In each octave there are eight white keys and five black keys, as seen in this diagram of the octave above middle c:

Example 1.11

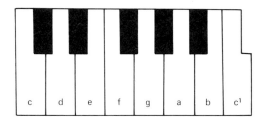

Notice that many of the white keys have black keys between them. When this is true, as in the case of the two white keys c and d, the interval between them is a *whole tone,* or *whole step.* The interval between c and the black key directly to its right is half as great and is called a *semitone,* or *half step.* White notes that have no black key between them, such as b and c^1, are also separated by a half step, the same interval that divides adjoining white and black keys. An octave, therefore, comprises twelve half-step intervals. In our Western music the half step is the smallest interval between two notes.

Accidentals

The lines and spaces of the staff represent the tones produced by the white keys of the keyboard. To indicate tones produced by the black keys, the notes on the staff are preceded by signs called *accidentals.* An accidental preceding a note indicates that the tone represented by that note should be raised or lowered in pitch to a tone produced by a black key. These accidental signs are the sharp (♯), which indicates that a pitch is to be *raised* by a half step; the flat (♭), which indicates that a pitch is to be *lowered* by a half step; and the natural (♮), which restores a note to its original, unaltered pitch. The note g, for example, is raised, restored, and lowered in the following manner:

Example 1.12

Enharmonics

On the keyboard diagram we saw that the notes c and d share a common black key. When the note for this black key is written as a half step higher than c it is called c-sharp; when it is written as a half step lower than d it is called d-flat. The sound of the black key is, of course, the same, whether it is called c-sharp or d-flat. When two tones have the same sound but can be written in different ways, they are said to be *enharmonic equivalents*.

Example 1.13

The Chromatic Scale

We have seen that on the keyboard each octave is divided into twelve tones (seven white and five black keys). These twelve tones, when sounded in consecutive order, make up the *chromatic scale*.

Example 1.14

Almost infinite variety is possible in the ways in which these twelve tones may be combined.

Major and Minor Scales

From the pitches available in the chromatic scale it is possible, by selection, to create other scales (a scale being simply an arrangement of tones in an order of ascending, or descending, pitches). If we were to play only the white keys of an octave on the keyboard, beginning with middle c, we would sound the *major diatonic scale*. Here we have divided the octave into a combination of whole and half steps.

Example 1.15

Notice that the half steps fall between the third and fourth and between the seventh and eighth tones of the scale. By maintaining this pattern of whole and half steps, the major diatonic scale can be *transposed* to any pitch. Beginning on the note d, for example, it appears as follows:

Example 1.16

In this case, the half-step intervals are maintained by raising the third and seventh steps.

The *major* scale can begin on any of the twelve tones of the chromatic scale. But regardless of the starting point, it follows the same arrangement of whole and half steps.

The *minor* scale has its own structure and character. The third tone (here a half step rather than a whole step above the second) imparts the distinctive minor quality. The upper part of the scale assumes one of *several* forms, depending upon the musical context. Often there is a half step between tones five and six and whole steps between tones six, seven, and eight. Frequently the seventh tone is raised to the line a half step below the eighth, in which case there is a one-and-a-half-step interval between tones six and seven.

Example 1.17

Duration

The duration of a tone refers to the length of time its vibrations are maintained or permitted to continue. Thus tones are not only high and low, but also long and short. Duration is a relative value. A tone is perceived as being long only when it is heard in a context of tones shorter than itself.

Duration Notation

A system of notation for indicating pitch was arrived at much earlier than a system for indicating duration. And it is in the area of duration that our notational system—accurate as it is—reveals some of its greatest imperfections. Our present-day notation is the result of centuries of experimentation, and changes are still being made to accommodate the demands of some modern music.

The length of time a composer intends a tone to sound is indicated by the shape and color of the written note and by additional stems, flags, dots, and ties attached to the notes. Usually the basic value against which all other values are measured is the whole note. Example 1.18 shows several ways the whole note can be subdivided.

Example 1.18

whole   half   quarter   eighth   sixteenth

Further subdivisions are possible, such as thirty-second (♪) and sixty-fourth (♪) notes, and other modifications can be made. Among the notes shown in Example 1.18, the eighth note represents half the value of the quarter note. But there is no note representing a third of its value. For this purpose the symbol for the eighth note is used, but is assigned a different value. Known as the *triplet,* it divides the quarter note into three equal parts (Ex. 1.19).

Example 1.19

Example 1.20

In the same way, a sixteenth note can be modified to divide the quarter note into five equal parts (Ex. 1.20).

Notes may be lengthened by the use of a *tie,* which combines the values of two notes, or a *dot,* which prolongs the value of a note by half of its original value (Ex. 1.21).

Example 1.21

Rests

No less important than musical sound is musical *silence.* Symbols for silences, called *rests,* have time values equivalent to those for musical sounds.

Example 1.22

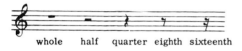

whole   half   quarter   eighth   sixteenth

Rests, like notes, may be used in combination—the larger preceding the smaller—or two of equal duration may take the place of one of the next higher value.

Intensity

All musical sounds have intensity—the quality of being relatively loud or soft. Between these two extremes many degrees of volume are possible. The intensity of a tone depends on the force with which its vibrations are produced and has no bearing on the pitch of a tone. The rate of vibrations for the note c, for example, remains constant no matter how loudly the note is played.

Another term for the intensity, or volume, of a musical sound is *dynamic level.* The terms and symbols used to express the possible gradations in dynamic level are called *dynamics.*

Intensity Notation

Of all the symbols of notation, those indicating dynamics are the least precise. As composers became less directly involved in supervising performances of their works, a system of notating intensity became a prime necessity in order for performers to understand the composers' intentions. Dynamic indications, like most musical terms, are traditionally expressed in Italian.

pianissimo	(pp)	Very soft
piano	(p)	Soft
mezzo piano	(mp)	Moderately soft
mezzo forte	(mf)	Moderately loud
forte	(f)	Loud
fortissimo	(ff)	Very loud

To express a gradual change from one dynamic level to another the following signs and terms are used.

crescendo	$<$	Becoming louder
decrescendo or diminuendo	$>$	Becoming softer
crescendo and decrescendo	$< \quad >$	Becoming louder and softer

The composer can prescribe only in the most approximate way the dynamic level he desires. There is no objective standard on which to calculate dynamics. Dynamic level and its graduations are a matter of interpretation and context. The execution of a specific dynamic is entirely in the hands of the player and is influenced by his judgment, his taste, and the degree of control he has over his instrument.

Color

A clarinet has a musical quality all its own; a violin sounds entirely different. One person's voice can easily be distinguished from another's, even though each sings the same notes. This quality, known as *tone color,* or *timbre* (pronounced tam′br), is determined by the nature of the sounding body of a particular voice or instrument. Thus, a reed, a string, or a vocal cord will each give the same pitch a different tone color.

Summary

In the preceding pages we have described the qualities of musical sound—those properties that distinguish musical sounds from simple random noises. Musical sounds have pitch, the quality of being high or low; they exist in durations of varying lengths; they can be produced at varying levels of intensity, or volume; and, depending on the manner in which they are produced, they are imbued with distinctive tone colors. In varying degrees of precision the pitch, duration, and intensity of musical sound can be expressed in a written system of notation.

Thus far we have been dealing with the raw material of music, not music itself. Individual sounds achieve musical significance only when one tone relates to another and groups of tones relate to other groups, organized in the time flow they create.

chapter 2

In Chapter 1 we considered sounds as individual, isolated elements. This chapter deals with the various kinds of relationships among musical sounds and the resulting musical elements known as melody, rhythm, harmony, and tonality.

Musical Relationships

Melodic Relationships

The most obvious and immediate relationship perceived by the listener occurs among pitches that sound one after another. This linear relationship of successive pitches is called a *melodic line*, or *melody*. Melody gives music a sense of movement up and down through space as it moves forward in time. Different melodies follow different patterns of movement. For example, even though it has some downward movement, the following melodic line gives the general impression of moving upward:

Example 2.1

On the other hand, a melody can convey a sense of downward movement:

Example 2.2

The following melody seems anchored in the middle. Its movement is evenly distributed around a melodic center:

Example 2.3

Melodic movement can be smooth and even, as the preceding examples show. It can also be jerky and angular, leaping over a wide span of musical space:

Example 2.4

13

When we listen to music, we are usually drawn first to its melodic content—the aspect of the flow of sound and time that we tend to follow with the greatest interest and ease. And, in general, it is the melodic qualities that linger with us. When we think of a piece of music, we tend to recall the melody or melodies that represent and symbolize for us the piece.

In a long work of music some melodies assume a greater importance than others. Melodies that contain central musical ideas are called *themes.* In the course of a musical composition important themes may be stated and restated in many different forms.

Any melody that we encounter is a fusion of two inseparable, interacting relationships—*pitch* and *duration.* Consider the following melody, for example:

Example 2.5

If we disregard duration and extract the purely melodic (pitch) content for the same melody, the result is as follows:

Example 2.6

In terms of pitch, the melody begins with a steady upward movement, followed by sudden downward and upward leaps (7, 8, 9). After a smooth descent (9 to 12), a peak is reached (13). The melody ends on a tone more or less in the middle of its range (15).

By eliminating the element of pitch from the melody, we can extract its durational content:

Example 2.7

These two components of the melody—its directional pitch line through space and its durational pattern in time—together create another element that constitutes a higher level of musical organization. We call it *rhythm.*

Rhythmic Relationships

When a person hears a melody, his mind instinctively organizes its sounds in terms of *time,* making it possible for him to comprehend the flow of sound. First, from among the initial tones of the melody, his mind selects a length of time that he uses as a basic measuring stick. This basic unit is referred to as the *beat.*

The lengths of individual tones in the melody are measured as equivalents, multiples, or divisions of the beat. For instance, in Example 2.5 the melody begins with a number of tones whose lengths are expressed in rhythmic notation as ♪, ♩, ♩., ♩, and ♩.. If this melody is played at a moderate speed, the length of time the mind will select as the basic unit is expressed by ♩. This being the case, the mind will measure ♪ as half a beat, ♩. as a beat and a half, ♩ as two beats, and ♩. as three beats.

Once this basic yardstick has been firmly established and begins to operate as the basis of expectation in his mind, the listener becomes accustomed to the regular flow of even, equal beats. He expects it to continue as the length by which he will be able to measure and comprehend all other individual lengths.

Of coures, the beat need not always be regular. It can be accelerated or slowed down. If the change is *gradual,* the listener can adjust his expectation. But, any radical or abrupt departure will result in confusion and loss of stability on the part of the listener. His expectation will be upset until he can select and adjust to a new beat.

Rhythmic Clusters

At virtually the same time that the listener selects the beat as the basic level of expectation, he also perceives the relationships of sound on a more complex level. He hears the music not only as a constant flow of equal beats, but also in *groups* of two or more beats.

When a person hears a melody, his mind instinctively organizes its elements in time and space. Among the individual tones in the melody, some appear more pronounced than others. Such tones are said to possess *aural prominence.* A tone may be aurally prominent in any of several ways. Long tones are generally more prominent than short ones. In the following example the second, fifth, and eighth notes stand out more than the others because of their longer duration.

Example 2.8

Example 2.9

A tone that deviates markedly in pitch, whether it is higher or lower than the others around it, will be perceived as being more important.

Example 2.10

A tone that is *accented,* or played at a greater volume than the tones immediately before or after it, will also attract greater attention.

The mind tends to perceive the melodic flow as a series of points of aural prominence. While beats are used to measure individual sounds, points of aural prominence are used to build larger units of time. Each unit begins with a tone of aural prominenace and ends immediately before the next tone of aural prominence, which, in turn, begins a new unit. These larger units are called *rhythmic clusters.* The smallest cluster consists of two beats. Usually the largest cluster the mind will accept as a simple, self-contained unit consists of five beats.

Most of the music we hear in the standard concert repertoire is generally based on regular rhythmic groupings. But not all music is characterized by a succession of equal groups of beats. Much pre-Baroque and modern music, for example, is based on shifting, diverse rhythmic grouping.

If we return to the melody in Example 2.5, we observe that it contains six rhythmic clusters of *varying* numbers of beats. A cluster of three beats is followed by a cluster of four, which in turn is followed by a cluster of three beats, and so on:

Example 2.11

Thus, the rhythmic structure of the melody is diverse (its rhythmic clusters are irregular in length). It is possible, however, to alter this melody so that the clusters will be equal to one another in length. To do this we retain the same pitch relationships, but change the durational relationships in the second and fourth clusters. As a result, we now observe a succession of six *equal* groups of beats.

Example 2.12

Meter

The usual musical term for what we have called a rhythmic cluster is a *measure*. When a piece of music is characterized by equal and regular clusters, it is said to be *metrical* and is based on one of the *simple meters:* in *duple* meter the measure (cluster) contains two beats, in *triple* meter it contains three, and in *quadruple* it contains four beats.

Meter is indicated by two notational devices. The *barline* marks the end of one measure and the beginning of the next. The *time signature* is a symbol, consisting of two numbers, written one above the other. The top number indicates the number of beats per measure, and the bottom number indicates the value of the note that represents one beat. The time signature ⁴/₄, for example, is interpreted as follows:

4 four beats to the measure (quadruple meter)
4 the quarter note (♩) represents the beat

The time signature ³/₂ is read in the same way:

3 three beats to the measure (triple meter)
2 the half note (♩) represents the beat

The simple meters are represented by such time signatures as ⁴/₄, ³/₂, ²/₂, ²/₄, and ³/₄. In addition, another symbol, **C** , is sometimes used to represent ⁴/₄ meter, and the same symbol with a line through it (**¢**) to represent ²/₂ meter.

In *compound* meters five, six, seven, or more beats may make up a measure. The compound duple meters are ⁶/₄ and ⁶/₈; the compound triple meters are ⁹/₄ and ⁹/₈; and the compound quadruple meters are ¹²/₄, ¹²/₈, and ¹²/₁₆. When the number of beats cannot be divided by either 2 or 3 (as in ⁵/₄ or ⁷/₄), the meter is said to be irregular. Such meters are usually felt as combinations of regular meters (⁵/₄ = ²/₄ + ³/₄, for example).

Ordinarily, the first beat of a measure is aurally prominent. Music in ³/₄ time, for example, has a ONE-two-three character (see Ex. 2.13a). In some pieces, however, the pulse of the meter is deliberately disturbed so that the emphasis does not occur where the listener expects it. In such cases the rhythm is said to be *syncopated*.

Syncopation is a rhythmic device used to disturb the listener's expectation of regular metrical groupings. The effect of syncopation is to change the length of the rhythmic cluster. This can be achieved in several ways. One way is to carry over a tone from one measure to the next so that the initial strong beat is not sounded (see Ex. 2.13b). Another way is to stop the sound by placing a rest on the strong beat (Ex. 2.13c).

Example 2.13

Once the mind observes a pattern of regularity—even for a brief period of time—it becomes comfortable with it and assumes that it will continue. This expectation is so strong that considerable manipulation is required to upset it. The listener can, however, be "surprised" by a sudden shortening or lengthening of the duration of the group. If there is an immediate return to the previous regularity, the upset is mild and momentary. If the departure is radical and persistent, the mind is forced to adjust to a new metrical order.

Some music maintains an almost equal balance between meter and rhythm. Other music emphasizes one aspect over the other. Marches and dance music, for example, tend to be heavily metrical. In other styles the rhythm is so strong that the meter is almost obscured.

Meter and rhythm are the two fundamental forces continually at work in musical time. Meter imposes regularity and equality. It controls, it regulates, and it provides the basic grouping within which the listener organizes sound. Rhythm is a larger concept. It opposes meter in the sense that it lends diversity and inequality to a piece of music. These two forces, however, are interdependent, with each providing the basis for the existence of the other.

Levels of Time

Rhythm and meter exist simultaneously on different levels. On the most fundamental level is the beat. The succession of even beats creates a regular flow of equal time lengths. But, as we have seen, some beats are more aurally prominent than others. This inequality results in the grouping of beats into a second, higher level of organization, the measure. The measure, in turn, becomes a concrete length in its own right, perceived as a series of regularly occurring equal lengths of time.

On a third and higher level the listener perceives larger segments of musical time consisting of several measures. These are called *phrases* and relate to measures and beats in the following way:

Example 2.14

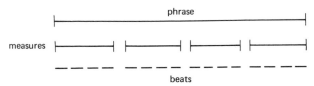

At this stage, after sounds have been grouped and regrouped into phrases, we enter the realm of musical *form*. Here the architecture of long stretches of musical time comes into play.

Musical Energy

The length of the beat determines the speed, or *tempo*, at which a piece of music moves. If the beat is short, the tempo is fast. If the beat is relatively long, the tempo is slow. If the length of the beat falls somewhere in between these two extremes, the tempo is moderate. The composer indicates tempo in one of two ways.

The first method of indicating tempo relies on a machine called the *metronome*. The metronome operates by electricity, by battery, or by means of an inverted pendulum with a weight that can be moved along a scale. By adjusting the weight, one can make the metronome beat out the desired tempo. For example, a piece of music may be marked ♩ = 80 or ♩ = M.M. 80. Either marking means that the desired tempo is 80 quarter-note-beats per minute. The initials M.M. stand for "Maelzel's Metronome," crediting the inventor Johannes Maelzel.

Before the nineteenth century, when the metronome was invented, composers had to rely on the more inexact method of describing the tempo with words such as *fast* or *slow*. Even after the metronome came into use, it was common to use verbal descriptions along with the metronome marking. Traditionally, but not always, the descriptive terminology is given in Italian:

Very slow:	*Largo* (broad)
	Grave (grave, solemn)
Slow:	*Lento*
	Adagio (leisurely; literally, at ease)
Moderate:	*Andante* (at a walking pace)
	Moderato
Fast:	*Allegretto*
	Allegro (faster than allegretto; literally, cheerful)
Very fast:	*Vivace* (vivacious)
	Presto (very quick)
	Prestissimo (as fast as possible)

These terms can be modified by adding such words as *molto* (very), *meno* (less), *poco* (a little), and *non troppo* (not too much). Thus, *molto largo* is very, very slow; *meno allegro* is less lively; *poco adagio* is just somewhat slow; and *allegro ma non troppo* is fast, but not too fast.

Once it is given, the tempo can be increased or slowed down. Gradual increases are indicated by the word *accelerando* (accelerating, getting faster), and gradual decreases by *ritardando* (slowing down, holding back). If, after changing the tempo, the composer wishes to return to the original rate of speed, he marks the music *a tempo*.

Tempo can also be disturbed in other ways. The word *rubato* indicates that a passage should be played with a deliberate unsteadiness, or elasticity, of tempo, alternately speeding up and slowing down. The *fermata* (⌢) indicates the prolongations of a note beyond its normal time value. Its effect is to suspend the flow of both beats and tempo.

No matter how the tempo is indicated, the final determination of how fast it will be played will be made by the performer. He takes into account many factors, including the size of the performing ensemble and the acoustical properties of the place of performance.

In addition to tempo, *density* (the amount and degree of musical activity) is an important element in musical speed. Two stretches of music that proceed at exactly the same tempo but contrast in density will seem to move at different speeds. The one with higher density will be busier, more energetic, and seem faster than the one of lower density. Music that gradually increases in density gives the impression of speeding up even though the tempo remains unchanged. A gradual reduction in density creates the effect of slowing down. Obviously, when density and tempo are combined in either speeding up or slowing down, the effect is that much more potent. Both tempo and density are important aspects of *musical energy*.

Harmonic Relationships

Virtually all Western music depends heavily on the element of harmony as an expressive quality and structural force. While melody constitutes the horizontal aspect of music, harmony represents the vertical. A *harmony* is a composite sound made up of two or more tones of different pitch that sound simultaneously. The smallest harmonic unit is the *interval*, consisting of two tones. The *chord* contains three or more tones. It is important to understand that the tones making up a harmony are not heard individually. Instead, they fuse into a composite sound that has its own distinctive characteristics and quality.

One important quality of a given harmony is its degree of *consonance*. A *consonant* harmony imparts a sense of stability, simplicity, and repose. In contrast, a *dissonant* harmony brings about tension, lack of stability, and the implication of movement. The degree of consonance or dissonance of a particular chord depends to a large degree on the context in which it is heard. A chord that sounds mildly dissonant in one context may seem consonant when heard with chords of much greater dissonance.

Most music we hear is predominantly consonant. Dissonance usually occurs only as a transient tension in a harmonic progression. The tension is immediately relieved by the *resolution* of the dissonant harmony into a

Example 2.15

consonant harmony. The music of the twentieth century, however, has a much greater degree of dissonance than that of earlier times. Indeed, one distinctive feature of modern music is that dissonances are employed independently and do not necessarily resolve into consonances.

Harmony, as an element, functions in a variety of ways. Often it serves as the underpinning for a melody. A particularly distinctive harmonic progression often achieves importance in its own right. Harmonies can appear in "solid" form (Ex. 2.15) or they can be "broken up," existing almost by implication (Ex. 2.16).

Example 2.16

This type of chord is said to be *arpeggiated.*

Harmony joins with the other elements in creating the flow of sound through musical time. Harmonic progressions contribute to the metrical and rhythmic aspects of musical structure. Often they are a crucial factor in delineating large segments of time, such as the phrase. In addition, harmonic movement contributes to musical density and energy.

One of harmony's most important functions is that which it performs in the realm of *tonality.*

Tonal Relationships

One of the striking characteristics of Western music is its reliance on the shaping force of the element of *tonality.* Although much of the music of the twentieth century either minimizes or eliminates tonality, the great bulk of the musical literature we are familiar with relies on the organizing power of the tonal center. The element of tonality is strongest in the music from the Baroque era through the Romantic period. Tonal music is characterized by its affirmation of a central tone, called the *tonic.* The tonic acts as a center of gravity, a kind of musical home base. It is the point of rest from which movement originates and toward which movement drives. At the end of a section of music it imparts a sense of convincing conclusion. Because of its sense of inevitability, tonality and the tonal center create another kind of expectation on the part of the listener—the expectation of the return to the tonic.

Returning again to Example 2.12, notice the effect produced by reversing the last two tones.

Example 2.17

Instead of ending on the note G, the melody now stops on F-sharp. But in this version the melody does not arrive at a conclusion. Rather, it ends "up in the air," making the listener feel a need to move forward. The original melody fulfilled the listener's expectation, but the altered ver-

Example 2.18

sion thwarts it. To reestablish a firm and convincing ending, we need only restore the tonic as the concluding tone.

Essentially, the music discussed here has depended on the major-minor system of keys and scales and the potent tonal relationship of first and fifth notes of those scales. When a piece of music is said to be in C major, this means that the prevailing tonic of the music is the pitch C and the prevailing tones are those of the C-major scale as opposed to the C-minor scale. In this system a chord is built on each degree of the scale. Each chord varies greatly in its relationship to the tonic. The *tonic note* is the first degree of the scale; the *dominant* is the fifth degree of the scale. The tonic is the point of rest, and the dominant is the note that most actively "seeks" or creates the expectation of movement to the tonic. This feeling of tonic and dominant is also present in the *chords* built on the first and fifth degrees of the scale; the dominant chord is the most active agent in establishing and driving toward a return to the tonic. Establishing a tonic chord at the beginning of a stretch of music and eventually returning to it form an extremely important aspect of musical structure. The return to the tonic acts to draw a section of music to a close by arriving at a point of rest. (The process of setting up and arriving at the tonic is *cadence.*)

In addition to the relationships among the tones of a melody and the relationship of chords to the tonal center, tonality includes the relationships among keys. A piece of music of any appreciable length seldom is confined to one key or to one tonal center. When we say that a work is in the key of C, we mean that the piece begins and ends in the key of C. Within the piece, additional tonal centers are usually touched upon through the process of *modulation*, or the gradual change from one key to another. In this sense C is the prevailing but not the only tonic. Very often large sections of music are set off from each other in a variety of ways, including contrast in key. One of the most frequent contrasts is that growing out of the tonic-dominant relationship.

Section A	Section B	Return of Section A
C major (tonic key)	G major (key of the dominant)	C major

During the Baroque and Classical periods tonality was a primary characteristic of musical composition. By the late nineteenth century tonal centers had become blurred as composers increased the number and frequency of modulations. In the twentieth century composers revolted against tonality and introduced *atonal* systems that had no key centers.

Summary

The melody of a piece of music is perhaps its most memorable aspect. Moving up and down in a horizontal direction through space, the melody may be smooth or angular. This directional line, or sequence of *pitches,* and the *durational* pattern of the music, are the two components of melody. Frequently a work contains several melodies, the most central of which are called *themes*.

A listener accustoms himself to the musical flow of a work by organizing it into basic units of time called *beats*. He also perceives the musical flow in terms of *rhythmic clusters* or *measures*, which are larger units separated by tones of *aural prominence*. If the measures are regular and equal, the music is said to be *metrical*. In each piece of music, the meter is designated by a *time signature*, showing the number of beats to the measure and the value of the note representing one beat. It is the length of the beat that determines *tempo*, or speed. This is indicated by metronome markings or by descriptive terminology.

Harmony is an expressive and structural force, representing the vertical aspect of music. Harmony may consist of two tones (an *interval*), or three or more tones (a *chord*). Its quality is generally described as *consonant*, or in repose; or *dissonant*, or in a state of tension and needing resolution.

Another structural principle of music is *tonality*, the affirmation of a central tone, or resting point, called the *tonic*. The *tonic note* is the first degree of the scale; the fifth degree of the scale is the *dominant note*, which is the note most actively anticipating the return to the tonic. Larger works often include *modulation* from one key to another.

chapter 3

Much as individual sounds are combined to produce the basic elements of music—melody, rhythm, harmony, and tonality—the elements themselves are combined, extended, and structured to create larger musical entities. From the shortest, simplest melody to the longest and most complex section of music, these elements provide the fundamental materials from which all music is structured.

Musical Organization

In Chapter 1 we say that "music is sound organized in time" and that it is "time defined by the sound that fills it." Let us now pursue these ideas a step further. The listener's sense of time passing is created by his perception of musical *change*. In much the same way that the changing events of the day create a sense of the passage of time, a change from one melody to another, a progression from one harmony to another, or a modulation from one key to another produce in the listener a general sense of the flow of time. This time flow is given character and structure by the way the elements function in the music.

Musical Texture

Like woven cloth, music has horizontal and vertical aspects. The way in which these aspects relate and balance in a piece of music is known as its *texture*. The two extremes in texture are known as *polyphony* and *homophony*.*

Polyphonic music is perceived as strata of simultaneous melodies. It is the result of the combination of two or more "independent" melodic lines that are roughly equal in their melodic and rhythmic activity. In Example 3.1, the melodic lines are independent of each other, with neither of them playing a secondary or accompanying role.

Sometimes, simultaneous melodic lines relate in such a way that they are equal in activity but are *not* independent of one another and, therefore, *not* polyphonic (see Example 3.2).

---

*Distinct from both polyphony and homophony is *monophony*, which literally means "one sound." Monophonic music consists of a single melodic line without accompanying material.

Example 3.1

Example 3.2

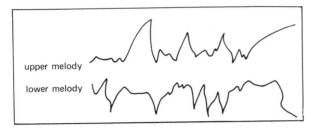

The melodies in Example 3.2 move at the same time and in the same direction, duplicating each other. The result is actually a thickening of *one* melodic line.

In Example 3.3, the two melodic lines are independent, but they are by no means "roughly equal" in melodic and rhythmic activity. The upper melody is markedly inferior to the lower melody in this respect. The upper melody is relatively static, and the action is in the lower melody.

Example 3.3

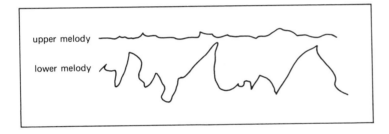

Example 3.4 also illustrates two independent melodies with a static voice playing against an active one. But midway the roles interchange so that the static voice becomes active and the active voice becomes static. By passing the relative activity from one voice to another, these melodies generate more or less equal interest. In this way they come closer to a polyphonic texture than do the melodies in Examples 3.2 and 3.3.

In Example 3.5 the two melodic lines never lose their vitality, even when one becomes somewhat less prominent than the other. Both are

Example 3.4

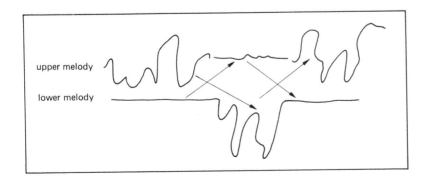

roughly equal in the degree of activity spread out over their entire length, and they are independent in that they do not move in the same direction at the same time. This is the essence of polyphony. The simultaneous strands are in opposition to each other, competing for the listener's attention, which shifts from one to the other, depending on which melodic line gains the upper hand at any given moment. This kind of interplay of melodies is also known as *counterpoint*. The interest of polyphonic (or contrapuntal) music lies in the relationship between the independent, simultaneous melodic lines.

Example 3.5

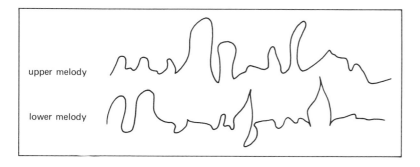

upper melody

lower melody

Homophony is at the opposite end of the spectrum of musical texture. In homophonic music a single melodic strand predominates. The principal melody may be located in an upper, middle, or lower voice. Or it may change from one voice to another. But wherever it is, it will have no serious competition from the other voice parts.

The listener is free to concentrate on the single melodic ingredient, perceiving all other elements as less significant. Rather than functioning independently, the other melodies blend into accompaniment, providing support for the main melodic line.

Actually, much music occupies a middle position between the two extremes of homophony and polyphony. Frequently, the texture of a piece of music alternates between homophonic and polyphonic stretches. Then an essentially homophonic stretch will be followed by a section that is basically polyphonic. Even in these stretches, however, the distinction may not be clear cut. One voice may dominate the section that is predominantly polyphonic, or the accompanying materials may assume an importance to compete with the main melodic line in the stretch of music that is generally homophonic.

Musical Structure

While musical texture concerns the relationship of simultaneous events, *musical structure* concerns the relationship of successive events. In order for the musical time-flow to hold the listener's attention, it must provide a series of events that are at the same time interesting and coherent. Interest depends upon the presence of variety, and coherence requires unifying factors. The elements of *unity* and *variety*, and the balance that exists between them, are basic to musical structure. Variety is the result of change; unity is achieved by repetition.

Musical Unity

Musical repetition varies greatly in the forms it takes and the ways it is applied.

Restatement is immediate repetition in the same voice part at the same pitch level:

A　　　A

Sequence is immediate repetition in the same voice part at different pitch levels:

A

　A

A

Imitation is immediate repetition by different voice parts at the same or different pitch levels:

First voice part:　A

Second voice part:　　A

Third voice part:　　　A

Stretto is repetition in which the second voice enters before the phrase is completed in the first voice part. The second part may be on the same or a different pitch level.

First voice part:　A

Second voice part:　　A

Reappearance is repetition in any voice part with contrasting material intervening between the statement and its repetition:

A　　B　　A　　C　　A

statement　(contrast)　reappearance　(contrast)　reappearance

Some of the types of repetition listed are commonly found in polyphonic music. Imitation, for example, is essentially a polyphonic device, and *imitative polyphony* is a particular type of polyphony. Three of the primary methods for organizing relatively long stretches of polyphonic music are the *canon*, the *ground bass*, and the *fugue*.

The *canon* is a contrapuntal sequence in which two or more voice parts imitate each other note for note throughout an entire piece:

First voice part:　A　B　C　D　E

Second voice part:　　A　B　C　D　E

In a canon the second voice part has exactly the same melody as the first, but begins later. A canon can also combine three voice parts, as follows:

First voice part:		A̲	B̲	C̲	D̲	E̲
Second voice part:	A̲	B̲	C̲	D̲	E̲	
Third voice part:		A̲	B̲	C̲	D̲	E

Again, the relationship among parts is one of exact imitation.

Often a two-part canon will be combined with a third part that does not join in the imitation, but remains outside the canon.

First voice part:	A̲	B̲	C̲	D̲	E̲
Second voice part:		free voice			
Third voice part:	A̲	B̲	C̲	D̲	E

Here the canonic first and third voices surround the free, second voice.

Most frequently, the canonic structure is located in the top two voices that are superimposed over an independent bass voice.

First voice part:		A̲	B̲	C̲
Second voice part:	A̲	B̲	C̲	
Bass voice part:		free voice		

Ground bass, or *basso ostinato*, is a procedure that makes flexible use of several types of repetition within a polyphonic texture. Its fundamental device is the constant restatement of a short melodic fragment in the bass, above which one or more voices have contrasting material. The upper voices sometimes employ imitation. At other times they move against each other freely, in a nonimitative but nevertheless polyphonic relationship.

The *fugue* is a polyphonic procedure that depends heavily on the imitation and reappearance of a short melodic theme, or *subject*. In addition to repetition and contrast in the melodic material, the fugue involves considerable modulation. It achieves tonal unity by the return to the key in which it began. The fugue is discussed in more detail in Chapter 10.

The ground bass, canon, and fugue employ their own methods of achieving unity and variety, and each has attained an important place in musical history. The organ fugues of Bach, the canons of Mozart, the ground bass technique employed by Brahms, and the polyphonic writing of Hindemith demonstrate the durability of the basic polyphonic procedures.

Like polyphony, homophony employs devices of musical repetition —particularly restatement and reappearance—to achieve coherence.

Musical Variety

Musical change varies in type, degree, and function. In its mildest form the change affects some relatively minor aspect of a repeated element.

For example, the following restatement differs only in its dynamic level:

$$\frac{A}{forte} \qquad \frac{A}{piaro}$$

When these two versions of a stretch of music are played one after the other, the change from loud to soft is what attracts the listener's attention.

However, if there is intervening material between the initial statement of A and its reappearance in a mildly modified form, the effect of the change in A is substantially lessened. In this case the stronger impression is created by the unifying force of the return of the familiar, known material.

$$\frac{A}{forte} \quad \underline{B} \quad \underline{C} \quad \frac{A}{piano}$$

When the techniques of both repetition and contrast are embodied in the same event, one usually makes a stronger impression because it takes place within the context of the other. Any repeition within a generally contrasting section will act as a unifying element. Conversely, any change within a context of repetition will contribute to the impression of contrast and variety.

Not only the occurrence of change, but also its degree and function are important features of homophonic music. Alterations of the same material can take many forms. A partial list would include:

$\frac{A}{piano} \quad \frac{A}{forte}$ $\frac{A}{strings} \quad \frac{A}{woodwinds}$	$\Big\}$	Change in volume and color
$\underline{A} \quad \frac{A}{shorter}$ $\underline{A} \quad \frac{A}{expanded}$ $\underline{A} \quad \frac{A}{decorated}$	$\Big\}$	Change of the melodic material

$\frac{A}{original\ harmony} \qquad \frac{A}{different\ harmony}$	Change in the material surrounding the melody
$\frac{A}{original\ meter} \qquad \frac{A}{different\ meter}$	Change in rhythm
$\frac{A}{original\ key} \qquad \frac{A}{different\ key}$	Change in tonality
$\frac{A}{major\ key} \qquad \frac{A}{minor\ key}$	Change in modality

All these contrasts concern changes formed within the context of the repetition of the same material (in this case the melodic material A). The degree of musical contrast resulting from these kinds of changes is relatively mild in comparison with the contrast that results when the material that follows A is sufficiently different to constitute completely *new* material:

<u>A</u>   <u>B</u>

Homophonic music employs both kinds of contrasts. Two basic procedures that use the principle of simple contrast are *binary form* and *ternary form.*

As its name suggests, binary form consists of two contrasting musical phrases, A and B. Usually, each section is repeated, resulting in an A A B B sequence. The A and B sections are related very specifically in terms of keys: the A section begins in the tonic and modulates to the dominant; the B section begins in the dominant and modulates back to the tonic.

Binary form is said to be *symmetrical* if the A and B sections are of equal length; *asymmetrical* if one section is longer than the other section; or *rounded* if the A section is repeated, in whole or in part, at the end of the B section. This expanded binary form, which rounds off the piece with the return to the original A material, strongly suggests ternary form.

Ternary form consists of three sections, A B A. The final A section is a repetition of the first. Unlike binary form, A does not end in the dominant, but in the tonic key, in which it began. The B section is in a contrasting key. Thus, with its contrasting melodic material and key, B is the element of variety, and the return of A in the tonic key provides the unifying force.

The ternary form (ABA) is the simplest example of the principle of *alternation.* Music built on this principle consists of a main section alternating with contrasting sections:

ABA   three-part form
ABACA   five-part form
ABACADA   seven-part form

The contrasting sections and their different keys provide the element of variety, while the unifying forces center on the reappearing A section in the principal key. Section A may appear in partial or modified form, but it nevertheless has the unifying effect that comes from the return of familiar material. It shapes the flow of time into a coherent pattern.

The Baroque *da capo* aria, the Classical minuet and trio, and the rondo, all of which we shall encounter in subsequent chapters, employ the principle of alternation.

While alternation is based on contrast between different materials, other formal procedures consist of the statement of a single idea and its subsequent variation. This procedure found its most potent manifestation in *theme and variations.* A theme, used as a point of departure, is followed by a series of variations, all based on it but each presenting the material in a different way:

Statement	Variation 1	Variation2	Variation 3	
Theme A	A^1	A^2	A^3	etc.

While the restatement of familiar thematic material is the unifying force, the successive changes maintain constant variety.

The numerous techniques and devices by which thematic material can be varied are best studied in connection with specific works. Whichever devices are employed, each variation usually utilizes the entire theme. Occasionally, however, only fragments of the original theme are employed.

Variation based on fragments are much more typical of the *development technique*. The technique is best seen in *sonata-allegro* form, which we shall study in detail in connection with the Classical era. In sonata-allegro form, two or more contrasting themes are first stated in what is known as an *exposition* section. After that, in the *development* section, fragments from one or both themes are expanded and explored. Elements from the contrasting themes may be combined and regrouped, and the character of the material may be altered in texture, harmony, or rhythm. In addition, the treatment of the material almost always includes modulation. Unity is inherent by virtue of the familiarity of the recurring material, and variety is provided by the changes that take place in the thematic material during its development.

Alternation, variation, and development are three of the principal organizing features characteristic of many periods of history. The twentieth century, however, has seen a radical revolt against these traditional techniques of composition. This revolt has led to what is called *serial technique*, based on the twelve-tone system developed by the German composer Arnold Schoenberg. In serial technique the composer utilizes the twelve tones of the chromatic scale in such a way that no one tone acquires the stability of a tonal center. This ordering of tones creates an abstract melody called the *tone row*. All melodic and harmonic materials for the specific composition are derived from the tone row. The twelve-tone technique and the varieties of serial techniques derived from it have constituted one of the significant forces in music of the twentieth century.

The elements of musical structure and musical texture are the materials with which music is made. The specific way in which these materials are combined in any musical piece determines the *style* of that work.

Musical Style

In any discussion of art the word *style* will appear in many contexts and with seemingly endless applications. Broadly defined, style is a manner of expression characteristic of an individual, a historical period, a school, or other identifiable group. In speaking of musical style, we are referring to the methods of treating the elements of melody, harmony, rhythm, form, tone color, and tonality.

Even in a musical context, the term is applied in several ways. Thus, we speak of the style of Beethoven's Ninth Symphony as compared with that of his Second Symphony; or the style of Debussy as compared with that of Ravel; or operatic style as distinguished from oratorio style. We also speak of instrumental style, vocal style, keyboard style, German style, Italian style, or the style of Western music as contrasted with Oriental music.

In a larger sense, the word *style* is applied to periods of music history. Every age presents new problems, makes new demands, and offers new possibilities; and every artist responds in his own way. Yet no matter how varied the stylistic traits of the artists of a particular era, when they are seen in historical perspective, a common manner of expression binds them together. Thus, we are able to identify the common practices of a specific period and distill from the individual works of that era a general stylistic statement.

A concept as many-faceted as style does not lend itself to precise definition. Scholars never completely agree on the boundary lines separating one period of style from another.

The following outline of the major periods of music history provides approximate dates. Each period had a unique means of expression.

600– 850	Early Middle Ages
850–1150	Romanesque
1150–1300	Early Gothic
1300–1450	Late Gothic
1450–1600	Renaissance
1600–1750	Baroque
1725–1775	Rococo
1775–1825	Classical
1820–1900	Romantic
1890–1915	Post-Romantic
1900–	Twentieth century

Style periods overlap; the new exists side by side with the old. Elements from an older style may be combined with new procedures to create what is sometimes called a *neo*-Classical, or *neo*-Baroque style. Although Italy was the very heart of the Renaissance spirit in literature and the visual arts, Renaissance music originated and developed in northern France and Belgium. The Baroque style appeared earlier in Italy than in Germany or England. Nevertheless, the style periods listed are a useful guide to the principal stylistic developments in Western music.

Summary

Musical time-flow is given character and structure by the way in which the elements of melody, rhythm, harmony, and tonality function in simultaneous and successive musical events.

The relationship between the vertical and horizontal aspects of a piece of music is known as its texture. Polyphonic music is perceived as strata of simultaneous melodies. Homophonic music is dominated by a single melodic strand, with the other elements blending into the accompaniment and serving as harmonic support.

To hold the listener's attention, music must present a coherent and interesting flow of time. Coherence is provided by musical unity, which is achieved by repetition. Interest is created by musical change, which varies in type, degree, and function.

The specific way in which the elements of musical structure and texture are combined in any piece determines the style of that work. Music has evolved through a series of style periods, each with general distinguishing characteristics. In the subsequent chapters of this book we shall trace the development of Western music from the early Middle Ages to the "new music" of the twentieth century.

chapter 4

We have examined the way in which musical sounds are produced, how they are related to one another, and how they are organized in time. This chapter examines the instruments that produce them. The first section discusses the instruments individually, and the second section deals with instrumental and vocal ensembles.

The Performing Media

Musical Instruments

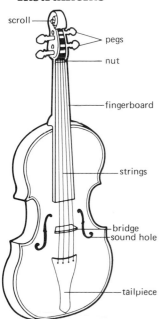

Figure 4.1   First developed by early-sixteenth-century Italians, violins have undergone little structural change since their invention.

The instruments available to composers offer a wide variety of pitch ranges, technical capabilities, and tone colors. They are commonly grouped into four families—strings, woodwinds, brasses, and percussion.

Strings

A stringed instrument produces sound when the player either plucks or bows one of its strings. Each string is stretched between two fixed points, with one end attached to a *peg* on the neck of the instrument and the other to a *tailpiece* at the base of the body. The midsections of the strings pass over a *bridge*, which is mounted on the body of the instrument (Fig. 4.1).

Individual strings vary in thickness. These dimensions, plus the nature of the material from which a particular string is made, determine the frequency at which a string will vibrate and, therefore, the pitch at which it will sound. The player can effectively reduce the portion of a string that is free to vibrate by pressing down the string against the *fingerboard* with the fingers of his left hand. This is known as *stopping* the string.

String Techniques   Many stringed instruments, including those of the violin and gamba families, are played by drawing a *bow*, held in the right hand, across the strings of the instrument, which is held with the left hand. The bow (Fig. 4.2) is a long, slender shaft of wood in which a bundle of strands of horsehair is stretched from end to end.

A variety of effects can be achieved by using *legato* and *staccato* bowing.

Figure 4.2   Horsehair bows are used to vibrate the strings of instruments of the violin and gamba families. The adjustable frog enables the artist to tighten the hair.

Legato bowing produces a smooth sound. In staccato playing, the notes are short and detached.

When the bow is moved rapidly back and forth across the strings, the effect called *tremolo* is produced. The bow may also be bounced off the strings, or the strings may be struck with the wooden part of the bow. *Double* and *triple stopping* are used to sound chords and intervals. To do this, the player presses two or three strings against the fingerboard at the same time while drawing his bow across them.

In pressing a string against the fingerboard, the player may also vibrate his hand back and forth rapidly. In so doing, he creates a slight fluctuation in pitch that is known as *vibrato*. This increases the "warmth" of the tone produced.

A velvety tone can be achieved by clamping a device called a *mute* to the top of the bridge. The mute produces a softer and less brilliant sound without affecting the pitch.

Instead of using the bow, the player may pluck the strings with his fingers. This technique, known as *pizzicato*, produces short, crisp tones.

Instruments of the string family that do not have bows—such as the guitar, lute, and harp—are played solely by plucking. Some of these instruments, including the guitar, use a plucking device known as a *plectrum*, which is made of a small piece of tortoise shell, ivory, or metal.

The Violin Family   The chief members of this family—the violin, viola, violoncello, and double bass—are among the most important instruments in all Western music. They constitute the backbone of the orchestra and are frequent members of chamber ensembles. In addition, all are solo instruments in their own right. The double bass is commonly used in jazz bands.

The highest in pitch, the *violin* is famous for its lyric and dramatic expressiveness. Its four strings are separated in pitch by the interval of a fifth. The player holds the instrument beneath his chin.

Slightly larger than the violin, the *viola* has longer, thicker, and heavier strings. Tuned a fifth lower than the violin, it is also held beneath the player's chin.

The *violoncello* is commonly called by its shortened name, *cello*. Tuned an octave below the viola, it is about twice the length of the violin. Because of its size, it rests on the floor and is held upright between the player's knees.

The *double bass*, also called the *bass viol* or *contrabass*, is the largest and lowest-voiced member of the family. Because of its size, the player must stand to play it.

Other Strings   Popular during the Renaissance and Baroque periods, the instruments of the *viole da gamba* family are now being revived to play music from those periods. They are similar to the modern violin family in appearance, but they have six strings. They are available in five sizes, and all are played in cello position, between the player's knees.

Figure 4.3 Having made his concert dêbut at age 7, Yehudi Menuhin has devoted his life to mastering the infinite complexities of the violin. (Columbia Artists Management, Inc.)

The largest member of this family, which is also the most popular, has roughly the same range as the modern cello. Like all viole da gamba, it produces a lighter, slightly more nasal tone than does its cousin in the violin family.

Among many instruments in which the strings are plucked are the harp, lute, and guitar. Both the harp and the lute have ancient origins in the Near East. The modern *harp*, which is often included in the symphony orchestra, has forty-seven strings stretched vertically in a triangular frame. Seven pedals at its base are used to alter the pitch of the strings.

The *lute* rose to its greatest prominence in the sixteenth century. Its present-day use is generally restricted to the performance of Renaissance and Baroque music. Lutes are easily recognized by their rounded backs.

Instruments that are similar in design to the lute but have flat backs are grouped in the *guitar* family. The six-stringed guitar, which has become extremely popular in recent years, is widely used in folk music.

Figure 4.5
The largest
of the violin
family, the
double bass—
played here by
Gary Karr—
is also the low-
est voiced.
Sheldon Soffer
Management,
Inc.)

*Figure 4.4   Unlike its violin
and viola cousins, the
violoncello—or cello—
(played here by Stephen
Kates) rests on the floor.
(CBS)*

*Figure 4.6   The instruments
of the viole da gamba family
are now enjoying a revival for
their parts in Renaissance
and Baroque music. (The
Bettmann Archive)*

Figure 4.7   Like this eighteenth-century harp, today's harps have foot pedals, which raise tones in varying amounts. (The Metropolitan Museum of Art)

Figure 4.9   Andrés Segovia plays the classical guitar, which he established as a concert instrument. Like all guitars, this classical guitar is of Spanish origin. (Wayne J. Shilkret)

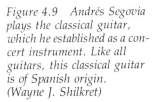

Figure 4.8   Joseph Iodone's lute might best be recognized for its part in Renaissance and Baroque music. Of ancient origin, the round-backed lute has five or more pairs of strings tuned either in unison or in octaves.

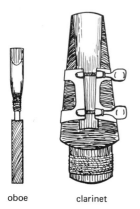

oboe   clarinet

Figure 4.10   The oboe requires a double reed, using air vibrations between its two reed parts to generate sound; the clarinet's single reed produces sound when air is blown between it and the open side of the mouthpiece.

Woodwinds

Although not all woodwinds are constructed of wood, the term applies to a family of instruments in which tone is produced by a column of air vibrating through a cylindrical pipe. In this group are the members of the flute, oboe, and clarinet families. Instruments such as the recorder and the saxophone are also classified as woodwinds.

All woodwinds have a pipelike shape, with fingerholes spaced along the side. The player changes the length of the column of air by closing or opening the finger holes with fingers or with the *keys*. In stopping the fingerholes the player lengthens the air column passing through the instrument and thereby lowers the pitch.

The vibrating column of air is produced by several different methods. In all of them the position of the player's lips, or *embouchure*, is of paramount importance in controlling the amount and direction of air.

A flute is *edge-blown* in somewhat the same manner as air is blown over the top of a bottle to produce sound. The player funnels a narrow stream of air to the opposite edge of the oval-shaped mouth hole. The air in the recorder is *end-blown* into a mouthpiece resembling that of a whistle.

Other instruments produce sound by the vibrations of a thin piece of material called a *reed* (Fig. 4.10). In *single-reed* instruments, such as the clarinet, the player blows a column of air between the reed and the open side of the mouthpiece. In *double-reed* instruments, such as the oboe, the player blows the air between two reeds.

The Woodwind Family   One of the oldest woodwinds, the *flute* is an extremely agile instrument, able to produce rapid scale passages and trills. The smallest and highest woodwind, the *piccolo* (*flauto piccolo* or little flute), is really a small flute. Despite its size, it produces one of the most penetrating sounds of all the instruments of the orchestra. It is pitched an octave higher than the flute.

The *oboe* has a nasal, plaintive timbre often used for pastoral or nostalgic effects.

The *English horn* is neither English nor a horn. Actually, it is an alto oboe, a double-reed instrument pitched a fifth lower than the oboe. Its timbre resembles that of the oboe.

The *bassoon* is the bass member of the oboe family. Because of its length, the instrument is bent back on itself. The bassoon has remarkably even tone color and is expressive in both its high and low ranges.

The woodwind counterpart of the double bass, the *contrabassoon*, is pitched an octave below the bassoon. Its sixteen-foot pipe is doubled back on itself three times.

The single-reed *clarinet* family has eleven members, but only four are regularly used. Fuller in tone than the oboe, the clarinet is capable of producing rapid runs and trills. The most common instrument in this family is the *clarinet in B-flat*. The *clarinet in A*, which is sometimes preferred for parts written in sharp keys, is pitched one-half step lower than the clarinet in B-flat. A fourth above the B-flat clarinet is the small *clarinet in E-flat*. An octave below the B♭ clarinet is the *bass clarinet*.

Figure 4.11   Both the piccolo and the flute are played by blowing air across the mouth hole. Although the two-foot-long flute cannot produce the piccolo's high notes, it is regarded as an extremely agile instrument. (Susan E. Meyer)

Figure 4.12   The oboe and its longer, deeper-toned cousin, the English horn. Because early oboes produced louder, coarser tones than do our modern versions, experts agree that the oboe was probably originally a hunting instrument. (Susan E. Meyer)

The flutelike *recorder* reached its final stage of development in the late Middle Ages. By the sixteenth century it had spawned a whole family. Modern recorders, the popularity of which has been revived in the twentieth century, are usually made in four sizes: soprano (or descant), alto (or treble), tenor, and bass.

Two rare oboes are the *oboe d'amore* and the *oboe da caccia*. Invented in the early eighteenth century, the oboe d'amore (oboe of love) got its name because it produced a sweeter sound than the other oboes. The oboe da caccia ("of the hunt" in Italian) was named for its curved hunting-horn shape.

The *saxophone*, invented by Adolphe Sax of Brussels in the mid-nineteenth century, is a hybrid instrument. It combines the single reed and mouthpiece of the clarinet with the conical shape and key arrangement of the oboe. Its timbre is somewhere between the softness of the woodwinds and the metallic qualities of the brasses. Although it is seldom seen in symphony orchestras, the saxophone is an important instrument in jazz and dance bands.

Figure 4.13   The added length of these bass members of the oboe family, the bassoon and the contrabassoon, affords even, mellow tones down to the lowest of the instruments' ranges. (Susan E. Meyer)

Figure 4.14   Three most popular members of the agile clarinet family—the E-flat, B-flat, and bass clarinets—produce fuller tones than the oboes. (Susan E. Meyer)

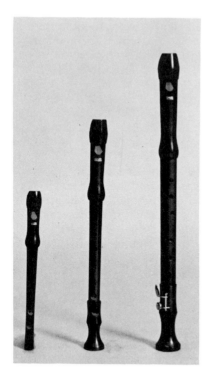

Figure 4.15 Products of a recent revival of interest in recorders, these soprano, alto, and tenor instruments have an ancestry dating back to the Middle Ages. (Susan E. Meyer)

Figure 4.17 The hunting-horn shape of the oboe da caccia supports the theory that oboes were originally a hunting instrument. (Smithsonian Institution)

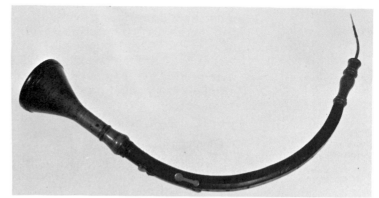

Figure 4.16 The many members of the oboe family give it a wide range of sounds embodying pastoral or nostalgic effects. (The Metropolitan Museum of Art, The Crosby Brown Collection of Musical Instruments, 1889)

Figure 4.18 Only a century old, the tenor saxophone represents a combination of clarinet and oboe features and gives a sound midway between that of woodwinds and brasses. (Susan E. Meyer)

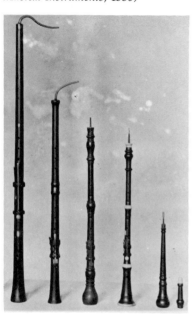

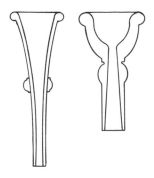

funnel-shaped
mouthpiece
(horn)

cup-shaped
mouthpiece
(trombone)

*Figure 4.19   Brass mouth-
pieces take one of these two
shapes. Regardless of which
is used, however, sound is
caused by the vibrations of
the player's lips rather than
by reed vibrations.*

Brasses

Like the woodwinds, brass instruments produce sound by sending a
vibrating column of air through pipe-shaped tubing. The significant difference, however, is where the vibrations come from. In a brass instrument the mouthpiece is shaped like either a cup or a funnel (Fig. 4.19).
As the player blows into the mouthpiece, the vibrations of his lips function much like the reed in the woodwinds.

Another difference involves the valves or, in the case of the trombone,
a sliding double tube. While the length of the air column in woodwinds
is controlled by keys in the side of the instrument, the brasses have
slides or valves to alter the length of the tubing.

Like stringed instruments, the brasses can be muted. Brass mutes look
like hollow cones, which the players insert into the bells of their instruments. The mutes tend to accentuate the higher resonances, resulting in
a more nasal tone color.

The modern orchestra includes trumpets, French horns, trombones,
and tubas in its brass section. The highest of these, the *trumpet*, has a
brilliant and penetrating timbre. Different notes are sounded by opening
combinations of the three valves and by adjusting the embouchure
against the cup-shaped mouthpiece. The trumpet is capable of techniques ranging from a smooth legato to a sharp staccato.

The *cornet* is a shorter version of the trumpet, with the same range of
pitch, but lacking the trumpet's brilliance of tone color.

Descended from the hunting horn, the *French horn* produces a full,
mellow tone. Its pitch is controlled by three valves and a funnel-shaped
mouthpiece.

*Figure 4.20   The D- and
B-flat trumpets are the
highest-pitched members of
an orchestra's brass section.
Different notes are produced
by combining valve work
with embouchure variations.
(Susan E. Meyer)*

*Figure 4.21   The mellow-
toned French horn tapers
from the funnel-shaped
mouthpiece at one end,
through many feet of metallic
curves and circles, to the flar-
ing bell at the other.
(Susan E. Meyer)*

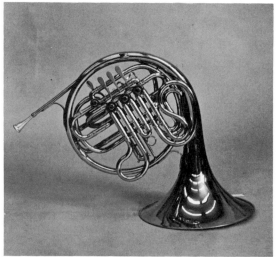

The *trombone* (which means "large trumpet" in Italian) has a cup-shaped mouthpiece, but no valves. Adjustments in pitch are made by changing the position of its long, U-shaped tubing. The tenor and bass trombones are most frequently seen in the modern orchestra, while the alto trombone is encountered less often.

The lowest member of the brass family, the *tuba*, corresponds to the double bass and the contrabassoon in the string and woodwind families. It has a cup-shaped mouthpiece and three to five valves. Tubas come in a variety of sizes, the most common of which are the E-flat, or bass, tuba and the BB-flat, or contrabass.

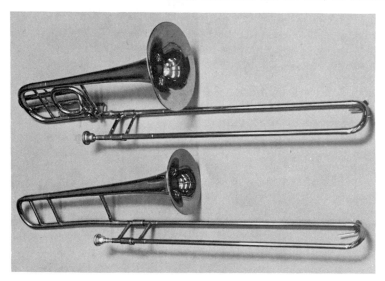

Figure 4.22   These tenor and bass trombones substitute sliding tubing for valves in the control of their sounds. A valved model has been developed, however, to accommodate the very rapid passages found in modern jazz. (Susan E. Meyer)

Figure 4.23   Serving an orchestral function comparable to that of the double bass and the contrabassoon, the E-flat, or bass, tuba helps anchor the brass section with its deep, sonorous tones. Comparatively new instruments, tubas were developed in the mid-nineteenth century. (Susan E. Meyer)

Percussion Instruments

Instruments that produce sound by being struck or shaken are by far the oldest known to man. Although the principles of their construction have not altered greatly over the centuries, the number of percussion instruments has grown steadily. Today the *battery*, as the percussion section is called, consists of a variety of instruments in two categories: those that produce sounds of definite pitch and those that do not.

The most important percussion instrument of definite pitch is the *kettledrum*. Named for its copper "kettle," this instrument produces sound by the vibrations of its calfskin *head*. The tension on the head can be adjusted by screws around the edge of the kettle and by pedals.

Figure 4.24 Percussion instruments that form the battery of a modern orchestra still employ the oldest sound-generating principles known to man. The percussionist can produce sounds of either definite or indefinite pitch by selecting the appropriate instrument. (Ludwig Industries)

Kettledrums, also called *timpani*, are available in a number of sizes, each with a basic range of a fifth. The kettledrum's roll can grow in intensity from a soft rumble to an awesome thunder.

The *glockenspiel* consists of two rows of steel slabs of varying sizes, tuned to the chromatic scale. The sound, produced by striking the slabs with a mallet, is crisp and bell-like. The *celesta*, a keyboard glockenspiel that looks like a small, upright piano, is used for a soft, light effect.

The *xylophone, marimba*, and *vibraphone* also resemble the glockenspiel in design. The xylophone producs a dry, hollow sound. The marimba, an instrument of African and South American origin, is used primarily for the performance of dance music. An electric xylophone favored by jazz musicians, the vibraphone is increasingly used by contemporary composers for the orchestra.

The *chimes* are a set of metal tubes suspended vertically in a frame. Struck with one or two wooden mallets, they are often used to imitate church bells.

The instruments that produce sounds of indefinite pitch include the *tambourine*, which is played by shaking and striking the head; the *castanets*, which are clicked together; the *triangle*, which is struck by a metal rod; the *gong*, which is struck in the center with a soft-headed stick; and the *cymbals*, which are struck together or hit by a stick.

Among the drums of indefinite pitch are the *bass drum*, the snare (or *side*) drum, and the *tenor drum*.

Keyboard Instruments

Although they can be classified in the wind, string, or percussion groups, keyboard instruments have a sufficient number of features in common to be considered separately.

Because it is capable of playing both loud and soft notes, the *piano* was originally named the *pianoforte*. The piano has some 230 strings. The strings are set in motion when they are *struck* by small hammers. Technically, therefore, it is classified as a percussion instrument.

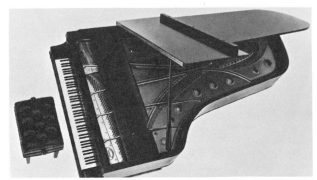

Figure 4.25 *Technically a percussion instrument, the piano has the greatest range of all instruments. The piano's extraordinary versatility is to be found not only in its range of pitch, but also in its pedal structure and its range of volume. (Baldwin Piano and Organ Co.)*

A complex chain of mechanisms connects the key on the keyboard to the strings, which then vibrate and produce the sound. The piano's range is greater than that of any other instrument, usually extending for more than seven octaves, and its dynamic capabilities are exceeded only by those of the organ.

Since the end of the eighteenth century the piano has been extremely popular in homes and concert halls. It is technically suited for lyric melodies, rapid scales and trills, and massive chordal combinations. Its lyric, harmonic, and percussive qualities make the piano a favorite instrument for solos, accompaniment, and ensembles alike.

The *organ* is a wind instrument in which air is released from a blower into a series of pipes. The player operates one or two keyboards with his hands, and another keyboard, in the forms of pedals, with his feet. By activating different *stops* and combinations of stops, a variety of sounds can be achieved.

The *harpsichord* has been revived in this century to play music from the Baroque and Renaissance periods. Because its strings are *plucked* by plectra of quill or leather, the harpsichord is classified as a stringed instrument. Consequently, its tone is quite unlike that of the piano, in which the strings are struck.

Figure 4.26 *Essentially wind instruments, organs require the manipulation of fingers, feet, and panels of stops (on each side of the manual keyboards). The pipes of a modern organ may range from 1 inch to 64 feet in length, and may vary in shape as well as material. (Aeolian-American Corp.)*

Figure 4.27 *The plucked strings of the harpsichord produce much softer sounds than a piano. Some modern composers are now writing especially for the harpsichord, although it is primarily popular for its part in Renaissance and Baroque music. (Susan E. Meyer)*

The *clavichord*, which was in use from the fifteenth throughout the eighteenth centuries, has strings that are struck. It produces a very soft sound, but variations in the force with which the keys are struck can produce degrees of loudness and softness.

The Human Voice

Because it produces sound by air under pressure, the human voice is fundamentally a wind instrument. Individual voices vary in their ranges, but vocal music is generally written for the following four ranges:

Soprano:	The highest female voice
Alto:	The lowest female voice
Tenor:	The highest male voice
Bass:	The lowest male voice

The Electronic Media

Music that is produced, modified, or amplified by electronic means has become increasingly important since World War II. Instruments range from the electronic organ, which simulates the sound produced by the pipe organ, to the computer. (Electronic music is covered in more detail in Chapter 29.)

Ensembles

Throughout the history of music, composers have written works that call for the use of instruments in a great variety of numbers, combinations, and groupings. These range from the solo, unaccompanied instrument to the large orchestra, consisting of more than a hundred players, often combined with a chorus and solo voices. Instrumental music falls into two broad categories: chamber music, in which one player executes each part; and orchestral music, which requires sections with more than one performer. Within the category of orchestral music there are again two major divisions: the small chamber orchestra and the large symphony orchestra.

Chamber Ensembles

Chamber music is classified by the number of instruments for which it is written. Thus we have *duos* for two performers, *trios* for three, *quartets*, *quintets*, *sextets*, *octets*, and so on. The combinations may be for a single type of instrument (such as a flute trio), instruments of the same family (such as a brass quintet consisting of trumpets, French horn, trombone, and tuba), or assortments of instruments.

The most important chamber combination, the *string quartet* has been widely used by composers from the middle of the eighteenth century into the modern period. The string quartet consists of a first and a second violin, a viola, and a cello.

Frequently a fifth instrument is added to the string quartet to create a quintet; ensembles of this type are named after the added instrument. Thus, a *clarinet quintet* is a string quartet plus a clarinet; a *piano quintet* is a string quartet plus a piano. Clarinet quintets have been written by Mozart and Brahms; and piano quintets by Schubert, Brahms, Dvořák, and Fauré. A quintet consisting of five strings is also common. Mozart, Beethoven, Mendelssohn, and Brahms have written works of this type for ensembles consisting of two violins, two violas, and a cello. Chamber groupings, some for larger ensembles, have continued to the present day. Igor Stravinsky, for example, wrote his *Octet for Wind Instruments* for two bassoons, two trombones, two trumpets, a flute, and a clarinet.

Figure 4.28   The New York Brass Quintet makes the most of the brass family's variations in range and tone. Chamber ensembles such as this have been popular with composers for several centuries. (Columbia Artists Management, Inc.)

Figure 4.29   The Guarneri String Quartet presents the classical combination of first and second violins, a viola, and a cello. When the background piano is added to their performance, the group is technically called a piano quintet. (RCA Records)

The Orchestra

Throughout its history the *orchestra* has varied in size and composition. As the creature of the composer, it is an ever-changing unit, not only in size but also in makeup.

One of the earliest orchestral ensembles was established in Paris by Jean-Baptiste Lully in the mid-seventeenth century. His orchestra was called *Les vingt-quatre violons du roi* (the twenty-four strings of the king). As its name implies, it consisted mainly of strings. During the first quarter of the eighteenth century, wind instruments, trumpets, and kettledrums were added.

In the mid-eighteenth century the orchestra became more standardized. German composers active in Mannheim wrote for an orchestral ensemble of more or less fixed proportions and makeup. In the Mannheim orchestra the strings remained dominant, but the woodwinds took on an increasingly important role.

In the early decades of the nineteenth century, many of the wind instruments underwent significant technical improvements. Around 1815, valves were added to the horns and trumpets, enabling them to sound all twelve notes of the chromatic scale. Improvements in the fingering mechanisms of the woodwinds made it possible for the performer to execute rapid passages. Composers were quick to take advantage of these technical improvements.

In the second half of the nineteenth century, the orchestra grew extensively in both size and makeup. Today's symphony orchestra consists of a nucleus of about one hundred players, with additions and subtractions being made to suit the requirements of individual pieces. The players are distributed according to the following plan:

Figure 4.30   The seating arrangement of the orchestra varies according to the preference of the conductor, but generally the strings are to the front, the woodwinds in the middle, and the brasses and percussion to the back.

Strings:
18 first violins
16 second violins
12 violas
10 cellos
10 basses
Harps

Woodwinds:
3 flutes, 1 piccolo
3 oboes, 1 English horn
3 clarinets, 1 bass clarinet
3 bassoons, 1 contrabassoon

Brass:
4 horns
3 trumpets
3 trombones
1 tuba

Percussion:
2 kettledrum players
3 players alternating on side, bass, and tenor drum, glockenspiel, celesta, triangle, cymbals

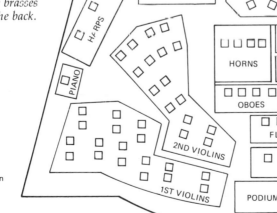

SEATING PLAN OF SYMPHONY ORCHESTRA

Figure 4.31 Leopold Stokowski conducts the American Symphony Orchestra. The conductor's left hand cues entrances and directs the subtler interpretations. (American Symphony Orchestra)

Figure 4.32 The Philadelphia Orchestra illustrates the concert seating pattern in use for the last century. Leopold Stokowski and Eugene Ormandy have conducted this long-established orchestra. (Columbia Records)

Vocal Ensembles

Chamber vocal ensembles vary in size and makeup in much the same way that chamber instrumental ensembles do. There are vocal trios, quartets, quintets, sextets, and so on. The vocal quartet usually consists of soprano, alto, tenor, and bass. So long as only one or two singers sing each part, the ensemble is essentially of chamber music proportions. However, when four or five or more singers are involved in each section, the ensemble is referred to as a *chorus* or *choir*. Several types of choruses are possible. A *women's chorus* usually consists of two soprano parts (first and second) and one or two alto sections—SSAA. A *men's chorus* is made up of two tenor sections (first and second), baritone, and bass—TTBB. The mixed chorus consists of both female and male voices, divided into soprano, alto, tenor, and bass. In church choirs before the nineteenth century, female voices were not generally used; soprano and alto parts were sung by boys whose voices had not yet changed.

The chorus can also be divided into more sections. A five-part chorus could consist of first and second soprano, alto, tenor, and bass—SSATB; or soprano, alto, first and second tenor, and bass—SATTB. A six-part chorus could subdivide both the soprano and tenor sections—SSATTB. Frequently, the chorus is divided into a *double chorus*—SSAATTBB. In performance the two choruses (SATB–SATB) generally sing *antiphonally*, one chorus answering the other.

Choral music is often intended for voices alone, without instrumental accompaniment, a style of performance called *a cappella*. But choral music is also frequently performed with instrumental accompaniment, e.g., piano, organ, or orchestra.

Like the orchestra, the chorus has varied greatly in size throughout its history. In the sixteenth century the choir of the papal chapel in Rome consisted of from nine to twenty-four singers. The sacred music of the period was performed by groups of this size, whereas solo performance—one singer to a part—seems to have been the practice for secular, or nonreligious, music. A chorus numbering no more than thirty appears to have been the norm during the Baroque period in the seventeenth century. Nineteenth-century composers wrote for a considerably expanded chorus. The *Requiems* of Brahms, Berlioz, and Verdi called for choruses numbering over one hundred singers. The twentieth century, generally, has seen a trend toward more modest performing groups, both choral and orchestral. Performance style has become more austere as the structure of the music has become more complex. The economics of musical performance today discourages large groups; they are too expensive to organize, rehearse, and perform.

Conductor

Large ensembles usually require the leadership of a conductor. Placed in front of the orchestra or chorus, usually on a podium, the conductor directs the ensemble and is responsible for all aspects of the performance. The craft of conducting is a complex one, and conducting techniques and styles are highly individual and vary widely. In

Figure 4.33 The famous Robert Shaw Chorale and Orchestra exemplifies the relatively small musical groupings popular today. The complexity of modern music and the economics of modern performances make such modestly sized groups both advantageous and practical.

general, the conductor's right hand indicates the tempo and basic metrical structure of the music. With his left hand, the conductor cues the entrances of instruments, the shadings of dynamics, and indicates other nuances relating to the expressive character of the music.

Summary

In this chapter we have examined, both individually and in groups, some of the most important instruments in Western music.

Instruments are usually classified into four groups —strings, woodwinds, brasses, and percussion. Although they can be classified as wind, string, or percussion instruments, keyboard instruments are often considered separately. Operated by air under pressure, the human voice is technically a wind instrument. Today the computer and other electronic media are being developed as new means of producing music.

A great number of combinations and groupings are possible with both instrumental and vocal music. Chamber ensembles include trios, quartets, and a number of other small groups, with usually one voice or instrument assigned to a part. Larger groupings, such as the orchestra and chorus, have several voices or instruments performing a single part.

chapter 5

Each of us is, to at least some extent, a "prisoner" of the culture in which he is born. Our physical, intellectual, and emotional lives are affected continuously by our surrounding social milieu. The food we consider most succulent, the art we enjoy, our patterns of friendship, family solidarity, and group identity are influenced by the cultural standards we absorb.

Ethnic Music

The same is true of music. A people's sense of their history, of their relationship to a deity, of their joy in life and sorrow in death are revealed by the use they make of musical materials.

And ideas of what music should be—how it should sound, when it should be heard, and who should perform it—are related directly to cultural backgrounds. In short, the "ear" of the listener is very much conditioned by his culture.

The Role and Function of Music in Non-Western Cultures

In most non-Western societies, music is almost completely integrated into the day-to-day lives of individuals. Musical performance is not considered the special province of highly trained professionals, nor is musical expression reserved for scheduled concerts and recitals. At work and at play, during worship or healing the sick, music assumes its place as a necessary accompaniment to most ceremonial and social functions.

Music and Religion

In Africa, much of the music is meant to be heard by the deity. The Dogon of Mali believe that music, specifically the drum, is the vehicle through which the sacred word is brought to man. More commonly, music is used to lift up men's prayers to a divinity. An African agricultural festival cannot be disbanded until the good will of the deity is ensured through the singing of special songs. Chants to bring rain and to guard against forest fires must also be included in any festival gathering if the threat of disaster is to be minimized. Similarly, American Indians believe music to be endowed with mystical qualities. Through music and ceremonial dancing, the benevolence of the gods can be secured.

The Hindu religion influences many forms of musical expression in India. The majority of Indian songs are devotional, expressing a love for the deity. The religious spirit expresses itself throughout a wide range of subjects, from the most personal and familiar to esoteric, abstract philosophy. Even the songs of erotic love often convey the bliss of union with the divine.

A unique blending of indigenous music with the established forms of worship has taken place recently in Mexico. At the altar of the Cathedral of Cuernavaca, the first "Mariachi Mass" was celebrated in 1966. Using the traditional mariachi ensemble—flutes, guitars, violins, trumpets, and voices—the words of the Catholic Mass are set to the rhythms and melodies of Mexican mariachi music. The mariachi band plays and sings the verses while the congregation joins in the musical response. In this instance, a form of musical expression considered "secular" has been given new life and meaning by being included as a valuable accompaniment to religious worship.

Music and the Progression of Life

Nowhere in the world is music more a part of the very process of living than in Africa. Music follows the African through each hour of his day and through all the changes and events of his life.

To ensure the delivery of a healthy baby, special songs are sung during the hours of childbirth. After the birth, the joy and thankfulness of the family finds expression in chants and dancing. The naming of the baby, the loss of a first tooth, and other incidents in the life of the child, from infancy through puberty, will be celebrated with music for the occasion. After puberty, when an African marries, his wedding will be celebrated with music. Even death has its own musical program. Songs of mourning for the dead are sung before burial. But after burial, a series of more joyful songs are considered necessary in order to turn the relatives' thoughts away from death. The well-known brass band of the American South, leading the mourners away from the cemetery with a nearly joyous rendition of *When the Saints Go Marching In*, is almost certainly a descendant of this African tradition.

Music and Group Identity

In addition to marking the stages of an African's life, music also deepens and defines his existence. Through songs and dances he is taught the language of his tribe, the traditions of family living, the obligations he

Figure 5.1 Throughout the wide range of cultures within the African continent, music helps mark every turning point of life. Here, Moroccans use their native Arab music to celebrate a marriage at Marrakech. (Sabine Weiss, Rapho Guillumette)

will be expected to fulfill, and even "the facts of life." The communal holidays and festivals he attends are celebrated through seasonal musical offerings. Should his tribe or nation be forced to wage war, music will be a part of the preparation for battle.

Very frequently the collective history of a people is conveyed and kept alive through epic "story songs." The ballads of the Argentinian gaucho reaffirm the common background shared by the patriotic descendants of Bartolome Hidalgo, the nineteenth-century revolutionary priest. Jews have fought, fasted, and died to the strains of *Hatikva,* sung to bolster their courage in the face of opposition, reenforcing their sense of a common destiny.

Music is also often used to chastise those whose actions are deemed unacceptable. American Indians sing songs of mockery to ridicule a member of society who fails to conform. The Eskimos use music to lessen tensions between individuals, tensions that could have dangerous consequences if left to fester. Should two members of an Eskimo community be unable to come to terms, they are given the opportunity to sing songs of ridicule in which they compete to achieve the most satisfying heights of character assassination and personal slander. When finally all aggression is spent, the song contest is discontinued.

At Work and at Play

To ease the strain of monotonous labor, peoples everywhere have sung their own work songs. African slaves working on the cotton plantations of the American South sang together of a better life "across the river." Today, in Africa, work songs that counter the dreariness of repetitive agricultural tasks or provide diversion from the dangers of gold and diamond mining are still being sung. When his work is done, the African relaxes by singing love songs or relaxing songs simply for the sheer pleasure of the sounds.

To heighten the excitement involved in games of chance, American Indians risked their treasures to the background sounds of gambling music. Athletic events among the Indian tribes were also given their own prelude and accompaniment.

In India, villagers dance to the accompaniment of a transverse flute, stringed and bowed instruments, and a variety of drums. Vertical, single-skin drums, small and large two-skinned drums, and wooden and pottery drums provide a wealth of percussive effects. Simple, lilting work songs, generally unaccompanied, are sung in India as the village inhabitants go about the chores of farming and fishing.

Politics and Protest

Through music, members of African cultures are informed of their political institutions and the laws of their community. Among the Banum people of the Cameroon, a specific piece of music is traditionally performed only at the hanging of a government minister. In some West African cultures, political music is considered so important to the general welfare that select groups of musicians, known as Griots, specialize in these songs of governmental and social information.

The African struggle for independence finds articulation in many songs of protest. Throughout their long history, Africans have sung and chanted to strengthen themselves for the battles they both desired and feared. Today, in America, we have a similar type of protest music coming from the young and the disestablished. When Buffy Saint-Marie, an American Indian, uses the musical idiom of her people to express outrage over their collective fate, one hears again the unique ability of music to mobilize discontent and turn it into active resistance.

Music as Healer

In many non-Western cultures the curative powers of music have become ritualized. Chants and dances are performed in Mexico and other South American countries to drive away the demon of disease, while in many African societies songs and wild "possession" dances performed to release a disturbed mind from its torment provide an ancient and hypnotically effective type of psychotherapy.

Figure 5.2 Music is often an integral part of the African community's political climate. In Nairobi, tribal musicians and dancers are called upon to rally support for both major political parties. (Frederick Ayer, Photo Researchers)

Characteristics of Ethnic Music

Although ethnic music is frequently composed by an individual, it is soon appropriated by the entire community. If a new song or chant captures a common feeling of joy or fear, jubilation or mourning, it is taken for the people's own, used freely whenever the occasion seems fitting, modified, and elaborated on at the group's discretion.

Perhaps some of the attraction of ethnic music evolves from this lack of any personal "ownership" of the songs. Because the individual composer does not insist that his name be linked with the products of his musical imagination, his compositions are free to become the possession of the people and are passed down over the generations in an essentially oral tradition.

Pitch

The scales employed in ethnic music are often markedly different from the diatonic tonality that Westerners have long accepted as "normal." During the ancient period, Chinese musicians and philosophers believed in the existence of one true "foundation tone" upon which the whole edifice of musical composition should be built. This foundation tone, or *huang chung*, was thought to have social, cosmological, and mystical significance. For many centuries, the disappearance of a dynasty was attributed to its inability to find the true *huang chung*. Several methods were used to discover the elusive tone. One method prescribed that the correct height for the pipe that would produce the true *huang chung* would be equal to ninety average-size grains of millet laid end to end. From this tone the pitch of the other tones in the Chinese musical system were derived by means of small bamboo tubes. These tubes, sized through an exact mathematical formula, produced twelve tones, or *lü*, which are roughly comparable to the twelve semitones of the Western scale. Acoustical science reveals that all the vibration frequencies of the twelve *lü* are powers of two and three, which in Chinese philosophy, are the numbers of earth and heaven. The *lü* also correspond to the twelve months of the year, so that each month has its tone. The twelve tones are never used chromatically as they are in Western music. Rather they provide a "free choice" from which the musician selects five tones to form a pentatonic scale. This scale, used widely in Chinese music, consists of any five tones that will reach the octave on the sixth degree. If we play the pentatonic scale of C D E G A (C) on the piano, we will quickly hear a characteristic "oriental" quality, produced by the pentatonic structure. The five black keys on the piano, another pentatonic scale, will also evoke the feeling of Far Eastern music. The five tones of the pentatonic scale were believed by the Chinese to correspond to the five elements: earth, air, water, fire, and metal.

The pentatonic scale was also prevalent in the music of the North and South American Indians. In South America, each tone of the pentatonic scale was given its own mode or characteristic treatment.

The close association between a scale and certain modes or types of melodic composition characterizes Arabian music. The Arabian scale, or *maqam*, is more than a series of tonal progressions. In practice, the *maqam* is the basis for the melodic formulas, rhythmic patterns, and ornamentations that are associated with it. Thus, to compose a piece in any given *maqam* means not only to choose a key but to choose a style as well.

The mystical and complex relationship between a key and the type of music that it naturally fosters is nowhere studied more closely than in India. Each of the seven notes, or *svars*, of the Hindu scale—*sa, re, ga, ma, pa, dha,* and *ni*—represent a basic mood. *Sa* and *ma* are associated with tranquility, *re* connotes harsh feelings, joy or gaiety is expressed in *pa*, sorrow is shown in *ni*, and solemn moods are expressed through *ga* and *dha*.

These seven notes, which correspond approximately to the Western diatonic scale, are modified through the use of *shrutis*. *Shrutis* alter the basic notes in much the way that accidentals in Western music change the notes. The *shrutis* can prescribe that a note be played in either its natural state, flat, very flat, sharp, or very sharp. These *shrutis*, or *microtones*, are very difficult for even the well-trained Western ear to distinguish. A person not trained in Indian music from childhood has difficulty hearing the subtle difference between a sharp *dha* and a very sharp *dha*.

From the seven basic tones and their modifications, melodic modes known as *ragas* have been developed. Ragas are governed by a complex musical system in which certain tonal combinations are permitted while others are strongly prohibited. For example, some ragas do not allow the notes *re* and *dha* to be used in an ascending melodic progression but permit their use in descending melodic progressions. Occasionally, a note that does not belong in the raga at all is sounded intentionally to heighten the tension and the poignancy of the melody.

Unlike the highly codified, almost mathematically exact, musical tradition that influences the ragas of India, Africa's songs and chants pour forth in a variety of styles and scale patterns. Music composed on a foundation of pentatonic or even heptatonic scales coexists with a large body of songs based on the diatonic pattern. It is the use of the diatonic scale that gives much of African music its folksong quality.

Harmony

Western music is steeped in its own harmonic laws. From the period of J. S. Bach through the nineteenth century, composers wrote music in which harmonic considerations were weighed equally with melodic claims.

However, in non-Western music, harmony, if it occurs at all, exists mainly as a by-product of melodic elaboration. The melodic exuberance

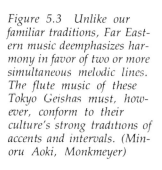

Figure 5.3 Unlike our familiar traditions, Far Eastern music deemphasizes harmony in favor of two or more simultaneous melodic lines. The flute music of these Tokyo Geishas must, however, conform to their culture's strong traditions of accents and intervals. (Minoru Aoki, Monkmeyer)

of African folk songs carries over into round-type polyphony or a simple harmonic structure in which one group of performers sustains the key tone of a melody while another group repeats the tune. At times, both groups are likely to sing the same melody at different pitches in what is known as heterophonic style.

Melody in Far Eastern music is the basis for a kind of polyphony in which two or more melodic lines proceeds simultaneously. All parts start the piece in unison and must arrive at the strong accents of the bar either in unison or in intervals of fourths or fifths, the pefect consonances. Although all intervals are permitted on weak beats, the resultant "chords" are not treated harmonically but rather as two or more unrelated notes of their own melodic lines.

To set off the melody of Indian ragas, a harmonic drone is played almost constantly throughout the piece. This drone consists of the key note for the raga, the note a fifth above, and the higher octave. For example, if the raga is played in C, the drone would include the tones C, G, and C. Or if the raga is constructed in E, the drone would be E, B, and E. This drone supplies the only harmonic element of Indian music. It serves an extremely important function by providing a harmonic frame of reference for both the audience and the performer.

Rhythm

As the drone holds an Indian raga together harmonically, the rhythmic cycle, or *tala*, unifies it metrically. Talas comprise a fixed number of beats, or *matras*, which are grouped together in an orderly arrangement. The tala known as *tintal* refers to a cycle of sixteen beats grouped in four (4–4–4–4). Save for a rhythmically free prelude known as the *alapana*, this rhythmic arrangement is continued throughout the raga. Another popular tala is *jhaptal*, in which ten beats are divided into four bars (2–3–2–3). In *sultal*, the same ten beats are divided into five bars (2–2–2–2–2). Although there are twenty talas in common use, the most frequently employed tala is tintal. While maintaining the strict division of the tala, the players are free to explore and improvise on their own rhythms, competing with each other in a back and forth contest of rhythmic virtuosity. The rhythmic tension is increased only by the requirement that all players reach the *saman*, or first beat of the cycle, exactly together. As the players attempt more and more daring cross-rhythms, and yet still manage to come out together on the saman, the audience begins to assist the performers by clapping out the beats of the tala.

The tempo, or speed, at which a raga is performed does not vary within a section. Indian music is played from beginning to end at a constant tempo. Indian music is generally performed in only one of three tempos: slow, moderate, and fast. The moderate tempo is exactly twice as fast as the slow tempo; the fast tempo is precisely twice as fast as the moderate tempo.

The unvarying pace with which Africans sing and play their music is both legendary and amazing. For minutes, even hours, African musicians are able to maintain an exact and constant speed. Within this

Figure 5.4 African musicians, such as these of the Southern Rhodesian Makishi tribe, can perform for hours with astonishing rhythmic regularity. By blending or opposing one rhythm with another, countless variations of tone and feeling can be conveyed. (Carl Frank, Photo Researchers)

framework of a steady, changeless tempo, Africans drum, sing, and play in spontaneous patterns of "rhythmic polyphony." Drums beat out rhythms that are imitated and varied by voices. Instruments play in one meter while a singer chants in another. This superimposition of one rhythmic structure upon another is customary in African music. When cross-rhythms work together to produce a particularly exciting passage, West Africans call it a "hot rhythm."

The rhythms of Far Eastern classical music are, by and large, duple ($^2/_4$, $^4/_4$). Triple rhythms are generally found only in the popular music. Rhythmic formulas in Eastern music are based on one or more of the traditional "cell units." In the Japanese music of the Noh theater, there are two hundred of these units. Rhythmic cell units, on first hearing, seem to be quite complex. In reality, they are simple rhythmic formulas ornamented by elaborate percussive effects.

Instruments

The particular way in which a culture invents, classifies, and employs musical instruments reveals a great deal about its musical traditions.

The immense size and diversity of ancient Chinese orchestras is well known. The orchestra of the Temple of the Ancestors at Peking included over 150 players. Musicologists have come to believe that the Chinese use of a variety of instrumental timbres represented an attempt to compensate for the absence of harmony in Chinese music. The existence of a variety of instruments also encouraged a "programmatic" style, in which the instruments were used to create realistic sound effects such as animal cries or roaring gales.

The musical instruments of China are classified according to the material from which they are made. Metal instruments include bells, gongs, chimes, and the carillon. The stone chime, constructed of small L-shaped plates, is grouped with the stone instruments. Of the silk instruments, the *ch'in,* or silk-stringed zither, is considered the most prestigious. Used as both a solo instrument and an accompaniment for solo song, the ch'in dates back to the Confucian period and is described as the "instrument of philosophers."

The transverse flute and the panpipe are bamboo instruments. The wood and skin instruments include a rich variety of percussive devices. The globular flute, an instrument similar to our ocarina, is defined as a clay instrument, while the *sheng* mouth organ fits into the category of gourd instruments. Important in the Chinese orchestra, the sheng consists of seventeen pipes set into a gourd wind chest. Its sound is said to imitate the cry of a phoenix bird and its shape resembles a phoenix with folded wings.

A number of Japanese musical instruments are derived from the Chinese. The *biwa,* a short-necked lute, is an offshoot of the Chinese *p'ip'a.* The *sho* mouth organ is closely related to the Chinese *sheng.* Of the two forms of the *koto* that exist in Japan, one style is considered authentic while the other is similar to the Chinese *ch'in.* The koto became popular in the seventeenth century and is still used as an instrument of art music. Over the koto's six-foot-long sounding board, thirteen waxed silk strings are stretched and anchored at both ends. Beneath the strings, movable bridges facilitate quick and complex adjustments in pitch. These adjustments are made throughout the performance so that even while the player is plucking the strings he is constantly repositioning the numerous bridges. Another well-known stringed instrument of Japan, the *samisen,* resembles a guitar without frets. The plectrum that is used to pluck the samisen is both picturesque and functional. Shaped like a large ax head, the samisen plectrum yields a heavy, almost percussive stroke.

From the thirteenth century, the favorite Arabian stringed instrument has remained the *'ud.* In its first form, the 'ud had four strings, the outer two bearing Persian names, the inner two named in Arabic. To obtain a full range of two octaves, a fifth string was later added. Today, the 'ud has ten or twelve strings grouped in twos and stretched over a sounding board without frets. Like the ch'in in China and the koto in Japan, the Arabian 'ud has been traditionally associated with scholarship and philosophic speculation.

Associated with Saraswati, the Indian goddess of music and learning, the *vina* is the oldest of the Indian stringed instruments. Still used in southern India, it is constructed of jackwood, rosewood, or ebony, and strung with seven strings controlled by pegs and two sets of movable bridges. Two hemispheric resonators fashioned from gourds amplify the sound. When played, the *vina* is either placed horizontally across the performer's knees or laid slanting against his left shoulder.

In the northern regions of India, the vina has been supplanted by the sitar, which is smaller and simpler to play. The sitar has a track of twenty metal frets, above which are the seven main strings. Below the frets, a set of thirteen sympathetic strings can be tuned to the pitches that will most advantageously pick up the main notes of the raga to be performed.

The drums of India are fashioned so that they will reenforce the most important tonal pitches of the raga. In the south, the *mridangam,* a single-piece drum with two heads is treated with tuning pastes so that various areas on the playing surface produce differing pitches. The *tabla* of the north is actually a set of two drums; the right-hand drum is tuned to the tonic, dominant, or subdominant of the raga, whereas the left-hand drum functions as the bass drum and is capable of producing many tones, which can be varied in response to the pressure of the performer's left hand.

The need for drums that can produce a variety of tones is nowhere felt more keenly than in Africa, for Africans use drums to express their every thought and feeling. Even intricate and complex messages are relayed by drumbeat. Because many of the African languages are tonal, or inflected, languages, in which the meaning of words is changed by delicate alterations of pitch, drums tuned to higher and lower tones can imitate the talking voice. The "talking drums" of the Ashanti people in Ghana are used to transmit messages from camp to camp. One of the most tonally flexible drums, the hourglass or *donno* drum, is a double-headed drum held in the player's left armpit. By squeezing his arm, the player alters the length of the strings that hold the two drum heads together, and he is thus able to raise and lower the drum's pitch.

Another popular African instrument possessing both percussive and tonal elements is the xylophone. Used both in instrumental ensembles and alone as a solo instrument, the African xylophone is constructed in one of many ways. In some xylophones, wooden planks or keys are set across banana trunks, while in others, wooden keys, each with their own gourd or calabash resonator, rest in a wooden frame.

The thumb piano, or *mbira*, of Africa is said to be second only to the drum in popularity. The soft and gentle sound of the *mbira* is produced when metal reeds, constructed of varying lengths and attached to a sounding board, are plucked.

The tremendous vitality and subtlety of African drumming are found in slightly different form among a people far removed geographically. The Indians of North America listened to the sound of their drums with both reverence and awe. They believed that through the sound of the drumbeat the rhythm of supernatural powers could be heard. In addition to ceremonial drums of all kinds, rattles made from gourds, turtle shells, and deer hoofs were often tied to dancers' legs.

Any materials that the American Indians had at hand eventually found their way into Indian instruments. Like early instrument-makers everywhere, the Indians were subject to the control of environmental availability.

Examples of Ethnic Music

The Far East

China From its beginnings, Chinese music was conceived of as a system that would reflect the surrounding cosmological order. Each of the twelve tones, or *lü*, represented either the yin or yang, male or female elements of the universe. The tones were also used to symbolize the hours of day and night and the revolving cycle of months in the yearly calendar. Because each tone was invested with mystical significance, Chinese music developed as a system in which the perfect performance of these individual tones was regarded as the highest art. Confucius himself played a stone slab on which only one note could be produced. Yet, he is said to have played it with such a full heart that its sound was captivating. The sophistication needed to enjoy subtle colorations and inflections on only one tone was, of course, not a universal gift among the ancient Chinese. Popular discontent with "scholarly music" was expressed by the Prince of Wen (426–387 B.C.): "When in full ceremonial dress I must listen to the Ancient Music, I think I shall fall asleep, but when I listen to the songs of Cheng and Wei, I never get tired."

From these secular, less "cultivated" song styles, a popular form developed in which sight and sound, voice and instruments were combined to produce "something for everyone." Presented originally in teahouses or outdoor arenas, Chinese opera evolved in an atmosphere of noisy informality. Today, the uniform loudness with which the operas are performed is thought to be a stylistic holdover from the days when players had to compete with squalling babies and clattering rickshaws for audience attention. To involve the audiences emotionally, singers and musicians presented operas in which characterization was the overriding concern.

To delineate the three basic emotional moods, three corresponding musical styles became customary. For scenes involving agitated emotions such as happiness, gaiety, or temporary distress a quick, a light style known as *hsi p'i* was employed. Music written in another style, *erh huang*, portrayed subdued, contemplative moods, whereas a character's despair or depression was conveyed through the *fan erh huang* style of composition.

Similarly, various dramatic situations came to be associated with certain melodic patterns. These stereotyped melodic formulas are still available to any composer who wishes to communicate one of the standard dramatic incidents common to Chinese operatic plots. Consequently, a number of operas are heard in which the same melodic material forms the basis for any set aria describing the anguish of the abandoned wife, a villain's intended vengeance, or the final triumph of good over evil.

The vocal quality and range in these arias also depends, to a large extent, on the type of character to be portrayed. Heroes are required to sing with a tight, controlled rasp, whereas heroines often produce a high, nasal sound that originated with the male singers who played the feminine parts until recently.

The scenes of an opera generally begin with percussion overtures. Percussive devices are used to accompany the recitative and to mark off one character's words from another's. In melodic passages, instruments of the orchestra—bowed and plucked lutes, fiddles, and flutes—play the main melody either in unison or at various pitches, in heterophonic style. The melody's termination is emphasized by the crashing of cymbals.

Japan The music of Japan is also closely interwoven with Japanese theatrical tradition. The Noh plays, first written and performed in the fourteenth century, are dependent on an integration of all the theatrical arts—music, dance, poetry, design, and costume—to achieve their intended effect of quiet, nearly religious sublimity.

The instrumental ensemble of the Noh play, the *hayashi*, is not hidden in a typical Western orchestra "pit" but is seated on stage along with the actors. In Japanese music, traditional regard is given to the gentle and self-restrained manner in which musical instruments should be played. Musicians are enjoined to perform gracefully so that aesthetic pleasure may be taken in their visual aspects as well as in the sounds they produce. The hayashi ensemble is made up of four instruments: a transverse flute, two hand-beaten drums, and one stick-beaten floor drum used mainly in dance pieces. The two hand drums provide a rhythmic framework in which singers can function flexibly. The flute part, played as a sort of accompaniment to the vocal line, bears little tonal or thematic relation to the music the singers perform. In the Noh music, voice and flute correlate with each other in a magical sense, but are not expected to join harmonically. Because these melodic lines are constructed with an elastic, flowing rhythm, the rhythmic patterns depend for further definition upon the "announcements" of the drummers, who periodically call out the beats.

From the early Noh plays, two popular forms of musical entertainment developed in the seventeenth century. The Bunraku puppet theater pleased a growing audience in the mercantile center of Edo (Tokyo). With a narration set to the accompaniment of samisen music, the Bunraku puppet theater took on a more flamboyant, spontaneous style.

Taking elements from both the Noh plays and the Bunraku theater, the Kabuki players used drama, dance, and vocal and instrumental music to create a new form. Kabuki theater preserves the convention of the on-stage instrumental ensemble. This ensemble is responsible for both instrumental interludes and certain song accompaniments. As in Bunraku, recitatives are accompanied by one *samisen*.

Finally, a third musical ensemble known as the *geza* functions as an off-stage musical index to the dramatic plot. Singers, flutes, drums, samisen, and a battery of bells and gongs used singly and in combination play musical patterns with a dramatic meaning. A given melody indicates the time and location of a scene. The *o daiko* barrel drum is symbolic of a rainstorm, a military battle, or a soft snowfall. Thus, in much the same way as a Western audience takes its clues from the ominous chords or gentle harmonies of a motion picture soundtrack, Japanese audiences respond to the precise dramatic indications of Kabuki music.

India

The ancient Vedic hymns of the second millenium B.C. are the source of Indian melody. Sung as incantations to the divinities or as sacred sacrificial formulas, the hymns were performed to ensure the order and stability of the universe.

The tradition and style of Vedic psalmody has been preserved through a collection known as the Rig Veda. Later, scholars of the sixth century A.D. drew upon the musical theories illustrated in the Rig Veda to form their own compilation of Indian musical theory known as the Natya Sastra. The Natya Sastra thus provides a bridge that connects the oldest musical traditions of India with the forms still in use today.

The basic motive force of Indian music has remained constant: Music must reflect the inherent order and majesty of the universe and contribute to a performer's own spiritual development. This deep and sustaining tie, which anchors Indian music to its mystical, philosophic framework, is reflected in the ordering of the ragas themselves. Each raga is related to a certain time of day or night. Indian historians tell of a musician at the court of the sixteenth-century emperor Akbar who sang a night raga at midday with such power and beauty that "darkness fell on the place where he stood." Each raga is associated also with a definite mood, a color, a festival, a diety, and certain specific natural events. Sexual differentiation of the ragas into male ragas and female raginis completes the unification of Indian music with the total surrounding cosmology.

A teacher of Indian music is considered a true guru, responsible not only for his students' musical progress but also for their spiritual development. The guru receives no money for his services. The knowledge and wisdom he imparts are thought to be priceless and far beyond any conceivable financial remuneration. Often, a student binds himself to one guru for a period of ten years or more. During that time he will be expected to memorize over sixty ragas and talas. The memorization is demanded not to ensure perfect reproduction of the ragas but to promote the complete familiarity and understanding needed to master the pinnacle of Indian musical art—the art of improvisation.

The ability of a performer to improvise and create his own music within the strict structure of the raga and tala is the standard by which Indian audiences judge the art of a musician. In order to leave room for the performer to improvise, the forms of Indian music have remained quite flexible. In a rhapsodic, rather free introduction to the raga, the performer gradually reveals the main notes of the raga. At some time during this introduction (the *alapana*) the drone softly begins to intone the raga's harmonic structure. Not until the rhythmic cycle, or tala, is set into motion does the main section of the raga get underway. Then, using his own unique style of *gamaka*, or melodic ornamentation, the performer begins the raga, varying and elaborating it with all the resources at his command.

If the raga is being performed by more than one musician, the competitive, improvisational rhythmic exploration of the tala cycle often becomes predominant. For an Indian audience, these feats of rhythmic and musical daring are more than mere pyrotechnics. Each time the performers reach the saman, or first beat of the tala cycle, with exact precision, it is as though the reality of universal order has once more been reaffirmed.

Arabia

As the Moslem conquerors streamed across the Middle East, they took with them Mohammed's injunction against purely secular music. Music was not to provide diversion from the religious impulse. Rather, the cantillations of the muezzin's call to prayer were to be the dominant form of "serious" musical expression.

The musical tradition of the pre-Islamic Arab world was essentially vocal. Bedouin camel drivers sang to themselves as they drove their

Figure 5.5 Berber tribesmen from Morocco's High Atlas mountains play traditional Arab music. (Carl Frank, Photo Researchers)

caravans across the desert. Their songs, known as *hudas*, imitated the rhythmic movements of the camel's hoofs and warded off the spirits of the desert. Similar to the hudas in musical style, funeral laments or *bukas* were sung to assuage the grief of bereavement, while before battles, warriors intoned supplicatory songs to plead for supernatural strength.

These songs, in which the vocal line unfolds against a simple, chordal accompaniment, are known as monodic. The interest of monodic music derives from the ebb and flow of its melodic contours and the beauty of the singing style. Because Arabian music is essentially monodic, audiences in the Middle East are sensitive to subtle nuances and colorations of the singing voice. The association between the music of the Arab peoples and a predominantly vocal form has also left its stamp on the shape of Arabian melody. Because each line of Arabic verse must be complete in itself, each phrase of any melody set to Arabian poetry must be similarly rounded off, or self-sufficient.

The first flowering of Islamic music in the seventh and eighth centuries A.D. evolved from this tradition of song. The solo lute song became the dominant mode of musical expression as Islamic music achieved its first classical period under the Umayyad caliphate (661–750 A.D.).

However, quarrels between musicians who advocated the introduction of newer, more modern forms and those who prescribed the use of unfamiliar or extravagant styles became rampant. A schism broke out in the ninth century between the ancient and modern schools of Arabian music. Ishaq al-Mausili (d. 850), one of Islam's greatest musicians, rigorously defended the preservation of the old music and protested all decadent and "effeminent" displays of virtuosity. Unable to control his own jealousy, Ishaq forced his greatest pupil, Ziryab, to leave Baghdad. Ziryab went to Spain, taking with him the living tradition of Islamic music. The transplantation of Islamic music to the soil of Moorish Spain brought the musical theories of the Middle East within the reach of European scholars. With the tide of Moslem migration, Arabian instruments were also carried to the European continent. Such instruments as the *'ud* and *rebab* are believed by many musicologists to be the precursors of the lute and the rebec.

Africa

Through drum, voice, and xylophone, mbira, and musical mouth bow, the African fills his days and nights with music for work, relaxation, instruction, information, and ritual. The African is far more apt to play an instrument or sing *with* others than *for* them. It is this ease of coming together to make music that results in the characteristic group performance of African music. Although there is solo singing and playing in the music of Africa, the most typical musical expression involves any number of singers and players.

The need to organize the musical efforts of many individuals into one cohesive expression has given African music some of its forms. Responsive singing, in which a leader calls out the verse and the group responds in chorus, exemplifies one form. Simple polyphonic forms in which half the group sustains the key tone or tonic while the other half proceeds with the next verse is another frequently used form. Rounds in two parts are also sung and played, and quite often the subsections of an African ensemble will perform the same melody simultaneously at different pitches in what is known as heterophonic style. At times, African music is so filled with separate simultaneous musical events that Westerners lose their way among the seemingly disparate elements. But to the African, polyphony and cross-rhythms are all the richer for their combination in new and often unpredictable improvised patterns.

The melodies that form the basis for ensemble singing or playing are generally quite short. This shortness of the melodic unit helps to keep the phrase easily workable and open to improvisation. Should one player "get hot," he can use the small melodic bit as the subject for his improvisation until another player attempts to outdo him with a still more complex and ingenious feat of virtuosity.

The flexibility with which Africans constantly reinvent their music evolves from their need to shape a satisfying composition to fit each changing occasion. Among the Watusi of Ruanda, whose lives are centered around the care of their livestock, there are literally hundreds of different songs relating to a cattleman's daily life. There are children's cattle songs, songs that glorify the royal cattle or songs that relate historical events in which cattle played a major role. No detail of a scene, a chore, or a way of life is considered too unimportant to merit its own music, composed spontaneously to fit the occasion.

North America

Although North American Indians do occasionally improvise new music, there is a seriousness of purpose about the Indian use of music which, to some extent, precludes easy, carefree invention. Music is imbued with almost supernatural powers. It is part of every act of worship, every important ritual to mark the passing of time and the coming of death. The chants and incantations that are used to heal the sick must be performed correctly; if they are not, the whole ceremony is invalidated. For this reason, much Indian music is practiced again and again until a perfect rendition is virtually assured. The emphasis given to correctness of performance preserves the many samples of Indian music; because the songs are removed from the realm of improvisation, they are thus passed down in a stable, relatively changeless form.

The process of composition is divided into two distinct "methods." In the first, a composer is "given" a piece of new music through supernatural means. He becomes, temporarily, a mouthpiece through which the music of the gods is revealed to his tribe. Among the Yuman Indians of the southwest, songs are thought to exist long before they are "untangled" from the elements by one perceptive musician.

The second method of composition is a far more prosaic and craftsmanlike process of piecing together new songs by using some fragments from old music, then perhaps adding a certain amount of original material, and concluding the piece with a traditional song from the tribe's musical past. Many of the Arapaho songs for the Peyote cult are composed in this manner.

Figure 5.6 Because American Indians believe that their music is endowed with supernatural powers, performances are practiced to perfection. The fact that costumes are very much a part of this musical tradition is evidenced by the finery worn by these dancers in their annual ceremony at Gallup, New Mexico. (Townsend Godsey, Monkmeyer)

Although the music of the North American Indians has several overall characteristics in common—it is, for the most part, vocal, monodic, and based on the pentatonic scale—the vast distances across the continent prevented the formation of one predominant style.

In the northwest coast area, the Eskimos employed a recitative-like singing style in which the melodic range rarely reached beyond the confines of a sixth. Nearby tribes to the south, such as the Nootka, the Kwakiutl, and the Makah, evolved a far more complex form in which percussion accompaniments to a melody were composed with an intricate rhythmic relationship to the vocal line. The use of such rudimentary polyphonic techniques as a drone or voices set in parallel motion also found a prominent place among the tribes of the northwest.

One striking trait that distinguished the music of the California Yuman tribes is the presence of a "rise" at the end of each composition. The rise is typically based on material taken from the main body of the song and transposed one octave above.

The tribes of the Great Basin area sang and played with comparative simplicity. Short forms in which each phrase was repeated once (Aa, Bb, Cc, etc.) were popular among the Shoshoni and Paiute nations. In the late nineteenth century, the style of the Great Basin tribes was carried eastward through a singular combination of events. Harrassed by the steady encroachment of white settlers, the Paiutes made one last effort in their desperate struggle for survival. A "prophet" among them promised that if a particular Ghost Dance were performed, it would return all the dead Indians and buffaloes to life and force the white invaders into the sea. Although the Ghost Dance was outlawed in 1891, the ceremony and its surrounding songs spread to the tribes of the Great Plains. The Apaches also brought with them the songs of accompaniment used by the Peyote cult as they migrated into the Plains area, and in this way another musical tradition filtered into the music of the Great Plains tribes.

The singing style of the Plains Indians—Blackfoot, Cheyenne, Crow, Dakota, Arapaho, and Comanche—used an extreme tension in the vocal cords and a steady, rhythmic pulsation on one tone. Among the Eastern tribes—Creeks, Cherokees, and Choctaws—it was not uncommon to shout before, during, or after the song while Apaches and Navahos of the Southwest often employed a high, falsetto type of vocal production.

The songs of the American Indians are set to both meaningful texts and meaningless syllables. Although the meaningless syllables do not communicate anything specific, they are arranged to create an abstract rhythmic pattern. For the most part, their order is considered inviolable. A Shawnee Peyote text uses the following design:

He ne ne yo yo (five times)
He ya ne, he yo ea, he ya ne (twice)
Yo ho ho, yo ho ho, he ya na
He yo wa ne hi ya na, he ne yo we.

When words are set to music it is not considered important that they create a regular meter or rhyme scheme. The words are simply small prose-poems—mystical, melancholy, or frighteningly fierce. An Arapaho vision-song is set to these gentle words:

The star-child is here.
It is through him that
our people are living.

Men of the Blackfoot tribe chanted the following menacing words as they departed on a war party:

White Dog [name of a Sioux Chief],
stay away from this tribe.
You will cry when they scalp you.

The value of this last song was directly proportional to its ability to buoy the spirits of the warriors and to frighten members of the enemy tribe who happened to overhear it. Its abstract "beauty" was of little concern. The American Indians deemed a song "good" or "powerful" only if it could accomplish its intended purpose.

South America

To uncover South America's musical past it is necessary to search for whatever remnants still survive of the indigenous, pre-Columbian songs and dances. Because this ancient music lacked written notation, almost all of it has been lost. Only the smallest scraps of historical information reveal what the musical practices of the vast Aztec and Incan empires must have been.

The Aztecs are known to have used music widely in all their social, political, and religious ceremonies. For public occasions, literally thousands of singers and dancers took part in the songs and chants. They were accompanied by numerous players of percussion and wind instruments. The Aztecs were fond of using notched bones scraped with a stick to provide what one Spanish chronicler described as *"musica muy triste"* (very sad music). Although the actual form and content of Aztec music is a matter of speculation, most musicologists agree that it was largely monophonic and that its melodies were based on the pentatonic scale.

Of the pre-Hispanic music in Peru we know very little. The Incas appear to have had a highly developed musical system and many varieties of musical instruments. The melodic capabilities of these instruments have confirmed the belief that Incan melody probably incorporated semitones in its elaborate patterns.

The sixteenth-century Spanish conquest of Central America and the northern portions of South America almost completely obliterated the indigenous music of the Indians. With stern missionary zeal, the conquistadores and the monks who followed them quickly set about substituting Roman Catholic plain chant for native religious music.

The Spanish conquest also sent white adventurers and colonialists streaming into the Caribbean Islands. In Dominica, the Spanish settlers were attracted to the *areito*, a common round dance. As the Spaniards accumulated vast plantations, they began the steady importation of slaves from West Africa to provide sufficient numbers of field laborers. The Africans brought their own musical style with them to the New World and strongly influenced the form and content of music on the islands. The marimbulla of Dominica, a popular xylophone-type instrument with metal tongues, is derived from the African marimba. African influence on the music of Haiti and Cuba is equally pronounced. The Haitian ritual dance known as the "moundongue" is a direct descendent of similar African ceremonies, whereas Cuban rhythmic variety and virtuosity, as exemplified in their bongo-drumming techniques, are certainly African-inspired.

The musical life of Brazil also reflects the influence of the large number of West African slaves transported by Portuguese plantation owners. Popular forms such as the *congada*, the *choro*, and the *samba* reveal a strong African influence.

The effort to recapture some of these early musical forms has been one of the major concerns of both the modern Brazilian composers and their colleagues throughout the South American continent. Heitor Villa-Lobos (1887–1959) sought first to repossess the treasures of Brazil's musical past through systematic musicological investigations. Subsequently, he introduced ancient forms into such compositions as *Bachianas Brasileiras* and *Choros*. "Choros"—based on the choros of pre-colonial Brazil—uses the old melodies, rhythms, and instruments to provide a modern synthesis of Brazilian folk and popular music.

In Mexico, too, the desire to reclaim the country's musical heritage has shaped its modern "national" style. Carlos Chavez, Mexico's foremost twentieth-century composer, attempted to incorporate many elements of the pre-Hispanic tradition into his musical works.

The increasing respect with which South American musicians view

Figure 5.7   These carnival musicians in Caracotu, Peru, participate in a musical tradition dating back to the Incan empire. Evidence presently indicates that considerable instrumental sophistication and melodic elaborateness have been part of that tradition for many hundreds of years. (Carl Frank, Photo Researchers)

their musical past finds expression not only in the symphonic works composed in nationalistic styles but also through a steady incorporation of indigenous forms into the liturgy of the Roman Catholic church.

Summary

The ways in which particular cultures create and perform their own music reveals a great deal about their communal life. In most non-Western societies, music is woven into the fabric of daily existence. Performance and composition are not reserved for highly trained professionals, and most songs and dances are considered communal property. The name of an individual composer is rarely attached to the piece he has written. Consequently, the music is set free for all to learn, enjoy, and modify as the occasion demands.

Although improvisation plays an extremely important role in non-Western music, musical composition is treated with seriousness and reverence, for in much of the non-Western world, music is considered a reflection of universal order and spiritual purity. The Chinese belief in one true tone and the traditional association of Indian ragas with moods and times of day exemplify the ways in which music often becomes an integral part of belief systems in non-Western cultures.

Technically, the melodies and rhythms of ethnic music are its strongest features. Harmony, if it has a role at all, occurs mainly as a by-product of melodic considerations. As a substitute for dense harmonic textures, a variety of instrumental and vocal timbres is employed. Plucked and bowed stringed instruments, flutes, trumpets, bells, rattles, and xylophones are only a few of the instruments crafted to enrich musical performance.

The musical forms of the various non-Western countries—the arias of the Peking opera, the rounds and talking drums of Africa, the Indian ragas, and the South American sambas—are only comparable in that each expresses a separate and unique culture.

A volume of Masses published by Attaingnant in 1532 depicts Francis I and the French court attending Mass. (Courtesy of the Österreichische Nationalbibliothek, Vienna)

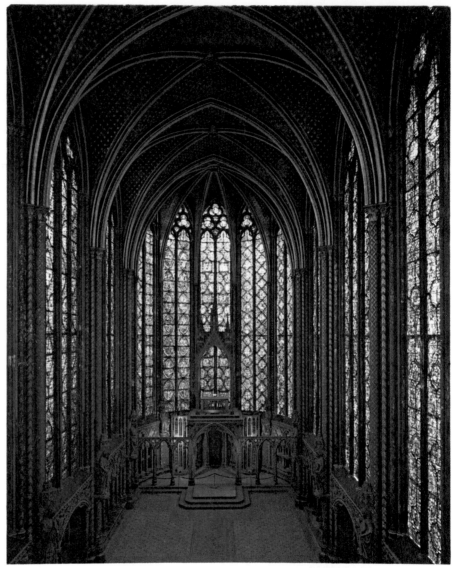

Plate 1.   Ste. Chapelle's airy, stained-glass elegance was made possible by the introduction of columns and pointed arches to support the weight of the roof. Here, thirteenth-century craftsmen depicted the Bible in stained glass. (Courtesy Rapho Guillumette, Ciccione)

Plate 2.   The bright colors and intricate designs of the medieval monks' illuminated manuscripts stand in sharp contrast to the austerity of the times. Decorations such as these were to be found in almost every kind of devotional work. (Courtesy Pierpont Morgan Library, manuscript 102, folio 100)

om tu dñs altissim' sup omñe terram:
nimis exaltatus es sup omnes deos.

Qui diligitis dñm odite malũ: custodit
dominus animas sctox suox de manu
peccatoris liberabit eos.

Lux orta est iusto: & rectis corde leticia.

Letamini iusti in dño: & confitemini
memorie sanctificationis eius

ANTATE
domino can
ticum nouũ:
quia mirabi
lia fecit.

Saluauit s
dextera eius:
& brachium sanctum eius.

Notũ fecit dñs salutare suũ: i conspec
tu gentiũ reuelauit iusticiã suam.

psalm 97

Plate 3.   Forerunner of the Italian Renaissance, Giotto di Bondone broke from tradition to make his paintings more realistic. Innovations such as the use of depth-creating shadows and perspective, as well as individualized faces and figures, are exemplified in The Mourning of Christ, Arena Chapel, Padua. (Courtesy Alinari-Art Reference Bureau)

Plate 4.   El Greco made excellent use of the exaggerated perspective, distorted proportion, and dissonant color schemes characteristic of late-Renaissance Mannerism. As seen in The Vision of St. John the Divine, these artistic techniques gave his expression of medieval religious intensity a convincing aura of mysticism. (Courtesy The Metropolitan Museum of Art, Rogers Fund, 1956)

part II   Music before 1600

Rome did not fall in a day, but slowly dissolved into hundreds of petty, isolated communities. After the Empire declined, however, the painting, sculpture, architecture, and even the clothing fashioned by the Romans remained the models until the Christian era was a thousand years old.

The Arts before 1600

During this period, the Church—which had replaced the Roman Empire as the unifying force of European civilization—was the only institution with enough stability, prestige, and wealth to commission new art in any quantity. For this reason, most of the surviving art is religious both in origin and in subject matter.

Churches and cathedrals were built like late Roman structures, with thick walls and tiny windows. This architecture prevailed partly because the fortresslike interiors served as refuges for the townspeople when barbarians sacked their villages and burned their wooden houses.

Within the monasteries, monks challenged the austerity of the times by decorating the pages of Bibles, Psalters, and other devotional works. Books of Gregorian chant were illuminated with paintings that were small but combined bright colors, intricate decoration, and a deeply felt religious zeal.

Although Western civilization was relatively stationary, people were not. Artisans traveled from town to town, perfecting their skills, learning the secrets of stone-masonry, goldsmithing, painting, and engaging in other specialized crafts. What they learned they brought with them when they returned home.

The goal of many of these journeymen was Constantinople, today called Istanbul. Constantinople was then the capital of the Byzantine Empire and the largest and wealthiest city in Europe. There the arts of the Greeks and Romans flourished and were blended with arts from the East. Throughout the West, kings and bishops eagerly sought the ornate ·

works of gold, enamel, ivory, and silk created by skilled Byzantine craftsmen. From them, Western craftsmen learned to make decorative objects for the new churches being built as Christianity spread throughout Europe.

Larger than any buildings constructed since Roman times, these churches and cathedrals exhibited a new richness of decoration and a new architecture characterized by high, vaulted ceilings supported by massive columns. Inside, these edifices were appropriate settings for the Gregorian chant, which remained the chief form of musical expression until the late Middle Ages.

By the twelfth century Christianity had replaced paganism, the barbarian invasions had ended, and forests had been cleared for agriculture. Increased trade led to the building of new cities where the citizens acquired a taste for such luxuries as spices, silks, and glassware, many of which were introduced to the West by returning Crusaders.

This was the climate in which Gothic art was born. The first pointed Gothic arches were constructed in the Abbey Church of St. Denis, completed in Paris in 1144. Within a hundred years the Gothic style had spread throughout Europe. Cities vied with one another to construct the highest, longest, and most elaborate churches. Guild halls, town halls, and the homes of the rich also reflected the Gothic influence. No longer was it necessary to build thick, massive walls; roofs were supported by soaring columns and pointed arches that could be extended almost indefinitely. As walls became structurally insignificant, windows grew in size and were filled with colored glass illustrating scenes from the Scriptures.

Like the architecture, the sculpture decorating Gothic churches became longer in shape and lighter in weight. So did figures in paintings. Even clothing became tight fitting, with tall hats and pointed shoes creating an elongated appearance.

For the first time in almost a thousand years large numbers of people had the leisure and confidence to think about more than mere survival and to pay attention to their own appearance and surroundings. Painters and sculptors began representing individuals rather than symbolic figures, even in religious art. Wealthy patrons who commissioned sacred paintings for a church had the artist include their own images, complete with warts, wrinkles, and costumes in the height of fashion. Artists—hitherto anonymous craftsmen—began to be known by name.

Music, like the visual arts, developed in new directions. The Gregorian chants were used as source materials for longer, more complex works. Formerly music had been almost exclusively in the service of the Church, but now it became somewhat secularized. Troubadours accompanied by stringed instruments sang verses about love and chivalry.

The Gothic style spread so widely that it unified Europe artistically as the continent had never been unified by politics or even by religion. Yet the very success of the Gothic style helped destroy it. Craftsmen elaborated details while ignoring the spirit of their works. Musicians were only concerned with embellishing their songs with complex passages to display their virtuosity. By the fifteenth century ornamentation existed for its own sake, and there was scarcely an inch of surface free of excessive and complex design.

Figure 6.1 The Cathedral of Tours exemplifies the impressive structures made possible by the innovations of Gothic architecture. Soaring columns and pointed arches made larger, more open, and more decorated churches the style throughout Europe. (French Cultural Services)

The Renaissance

In the fourteenth century, however, a new age had begun in the arts. Its forerunner was Giotto di Bondone (1266?–1337), known as Giotto. Gothic painting had been flat, as if the figures were pasted on the background. By using shadows and other effects, Giotto made figures stand out from the background. He painted scenes that gave the illusion of dimension and depth. Not only did he overlap figures in a group, but he individualized their expressions of sorrow, love, anger, and pity. Unlike many innovators, Giotto was recognized by his contemporaries as a genius and reformer. Other painters patterned their techniques on his and, more important, added their own. The result was the beginning of the Italian Renaissance. (Plate 3.)

The Renaissance was a period of spectacular artistic achievement. Literally meaning rebirth, it brought to Europe a spirit of humanism that had been dormant since Greek and Roman times. In art, philosophy, and literature, it centered on man rather than God, and life on earth rather than life in the hereafter.

Contributing to Renaissance humanism was the rediscovery of Greek and Roman sculpture, in which human proportions and features were faithfully rendered. Another influence was the rediscovery of ancient literature, particularly the Greek tragedies and the epic poems of Homer, which portrayed man struggling against a fate ordained by capricious destiny. This tragic sense is often a part of Renaissance art. In Masaccio's painting of the *Expulsion from the Garden of Eden*, Adam and Eve are pictured not only as figures derived from classical sculpture, but also as humans who have lost their innocence and therefore must leave Paradise weighed down by the responsibility of their acts.

Other Greek ideals accepted by Renaissance artists were those of harmony and balance. Since nature is seldom harmonious or balanced, artists freely rearranged figures and landscapes to make nature suit their ideals. In Antonio Pollaiuolo's painting *The Martyrdom of St. Sebastian*, the artist has arranged the figures to form a triangle. The composition is so well balanced that the left and right halves are almost mirror images of each other. When you notice that the two archers in the center are standing behind the others, the triangle becomes a pyramid, which had been considered an ideal form since the time of the Egyptians.

Under the enlightened despotism of the ruling Medici family, the Italian city of Florence was the major center for literature and art during the Renaissance. Sculptors Donatello and Verrocchio carved statues of saints and patriarchs in realistic poses which suggest that their action might continue when the viewer looks away. In architecture there was a return to the harmony and balance of classical Roman structure; builders relearned how to construct domes atop buildings. Instead of soaring to the heavens like Gothic churches, Renaissance churches were fixed solidly to the earth.

The classic revival created a wholly new art form in music. Scholars believed that in ancient Greece actors had sung lyric passages of the plays to musical accompaniment and that the chorus danced while chanting their passages. Attempting to recreate such performances, composers in Florence set literature and plays to music.

Songs for their own sakes also flourished. Composers wrote verses of love, which were sung in the vernacular. The refrains reflected the humor or the bawdy earthiness of the day.

The visual arts of the Renaissance, though highly and diversely creative, were technically based on mathematical principles. The aim was to achieve an effect of realism. The discovery of the principles of perspective allowed painters to create the illusion of buildings, trees, fields, and hills receding to infinity. Landscape painting was the result of the careful observation of nature by artists. Leonardo da Vinci filled notebooks with detailed studies of plants, animals, rocks, and human anatomy. Such works as the painting *Mona Lisa* by Leonardo da Vinci and the

Figure 6.2 Masaccio's Expulsion from the Garden of Eden *offers a sympathetic, human interpretation of a classical religious story. Man's heavy responsibilities and his struggle against fate were dominant themes of Renaissance humanism. (Alinari-Art Reference Bureau)*

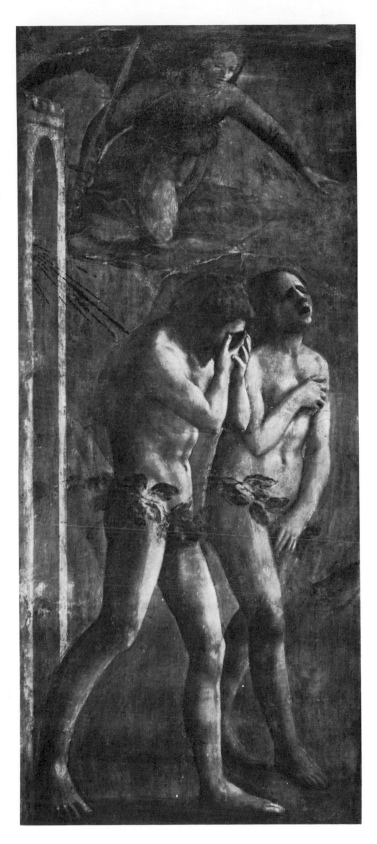

Figure 6.4 Verrocchio's statue "Christ and St. Thomas" is typical of the new realism characteristic of Renaissance sculpture. Although the subjects remained the traditional religious saints and patriarchs, their poses were convincingly lifelike. (Alinari-Art Reference Bureau)

Figure 6.5 The Renaissance church of St. Andrea reflects a return to the harmony and balance of classical Roman structures. Architectural simplicity and solidity replaced the soaring towers and flying buttresses of the Gothic period. (Alinari-Art Reference Bureau)

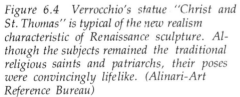

Figure 6.3 Antonio Pollaiuolo's The Martyrdom of St. Sebastian *exemplifies the Renaissance artist's commitment to harmony and balance. The obvious triangularity and mirror-image quality of this design illustrate how symmetry was sometimes forced on nature in the spirit of classical revival. (The National Gallery, London)*

statue *David* by Michelangelo were faithful to outward appearance while portraying with equal fidelity the spirit or personality of the subject.

The Renaissance was not limited to Florence. To the north, especially in Flanders, the Gothic tradition was altered to accommodate perspective, landscape, and portraiture, though Flemish artists remained preoccupied with meticulous rendering of details and still painted somewhat elongated figures.

In the early fifteenth century a Flemish artist, Jan van Eyck, invented oil painting. Oil allowed the artist to work spontaneously, to repaint sections, and to create a rich surface and subtle variations in color. These qualities characterized the great Renaissance painters of Venice—Bellini, Titian, Georgione, Tintoretto, and Veronese.

The artists of the sixteenth century recognized the achievements of Leonardo and Michelangelo by making technically brilliant but artistically second-rate imitations of the masters' works. In the late sixteenth century, as England reached the heights of the Elizabethan Age, the Renaissance declined in Italy. Exaggerated perspective distorted proportion, and dissonant color schemes were the outward masks of the late Renaissance style appropriately known as Mannerism. Turning away from realistic portrayal, artists became obsessed with personal fantasy and secret symbolic visions. For El Greco, however, Mannerism seemed the appropriate vehicle to convey his medieval religious intensity. His elongated figures and supernatural settings evoked a former age of mysticism. (Plate 4.)

chapter 7

The beginnings of our musical heritage are lost in the shadows of prehistoric times. But relics of musical instruments and pictures of musical performances indicate the central role music played in the life of earliest man. The Bible, too, makes frequent reference to music: David singing

Music before 1600

psalms while accompanying himself on the harp, the trumpets leveling the walls of Jericho. Ancient Greek philosophers and theorists wrote endlessly about music, and ancient Greek and Roman art abounds with illustrations concerning music and dance.

The earliest preserved fragments of written music are scattered, indecipherable, and impossible to date precisely. It was not until around A.D. 1000 that the melodies of the Roman Catholic church, known as *Gregorian chants*, began to be written down in a decipherable notation and preserved for posterity.

Gregorian Chant

Record 1/Side 1

The music that accompanies the Roman Catholic Mass is called *Gregorian chant*, after Pope Gregory I, who was pope from 590 to 604. Gregory's papacy saw the codification of nearly three thousand melodies, particular chants assigned to specific services in the Church calendar. At the time they were codified, however, the melodies were not written down. Until a notation capable of preserving the melodies in fixed form was developed, they were passed on by oral tradition to the priests and monks of succeeding generations. Finally, in the eleventh century, a system was devised for notating them. When we listen to the chants today, it is impossible to know what changes may have taken place during the intervening centuries.

Figure 7.1 Wandering bands of musicians, such as this sixteenth-century group, were very important to Renaissance music. Following the vernacular, often bawdy, musical tradition of earlier wanderers, this group may have sung madrigals, chansons, or lieder throughout the European countryside. (Culver Pictures)

The Chant Melodies

The chants, also known as *plainsong* or *plainchant*, are *monophonic*, or single-line melodies, sung without instrumental accompaniment. The texts are in Latin and are taken from the Bible, particularly from the Book of Psalms.

The rhythm of Gregorian chant is unmeasured. The tempos are flexible and follow the natural accents that the text would have if it were spoken.

The chants are based on scale systems called *church modes*. The melodies are built by stringing together short groups of two, three, and four notes. Their range is not great, usually encompassing no more than an octave.

The melodies achieve their sensuous beauty with the barest of means. They have an undulating, wavelike quality, an austerity, and a simple beauty that is wholly in keeping with their religious intent. They were not written to be listened to as music per se, but as a functional adjunct to early Christian worship.

Figure 7.2 This ninth-century Mass-book illustration depicts Pope Gregory I. Historians attribute the preservation of ancient Church melodies to Gregory's formal assignment of particular chants to specific services of the Roman Catholic church calendar. (Culver Pictures)

The Mass

The Mass is the most solemn service of the Roman Catholic church. It is the commemoration and symbolic reenactment of the Last Supper of Christ. The *liturgy* of the Mass, the prescribed ceremony, is divided into two parts: the *Ordinary* (those items that do not change from day to day) and the *Proper* (those items that vary according to the religious nature of the specific day in the Church year). The Mass combines the items from the Ordinary and the Proper according to the following plan.

THE LITURGY OF THE MASS

Proper	Ordinary
1. *Introit* (processional)	
	2. *Kyrie eleison* "Lord have mercy on us"
	3. *Gloria in excelsis Deo* "Glory to God in the highest"
4. *Collect* (prayer on behalf of the congregation)	
5. *Epistle* (from the Epistles of the New Testament)	
6. *Gradual* (a psalm verse)	
7. *Alleluia* (or *Tract*) (During times of penitence, such as Lent, the Alleluia is replaced by a psalm, called the Tract.)	
8. *Sequence* (a form of hymn)	
9. *Gospel* (from one of New Testament Gospels)	
	10. *Credo (in unum Deum)* "I believe in one God"
11. *Offertory*	
	12. *Sanctus* "Holy, holy, holy"
	13. *Benedictus qui venit* "Blessed is he that cometh"
	14. *Canon* (a series of prayers said by the priest in a low voice during the consecration of the bread and wine)
	15. *Agnus Dei (qui tollis peccata mundi)* "Lamb of God, who taketh away the sins of the world"
16. *Communion*	
17. *Post-Communion* (a prayer of prayers)	
	18. *Ite missa est* "Go" (the congregation is dismissed)

Example 7.1

Salve Regina

HERMANNUS CONTRACTUS

Hail, Holy Queen, Mother of mercy, our life, our sweetness, and our hope. To thee do we cry, poor banished children of Eve. To thee do we send up our sighs, mourning and weeping in this valley of tears. Turn then, most gracious advocate, thine eyes of mercy toward us; and after this our exile, show unto us the blessed fruit of thy womb, Jesus. O clement, O loving, O sweet Virgin Mary!

Many of the items for the Ordinary and the Proper were sung to a chant melody. Chants were also composed for the *Office Hours*, or prayer services, that were held at specified times throughout the day. From a musical point of view, the most important Offices were the *Matins, Lauds, Vespers*, and *Compline*.

The Chants as Source Materials

The chant melodies were important in their own right and were a rich source of materials used by composers throughout the Middle Ages and Renaissance. Composers used the chants as the basis for longer polyphonic compositions. Even when they made melodic and rhythmic changes, the essential melodic outlines usually remained intact.

The chant *Salve Regina*, a hymn of praise to the Virgin, was sung during the Church year from the week following Pentecost to Advent Sunday. It was customarily sung during the vespers. The *Salve Regina* attracted the greatest composers of the Renaissance, who used the melody for polyphonic compositions.

The melody and text were written by Hermannus Contractus, a Benedictine monk who lived during the first half of the eleventh century. The grave and expressive melody was cast in the *Dorian mode*, that begins on D and extends upward for an octave. *Salve Regina* illustrates the typical manner in which a text was set to a chant melody.

Short *syllabic* groupings (in which each syllable of text is given one note) alternate freely with longer *melismatic* passages (in which one syllable is spread over several notes). The piece is made up of six sections, the first of which (A) consists of a phrase and its immediate restatement with different words. Each subsequent section consists of a line of text with its own melodic phrase. The concluding section (F) is of particular interest because of the expressiveness resulting from the melismatically extended "O," the last of which constitutes the longest melisma in the entire piece.

Secular Music

In addition to the music of the Church, the Middle Ages witnessed the growth of a rich tradition of nonreligious, or *secular*, music. Gregorian chants used only Latin, but secular music came to emphasize texts in the vernacular language of the country in which they were written. Often these texts concerned the subject of love. Other texts were humorous or obscene; some were political or told stories of vagabonds. The most important early secular vocal music was created and performed by poet-musicians called *trouvères* in northern France, *troubadours* in southern France, and *minnesingers* in Germany. Their ranks included many members of the nobility who traversed the countryside as court musicians, poets, and sometimes even jugglers. The number of musical and poetic works created by these wanderers is enormous. The melodies of their songs, like the melodies of the chant, were monophonic and simple in design. But they were probably sung with some kind of instrumental accompaniment. The songs were mainly *strophic*; that is, all the stanzas were sung to the same music.

Polyphony and Measured Rhythm

Music, both sacred and secular, remained monophonic until the tenth century, when two or more voice parts began appearing in combination. This new method of composition, called *polyphony*, went through a number of stages over a long period of time. At first, two melodic lines

Figure 7.3   The evolution of the writing of musical notes has taken nearly a thousand years. Not only has the style changed, but rhythm has become increasingly regulated, with precise time values related to each other. (Culver Pictures)

simply duplicated each other at different pitch levels. They moved in *parallel motion;* that is, at the same time and in the same melodic direction. If one line went up, the other line went up, and so forth. Gradually *contrary motion* was introduced to provide variety—one voice might move up, the other would move down. The two voice parts began to be *melodically* independent; that is, they moved in different directions, but at the same time. These early polyphonic compositions were called *organa* (singular, *organum*).

The rhythm of the earliest organa was, like that of the monophonic chant, unmeasured. It remained so as long as the two melodies moved at the same time. But eventually the two voices assumed *rhythmic* independence. They not only moved in parallel and contrary melodic motion, but in *different time patterns.* This diversity between the two parts made it necessary to develop a new type of rhythmic notation so that each voice could be accurately coordinated with the other. *Mensural notation* appeared, in which the precise length of time of each part was indicated. Later organa employed three and even four voice parts.

Thus, two major changes took place in Western music: (1) the change from monophony to polyphony, and (2) the change from unmeasured, relatively "free," rhythm to more regulated rhythm in which precise time values were related to each other. These principles of polyphony and measured rhythm were fully developed in the motet and in the polyphonic setting of the Mass.

The Motet

Much as the organa had added an independent line of music to the chant, the *motet* added a second set of words (the name *motet* comes from the French word *mot,* meaning word). Originally a form of religious music, it grew out of the two-part organa in the thirteenth century. While the lower voice continued to sing the words and music of the chant, a second text was sung in the upper voice. The second text at first paraphrased the chant text being sung below.

The motet was soon also employed for secular occasions. As its form evolved, the upper voice began to sing in the vernacular. The subject matter was usually secular, and sometimes obscene.

Gradually, composers added a third and even a fourth voice part. The French motet *Quant voi* was typical of those written in the thirteenth century. In it the top voice carries a secular text in the vernacular and the bottom two voices carry religious texts in Latin. The chant melody is incorporated in the bottom part.

Triplum, or top part:

Quant voi revenir	*When I see returning*
D'este la saison	*The summer season*
Que le bois font retenir	*And all the little birds*
Tuit cil oisillon,	*Make the woods resound,*
Adonc pleur et souspir	*Then I weep and sigh*
Pour le grant desir	*For the great desire*
Qu'ai de la belle Marion,	*Which I have for the fair Marion,*
Qui mon cuer a en prison.	*Who holds my heart imprisoned.*

Motet, or middle part:

Virgo virginum	*Virgin of virgins,*
Lumen luminum,	*Light of lights,*
Restauratrix hominum,	*Restorer of men,*
Qui portasti Dominum:	*Who bore the Lord:*
Per te Maria,	*Through Thee, Mary,*
Detur venia	*Let grace be given*
Angelo nunciante,	*As the angel announced,*
Virgo es post et ante.	*Thou are Virgin before and after.*

Tenor, or bottom part:

Hec dies	*This is the day (which the Lord hath made)*

By the fourteenth century the motet had increased in length and had become more elaborate in its melodic and rhythmic structure. But even with the increased number of melodic lines and texts the range of voices remained narrow, and the chant was almost always retained in some form in the lowest voice part. Without question, the most important composer of the fourteenth century was Guillaume de Machaut (ca. 1300–ca. 1377). In addition to large quantities of secular music and motets, he wrote the earliest polyphonic setting of the entire Ordinary of the Mass.

By the fifteenth century the motet had evolved full circle. Once again it became primarily a religious form, using one text for all voices. The text was almost always taken from the Bible. One of the leading motet composers of the fifteenth century was Guillaume Dufay (ca. 1400–1474). His motet, based on the chant *Salve Regina,* is typical of motet composition of his time. Dufay's *Salve Regina* opens with the first notes of the chant in the soprano. In contrast to earlier medieval motets, all voices share the same text. The top part carries the actual chant melody, which is sung in measured rhythm. The lower three parts carry independently moving lines that come together at cadence points.

In its return to a sacred form, the motet became a primary source for the polyphonic setting of the Mass. At first the Proper and isolated portions of the Ordinary appeared in polyphonic form. Later the entire Ordinary was set in polyphony.

During the Renaissance, secular melodies were introduced into the Mass and the traditional chant forms were moved freely from one part of the Liturgy to another.

Renaissance Sacred Music

The Renaissance in literature and the visual arts began in the fourteenth century and centered in Italy. The Renaissance in music began in the fifteenth century in what is today northern France, Holland, and Belgium. The Franco-Flemish style developed in these countries and then became international and spread to all parts of the Continent.

In addition to Guillaume Dufay, whose motet *Salve Regina* is shown in Example 7.2, the outstanding members of this early Flemish school were Johannes Ockeghem (ca. 1430–1495), Jacob Obrecht (1452–1505), and Josquin des Prez (ca. 1450–1521). In their Masses and motets, four-part writing became standard. An independent bass part was added beneath

Example 7.2

Salve Regina

DUFAY

Hail, Queen, Mother of mercy, our life. ✘ = notes of the chant employed in the soprano part.

the chant for the first time, so that the chant was no longer the lowest voice part. In addition, the use and treatment of the chant as a basic material became much freer and at times was abandoned altogether. The practice of using secular tunes as the musical raw material for sacred compositions became extremely popular. The polyphonic style emphasized the true independence of each of the four parts.

Josquin des Prez

Record 1 / Side 1

The greatest representative of the Franco-Flemish school was Josquin des Prez, who spent most of his creative life outside his native country, Belgium. In 1475 he was a member of the choir at the court of the Duke

Example 7.3

Ave Maria

JOSQUIN DES PREZ

Hail Mary, full of grace, the Lord (is with thee).

Figure 7.4   Josquin des Prez was the grand master of the complex Franco-Flemish style. His use of imitation, voice pairing, through-composing, and counterpoint distinguished his style. (Culver Pictures)

of Szorfa in Milan and later he joined the Papal Choir in Rome. He was also active in the Italian cities of Florence, Ferrara, and Modena. In the last years of his life he returned to northern Europe.

Josquin was acknowledged by his contemporaries to be the greatest master of the time, and he developed the complex Franco-Flemish style to its highest point. In much of his secular music he employed a lighter, more homophonic style, then popular in Italy. His polyphonic style is distinguished by the use of *imitation*, wherein a melodic fragment stated in one voice is repeated or imitated by another voice a measure or two later. Examples of imitative polyphony appear earlier than Josquin, but he was the first to apply the principle consistently.

Josquin's motet *Ave Maria (Hail Mary)* is typical of his motet writing in the following ways:

1. The melodic material is freely based on a Gregorian chant, in this case *Ave Maria, gratia plena.*
2. It is a four-part composition in which the voices are often paired, the two upper voices being pitted against the two lower voices.
3. The text is *through-composed,* which means that each unit is given a separate musical setting. (This contrasts to *strophic* music, where each stanza of text is sung to the same melody.) A feeling of continuity is achieved through the device of overlapping phrases: before one phrase ends, another voice begins a new phrase, so that there is seldom a cadence when all four voices come to a stop. This continuous flow is characteristic of later Renaissance polyphony.
4. Contrapuntal passages alternate with homophonic sections, another hallmark of Josquin's style. Despite the complexity of the contrapuntal writing, the text remains clear, for Josquin assigns to the homophonic sections the expressive parts of the text.

A prolific composer, Josquin left many motets, many Masses, and a considerable amount of secular music. He was also a gifted teacher, and many of his pupils became outstanding figures in the next generation of composers.

Figure 7.5 As choirmaster of St. Peter's in Rome, Palestrina is credited with dissuading Catholic church officials from abolishing the polyphonic style by returning church music to the simplicity and purity of earlier days. (The Bettmann Archive)

Palestrina

One of the most distinguished of Josquin's successors was Giovanni Pierluigi da Palestrina (1524–1594), who spent the greater part of his life as choirmaster of St. Peter's in Rome. Palestrina's great contribution was to return church music to the simplicity and purity of earlier times. Although his motets are masterpieces of composition, his Masses constitute his most important work.

Palestrina lived and worked during the Counter-Reformation, the reaction by the Catholic church to the spread of Protestantism. Central to this reaction was the Council of Trent, which met from 1545 to 1563 to formulate and execute the means by which church reform could be accomplished. The Council investigated every aspect of religious discipline, including church music. It was the opinion of the Council that sacred music had become corrupted by complex polyphonic devices that obscured the text and diverted attention from the act of worship. To remedy this situation the Council called for a return to a simpler vocal style, one that would preserve the sanctity of the text and discourage frivolous displays of virtuosity by the singers.

Legend has it that Palestrina, in order to prevent the Council from abolishing the polyphonic style entirely, composed a Mass of such beauty and simplicity that he was able to dissuade the cardinals from taking this drastic step. Without abandoning polyphony, Palestrina created a style that was less intricate than that of his predecessors.

A prolific composer, Palestrina wrote more than a hundred Mass settings. One of his relatively late Masses was based on the same chant melody, *Salve Regina,* that Dufay had used. The Mass, which is an excellent example of late Renaissance polyphony, employs elements of the chant in each movement.

Example 7.4

Kyrie from Missa Salve Regina

PALESTRINA

Lord have mercy on us.
✗ = notes of the chant incorporated into each vocal part.

1. All the voice parts (five in this case) are of equal importance. Each participates fully in singing the text.
2. The general style is imitative polyphony, with occasional homophonic sections.
3. Strong cadences set off sections from each other.
4. The text is treated in the simplest and most sensitive way permitted by the polyphonic texture.

Palestrina's sacred music was performed *a cappella,* without instruments, but this was the exception rather than the rule. Although no instrumental parts were written, it is well known that instruments frequently played along with or substituted for a voice in one or more of the parts. The degree to which instruments were employed in the performance of sacred music is a matter of considerable debate. In any event, the music was conceived for the voice and is whole and complete without the use of instruments.

Roland de Lassus

Record 1/Side 1

Palestrina's great contemporary, Roland de Lassus (1532–1594), was born in Mons, Belgium, and began his musical career as a member of the choir in the Mons Cathedral. So beautiful was his voice that he was kidnapped three times to sing in other choirs. A truly international musical figure, he was equally well known by the Italian and Latin forms of his name—Orlando di Lasso and Orlandus Lassus. Lassus' music included all the national genres of the time. He wrote Latin motets and Masses, Italian madrigals, German lieder, and French chansons. His sacred style is most clearly shown in his motets. Lassus' setting of *Salve Regina* demonstrates the fact that his music is less imitative and has a richer harmonic quality than Josquin's.

Example 7.5

Salve Regina

LASSUS

Hail Queen of mercy.
✗ = notes of the chant melody occurring in the bass voice.

Renaissance Secular Music

In addition to being a period of great piety, the sixteenth century was also a period of bawdy earthiness, irreverent humor, and celebration of sensual love. The same composers who created works "for the greater glory of God" also wrote compositions of an entirely different character. In Italy and England the principal form of secular music was the *madrigal*; in France it was the *chanson*; in Germany it was the *lied*.

The Madrigal

The Renaissance madrigal is a poem set to music. It had its beginnings in the fourteenth century among the aristocrats of the small Italian courts. The texts, written in the vernacular, were often twelve-line poems whose subject was sentimental or erotic love. The early madrigal was written in a predominantly homophonic style. It was usually in three, but sometimes four, parts, and its expressive qualities were subdued and restrained. The so-called *classical madrigal*, a product of the mid-sixteenth century, was written usually for five and sometimes for four or six voices. Its texture was more polyphonic than the early madrigal, and a greater attempt was made to capture in the music the expressive possibilities of the words.

The final flowering of the madrigal took place during the closing decades of the sixteenth century. The late madrigal is an elaborate composition, invariably through-composed, with a mixture of homophonic and polyphonic textures. It used notes from the chromatic scale (all twelve notes in the octave) for bold effects, often to express sadness. The compositions also used coloristic and dramatic effects. One of the most interesting elements of the madrigal style was *word painting*, which attempted to represent the literal meaning of the text through music. Thus, the melody would ascend for the word "heaven," and a wavelike melody would depict the word "water." Examples of word painting exist throughout the history of music, but as an aesthetic principle it belongs mainly to the music of the late Renaissance and the Baroque periods.

Around the middle of the sixteenth century the Italian madrigal was brought to England. There it flourished under a variety of names—song, sonnet, canzonet, and ayre. William Byrd (1543–1623) and Thomas Morley (1557–1603) were the first English composers to cultivate the genre. Morley wrote simplified versions of the madrigal, known as *ballets*. Adapted from the Italian *belletti*, they were usually characterized by a *fa-la-la* refrain of the type that appears in the English carol "Deck the Halls." Enlivened by accents and a regular beat, the music was largely homophonic.

The Chanson

In the sixteenth century the *chanson* (the French word for "song") was to France what the madrigal was to Italy and England. Early chansons developed with the work of Clément Jannequin (ca. 1485–ca. 1560), Claudin de Sermisy (ca. 1490–1562), and Pierre Certon (ca. 1510–1572).

Chansons modified the motet style with strong accented rhythms, frequent repetitions, and short phrases ending simultaneously in all parts. They were usually sung by three, four, or five voices, and sections of simple imitation alternated with sections that were essentially homophonic.

Word painting occured frequently in the early chansons. Jannequin wrote several *program chansons,* in which a nonmusical idea was literally interpreted. An example is his *Chant des Oiseaux (Song of the Birds),* in which the singers' voices imitate the sounds of birds.

The Lied

In Germany the counterpart to the French chanson was the *lied,* also meaning "song." The lied (plural, lieder) dates from the middle of the fifteenth century, when both monophonic melodies and three-part settings appeared. The early lieder, which were heavily influenced by the Netherlands' polyphonic style, later provided the Lutheran church with many melodies for chorale tunes. The first important lied composer was Heinrich Isaac (ca. 1450–1517).

In the sixteenth century Germany looked to Italy and France for musicians to staff her courts and municipalities. As a result, lied composers turned from the Franco-Flemish styles to the chanson and madrigal as their new models. In these lieder the text was treated in the manner of the madrigals, and the various melodies were set in imitative counterpoint.

Renaissance Instrumental Music

Although most of the music of the Renaissance was written for voices, the role of instrumental music should not be underestimated. Instruments were used in church, at many festive and social occasions, as part of theatrical productions, and in private homes.

The earliest music played on instruments was sacred or secular vocal music. During the Renaissance some music was written specifically for instruments. Most of it was dance music, as dancing was an important part of Renaissance social life. A fairly large collection of this music has been preserved, but apparently much of it was improvised on well-known or harmonic bass patterns, much as jazz is today.

The most popular instrument of the fifteenth and sixteenth centuries was the lute. The earliest lute music consisted of transcriptions of vocal pieces and dance music, but in the sixteenth century composers began to write original pieces for lute. These *ricercari*, or *fantasias*, were elaborate, difficult, and often polyphonic pieces that demonstrated the virtuosity of the performer, who was often the composer. Beginning in the 1530s, volumes of solo music for the lute were published in Italy, France, Germany, England, and Spain.

Keyboard instruments, especially the harpsichord and the organ, were also popular during the Renaissance. Keyboard music evolved through the same states as lute music, from vocal music to dance music, and then to original compositions, which were increasingly complex.

Small chamber music ensembles, called consorts, were favored among those who performed music in their homes. One of the favorite groupings, especially in England, was a consort of several viole da gamba. Polyphonic pieces for such consorts of two to five or more were written by some of England's greatest composers, including William Byrd (1543–1623) and Orlando Gibbons (1583–1625). Similar pieces were also played by consorts of recorders and other woodwinds. Music for brass and reed instruments was popular for outdoor occasions and for festive church ceremonies.

Summary

Western music grew out of the religious music of the Middle Ages. Chants, closely allied with the Roman Catholic Liturgy, were codified and compiled during the time of Pope Gregory. In the following centuries the simple, monophonic form of these chants evolved into the more complex, polyphonic forms of the organa and the motet. These forms, in turn, were further developed by Machaut and Dufay, and the sacred music of the Renaissance culminated in the works of des Pres, Lassus, and Palestrina.

Together with the sacred music, secular music was also developing. Early vocal music was performed by trouvères in northern France, troubadours in southern France, and minnesingers in Germany. The vernacular, and sometimes bawdy, tradition of their songs was preserved in the madrigals, chansons, and lieder of the Renaissance.

**Part II
Suggested
Listening**

Musical Organizations

Capella antiqua (Munich). Directed by Konrad Ruhland, this group employs original instruments of the Renaissance or modern copies. Its performances are attempts at reconstructing the original musical practices of the times. (Telefunken Records, *Das Alte Werk* series.)

The Early Music Quartet (Munich). This vocal and instrumental ensemble of three Americans and one German specializes chiefly in medieval song literature. (Telefunken Records, *Das Alte Werk* series.)

New York Pro Musica. Founded in 1952 by Noah Greenberg and subsequently directed by LaNoue Davenport and John White, this group is one of the oldest and most prominent of American early music groups. (Decca Records.)

Choir of the Monks of the Abbey of Saint Pierre de Solesmes (Solesmes, France). The performances of chant by this Benedictine Order are considered by many scholars to be among the best, historically as well as musically. (Deutsche Grammophon Gesellschaft, DGG, Archive series.)

Medieval Secular Music

John Dunstable, *O Rosa bella.* Though Dunstable was an English composer, he spent much of his life on the Continent; some of his vocal works employ French or Italian texts.

Medieval Sacred Music

Guillaume de Machaut, *Messe de Nostre Dame (Mass of Our Lady).* One of the earliest and best known polyphonic settings of the Ordinary of the Mass. The five interrelated movements demonstrate most of the important compositional techniques of the late medieval period.

Renaissance Secular Music

Roland de Lassus, *Matona, mia cara (Matona, Lovely Maiden).* One of the best-known of Renaissance satirical pieces, this madrigal for four voices makes fun of the German soldiers occupying much of sixteenth-century Italy by—among other things—mocking their pronunciation of Italian ("Matona" for "Madonna").

Orlando Gibbons, *The Silver Swan.* One of the loveliest vocal compositions ever written, this melancholy work is an outstanding example of English madrigal style.

Renaissance Sacred Music

Guillaume Dufay, *Missa Se la face ay pale (Mass on "If My Face Is Pale").* A classic example of early Renaissance polyphonic style, this four-voice setting of the Ordinary takes its rather odd name from the title of the chanson melody upon which it is based.

Josquin des Prez, *Missa Pange lingua (Mass on "Sing, My Tongue").* One of the great masterpieces of the Renaissance, this work is based on the plain-song hymn for the Feast of Corpus Christi.

Giovanni Pierluigi da Palestrina, *Sicut cervus desiderat (Like as the Hart Desireth)* One of Palestrina's most expressive and technically perfect works, this motet, its text taken from Psalm 42, is a classic example of Palestrina-style harmonic and melodic construction.

Title page of Handel's Alexander was published by Cluer in 1726. (Courtesy of the British Museum, London)

Plate 5.   Caravaggio's Calling of St. Matthew not only demonstrates the innovative lighting for which he is famous, but also exemplifies Baroque freedom from Renaissance constraints of ideal form and harmony. Caravaggio declared early in his career that nature—not tradition—would be his teacher. (Courtesy Alinari-Art Reference Bureau)

Plate 6. Baroque churches north of Italy are characterized by their lavish appearance and ornate styling. The elaborate interior of this Monastary Church in Melk, Austria, was clearly designed to overwhelm the viewer. (Courtesy Rapho Guillumette, Serrailier)

Plate 7. The relaxed, almost random movement in Rembrandt's The Night Watch reflected a sharp break with tradition. The diffused lighting characteristic of Rembrandt's works served not only to unify the painting's elements, but also to highlight the realistic personalities he portrayed. (Courtesy Rapho Guillumette, Seut)

Plate 8. The Hall of Mirrors in the Palace of Versailles was Louis XIV's successful attempt to impress his royal status upon his visitors. The academies and factories Louis established to ensure the "correctness" of the styles used here had far-ranging influence. (Courtesy Rapho Guillumette, Belzeaux)

part III   Music of the Baroque Era

Baroque is the name given to the style of music and the visual arts that grew directly out of the Renaissance and flourished from about 1600 to 1750. Historically, the period included the Thirty Years' War, the spread of Protestantism,

The Arts of the Baroque Era

the efforts of the Roman Catholic church to retain its supreme religious authority, and the exploration and colonization of the New World. Politically and socially, such basic changes occurred as the end of feudalism, the emergence of the middle class, and the rise of nations, such as England, France, Holland, and Spain.

Europeans discovered and assimilated new worlds. The Italian astronomer Galileo discovered the mountains of the moon and the satellites of Jupiter. The Dutchman Anton van Leeuwenhoek discovered bacteria and cells through his microscope. The Englishman Sir Isaac Newton formulated laws of gravitation and motion and also discovered the nature of light and color. This was an age of violence and change on a vast scale. The arts of the times reflected this change.

The word *baroque* comes from a Portuguese word for a large and irregularly shaped pearl. The origin of this word is interesting for two reasons. First, it indicated a departure from the Renaissance artistic standard of ideal form and harmony. Second, it implied that a huge, irregular work of art could be beautiful. Each new work of art had to be judged on its own merit, not by a preconceived aesthetic formula. People who looked at art—and what is even more significant, paid the artist for it—had highly individualistic standards.

This individualistic approach to art was a reflection of the Protestant Reformation. The essence of Protestantism was that a Christian should answer only to God, and not to the Church. Before 1517, when Martin

111

Luther openly challenged its authority, the Roman Catholic church was synonymous with Christianity in most of Europe. Within fifty years, much of Northern Europe had become Protestant, and the Catholic church had retaliated with the Counter-Reformation. Sculptors, architects, painters, and composers were pressed into service by the forces of the Reformation and Counter-Reformation.

Baroque visual art aspires to persuade the observer by overwhelming him with the feeling that he is participating in a scene and not merely watching it from a distance. Few Baroque artists were more successful in this than the Italian architect and sculptor Giovanni Lorenzo Bernini (1598–1680). In his statue *St. Theresa in Ecstasy,* Bernini depicts the moment of a religious exaltation in which Saint Theresa had a vision of an angel piercing her heart with a golden arrow. The angel holds the arrow, while the saint swoons on a cloud that looks airy and fragile, although it is carved of marble. Both figures appear to be ascending to heaven. Even the most apathetic viewer senses the ecstasy of the saint and feels the impulse to rise heavenward with her.

Figure 8.1 Bernini's St. Theresa in Ecstasy *exemplifies the Baroque attempt to involve the viewer in the art. Here, the restless figures' flowing lines and soft expressions belie the marble's hardness. (Alinari-Art Reference Bureau)*

Figure 8.2   Despite its relatively diminutive size, Borromini's church of San Carlo alle Quattro Fontane represents the Baroque architectural spirit. Its slightly curved facade juts out to engage the viewer and beckons him to enter. (Alinari-Art Reference Bureau)

Baroque architecture also arouses a feeling of participation on the part of the viewer. Perhaps the best-known example is also by Bernini—the double row of columns extending in front of St. Peter's in Rome and enclosing the square. This colonnade has been likened to the arms of the Church enfolding the faithful and compelling them to move toward the church itself. On a smaller scale, a similar effect was achieved by a contemporary of Bernini, Francesco Borromini. His entire church of San Carlo alle Quattro Fontane would fit inside one of the columns holding up the dome of St. Peter's. Borromini's curved facade juts forward, meets the viewer halfway, and compels him to enter. It is as if the church were built not of stone, but of some pliable material. Yet a feeling of stability is provided by the overall symmetry of the façade and the solid classical columns.

Baroque church architecture became popular in Germany and Austria as well as in Italy. In the North, Baroque church interiors were lavishly decorated with statues of multicolored stone (or plaster painted to resemble stone), gilded altars, painted ceilings, and elaborately carved pulpits, all calculated to awe the viewer (Plate 6). Equally moving was the music, which was produced by virtuoso organists, church orchestras, vocal soloists, and choirs.

In music the Baroque came to be dominated by the late Baroque composers, George Frederich Handel (1685–1759) and Johann Sebastian Bach (1685–1750). Handel, a German, made his greatest contribution in the composition of oratorios and other secular music in England. Bach, who spent the major part of his career as a church musician in Leipzig, left a vast legacy of sacred vocal and instrumental music.

In painting there was an attempt, similar to that found in sculpture of the era, to involve the viewer in the action. The artist whose work stands as the model of Baroque painting is Peter Paul Rubens (1577–1640). Rubens was born in Flanders, where he absorbed the Northern tradition of meticulous attention to detail, particularly in suggesting the sensual textures of fabric, fur, foliage, and flesh. He created a synthesis of Northern and Southern art that influenced painters until the nineteenth century. In his own lifetime Rubens was recognized as a supreme master, and was on friendly terms with kings and cardinals, who competed with one another for his paintings.

Typical of Rubens' paintings is *The Raising of the Cross*. Before Rubens, most painters showed Christ hanging from a cross planted firmly in the ground, inviting the viewer to contemplate Christ's sacrifice. Rubens shows the moment the cross is being raised to an upright position. From the strained postures and bulging muscles of the men who lift the cross,

Figure 8.3 The Raising of the Cross *shows the meticulous detail and sensuous texture for which Peter Paul Rubens is famous. Rubens' dynamic interpretation of the classical Renaissance pyramidal form attempts to involve the viewer in the scene's action.*
(A.C.L., Brussels)

the viewer can sense not only their physical effort but also their moral burden. There is much activity, but no chaos. Rubens has arranged the elements in the form of a pyramid, with Christ's left arm at the top, the foot of the soldier at the left corner, and the knee of the man kneeling at the right. The form of the pyramid is reinforced by the light shining from the right. What could be more stable than a pyramid? Yet the motion Rubens introduces into his painting gives the pyramid a feeling of toppling over. Thus, he has taken an ideal Renaissance form (the pyramid) and reinterpreted it in a dynamic way.

Throughout Europe painters learned from Rubens. In Spain, Diego Velazquez (1599–1660), the court painter, transformed portraits of a dull-looking royal family into paintings that glowed with light and movement. His greatest work, *The Maids of Honor*, shows a moment when the artist, brush in hand, is interrupted by a visit from the king and queen while painting a portrait of a princess; the royal likenesses are dimly reflected in a mirror. If this were a real scene and not a painting, the king would stand in the same spot as the viewer does when he looks at *The Maids of Honor*. Is the king the viewer or is the viewer the king?

Figure 8.4 Light and movement enliven this royal portrait, The Maids of Honor, *by Diego Velazquez. The painting's momentariness and informality do much to actualize the Baroque ideal of viewer involvement. (Museo del Prado, Madrid)*

The answer is either or both. The uncertainty gives the painting added drama.

Unlike Spain, the Netherlands had no king or nobility to commission art; during the Baroque era it was a republic and almost wholly Protestant. But a wealthy middle class created a market for portraits, biblical scenes, still lifes, and landscapes. The greatest Dutch painter was Rembrandt van Rijn (1606–1669), who died sixteen years before Johann Sebastian Bach was born. To the realism and atmospheric lighting of Caravaggio and the dynamic composition of Rubens, Rembrandt added the psychological characteristics of the personalities he painted. His painting *The Night Watch* (Plate 7), a group portrait of a company of soldiers, combines all these qualities. Before Rembrandt, such paintings had shown the figures formally lined up in a row, with everyone staring at the viewer. Rembrandt shows them strolling among the people of Amsterdam, carrying their rifles and pikes. It is a scene of apparently random movement, yet the elements of the painting are held together by the play of light across faces and uniforms. Unfortunately for Rembrandt, his patrons were not impressed by his virtuosity; each soldier had paid the same fee, but the ones hidden by the shadows complained that they were not getting their money's worth.

Artists have always had to please the people who paid the bills. Increasingly these bills were no longer paid by the Church, with its established tradition of religious painting, but by rising middle-class citizens who wanted "something nice" to reflect their new social position. Another class with new status was royalty. Previously, kings had been little better than chief nobles, but as feudalism waned, the power of the nobility was concentrated in the hands of a few rulers. Like the middle class, kings wanted art to reflect their new social position. The most grandiose king was Louis XIV (1638–1715) of France, and the most opulent artistic achievement was his palace at Versailles.

Architects, stonemasons, sculptors, painters, tapestry weavers, furniture makers, and landscape architects were used by Louis XIV to build Versailles. All were adequately paid and enjoyed a heightened social status as servants of the king. In return, they were expected to enhance the king's prestige. To make sure this was done efficiently, Louis founded royal academies in which "acceptable" styles were codified and taught and factories in which decorative arts were produced. Surely a visitor to the Hall of Mirrors (Plate 8) felt as awed by the wealth and power of the king who built this palace as the visitor entering St. Peter's was awed by the authority of the pope who built the church. When a visitor to Versailles was a ruler of another nation, he often built his own version of Versailles as soon as he could get home and levy another tax.

Since all the arts were utilized to glorify kings, it is no surprise that kings were among the chief patrons of a new art form, opera, that involved many arts—dance, scene-painting, costuming, as well as vocal and instrumental music.

In the Baroque era, the production of a new opera became the appropriate way to celebrate an important occasion, such as the betrothal of a prince, the birth of an heir to the throne, or a military victory. The productions brought into play all the elements of Baroque painting, sculpture, and architecture.

Figure 8.5 Bibiena's theater designs for Vienna's Imperial Opera were among the most grandiose of the Baroque period. The operatic combination of many Baroque art forms proved a popular medium for commemorating important state events.

Among the most spectacular theatrical productions were those created for the Imperial Opera in Vienna by the Bibiena family of set designers, who originally came from Italy. The last and best known, Giuseppe Galli Bibiena (1696–1757), created fantasies only hinted at in the architecture of Borromini and the sculpture of Bernini. With such grandiose effects the Baroque style in the visual arts exhausted itself—and possibly its audience.

chapter 9

The Baroque era, spanning the century and a half between the performance of the first opera in 1600 and the death of Johann Sebastian Bach in 1750, was a period of vast significance in the history of Western music. Stylistically, the early Baroque era was characterized by a change from the many-voiced polyphony of the Renaissance to chordal homophony, in which a single melodic line predominated. New

Baroque Vocal Music

forms of composition emerged, including the opera, the cantata, and the oratorio in vocal music, and the concerto, the concerto grosso, and the sonata in instrumental music. Instrumental music rose to hold a place of equal importance with the vocal idiom, developing a literature of its own apart from vocal music. The new interest in chordal homophony led to one of the most important changes in music history—a shift from the Medieval church modes to the major-minor system which was to dominate Western music for the next three hundred years.

The New Music

Around 1600 in Italy a group of composers called the Camerata reacted against the polyphonic proliferations of the Renaissance. They wanted music to intensify the expressiveness of the text rather than obscure it by elaborate decoration. During the sixteenth century, composers had focused their attention on the simultaneous musical lines and the interplay between voice parts. Often, various parts sang different words at the same time with the result that no words could be heard distinctly. And in a single part a word frequently was stretched out over so many tones that its identity and meaning were lost.

The poets and musicians in the Camerata sought to resurrect the spirit of ancient Greek drama as they envisioned it. An important member of this group was Giulio Caccini (1546–1618), whose compositions provided the basis for a new musical style.

119

The Major-Minor System

One of the most important aspects of the "new music" was that Baroque composers began to think vertically instead of horizontally. They were concerned with the harmonic organization of music. Gradually they evolved a system of harmony based on the idea of a *tonal center*, or *tonic*, using chords beneath the melodic line to establish a tonal center.

The tonic note established the key of the piece, and all other notes were ranked according to how closely they related to the tonic. The closest were the fifth note of the scale, the *dominant*, and the fourth, the *subdominant*. The dominant, or active, chord (V) tends to resolve to the tonic, or rest, chord (I). Without this resolution the music sounds incomplete; the inherent tension of the dominant-tonic relationship gives special impulse to harmonic progression.

This important dominant-tonic relationship enabled composers to establish a firm home base in the tonic key. Tension could be created by using a chord sequence that moves away from the tonic key. This tension could be eased by returning to the tonic. This movement from the tonic to the dominant and back to the tonic opened up a new way of organizing musical time-flow. It permitted the development of larger structures, for the expectation of eventual return to the tonic key could support a fairly long excursion away from it. Most pieces leave their original tonics and establish one or more secondary tonics in the middle of the work—the new keys providing variety and making the return to the original key more significant. Baroque composers exploited this relationship in their vocal as well as in their instrumental music.

With the new emphasis on harmony, *modes*, the basic organizing force of melodically oriented music, lost their importance. The number of modes in common use decreased from the eight or ten of the Renaissance to just two: *major* and *minor*.

The evolution of chordal homophony and its subsequent effects took hold gradually through the early Baroque. And though we may be more familiar with the profound changes through instrumental music, the changes began in vocal music.

The Monodic Style

The "new music" was founded on the premise that the music should serve the text, both in its pattern of accents and its emotional quality. It was the function of the music to reflect, enforce, and enhance the meaning of the words.

Out of this concept grew what has become known as the *monodic style*. The monodic style centered on solo singing in which the vocal line was predominant. Essentially, the composer wrote a two-part structure consisting of a melodic line for the voice and a simple bass. The bass was played by the left hand of a harpsichordist and by a bass instrument such as the viole da gamba or cello. Above the bass line the harpsichordist filled in harmonies with his right hand. This combination of instruments and the function it performs is called *basso continuo*, or simply *continuo*. The harmonies were improvised by the keyboard player; that is, they were not written out, but had to be deduced by him from

Example 9.1

symbols in the notation. Numbers written below the bass line indicated to the harpsichordist which harmonies were to be filled in (Example 9.1). These symbols constituted an ingenious shorthand called *figured bass,* or *thorough-bass.*

While the basso continuo originated in the vocal music of the early Baroque, it came to be applied to virtually all music in the period, both vocal and instrumental. So prevalent was the continuo practice that the Baroque was later nicknamed the "continuo period."

The monodic style, with its emphasis on the importance of the words, consisted of essentially two different types of vocal expression, the *recitative* and the *arioso.*

Recitative

The recitative is a kind of singing speech in which the rhythm is dictated by the natural inflection of the words. In contrast to the Renaissance idea of an even flow of music, the recitative is sung in free, flexible rhythm with continuo accompaniment. The performer slows down or speeds up the tempo according to his interpretation of the text.

Within Baroque opera and oratorio, the recitative primarily served to heighten dramatic impact or to further the action of the story. As it evolved through the Baroque, the recitative acquired greater dramatic importance. The simple recitative with only continuo accompaniment, known as *secco recitative,* usually introduced an aria or appeared in the less dramatic moments of a piece. The *stromento recitative,* in which the voice is accompanied by instruments aside from continuo, produced a more powerful effect. Both types of recitatives gradually acquired stock endings: In one, the voice part dropped down a fourth, and in the other the voice part ended on a descending scale. In both endings, after the voices had concluded their parts, the instruments sounded two final punctuating chords: a dominant chord, followed by a tonic chord.

Arioso

More lyrical and expressive than the recitative, the arioso tends to dwell on one aspect of the action or develops the feelings or state of mind of a character. The rhythm of the arioso is determined by musical as well as textual considerations. Thus, its tempo is less flexible than that of the recitative and is maintained steadily throughout.

The lyrical arioso was expanded gradually into the *aria.* In its most common form the aria has a three-part, *da capo* stucture consisting of two sections followed by a repetition of the first in an ABA sequence.

The first section (A) of the da capo aria was followed by a contrasting section (B). The conclusion of the B section was marked by the words "da capo," which instructed the performers to return to the beginning and repeat section A. This closed form made the aria even more dramatically static than the arioso. Although it was not suitable for swift action, it was superbly structured for lyrical expression.

As performed in the Baroque period, the repeated A section differed considerably the second time around. Performers decorated, or-namented, and otherwise altered the music to display their vocal techniques and to further intensify the spirit of the words. This style of singing became an inherent part of the opera and the oratorio of the later Baroque period. Solo performers, raised to new prominence by the monodic style, added intricate runs and trills to dress up the music. In fact, virtuosity was sometimes exaggerated to the point of overshadowing the music and drama.

Out of the monodic style, with its emphasis on the solo voice, continuo accompaniment, and lyrical projection of the text, came some of the principal ingredients for the three important forms of Baroque vocal music—the opera, the oratorio, and the cantata.

The early Baroque *opera* was a dramatic form based on secular themes and written in Italian. Sung primarily by solo voices, operas were fully staged with costuming, scenery, acting, and instrumental or orchestral accompaniment.

The early *oratorio* was also a dramatic work, but did not include scenery, costuming, or stage action. Texts were usually in Latin, almost invariably taken from the Old Testament. In addition to the solo voices, which portrayed roles, there was a narrator who explained the dramatic action. And, unlike early opera, the oratorio was characterized by the involvement of a chorus.

The *cantata* occupied a middle position between the opera and the oratorio. Either sacred or secular, it was shorter and used fewer performers than the other two forms. Usually written in Italian rather than Latin, cantatas emphasized solo voices in recitative style.

Early Opera

The earliest surviving opera was written by a member of the Camerata named Jacopo Peri (1561–1633), whose *Eurydice* dates from the year 1600. Based on the Greek legend of Orpheus and Eurydice, it consists almost entirely of recitative with continuo accompaniment. In accordance with the principles of the Camerata, Peri wrote in the foreword to his opera that its style was intended to "imitate speech in song."

Claudio Monteverdi

It was another Italian, however, who introduced to opera the full resources of music and the theater. His name was Claudio Monteverdi (1567–1643), and his treatment of the Orpheus legend, *La favola d'Orfeo,* marks the real beginning of opera. First performed in Mantua in 1607, *Orfeo* had elaborate costuming, staging, and lighting effects; an instrumental ensemble of forty players; and a chorus of singers and dancers. Another important innovation in *Orfeo* was the operatic overture. This type of orchestral introduction, known as a *sinfonia,* became standard in later operas.

In addition to *Orfeo,* Monteverdi wrote several other operas. Among the most successful were *Il ritorno di Ulisse in patria (The Return of Ulysses to His Homeland,* (1641) and *L'Incoronazione di Poppea (The Coronation of Poppea,* 1642). Like those of his contemporaries, Monteverdi's operas were written in Italian. They drew mainly upon Greek and Roman legends for their plots, which were adapted by poets into *librettos,* or operatic texts.

Originally performed for aristocratic gatherings, opera became a popular form of entertainment among the middle classes. Public opera houses were built in major Italian cities, and composers and librettists adapted their art to a wider and more varied audiences. During the Baroque period, Italian opera spread throughout Europe, reaching its heights in the Italian operas of Handel in England. The Italian style had less influence in France where the composer Jean-Baptiste Lully (1632–1687), ironically an Italian, headed the faction that created and supported French opera.

The Oratorio

In the early Baroque era the oratorios took two forms—the *Latin oratorio* and the *oratorio volgare,* which used Italian texts. The Latin oratorio reached its peak in the works of the Roman composer Giaccomo Carissimi (1605–1674). The finest of his fifteen oratorios, *Jepthe* (ca. 1649), was based on an Old Testament story from the Book of Judges.

Carissimi's pupil Alessandro Scarlatti (1660–1725) was one of the principal composers of the *oratorio volgare.* In the hands of Scarlatti, the oratorio became musically indistinct from opera. While the themes were still religious, the texts were in Italian, the role of the narrator was eliminated, and the chorus was abandoned. Actually, the oratorio was little more than a substitution for opera, theatrical performances of which were banned by the church during Lent.

The oratorio spread from Italy to the other countries of Europe. Heinrich Schütz (1585–1672), who studied in Italy, introduced the oratorio to Germany, and Marc-Antoine Charpentier (1634–1704), a pupil of Carissimi, was the principal oratorio composer in France. But the oratorio rose to its height in England in the monumental works of George Frederich Handel.

Handel (1685–1759)

The Bettmann Archive

George Frederich Handel was born in Halle, a trading center some eighty miles southwest of Berlin, the son of a prosperous barber-surgeon attached to the court of the duke of Saxony. His father had in mind a legal career for the boy but did allow him to begin music study at age eight with the organist of the town's principal Lutheran church. Aside from learning to play the organ, harpsichord, violin, and oboe, young Handel also studied composition, writing church cantatas and numerous small-scale instrumental works.

Out of respect for his father's wish, Handel enrolled at the University of Halle in 1702. At the end of his first year, however, he withdrew from the university and went to Hamburg to pursue his interest in music.

Musical activity in Hamburg, as in most cosmopolitan cities of the time, centered around the opera house, where Italian opera thrived. Soon after Handel arrived in Hamburg in 1703, he obtained a position as violinist in the theater orchestra and industriously set about learning the craft of opera composition. His first opera, *Almira* (1704), reflected the curious mixture of native German and imported Italian musical styles then prevalent in Hamburg: the recitatives were set in German, the arias in Italian. The work was a popular success and three other operas soon followed. In 1706, feeling that he had learned all that Hamburg had to offer, Handel decided to go to Italy.

His three-year stay in Italy was amazingly successful. Traveling back and forth between Florence, Venice, Rome, and Naples, he met many of Italy's greatest composers and was the frequent guest of cardinals, princes, and ambassadors. Much of his popularity stemmed from the success of his operas *Rodrigo* (Florence, 1708) and *Agrippina* (Venice, 1709). For the ecclesiastical nobility of Rome, Handel composed two oratorios, *La resurrezione* (*The Resurrection*, 1708) and *Il Trionfe del tempo e del disinganno* (*The Triumph of Time and Truth*, 1708).

Through one of the friends he met in Italy, Handel obtained the position of musical director to the Electoral Court of Hanover, Germany. He had just taken up his duties in 1710, however, when he asked permission from Elector Georg Ludwig to visit London. Italian opera was then in great vogue with the English aristocracy, and the success of his opera *Rinaldo* (1711) led Handel to ask permission for another leave of absence the following year. Though promising to return "within a reasonable time," Handel stretched out his second London visit indefinitely.

In 1714 Queen Anne died, and Elector Georg Ludwig of Hanover ascended to the throne as George I of England. How Handel settled the embarrassing problem of his long-neglected contract with the Electoral Court is unknown. But the annual pension Queen Anne had given him was continued and even increased by George I, and within several years he was in high favor at the royal court.

During his years in England (he became a subject in 1726) Handel was involved in no less than four operatic enterprises. The most significant of these, the Royal Academy of Music, was organized by British nobility under the sponsorship of the king. During its eight-year existence (1720–1728), Handel's career as an opera composer reached its highest point.

Despite Handel's many personal successes, each of his four opera companies collapsed. A major reason for their collapse was the declining taste of the English for Italian opera. The enormously successful production, in 1728, of John Gay's *The Beggar's Opera* undoubtedly hastened the extinction of Italian opera in England. A parody of Italian style, *The Beggar's Opera* was widely imitated and a new form of light, popular musical entertainment was created in English.

Though Handel continued to compose Italian operas for more than a decade after *The Beggar's Opera,* he turned increasingly to another type of music drama that had originated in Italy—the oratorio.

His first English oratorio, *Haman and Mordecai* (later revised and renamed *Esther*), was composed in 1720. Others followed during the 1730s, but it was not until 1739, with the completion of *Saul* and *Israel in Egypt,* that he seemed to sense the full musical and dramatic possibilities inherent in this genre. Neither of these works was an immediate success, but others that followed were. In 1742, *Messiah* received high critical praise after its first performance in Dublin. By 1746, with the performance of *Judas Maccabaeus*, Handel had found a new public in the growing English middle class.

In his last years Handel was universally recognized as England's greatest composer. His popularity with all segments of English society steadily grew, and the royal patronage of George I was followed by that of George II. Despite declining health and the eventual loss of his eyesight, Handel continued to maintain a heavy schedule of oratorio performances, which he conducted himself from the keyboard. While attending a performance of *Messiah* on March 30, 1759, he suddenly grew faint and had to be taken home. He died two weeks later and was buried with state honors in Westminster Abbey. His will revealed that he had accumulated a substantial private fortune, which was dispersed—along with his music manuscripts—among friends.

His Work

Handel's fame today rests largely on the half-dozen oratorios—particularly *Messiah*—still in concert repertory, several *concerti grossi*, a like number of organ concertos, and two orchestral suites, *Water Music* and *Royal Fireworks Music*. These amount to only a fraction of his total work, which fills one hundred volumes in the collected edition of his music. Included in this edition are more than forty operas, twenty-six oratorios in English, seventeen church anthems, seventy-nine cantatas for one or two solo voices, forty-six concertos for various instrumental combinations, twenty-seven sonatas for miscellaneous chamber ensembles, two settings of the Passion in German, and a host of church choruses, vocal duets, pieces for harpsichord, serenades, masques, odes, pastorals, and orchestral overtures.

Opera   With few exceptions, Handel's operas followed the pattern laid down by Italian composers of the seventeenth century. Their plots, drawn from classical mythology, were developed through a series of paired recitatives and arias. Although Handel's operas are seldom performed today, they were considerably better than those composed by his contemporaries. His gifts for melody and his imaginative, resourceful orchestration were acclaimed in his own time, and his ability to dramatize in music the psychological and emotional states of his characters was perhaps unexcelled.

Oratorios   It is primarily through his oratorios that Handel's popularity has persisted. The bulk of Handel's oratorios are dramatic, portraying dramatic conflict, progress, and resolution, and they concern themselves with specific characters and events. Most of them, including *Samson, Saul, Solomon, Belshazzar, Judas Maccabaeus,* and *Jeptha*, are based on stories drawn from the Old Testament. Some, like *Hercules*, however, are drawn from mythology. But whatever the original source, Handel instructed his librettists to produce dramatic plots, and Handel himself referred to these works as "dramatic oratorios" or "music dramas."

While the majority of Handel's oratorios are fashioned along the lines of drama with definite characters and plots, two works—*Israel in Egypt* and *Messiah*—are notable exceptions.

Israel in Egypt is really a long, enormous anthem in which the chorus, taking over the elements of narration and depiction, almost completely dominates the entire work. The solo voices do not represent specific characters as they would in a dramatic oratorio. Instead, they complement and act as a foil for the chorus. The orchestra is used brilliantly in the depiction of the plagues, particularly in the sections representing the buzzing of the flies, and the fire and hailstones.

Handel's other nondramatic oratorio, *Messiah*, tells the story of the life of Christ from prophecy to resurrection. But rather than telling the story dramatically, as in *Saul*, or through pictorial narration, as in *Israel in Egypt*, it relates the events in Christ's life symbolically, by indirection. In *Messiah* there are no "characters." Christ never appears, nor do Mary, Joseph, Pilate, or Judas. The solo voices (with the exception of the scene in which the angel appears to the shepherds) do not represent characters in a plot. Rather they are detached, disembodied. The text itself is not taken from the Gospels of the New Testament, where the life of Christ is recorded, but is almost entirely from the Old Testament. As a result, it mirrors the events in Christ's life in an oblique, mystical way, with almost no direct reference to actual people or concrete events.

Although written in only twenty-four days, *Messiah*, with its brilliantly structured text by Charles Jennens and Handel's mastery of the musical materials, is one of the world's great works. At its first London performance in 1743, King George II was so impressed that he stood during the "Hallelujah Chorus" at the end of Part II, a precedent that audiences have followed to the present day.

Altogether it represents nearly three hours of music for four solo voices (SATB), chorus (SATB), and orchestra. Its three parts comprise fifty-three movements, including arias, recitatives, choruses, and orchestral movements.

Record 1/Side 2

Arias   The aria received ingenious treatment in the oratorios of Handel. In *Messiah* the variety of arias is astounding. Handel modifies and adapts the da capo form in various ways, always avoiding the mechanical return to, and literal repetition of, the first section.

The bass aria "But who may abide" is an example of Handel's alteration of the da capo form. After the repeat of section A, in which the audience is led to believe it is listening to the standard da capo form, there is a sudden and unexpected plunge into a repetition of the B section. Thus, the form is ABAB rather than ABA. Handel made the effect even more startling by making the B section radically different from the A section. The meter changes from $3/8$ to $4/4$, and the tempo from larghetto to prestissimo. Violent sixteenth notes in the strings underlie the vocal text "For He is like a refiner's fire" in the B section.

In the alto aria "He was despised," Handel comes close to employing the da capo form. But still there is a difference. The aria begins with a long A section in which the voice and strings alternate, only rarely sounding at the same time. After a firm cadence and pause, the B section begins. Instead of the flowing, alternating melodies heard in A, the strings provide a continuous, agitated background against which the voice sings short, clipped pronouncements.

Example 9.2

He gave his back to the smi-ters, he gave his back to the smi-ters and his cheeks to them

There is hardly any "melodic" interest at all. At the end of the B section, the orchestra ceases while the alto sings a stock *recitative* ending on "with shame and spitting," followed by a two-chord confirmation by the orchestra. In reality the B section is actually an accompanied recitative, the ending of which introduces the return of section A.

The stirring aria for bass, "The trumpet shall sound," adheres to the standard ABA form. However, much of the A section is in the nature of a duet, with the solo bass and trumpet having equal roles, either alternating or working together. The contrasting B section utilizes only voice and continuo. Instead of being followed by the very beginning of A, however, the music returns to the point after the instrumental introduction where the voice enters with its trumpetlike melody.

Example 9.3

The trum-pet shall sound,———

In addition to these, a variety of other aria forms occur in *Messiah*. The alto aria "O Thou that tellest good tidings to Zion" does not end with the solo alto, but builds to a joyous climax, with the chorus taking up the same material sung earlier by the solo voice. The tenor aria "Every valley shall be exalted" exhibits virtuoso runs on the word "exalted," enhancing the meaning of the word.

Example 9.4

Shall be——— ex - al - - - - - -

ted

The exquisite "He shall feed his flock" is a "shared aria" between the alto and soprano soloists.

Recitatives   The recitative is less important in *Messiah* than it is in the dramatic oratorios. Thus, the stirring recitatives of the enraged Saul, the distraught Jeptha, or the tortured Hercules are not found here. In *Messiah*, recitatives serve primarily to introduce arias, or sometimes a chorus. However, aside from this function, some of the recitatives assume an importance and beauty of their own.

The tenor recitative "Comfort ye" illustrates Handel's use of the solo voice and orchestra to reinforce each other. Structurally, it consists of

Example 9.5

Violin I

two parts. The first is dominated by the instruments that focus on the melody:

The second part centers on the solo voice, with the orchestra punctuating the vocal line.

The four recitatives that lead into the chorus "Glory to God in the highest" are an excellent example of Handel's use of the recitative. Together they show how he alternated *secco* and *stromento* recitatives to emphasize the emotional qualities of the words.

The first recitative in this series, "There were shepherds," has a simple secco (continuo) accompaniment to reinforce its pastoral, relaxed feeling. A second recitative follows, "And lo! the angel of the Lord," in which a stromento accompaniment of sixteenth notes heightens the emotional effect of the appearance of the angel.

The return of the secco accompaniment signals the calm of the third recitative, "And the angel said unto them." This recitative is also interesting because in it the soprano represents the angel. The section that begins with the words "Fear not" is the only place in *Messiah* where Handel assigns a particular role to one of his soloists.

The final recitative, "And suddenly there was with the angel," returns to the stromento accompaniment as it builds to the climactic entrance of the chorus "Glory to God."

Choruses   The primary factor that stamps Handel's oratorios as historically unique is his use of the chorus as a major element in the musical and dramatic structure.

Handel's choral writing displays remarkable flexibility and versatility, absorbing the solid English choral tradition that Handel found in the works of such gifted writers as Henry Purcell (1659–1695), one of England's finest composers. Handel juxtaposes polyphonic and homophonic sections of music with sections that usually begin with imitative entrances (polyphonic) and gradually become homophonic, culminating in a climaxing cadence. This technique is clearly evident in the chorus "Glory to God in the highest."

The movement opens with one of Handel's favorite devices, alternating high and low voices. Here they reflect the contrasting ideas of "highest" (high voices) and "peace on earth" (with the low voices representing earth). After this contrast is presented twice, the texture changes to one of polyphony as the voices have successive imitative entrances on "good will towards men." After several entrances, all the voice parts join to build to a climactic cadence in a homophonic texture that culminates in the reappearance of the "Glory to God" material, this time stated by the entire chorus. Here we see the massive chordal harmony that gives Handel's choruses their power and majesty.

Handel's skill at producing a climax in the context of a choral movement is beautifully displayed in the chorus "For unto us a child is born." After several statements of the opening text, "For unto us a child is born," with a long *melisma* (many notes on one syllable) on "born," the tenors take up a new line of text with new melodic material. After this is repeated by the soprano section, the altos and basses, gradually joined by sopranos and finally tenors, extend the phrase by adding "and his name shall be called," now no longer in jagged dotted rhythm but with all the voices working together and building energy. At "called," the violins, which have been silent during this section, enter with a rising sixteenth note passage to add weight and brilliance to the choral proclamation on "Wonderful! Counselor! the mighty God, the everlasting Father, the Prince of Peace," releasing the accumulated energy in a powerful climax. The rest of the movement is devoted to successive climaxes on this text, each coming with increased strength and power.

The device of alternating forces and textures occasionally is expanded into a technique of more far-reaching structural importance. The chorus "Since by man came death" is a good example. Its two sections contrast sharply in dynamics, tempo, and key to reflect the meaning of the words.

The text "since by man came death" is sung by only half the chorus without instrumental accompaniment. The minor key (which the Baroque had begun to associate with subdued or tragic moods), slow (*grave*) tempo, and restrained dynamic level and stark forces all contrive to convey the quality of "death." In contrast, the music brightens to reflect the spirit of the text "by man came also the resurrection," as the tempo changes to allegro, a major key is used, and the orchestra joins the chorus—*forte*. This same idea of highly contrasting sections is used for the rest of the movement in the text: "For as in Adam all die, Even so in Christ shall all be made alive." Many choral movements finish with the characteristic short adagio ending frequently employed by Handel. In *Messiah*, no fewer than seven choral movements, including the stirring "Hallelujah," close with this kind of short, confirming statement.

The choruses in *Messiah* function in several ways. First, they are sometimes the climactic element in a three-part complex consisting of a recitative, an aria, and a chorus. This pattern dominates the first part of the oratorio. For example, the recitative "Comfort ye" is followed by the aria "Every valley" and culminates in the chorus "And the glory."

A second use of the chorus is as a structural "frame" beginning and ending a large section. Part II of *Messiah*, for instance, begins with the restrained and foreboding "Behold the Lamb of God" and concludes with the joyous and triumphant "Hallelujah Chorus." These two choruses constitute a frame for the entire section.

Handel also joins one chorus to another, so that each chorus depends upon the one immediately preceding or following it. Thus, each chorus is a unit in a larger complex of several choruses.

The chorus "Surely he hath borne our griefs" in Part II is the first of three interdependent choral movements. Although it ends with a definite cadence, it lacks a feeling of finality because the ending key (A flat major) is different from the F minor key in which it began. Its real completion requires the return to F minor, which is supplied by the beginning of the next chorus, "And with his stripes we are healed."

In this second chorus, Handel uses a favorite Baroque procedure, the fugue, which the next chapter discusses in detail. The voices in this chorus each present, in turn, the theme, and then weave an elaborate counterpoint around it.

Unlike the first chorus, the second does not end on a concluding tonic chord, but stops on a dominant chord that requires resolution. This resolution comes at the beginning of the third chorus, "All we like sheep have gone astray," which begins in F major, thus tying the three-movement complex together.

Orchestra   Because of the limited orchestral resources available to him in Dublin, where *Messiah* was to be performed for the first time, Handel employed a modest instrumental ensemble consisting of only oboes, bassoon, trumpets, timpani, strings, and continuo. The only independent movements for orchestra are the introductory "Sinfonia" and the short, eloquent "Pastorale" in Part I.

Handel's oratorios contrasted sharply with the choral works of the other giant of the late Baroque, Johann Sebastian Bach. While Handel's works were written to be performed in public concert halls before audiences seeking entertainment, Bach's were intended for performance as part of a religious ceremony.

The Passion

One of the most important forms of religious music in Lutheran Germany was the Passion, the story of the suffering and death of Christ. The Passion was particularly important during Holy Week, especially on Good Friday.

Throughout musical history, settings of the Passion have reflected the prevailing styles of the age in which they were written. In medieval times the Passion was sung in plain chant. Motet settings were common in the Renaissance. And in the Baroque period, settings of the Passion made full use of the aria, the recitative, the chorus, and the orchestra —the full dramatic range of the "new music." Consequently, the Baroque Passion is often referred to as the *oratorio* Passion.

Prior to the Baroque period, settings of the Passion had relied almost exclusively on the four Gospels for their texts. In the eighteenth century, particularly in Germany, it became the practice to treat the Gospel text freely and to add nonbiblical text.

Johann Sebastian Bach's setting of the *Passion According to Saint Matthew* is probably the finest example of the Baroque oratorio Passion. In it the Gospel text is used as the dramatic frame around which the work is built. The Gospel text is sung by a set of solo voices representing the characters in the story: Christ, Judas, Pilate, individual disciples, and the Evangelist (narrator), who has a central role.

These solo voices sing in secco recitative, with the exception of Christ, who is accompanied by continuo and strings. The chorus, accompanied by the orchestra, represents the disciples, the high priests, the scribes, and the crowd.

The nonbiblical texts take the musical form of accompanied recitatives and arias and chorales (simple hymn tunes). The recitatives and arias are sung by a separate group of soloists who do not represent characters in the drama but serve instead as commentators drawing religious inferences from the story as it unfolds. The chorales are sung by the chorus and the congregation. The congregation, in this way, actually participates in the performances. The added nonbiblical texts are highly theological and interpret the events from a specifically Lutheran point of view.

Bach's *St. Matthew Passion* joins *Messiah* in representing the culmination of Baroque vocal music.

The Chorale

The German chorale grew out of the reforms that began the Protestant movement. Martin Luther (1483–1546) and his aides developed chorales both to instruct and involve the congregation. Luther believed that people should participate in the act of worship. To this end, he inaugurated religious services in the native language and composed "German psalms" for the congregation to sing.

The chorale melodies came from a variety of sources. Some were adapted from Gregorian chants, others came from secular tunes popular at the time, and many were newly composed. Usually in four-part harmony with a simple rhythmic structure, they were characterized by a clear melody in the soprano that could be sung by the musically untrained. Luther's famous *"Ein' Feste Burg ist Unser Gott"* (A Mighty Fortress Is Our God), typifies the strength and solidity of the chorale.

In the Baroque era, chorale melodies provided a rich body of sturdy materials from which larger musical structures could be built. In this way, they functioned in much the same way in the Lutheran church as the Gregorian chant had functioned in the Roman Catholic church during the Renaissance.

The Cantata

The simplicity of the chorale as a unifying theme was especially suited to the *cantata*. In Germany, the cantata developed into a religious form that served as an integral part of the Lutheran service. Like the opera and oratorio, the cantata went through considerable transformation during the Baroque era, reaching its height in the works of Dietrich Buxtehude (ca. 1637–1707) and Johann Sebastian Bach. By Bach's time (1685–1750), the cantata often combined the standard Baroque elements of aria, recitative, chorus, and instrumental accompaniment. Frequently, cantatas were built upon a simple chorale tune.

Cantata texts related to specific feast days of the church year. For church musicians such as Bach, the writing of cantatas was a professional obligation. Between 1704 and 1740, with but a few brief interruptions, Bach produced cantatas on a weekly basis for the churches he served. He is believed to have written more than three hundred, although only one hundred ninety-five have been preserved. Bach's cantatas contain several movements and are scored for soloists, chorus, and instruments.

Cantata No. 4: *Christ Lag in Todesbanden* (*Christ Lay in Death's Bondage*)

Record 2/Side 1

Bach's Cantata No. 4 was written early in his career, before the Italian influence had made its full impact on him. Thus, it does not employ the da capo aria or the recitative. Using as its theme the chorale tune and text "Christ Lag in Todesbanden," it is an early example of Bach's contrapuntal technique, a skill that ultimately marked him as one of the great musical craftsmen in history.

The work is scored for four soloists (SATB), a four-part chorus (SATB), and a string instrumental ensemble with continuo. It comprises seven movements and an introductory sinfonia, according to the following plan:

Sinfonia	Verse I	II	III	IV	V	VI	VII
	chorus	duet	solo	quartet	solo	duet	chorus
	SATB	SA	T	SATB	B	ST	with congregation

Christ Lag in Todesbanden

VERSUS I

Christ lag in Todesbanden
Für unsre Sünd gegeben,
Er ist wieder erstanden
Und hat uns bracht das Leben;
Des wir sollen fröhlich sein,
Gott loben und ihm dankbar sein
Und singen Halleluja,
Halleluja!

VERSUS II

Den Tod niemand zwingen kunnt
Bei allen Menschenkinden,
Das macht alles unsre Sünd,
Kein Unschuld war zu finden.
Davon kam der Tod so bald
Und nahm über uns Gewalt,
Hielt uns in seinem Reich gefangen,
Halleluja!

VERSUS III

Jesus Christus, Gottes Sohn,
An unser Statt ist kommen
Und hat die Sünde weggetan,
Damit dem Tod genommen
All sein Recht und sein Gewalt,
Da bleibet nichts denn Todsgestalt,

Den Stachl hat er verloren.
Halleluja!

VERSUS IV

Es war ein wunderlicher Krieg,
Da Tod und Leben rungen,
Das Leben behielt den Sieg,
Es hat den Tod verschlungen.
Die Schrift hat verkündigt das,
Wie ein Tod den andern frass,
Ein Spott aus dem Tod ist worden.
Halleluja!

Christ Lay in Death's Bondage

VERSE I

Christ lay in death's bondage,
For our sins given;
He is again arisen
And has brought us life;
For which we should rejoice,
Praise God and give him thanks,
And sing Hallelujah,
Hallelujah!

VERSE II

No one could overcome Death
Among all mortal children;
This was caused by all our sins,
No innocence was to be found.
Hence came Death so soon
And over us achieved dominion,
Held us in his realm imprisoned,
Hallelujah!

VERSE III

Jesus Christ, God's Son,
In our stead has come
And had done away with sin;
Thus from Death seizing
All its perogatives and power;
There remains nothing but
*   Death's image,*
Its sting has been lost.
Hallelujah!

VERSE IV

It was a wondrous war,
With Death and Life embattled;
Life achieved the victory,
It swallowed up Death.
The scripture has proclaimed this,
How one Death consumed another;
A mockery has Death become.
Hallelujah!

VERSUS V	VERSE V
Hier ist das rechte Osterlamm,	*Here is the true Easter lamb*
Davon hat Gott geboten,	*That God has offered us,*
Das ist hoch an des Kreuzes Stamm	*Which high on the stem of the cross*
In heisser Lieb gebraten,	*Is roasted in burning love;*
Das Blut zeichnet unser Tür,	*His blood marks our door,*
Das hält der Glaub dem Tode für,	*Faith holds this up to death,*
Der Würger kann uns nicht mehr	*The destroyer can no longer*
schaden.	*harm us.*
Halleluja!	*Hallelujah!*

VERSUS VI	VERSE VI
So feiern wir das hohe Fest	*Therefore we celebrate the high feast*
Mit Herzensfreud und Wonne,	*With joyous heart and rapture,*
Das uns der Herre scheinen lässt,	*Which the Lord lets shine for us;*
Er ist selber die Sonne,	*He is himself the sun,*
Der durch seiner Gnade Glanz	*Who through the splendor of his grace*
Erleuchtet unsre Herzen ganz,	*Fully illumines our hearts,*
Der Sünden Nacht ist verschwunden.	*The night of sin has disappeared.*
Halleluja!	*Hallelujah!*

VERSUS VII	VERSE VII
Wir essen und leben wohl	*We eat and live well*
In rechten Osterfladen,	*By the true Passover bread,*
Der alte Sauerteig nicht soll	*The old leaven shall not endure*
Sein bei dem Wort der Gnaden,	*Beside the word of grace;*
Christus will die Koste sein	*Christ will be the feast*
Und speisen die Seel allein,	*And he alone will feed the soul,*
Der Glaub will keins andern Leben.	*Faith is sustained through no other.*
Halleluja!	*Hallelujah!*

—Martin Luther

Although the chorale melody is the unifying element, each movement uses it in a different way. Throughout most of Verse I, the sopranos of the chorus state the melody in long, sustained tones, while the other voice parts sound more active contrapuntal material. Each new phrase in the soprano is preceded by several statements of the same phrase by the other voice parts in imitation, using short note values. At times the orchestra doubles the voice parts, but most of the time it has active contrapuntal material of its own.

At the word "Hallelujah," there is an abrupt change in tempo, while the four parts of the chorus have short, imitative entrances of the Hallelujah phrase of the chorale tune. The increase in the tempo gives the movement an ending of excitement and joy, reflecting the usual meaning of "Hallelujah."

Verse II employs a rhythmic bass *ostinato*, against which the soprano and alto sing a variation of the chorale tune. This time the Hallelujah takes on the quality of lamentation that has characterized the rest of the movement.

Example 9.6

In contrast, Verse III is joyous, reflecting the text. The violins have a rapidly moving pattern of sixteenth notes.

Example 9.7

The bass again has a kind of ostinato figure.

Example 9.8

The tenor states the chorale tune in its original form until the Hallelujah, where the chorale tune is decorated in a manner that gives it the character of the violin figure. The constant driving motion of this movement is abruptly suspended to dramatize the text (death's image), after which the rigorous texture is resumed, for "death has lost its sting."

In Verse IV the chorale tune is sung by the alto, while the other voice parts sing snatches of the chorale tune in shorter note values as part of the counterpoint against the alto.

Verse V uses the entire instrumental ensemble against the solo bass voice. The movement is in triple meter, and the chorale tune takes on a more lyrical quality. For most of the movement the solo bass alternates with the first violin in stating the phrases of the chorale tune, while the rest of the strings and continuo provide harmony (see Example 9.9). The verse displays *word painting,* another device favored by Baroque composers, in which the music attempts to simulate the idea or object represented. *"Kreuzes"* ("cross") is emphasized by a lengthening and decoration of the note of the chorale tune on which the word occurs.

Example 9.10

Example 9.11

And of special interest is the setting of the words *"dem Todefür,"* with its emphasis on *Tode* (death).

Example 9.9

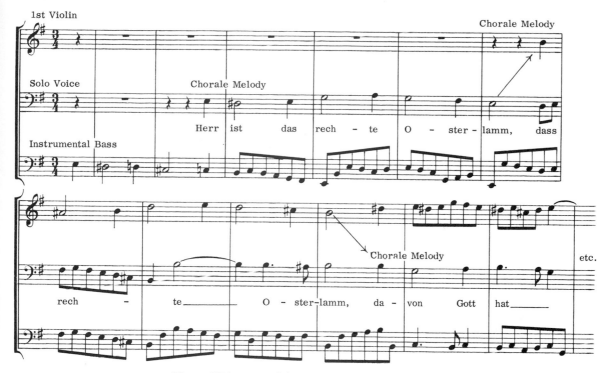

Verse VI is scored for soprano and tenor duet with continuo accompaniment and displays yet another variation of the chorale melody, in which each phrase is decorated and extended by a triplet figure.

Verse VII is a straightforward statement of the chorale tune in the soprano, the rest of the chorus providing a simple harmonic support doubled by instruments.

Example 9.12

In comparison to the elaborate settings in the previous movements, the final verse is considerably less complex, allowing the congregation to join the choir in singing the last verse of the cantata. This participation provides the religious and spiritual fulfillment of the experience as a whole.

With the sparsest of means—the chorale melody and its text—Bach has created a multimovement work, unified by the presence of the melody in each movement, yet highly diversified by the variety of treatments the chorale tune receives.

Summary

The Baroque era was a period of significant development in the history of music. It began in Italy around 1600, when composers created the new monadic style (in reaction to the polyphonic forms of the Renaissance). Recitatives, ariosos, and arias were written in the style of the "new music," which employed chordal relationships built around a clear tonal center.

The opera, the oratorio, and the cantata were the three important forms of Baroque vocal music. The beginnings of modern opera date from the early seventeenth century, when *Orfeo*, by Claudio Monteverdi, was performed in Italy. The oratorio rose to its height in England, in *Messiah* and other monumental works of George Frederich Handel. The cantata is best exemplified in the many works that Johann Sebastian Bach organized around German chorale tunes.

chapter 10

The Baroque era was not only a period of magnificent achievement in vocal composition. It also saw the gradual development of the instrumental idiom and the growth of the first significant body of instrumental music. The Baroque was the age of the great violin makers, among them the

Baroque Instrumental Music

members of the Stradivari family. Improvements were made in the construction of virtually every wind and brass instrument, and the organ and the harpsichord became the basic keyboard instruments. By the end of the Baroque era, instrumental music had gradually equalled and surpassed vocal music in importance, and the style of vocal music itself was very much influenced by the instrumental idiom.

Equal Temperament

Fundamental to the development of instrumental music (particularly that written for keyboard instruments) was the need to devise a system of tuning so that the keyboard instruments could play equally in tune in all keys without having to be retuned. Before 1700, all attempts to develop such a system had achieved only partial success and it was left for Baroque composers and music theorists to construct a completely satisfactory method of tuning that would facilitate frequent modulation to distant keys. This method of tuning is called *equal temperament*.

In the system of equal temperament, instruments are tuned so that all half steps are exactly the same size. As a result, each of these half steps is minutely larger or smaller than the "pure" half step. Indeed, with the exception of the octave and the unison, all intervals are proportionally "out of tune." But the imperfections are so slight that the ear accepts the intervals as being in tune. The application of this method of tuning made it possible for keyboard instruments to play equally well in every

137

Figure 10.1   Vast technical improvements in the wind, brass, and percussion instruments and the development of the violin encouraged the growth of instrumental music during the Baroque era. A cantata performance such as this created new demands for Baroque composers. (The Bettmann Archive)

key without retuning, an advantage that far outweighed the slight impurities inherent in the system.

Although modern listeners have become completely adjusted to the tempered scale, musicians in the eighteenth century had to be convinced that the gains in flexibility were worth the loss of perfectly tuned intervals. Bach's *Das Wohltemperierte Klavier (The Well-Tempered Clavier)*, which consisted of two sets of preludes and fugues in all possible keys, was designed in part to demonstrate the advantages of the new system.

Keyboard Music

A large body of keyboard music, especially for organ and harpsichord, was produced during the Baroque period. These pieces appeared with various titles—fantasia, capriccio, prelude, toccata—that were carryovers from the names given to lute music in the sixteenth century. The terms described the style and character of a piece rather than its form, for all the pieces bearing these titles were cast in "free form," with no standard formal design.

The *fantasia* was an improvisatory piece, characterized by displays of virtuosity in composition and performance. Although frequently an independent piece, the fantasia often served as a preliminary to a fugue.

A *capriccio* (caprice) is a short, improvisatory piece often used to precede a fugue. It tends to be humorous and lighthearted. An outstanding composer of the fantasia and capriccio was Girolamo Frescobaldi (1583–1643), organist at St. Peter's in Rome.

Originally the *prelude* was also an improvised piece played on the lute or a keyboard instrument. In the Renaissance prelude, a melodic or rhythmic motif was expanded freely. By the mid-seventeenth century the prelude customarily introduced another piece or group of pieces. Bach used it in combination with the fugue in his collection of forty-eight preludes and fugues (*Wohltemperierte Klavier*). The two styles represented the extremes of formal procedure: the prelude, in free form, contrasted with the highly organized and controlled formal structure of the fugue.

The term *toccata* derives from the Italian verb *toccare* ("to touch") and describes a piece full of scale passages, rapid runs and trills, and massive chords. Frequently one hand sustains a chord while the other performs embellishments on the chord tones. Like the prelude, the toccata was also often followed by a fugue. Originally developed in Italy, the toccata spread to Germany, where it was adopted and expanded by such composers as Dietrich Buxtehude (ca. 1637–1707).

All these keyboard styles served as introductory pieces to the fugue, one of the great intellectual musical structures of the Baroque era.

The Fugue

The fugue was by far the most magnificent and complex polyphonic keyboard piece of the Baroque period. The fugue is not a form that can be described precisely; it is, rather, a collection of general procedures, only some of which are found in any particular composition. All fugues, however, have two characteristics in common: their contrapuntal treatment of a theme (called a *subject*) and their dependence on a clear dominant-tonic relationship. This underlying tonality largely determines what the various contrapuntal parts, or *voices*, are allowed to do. This subordination of melodic to harmonic structure was an important departure from Renaissance counterpoint, in which the shape of each melodic line was the primary structural factor.

The subject of a fugue is stated first in the tonic key. A second statement, called the *answer*, follows, stated by the second voice part in the dominant key. Sometimes the answer is slightly altered to suit the harmonic requirements of the piece. As each successive voice of the fugue enters with the subject or answer, the preceding voices continue with other material. The number of voices may vary from two to five or more, although four is probably the most common. When all the voices have been presented, the *exposition* of the fugue is complete.

Almost all fugues have *episodes* inserted to relieve the steady presentation of the subject. An episode can be derived from the subject or based on entirely new material. It often involves a change in musical texture.

Another procedure common to many fugues is the use of a *countersubject*, a second theme that is played simultaneously with the main subject. The countersubject appears first as the continuation of the first voice and is answered by the second voice.

Several other devices may be used in the course of a fugue to vary the manner in which the subject is treated. The theme can be played very slowly, in longer notes (*augmentation*), faster than originally (*diminution*), or even turned upside down (*inversion*). Toward the end of a fugue, the entries of the voices can be permitted to overlap and pile up on each other; this is called *stretto* and usually produces a very impressive climax. The unchallenged master of fugal procedure was Johann Sebastian Bach.

Bach (1685–1750)

The Bettmann Archive

Johann Sebastian Bach was the most distinguished member of a family of musicians that reached back four generations before him and was carried forward by three of his sons. His father, Johann Ambrosius, was a musician in service to the town council of Eisenach, a small community in Thuringia—now part of East Germany. Little is known about Bach's early life, but it seems that his father, an excellent violinist, taught him to play stringed instruments, and another relative, the organist of Eisenach's leading church, began instructing him at the organ.

Orphaned when he was only ten, Bach was sent to live with his eldest brother, Johann Christoph, an organist at the nearby town of Ohrdruf. He remained there five years, taking organ and harpsichord lessons from his brother, earning some money as a boy soprano, and studying at the town's famed grammar school. He did so well at the school that he was offered a scholarship at St. Michael's, a secondary school in Luneburg, a city in northern Germany.

In 1703 Bach obtained his first musical position as violinist in the small chamber orchestra of the ducal court of Weimar, but when a post as church organist became available in Arnstadt in August of 1703, he accepted the position. Dissatisfied with working conditions in Arnstadt and the poor state of the church choir, Bach left in 1707 to become organist at the church of St. Blasius in the Free Imperial City of Muhlhausen. In that same year he married a cousin, Maria Barbara Bach.

Soon entangled in a feud between factions within the Lutheran church, he left Muhlhausen in 1708 to become court organist, and later concertmaster, in the ducal chapel of Weimar. His nine years in Weimar constitute his first major creative period. Here he composed a number of cantatas and many of his greatest organ works, and he worked intensively with singers and instrumentalists as a conductor.

Because of his evident talent as a composer, performer, and conductor, Bach expected to be offered the top position of *Kapellmeister* (chapelmaster) at Weimar when it became available in 1716. However, he was passed over in favor of another. The following year he accepted the position of court conductor to the small principality of Anhalt-Cöthen.

Bach had enjoyed a growing reputation as an organist and composer of church cantatas and had made annual performing tours to important centers such as Kassel, Leipzig, and Dresden. His duties at Cöthen, as conductor and composer for the eighteen-member court orchestra, led to a shift in emphasis toward instrumental music. Much of his finest orchestral music dates from this period, including the six Brandenburg Concertos.

The happy and productive years at Cöthen were marred by the death of his wife in 1720. Bach soon remarried, however, and his new wife, Anna Magdalena, proved to be a hard-working, cheerful companion who raised Bach's four children by Maria Barbara along with her own. She gave birth to thirteen children in all, six of whom survived.

In 1723 Bach was offered the position of cantor (director of music) at St. Thomas Church in Leipzig, one of the most important musical posts in Protestant Germany. However, it was not a completely auspicious beginning for Bach, as the city council turned to him only after it had received refusals from two other composers. His duties included composing cantatas for St. Nicholas Church as well as St. Thomas Church, supervising the musical programs in all the municipal churches, and teaching Latin in the St. Thomas choir school.

Despite the irksome nature of some of his duties and his uneasy relationship with his superiors, the Leipzig town council, Bach remained in Leipzig for the rest of his life. He personally supervised the musical education of his most gifted sons, Wilhelm Friedemann, Carl Philipp Emanuel, and Johann Christian, and saw them embark on promising musical careers. Though, like Handel, he went blind in old age, his creative powers remained undimmed. His last composition, dictated to a son-in-law a few days before his death, was a chorale prelude, "Before Thy Throne, My God, I Stand."

His Work

Bach's profound genius extended to nearly every form of musical composition prevalent in the Baroque period. His vocal music is best repre-

Figure 10.3 Bach's organ in St. Thomas Church, Leipzig. This superb instrument stimulated Bach's musical genius for more than a quarter century. (The Bettmann Archive)

sented by his *B Minor Mass*, his Passions, and his many chorales and cantatas. His instrumental music is equally prolific and far-ranging in style. His consummate skill with contrapuntal technique is clearly seen in the Fugue in G Minor, subtitled "The Little" to distinguish it from his longer fugue in the same key.

Fugue in G Minor ("The Little")

Record 2 / Side 1

The Fugue in G Minor is a four-voice fugue. A relatively lengthy subject is stated in the top voice and answered in the alto, while the top voice continues with a countersubject. After the subject has been stated in each of the four voices, the exposition comes to a close. The episode that follows is brief and is based on a figure derived from the first three notes of the subject. After it modulates to D minor (the key of the dominant), a restatement of the subject begins. But the full restatement does not begin until the next measure, where the first two notes of the subject are hidden within the complex texture. The voice that began the restatement continues with the countersubject. The bass sustains a long note, over which changing harmonies are sounded. This *pedal point* is one of the characteristic elements of the fugue.

A second episode, again about three measures long, prepares a statement of the subject in the key of B flat, the relative major to G minor. Subject and countersubject are each presented once. The third episode, which follows, does not modulate, but affirms the key of B flat, and subject and countersubject are sounded once more in that key. Episode IV, which is based on the material used in episode I, modulates to the subdominant, the key of C minor, and the subject is again sounded in that key. Not only is the subject presented here in a new key, but its rhythmic placement is changed also. Instead of starting on the first beat of the measure, as it had previously done, the subject now starts on the third beat of the measure. The lengthy episode that follows episode V is harmonically very active and is written in many different keys; it climaxes with a rising chromatic scale passage in the bass that ends with a firm cadence in the original key of G minor. The final statement of the subject is placed, prominently, in the bass.

Bach's last work, and one of his greatest, *Die Kunst der Fuge* (*The Art of the Fugue*), consists of twenty fugues and canons, called *contrapuncti*, all based on the same subject. Every possible device of counterpoint is demonstrated in this work which, far from being a mere manual of contrapuntal technique, is one of Bach's supreme achievements. *The Art of the Fugue* is the final summation of three hundred years of contrapuntal writing.

Many works that cannot be classified as real fugues nevertheless demonstrate many of the techniques and devices of the fugue. They employ the fugal procedure—subject and answer, exposition sections contrasting with episodic sections—which was one of the staples of Baroque composition. It was used everywhere as an organizing device and took many different shapes in the hands of many different composers.

Works Based on a Given Melody

As a prologue to the singing of the chorale, which occupied a central place in Lutheran church music, church organists would frequently improvise pieces using the chorale melody as a point of departure. From this practice grew the chorale prelude, chorale partita, and chorale fantasia. In the *chorale prelude* the chorale melody is placed in a contrapuntal texture that may or may not be based on motives derived from the chorale melody. The *chorale partita* is a set of variations on the chorale melody. In the *chorale fantasia*, the melody is treated much more freely, being embellished with highly ornamental figurations. The chorale fantasia was designed to display the virtuosity of the performer.

Two other keyboard forms that employed given melodic material were the *passacaglia* and the *chaconne*. Both made use of *basso ostinato*, one of the most important unifying devices of the Baroque music. A short melodic phrase would be repeated over and over in the bass, while the upper voices unfolded continually varied material. The distinctions between passacaglia and chaconne have occasionally been obscured because composers have used the terms interchangeably. Strictly speaking, however, in the passacaglia the basso ostinato is a melodic phrase of usually four or eight measures, while in the chaccone the ostinato element is a series of harmonies that are repeated over and over again.

Pieces Based on Dance Rhythms

A favorite form of keyboard music of many Baroque composers was the *suite*. The suite is a series of movements, each based on a particular dance rhythm. Usually it consisted of an allemande, a courante, a saraband, and a gigue. The first movement, the *allemande*, followed a rather stately duple meter that began with a short upbeat and frequently employed running figures in eighth and sixteenth notes. Contrast was provided by the *courante*, a quick dance in triple meter, in which the melodic interest shifted from voice to voice. The *saraband* following the courante was in a slow, dignified triple meter. The concluding *gigue*, which evolved from the English and Irish jig, was a rapid dance in either ⁶/₈ or ⁶/₄ that employed the fugal procedure. Its melody, usually based on wide leaps, made considerable use of dotted rhythms. Although other multimovement forms used contrasting keys, the suite retained the same key throughout.

The dance movements of the suite, of course, were not intended to accompany actual dancing. Composers simply borrowed the rhythms of the dances, turning them into fine works of art meant for listening. Bach wrote three sets of suites: two for keyboard—the so-called French and English Suites—and one for orchestra. He also wrote four orchestral suites, but called them overtures because their first movements, the overtures, were the longest and musically most significant.

It has not been definitely established whether the suites were written while Bach was at Cöthen or Leipzig, but they nonetheless exhibit a uniform method of procedure. All open in French overture style with a stately largo section followed by a brisk, fugal allegro. The movements that follow are based on dance forms, in particular the *bourree*, *gavotte*, and *minuet*.

Suite No. 3 in D Major

The third orchestral suite, in D major, is the best known of the set, principally because of its lovely second movement, which has come to be known as the *Air on the G String*. The work is scored for two oboes, three trumpets, timpani, and strings.

The first movement, the overture, employs all the instruments. It alternates a slow pompous section using dotted rhythm with one that is rhythmically lively, fast in tempo, and polyphonic throughout. Frequently the first violin section is treated as a solo "instrument," with the rest of the orchestra providing light accompaniment. The form of the movement is:

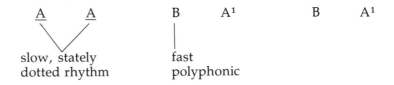

The second movement is a beautifully lyrical air with a long melody spun out in the first violin section. It is slow in tempo, quiet in dynamics, and it uses only strings and continuo. It uses the binary form AABB.

The third movement is a lively gavotte in which the full ensemble alternates with passages scored only for strings and oboes. It is in da capo form, with all sections repeated: AA BB AA.

The fourth and fifth movements are also lighthearted dance forms: the *bourree,* in duple meter and binary form (AB); and the *gigue,* in a lilting triple meter and also in binary form.

The dance forms played an important part in Baroque instrumental and vocal music. In the hands of Bach and his contemporaries, they provided individual movements for stylized concert pieces.

Concerto Grosso

The *concerto grosso* is a multimovement work for instruments in which a solo group called the *concertino* and a full ensemble called the *ripieno* (Italian for "full") are pitted against each other. In the early concerto grosso the concertino generally consisted of two violins and continuo (cello and harpsichord). The ripieno was usually a small string orchestra with its own continuo.

The first important examples of the concerto grosso appeared in the works of the Italian composer Arcangelo Corelli (1653–1713). Corelli's concertos had no fixed number of movements and no set plan of contrast between the movements. He made very little distinction between the material given to the solo group and that given to the ripieno; the contrast was essentially one of weight—two violins and continuo against the full string ensemble.

Another Italian, Antonio Vivaldi (1669–1741), was the first great master of the genre. Vivaldi systematized the structure of the concerto grosso by standardizing a three-movement form. Vivaldi was a prolific composer of instrumental music, and over 450 of his concertos have been preserved. His concertos are consistently in three movements: the first is fast and long, produced by the full instrumental ensemble; the second is slow and short, played by a reduced ensemble; and the third, like the first, is fast, long, and written for the full ensemble. Vivaldi made a greater distinction between the solo and ensemble groups both in timbre and in complexity of musical material than did his predecessors.

Vivaldi's concertos strongly influenced Bach, who often transcribed for keyboard the works, especially the concertos, of Italian composers. Between 1714 and 1717, Bach transcribed nine Vivaldi concertos for solo organ or harpsichord and orchestra. In his own concerti grossi, Bach achieved an even stronger contrast between the concertino and the ripieno in instrumental color and the degree of complexity of the music for each group.

In 1721 Bach completed six concertos for orchestra. He dedicated them to Christian Ludwig, the Margrave of Brandenburg, who had requested Bach to write some pieces for the Brandenburg court orchestra. These works have been called the Brandenburg Concertos, although Bach referred to them as "concertos for several instruments." Three of these concertos (Nos. 2, 4, and 5) are concerti grossi that highlight a group of solo instruments against a full ensemble; all but the first follow Vivaldi's three-movement plan.

Brandenburg Concerto No. 2 in F Major

Record 2/Side 1

The Brandenburg Concerto No. 2 is scored for a concertino consisting of a recorder, oboe, trumpet, and violin. The ripieno is the usual string ensemble with continuo.

First Movement   The first movement is cast in *ritornello* form, a characteristic form for the first and sometimes the last movement of the concerto grosso. In ritornello (from the Italian word meaning "return") form the thematic material given to the ripieno returns between the passages played by the soloists. In broad outline, the plan of the first movement consists of the following pattern:

A	B	A	C	A
ritornello	concertino	ritornello	concertino	ritornello

The ritornello secton may be shortened or lengthened during the course of the movement.

The first movement, in F major, opens with the material of the ritornello played *tutti* (by the concertino and ripieno together). This is followed by a short statement of contrasting material by the solo violin, accompanied by continuo. An abbreviated ritornello leads to another concertino section in which the oboe picks up the material previously heard in the violin and the violin plays a countermelody. After another short ritornello, the original solo material shifts to the recorder, and the oboe plays the violin's countermelody. Finally, the trumpet makes its statement of the opening solo melody with the recorder playing the countermelody. Thus, Bach introduces each solo instrument of the concertino.

The instruments of the concertino continue to restate and develop the solo material and the ritornello material, sometimes lightly accompanied by, and sometimes duplicated by, the ripieno. At one point the ripieno drops out except for the continuo, and the solo instruments again concentrate on statements of the material with which they began the movement. First the recorder and violin are paired, to be joined in turn by the oboe and then the trumpet, leading to another entrance of the ripieno. The movement is polyphonic throughout.

An important aspect of much Baroque instrumental music is what has been called unflagging rhythm, the constant spinning out of music with no stopping points, giving a relentless rhythmic drive to the piece. This movement is an excellent example. Not until very late in the movement do all the parts cadence (come to a full stop) at the same time, and here the stop is to emphasize the final statement or the ritornello material. Another characteristic of Baroque music is the constancy of tempo within a movement or section. Once a tempo has been established, it is almost always maintained throughout a movement or a section of a piece, as is evident in this movement. However, Baroque composers did create contrast by varying the dynamic levels. Their music shifts suddenly from loud to soft, soft to loud, seldom progressing gradually from one level to the other. This suddenly shifting dynamic level is a strong element in the concerto grosso, where it is intensified by the opposing small and large groups of instruments.

Second Movement   The second movement is slow (andante) and in a contrasting key (D minor). It is also much thinner in texture since it uses only the solo recorder, oboe, and violin accompanied by continuo; the solo trumpet and the ripieno do not appear. This extreme contrast between the slow middle movement and the first and last movements is by no means unusual. Often, the second movement is scored for only the concertino and continuo.

In this particular movement the three upper parts weave a constantly spinning, almost hypnotic, web of counterpoint above a basso ostinato. They imitate one another, they answer back and forth, they constantly exchange material, using a basic set of two melodic fragments and their variants:

Example 10.1

All the while, the bass continues its insistent rhythmic movement as background and harmonic support for the upper voices.

Third Movement   The last movement is a four-part fugue for the concertino in a fast (*allegro assai*) tempo, which returns to the original F major key. The fugue subject is stated successively by the trumpet, oboe, recorder, and violin. The ripieno has little melodic significance; it supplies light, unobtrusive accompaniment and harmonic support for the concertino. The unflagging rhythmic drive of the piece propels it forward from the opening statement of the fugue subject by the trumpet to its final brilliant statement by the same instrument.

The essence of the concerto grosso is contrast: contrast in tone color, texture, tempo, and material. The same principle is true for the concerto for solo instrument and orchestra.

Solo Concerto

In all respects except one, the solo concerto is the same as the concerto grosso. It is cast in three movements, fast-slow-fast. Its first and last movements are often in ritornello form. It emphasizes contrast between concertino and tutti. In the solo concerto, however, the concertino consists of only one instrument, which in the Baroque period was most often the violin. Vivaldi, whose contribution to the solo concerto was as important as his development of the concerto grosso, wrote hundreds of solo concertos. His works in this genre became the models for later Baroque composers, notably Handel and Bach.

Of all Vivaldi's concertos, the group called *Le Quattro Stagione* (*The Four Seasons*) is perhaps the most interesting because of the extramusical basis of its inspiration. Vivaldi was one of the first to try to depict by musical means the feelings and sounds of the changing seasons. His four concertos are an early form of Baroque descriptive or program music, and the music for the solo violin, which calls for virtuoso playing, demonstrates Vivaldi's skill at writing for the instrument.

Each of the four concertos bears the title of one of the seasons —spring, summer, winter, fall—and each is preceded by a sonnet describing that particular season. For instance, the concerto entitled *Spring* has the following introduction:

Spring has come, and the birds greet it with joyous songs, and at the same time the streams run softly murmuring to the breathing of gentle breezes . . .

The song of the birds, the murmuring streams, and the gentle breezes all receive vivid musical representation by the solo violin and the full ensemble. But all of this takes place within the three movements of the basic concerto structure. And the ritornello structure of the first and last movements is also maintained.

Descriptive music has attracted composers of every age. We have already mentioned the program chansons of Jannequin in the Renaissance, and an entire chapter is devoted to descriptive music in the Romantic period.

The Sonata

In the Baroque era, the name *sonata* was given to pieces that varied widely in structure, character, and medium of performance. Usually scored for one or more instruments, the sonata opened with a fast fugal movement, was followed by a slower, homophonic movement of a dancelike nature, and closed with a final movement that resembled the first. Additional movements, however, were frequently included.

The early sonata existed in two forms: the *sonata da camera* (the chamber sonata) and the *sonata da chiesa* (the church sonata). Originally these sonatas differed only in the place of performance, but later the two terms indicated formal distinctions. The sonata da camera became a suite with an introduction and three or four dance movements, and the sonata da chiesa, a four-movement work in which the movements alternated: slow-fast-slow-fast.

In the later Baroque period, the sonata could be divided according to the medium of performance into four categories: those written for one part, those for two, those for three, and those for four or more. The most remarkable of the sonatas for one part were the unaccompanied violin and cello sonatas by Bach. The sonatas for two parts usually required three players, one to play the solo instrument and two, usually playing the cello and the keyboard, for the continuo. The sonata for three parts, the *trio sonata*, was the most important type of Baroque chamber music. It required four instruments: two violins for the upper parts, and a cello and a keyboard instrument for the continuo. Corelli, Purcell, Handel, Vivaldi, and Bach all contributed to the trio sonata literature.

Sonatas for four or more parts were intended for small orchestral ensembles. These were often called *sinfonie*, and often acted as overtures to or interludes within larger works such as operas or oratorios. Bach used the term sinfonia in quite another way to title his two- and three-part *Inventions*, keyboard pieces in contrapuntal style.

Summary

Baroque composers generally tailored their works to fit a specific need. Thus, Handel wrote for the stage and concert hall, while Bach wrote primarily for the churches he served.

The Baroque era was a period of great progress in instrumental music. Instruments were improved technically, qualifying them to play serious music. Keyboard instruments in particular enjoyed greater versatility after the development of *equal temperament* enabled them to perform equally well in every key. The most important keyboard instruments during the period were the harpsichord and the organ.

A large body of keyboard music was produced during the Baroque period. The fantasia, capriccio, prelude, and toccata were carryovers from styles originally developed for the lute, the most popular instrument during the Renaissance. The prelude and toccata often served as preliminaries to the fugue, a musical procedure that attained its greatest heights in the works of Bach.

Another form of keyboard music, the suite, was based on dance music. Usually the four movements of a suite consisted of an allemande, a courante, a saraband, and a gigue.

The concerto grosso was a multimovement work that pitted a small group, called the concertino, against a full ensemble, called a ripieno. A solo concerto differed from the concerto grosso only by the fact that the concertino was reduced to a single instrument. The concerto's three-movement pattern (fast-slow-fast) became standardized during the Baroque period and influenced the development of Classical musical forms.

**Part III
Suggested
Listening**

Bach, Johann Sebastian

Magnifcat in D. Composed shortly after he settled in Leipzig, this concise setting of the Latin canticle of the Virgin Mary is one of Bach's finest and most melodious works; it is scored for five-part chorus, four soloists, and orchestra.

Mass in B Minor. Actually a compilation of separate movements, this immense composition encompasses all of the major choral and vocal techniques developed over the preceding century and a half.

Organ Works. Toccata in D Minor; Passacaglia in C Minor; Fantasia and Fugue in G Minor; Prelude and Fugue in E-Flat Major (St. Anne). This quartet of works, spanning Bach's most active period of organ composition, demonstrates the major Baroque techniques of keyboard writing.

Musikalisches Opfer (A Musical Offering). In 1747, Bach visited Frederick the Great of Prussia and improvised at the keyboard upon a theme proposed by the King; after returning to Leipzig, he revised and wrote his improvisations. It is a cycle of canons, two ricercari, and a trio sonata for flute, violin, and continuo.

Handel, George Frederich

Israel in Egypt. An oratorio in three sections. Unlike most of Handel's oratorios, the solo voices complement the more dominant chorus in this work. Of particular interest is the description of the plagues.

Orchestral Suites: Water Music; Fireworks Music.   The *Water Music*, actually a compilation of three individual suites, was first performed at a royal boating party. The *Fireworks Music*, a much shorter work, originally scored for a large wind band and later revised to include strings, was composed to celebrate the Peace of Aix-la-Chapelle.

Schütz, Heinrich

Historia von der Geburt Jesu Christi (The Christmas Story).   One of the earliest masterpieces of Baroque oratorio, this work is divided into eight parts, with an introductory and concluding chorus.

Vivaldi, Antonio

Concerto in D Major for Flute, Op. 10, No. 3 (Il gardellino).   One of Vivaldi's thirty solo concertos for flute, *Il gardellino (The Goldfinch)* shows his ability to use an instrument's potential to full advantage.

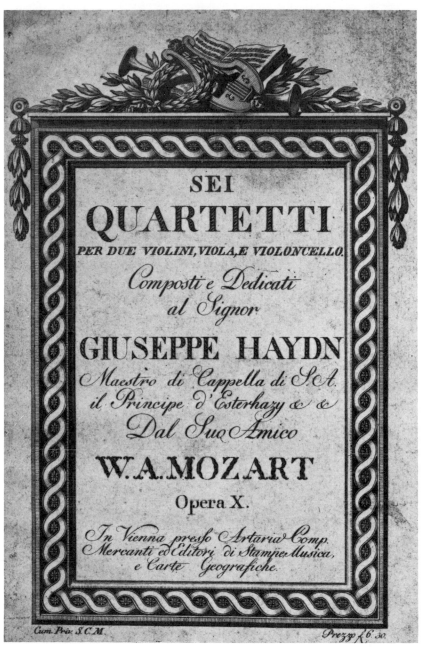

Title page of string quartets by Mozart that he dedicated to Joseph Haydn. (Courtesy of the British Museum, London)

Plate 9.   Sir Joshua Reynolds' portrait of Colonel George
K. H. Coussmaker, Grenadier Guards reflects the preoccupation with "good taste" and technique throughout the
Classical Era. Rather than striving for psychological insight, fashionable artists sought detachment, strict objectivity, and high commissions. (Courtesy The Metropolitan
Museum of Art, Bequest of William K. Vanderbilt, 1920)

Plate 10.   Paintings such as Goya's The Third of May exemplify the dramatic post-Revolution shift toward the artist's involvement in human situations. Goya's concern for portraying heightened emotion and social injustice has a modern flavor. (Courtesy Rapho Guillumette, Giraudon)

part IV   Music of the Classical Era

The Classical era in art* lasted from about 1770 to 1828 (the year of the death of Francisco Goya). Its single most important historical event was the French Revolution in 1789, which cut it sharply in half. In the decades before the Revolution, philosophers, writers, artists, and even rulers sought to substitute a faith in reason for the old traditions

The Arts of the Classical Era

and superstitions that had lasted since the Middle Ages. But the irrational acts of violence and terror committed by the leaders of the French Revolution led to the rise of Napoleon and the continuation of twenty years of warfare. Inevitably, people began to think that the period leading to these events was one of self-delusion rather than reason, that those who had preached faith in reason were naive at best, hypocrites at worst.

Before the Revolution

Nevertheless, the four or five decades before the French Revolution did witness improvements in the lives of many people. In particular, the middle class grew larger and more powerful. Social mobility was easier, as was physical mobility—roads were built and improved and stagecoaches regularly carried people and mail far from home. Indeed, the letters of Mme. de Sévigné, Horace Walpole, and Mozart rank among the important literature of the period. New ideas spread and were quickly accepted. The bases of scientific studies as we know them were laid down in physics, chemistry, geology, botany, zoology, and medicine.

The privileged members of society were living in an age of comfort. Some philosophers believed that man could shortly attain perfection by

*In music, the Classical era is generally considered to have begun about 1770 (the year Ludwig van Beethoven was born).

applying common sense to the problems of society. This optimistic view was championed by the German philosopher and mathematician Leibnitz (and brutally satirized by the French philosopher Voltaire in *Candide*). Still others adopted the views of the French writer Rousseau, who said that primitive man had enjoyed a perfection that civilization had adulterated. He believed that man could attain perfection again only if he returned to his instinctive behavior. The rational outlook of Leibnitz and the instinctive view of Rousseau seem to be opposites, yet they share the belief that the human condition can be improved.

The idea that an individual should reach his full potential, but with an emphasis on his responsibility to society, was expressed in other areas as well. In economics it was reflected in the doctrine of laissez-faire, which advocated the freedom of business from government restrictions. In politics it was echoed in the idea of the social contract, under which the power of a monarch or government depended on the will of the people—a view which strongly influenced the writers of the American Declaration of Independence.

The idea that standards could no longer be imposed arbitrarily from above strongly influenced artists. Instead of glorifying the Church or a king, artists and musicians had to satisfy the requirements of the middle class who bought their paintings and tickets to their concerts. Rulers still employed private orchestras and court painters, but increasingly artists, composers, and performers had to achieve a reputation through popular success. For example, the composer Haydn divided his time between writing music for the private entertainment of Prince Esterhazy and touring Europe to conduct public concerts of his new works, commissioned by managers who knew what the public wanted. Artists tried to please this new popular audience and the history of art in the eighteenth century reflects their efforts to do so.

To get the attention of the public, the English painter William Hogarth (1697–1764) developed a new type of painting. In Hogarth's time there was no tradition of painting in England; the Puritan notion that art was frivolous, if not immoral, was widespread in the middle class, and upper-class collectors preferred to buy the works of Italians. Hogarth shrewdly realized that if he could demonstrate that his art had a "purpose" it would find a market. To this end he painted moral scenes depicting the rewards of virtue and the penalties of sin. Because sin was more pictorial than virtue, Hogarth's series *The Rake's Progress* became sensationally popular; it shows graphically how an excess of vice leads to madness and death. With such works Hogarth titillated and instructed the public, became wealthy through the sale of engravings of his paintings, and made painting acceptable in England.

Two paintings from *The Rake's Progress* show the Rake at the height of his debauchery and at his death, chained to the floor of Bedlam, the insane asylum. Taken together they tell us some interesting things about the eighteenth century and its art. Hogarth's Puritan audience might have been offended by his candid depiction of wenching, gambling, and drinking in *The Orgy*, but by juxtaposing it with the Rake's death, Hogarth provided moral justification for showing the excesses. Similarly, in Mozart's opera *Don Giovanni*, the Don's debauchery is first shown in detail and then punished by a horrible death.

Figure 11.1   William Hogarth popularized painting in Puritan England by ensuring that his works had a "purpose." It was permissible to sensationalize "The Orgy" from the series The Rake's Progress *as long as the painting had a moral. (Trustees of Sir John Soane's Museum)*

Figure 11.2   Hogarth showed that the just reward for debauchery was this shackled madman's death in "The Madhouse" from The Rake's Progress. *Hogarth's stark realism and candid detail reveal the social values of eighteenth-century England. (Trustees of Sir John Soane's Museum)*

For the most part, Hogarth dispensed with the exaggerated and twisted figures of Baroque art to engage the viewer's attention. Instead he used stark realism and familiar detail. But he applied the lessons of the Baroque masters to create an effect, for example, the figure of the dying Rake, starkly illuminated by a mysterious light, shows the influence of Caravaggio's Baroque painting, *Calling of St. Matthew* (Plate 5). Finally, Hogarth's choice of a setting for the Rake's death reflects the preoccupation with madness during the Age of Reason. It was a fashionable diversion to look at the lunatics at Bedlam, much as we go to see animals at the zoo. The two elegantly dressed ladies in Figure 11.2 are tourists. Their cool detachment emphasizes the poignancy of the surrounding madness. It is as though the old maxim, "In the midst of life we are in death," had been transliterated for the age as, "In the midst of reason we are in madness."

The Renaissance and Baroque tradition of portraiture was maintained in the eighteenth century, but with a difference. What is most admired today in the portraits of painters like Sir Joshua Reynolds and Thomas Gainsborough is their brilliant technique rather than any profound insight into the character of the sitters (Plate 9). To have revealed depth of character would have been considered poor taste on the part of the artist and the sitter. "Good taste" was the standard of the fashionable world. Taste reflected reason and reason opposed extravagance; the artist's objective was the unemotional rendering of nature's appearance.

Figure 11.3   Thomas Gainsborough rivaled Joshua Reynolds as the most fashionable portrait painter of the Classical Era. This Portrait of Queen Charlotte *shows both the technique and the clientele for which Gainsborough was famous. (The Metropolitan Museum of Art, The Jules S. Bache Collection, 1949)*

Similar standards of taste also determined the appearance of buildings. Unlike such Baroque palaces as Versailles, eighteenth-century buildings emphasized comfort. Rooms were smaller, less imposing, and designed to entertain small groups with witty conversation and chamber music. For many years, taste dictated that the style for these houses should be based on the classical buildings of Greece and Rome, as described in the textbooks of the Renaissance architect Andrea Palladio and as discovered in the excavations of the ancient city of Pompeii.

Figure 11.4 Thomas Jefferson's home, Monticello, typifies the elegant simplicity and symmetry characteristic of most of the architecture from the Classical Era. Emphasis was on comfort and intimacy rather than the spacious grandeur of the Baroque palaces. (Monkmeyer, Pace)

Heavy, massive furniture was replaced by light and comfortable pieces designed and made by such distinguished English cabinetmakers as Thomas Chippendale and Thomas Sheraton. An equally high level of craftsmanship was attained by ceramic makers, whose porcelain figurines and tableware are still copied. Such famous workshops as Sèvres, Meissen, Nymphenburg, Frankenthal, Chelsea, Derby, and Wedgewood originated at this time.

Toward the end of the century there was a reaction to the symmetry and simplicity of Classicism. A rather eccentric Englishman, Horace Walpole, decided to build his country home, Strawberry Hill, in the Gothic style, which had been dormant for two centuries. The Gothic revival swept England and then Europe, continuing into the twentieth century (Figure 11.5).

The Near East and the Far East as well as the past were plundered for new styles. For a time it became the rage to collect Chinese porcelain and exhibit it in rooms with Chinese decor. Travelers stopping in Constantinople brought back Turkish fashions and soon ladies were wearing feathered turbans and pantaloons. The Turkish style found its way into European music in Mozart's Violin Concerto No. 5 and Beethoven's *Turkish March* and *Choral Symphony*. Napoleon's conquest of Egypt and the consequent discovery of Egyptian art resulted in some artistic and ornamental extremes, such as in sphinx heads and hieroglyphics carved in furniture. Perhaps the most outlandish example of eclectic exoticism was the Royal Pavilion built at Brighton for the Prince Regent

Figure 11.5 Horace Walpole built Strawberry Hill in the Gothic tradition, thereby sparking a revival of the medieval Gothic style which was to dominate much of Europe for the next century. (Louis H. Frohman)

Figure 11.6 The Royal Pavilion at Brighton Beach is an attempt to combine the then-fashionable styles from India, Egypt, China, and the tropics. Though extreme, such architectural fantasy demonstrated the public's determined reaction to excesses of Classical simplicity. (Rapho Guillumette, J. Allan Cash)

of England. Its fantasy architecture boasts Indian cupolas, Egyptian minarets, Chinese interiors, and a garden full of palm trees forced to survive in the English climate (Figure 11.6).

As long as Classicism was the prevailing taste, elegance and gracefulness were the distinguishing features of music and art. Artists, poets, and composers concentrated on skillful variations on Classical forms.

The music of Haydn and Mozart reflects their genius in perfecting existing forms; and even Beethoven wrote in the conventional forms of the symphony, sonata, and concerto.

After the Revolution

By its excesses, the French Revolution made a mockery of the worship of reason. Art became charged with suppressed emotions, and feeling became the subject matter of art. Poets still wrote meticulously rhymed

Figure 11.7   Goya's etching The Sleep of Reason Creates Monsters *served as an allegory of his age: the violence and bloodshed which interrupted the ''age of reason'' overpowered Europe much like a nightmare engulfs a defenseless sleeper. (Prints Division, The New York Library, Astor, Lenox and Tilden Foundations)*

stanzas, but they wrote about the sufferings of unrequited love; novelists invented tales of revenge, intrigue, and the supernatural.

No artist reflects this shift in sensibility more strongly than the Spanish painter Francisco Goya (1746–1828). As a young man Goya painted inoffensive scenes of daily life. His work changed profoundly during the Napoleonic Wars in Spain. These wars were complicated by a Spanish civil war, with atrocities committed by all sides. Goya depicted these atrocities in some of his greatest works, including a series of etchings, *The Horrors of War*, and his painting *The Third of May*, which commemorates the shooting of Spanish civilians by French soldiers (Plate 10). While the dramatic lighting of *The Third of May* is reminiscent of Baroque painting, the pity and terror conveyed by the victims confronting their faceless executioners are completely modern.

In one of his many etchings, *The Sleep of Reason Creates Monsters*, Goya created an allegory of his age. It shows both the dreamer and his dream. The cat, like the sleeper, has her feet on the ground and may be as real as he; but the cat's predatory expression is repeated on the faces of the owls, and the owls' outspread wings are echoed in the shadowy bats' wings. These monsters, though springing from the mind of the sleeping artist, are equally real and unreal. Though Hogarth was fascinated by the irrational, there is no touch of it in his painting of the Rake in Bedlam; in Goya's etching, however, the irrational becomes the subject matter and the Age of Reason becomes a dream.

chapter 12

The term *classical* is applied to music in several different ways. In one sense, we speak of a "classic" as any work of lasting value. "Classical" sometimes designates so-called *serious* or art music, as opposed to *popular* music. In this case the term is applied without regard to historical or stylistic

Mozart and Haydn

factors, so that composers of different style periods—Bach, Beethoven, and Tchaikovsky, for example—may all be considered "classical" composers.

In a narrower and more accurate sense, the term *classical* is applied to music in either of two meanings: First, it describes those periods in music history when style emphasized formal clarity, balance and structure, lucid design, objectivity, and traditionalism as opposed to the romantic qualities of sentimentalism, exaggerated emotionalism, subjectivism, and experimentation. (Seen in this light, the late Renaissance and late Baroque periods, when the art of polyphony was brought to its greatest heights, were periods of classicism.) The second meaning designates the music of the Viennese classic school (that is, the music of Haydn, Mozart, and to an extent, Beethoven and Schubert) from about 1770 to 1830.

Early Classical Music

The transition from the Baroque to the Classical style of the Viennese school began in the early decades of the eighteenth century. While Bach and Handel were creating their late Baroque masterpieces, new stylistic trends emerged that abandoned the forms and elaborate polyphonic texture of the Baroque period. Although unimportant in themselves, these lesser stylistic movements led to the first flowering of the Classical style in the 1770s in the works of Haydn and Mozart.

One of these new styles developed in France and was called *style galant*, or gallant style. Essentially a secular style, it was light and elegant in form. In instrumental music the *style galant* rejected Baroque principles, which limited the composer to expressing only one mood, and espoused the idea that a variety of moods is more in keeping with the natural emotions of man. Tenderness and delicacy were stressed. Polyphonic fugal procedures gave way to a homophonic style in which the melody, consisting of short, balanced phrases and its accompaniment were clearly evident.

As noted in Chapter 8, European culture in the early eighteenth century was patterned after the French. Thus the *style galant* exerted a strong influence on pre-Classical German composers, who developed a distinct style called *Empfindsamer Stil* ("sentiment"). Like the French style, it broke away from the Baroque to emphasize "true and natural" feelings.

One of the most gifted exponents of the new German style was Carl Philipp Emanuel Bach (1714–1788), son of Johann Sebastian. While Johann Sebastian was writing his final testaments to the polyphonic art—*The Musical Offering* and *The Art of the Fugue*—Carl Philipp Emanuel was producing keyboard sonatas in a markedly different style.

The younger Bach used themes of various and contrasting moods. The melodic motives introduced in his works were developed in new and frequently surprising rhythms and harmonies. Dissonances, chromatic harmonies, sudden changes in key and dynamics, and sections in free rhythm were all elements of his style. Equally important, the younger Bach made extensive use of two distinct themes within a piece. He contrasted one theme with another and then developed them by putting the themes in different rhythmic and harmonic contexts. The themes then reappeared in their original setting.

Composers began to apply this scheme to the first movements of instrumental sonatas in three or four movements. Since the first movement invariably had a fast tempo (allegro), the scheme came to be known as first-movement form or sonata-allegro form.

Sonata-Allegro Form

Sonata-allegro form consists of three sections: (1) the exposition, (2) the development, and (3) the recapitulation.

The function of the *exposition* is to state thematic material, to fix it firmly in the listener's memory so that he will be able to participate in the drama and excitement of the development process. This section is based on at least two themes, or groups of themes, which contrast in key and in general character, the first often being rhythmic and vital, the second being more lyrical. The themes are connected by a bridge, a section characterized by modulation to a new key. If the first theme is in a major key, the second will nearly always be in its dominant key, a fifth higher; for example, if the first theme is in C major, the second will be in G major. If, on the other hand, the first theme is written in a minor key, the second will usually appear in its relative major, a step and a half higher in pitch. Thus, if the original theme is in C minor, the second will be in E flat major.

When the thematic material of the exposition has been stated, it is usually repeated. A closing section is often used to bring the section to an end.

In some works the exposition is preceded by a slow introduction. The introduction, however, is not part of sonata-allegro form and is not included in the repetition of the exposition.

The *development* is the central section of the movement. In this section, some of the material from the exposition is reworked in a variety of ways. Many techniques are available with which thematic material can be developed. Fragmentation of melodies, expansion of small motives, the addition of counterpoint, and changes in timbre, rhythm, and dynamics are only a few that could be applied; modulation through a series of keys was an indispensable aspect of developmental technique.

The *recapitulation* is essentially a restatement of the material presented in the exposition. Bridge passages between the themes are usually longer, and the second theme is stated in the *original tonic* key, not, as in the exposition, in the dominant or relative key.

When a *coda* is included, it is usually brief and often based on material drawn from the exposition.

Sonata-allegro form, which involves only *one* movement, should not be confused with the term *sonata*, which refers to an entire composition consisting of several movements.

Other Movements of Large Works

While the first movement of the Classical sonata (the sonata-allegro movement) is invariably in a fast tempo, the second movement is in a slow tempo and cast either in the form of theme and variations or in an alternating form such as ABA song form. Occasionally the second movement will be cast in sonata-allegro form. The key of the second movement contrasts with that of the first.

The third movement, which returns to the key of the first movement, is invariably a minuet and trio. The fourth and last movement is also in the key of the first and is usually a rondo or sonata-allegro form. Occasionally it is a combination of the two.

This four-movement plan became the basis of the symphony (sonata for orchestra) and the string quartet (sonata for four stringed instruments). A three-movement scheme in which the minuet and trio was omitted was typical of works for solo piano, for solo instruments and the piano, and for concertos (works for solo instrument and orchestra).

The Orchestra

In the Baroque era instrumental music had become an independent idiom, and a vast literature for instrumental ensembles was produced. But the Baroque orchestra, aside from the usual complement of strings, had no fixed makeup.

In the Classical era the makeup of the orchestra became standardized to a great extent. Its development was largely the work of Johann Stamitz (1717–1757), a violinist, composer, and conductor of the orchestra at Mannheim. Under his direction it became the most celebrated musical ensemble in Europe. The excellence of its playing was praised by the leading composers of the day, Mozart among them.

By Baroque standards the Mannheim orchestra was of rather large dimensions. In 1756 it consisted of twenty violins, four violas, four cellos, and four basses. The wind section included four horns in addition to flutes, oboes, clarinets, and bassoons. Trumpets and timpani were also used.

The Mannheim orchestra was capable of achieving a great variety of startling effects. Chief among these were the Mannheim "rocket," crescendo, the string tremolo, and a forte of shattering impact. The German poet and musician D. F. D. Schubert (1739–1791) recorded his impressions of the orchestra in his *Essay on Musical Esthetics:*

No orchestra in the world ever equalled the Mannheimers' execution. Its forte is like thunder, its crescendo like a mighty waterfall, its diminuendo a gentle river disappearing into the distance, its piano is a breath of spring. The wind instruments could not be used to better advantage; they lift and carry, they reinforce and give life to the storm for violins.

While the technical improvement of the instruments during the Baroque period contributed to the creation of a significant body of solo and chamber music, the development of this collective instrument, the orchestra enabled the growth of a vast body of symphonic compositions.

The Symphony

Symphonic composition centered in the cities of Berlin, Mannheim, and Vienna. The Berlin, or North German composers, of whom C. P. E. Bach was the leading figure, retained the more conservative three-movement structure and preserved elements of the contrapuntal style. The Mannheim group, under the leadership of Stamitz, employed the four-movement structure. The Viennese symphonists also favored the four-movement form. One of the greatest of the Viennese symphonic composers was Wolfgang Amadeus Mozart.

Mozart (1756–1791)

The Bettmann Archive

Born in Salzburg, Austria, Wolfgang Amadeus Mozart began his musical career as one of the most celebrated child prodigies in eighteenth-century Europe. His father, Leopold, a highly respected composer and violinist, recognized his son's extraordinary talent and carefully supervised his musical education. Mozart began harpsichord lessons when he was four and wrote his first compositions when he was five. At the age of six he and his older sister, Maria Anna ("Nannerl"), were taken by their father on a concert tour of Munich and Vienna.

From this first public performance until he was fifteen, Mozart was almost constantly on tour, playing prepared works and improvising. While the harpsichord and later the piano remained Mozart's principal instruments, he also mastered the violin and the organ. In addition to keyboard pieces, he wrote church works, symphonies, string quartets, and operas. In 1769, on a long trip to Italy, Mozart composed his first major opera, *Mitridate*, which was performed in Milan in 1770. His success in Italy, as triumphant as Handel's had been some sixty years earlier, brought him a number of commissions for operas.

His father, court composer and vice chapelmaster to the Archbishop of Salzburg, obtained a position for his son as concertmaster in the Archbishop's orchestra. But the new Archbishop of Salzburg, installed in 1772, failed to appreciate Mozart's genius. Relations between the haughty churchman and the high-spirited young composer steadily deteriorated until, in 1781, despite his father's objections, Mozart quit his position and settled in Vienna.

The first years in Vienna were fairly prosperous. Mozart was in great demand as a teacher; he gave numerous concerts, and his German *Singspiel, Die Entführung aus dem Serail* (*The Abduction from the Harem*) (1782), was a success. He married Constanze Weber, a woman he had met several years earlier on a concert tour, and looked forward to a happy family life, but Constanze was a careless housekeeper, and Mozart was a poor manager of finances. Intrigues at the Viennese court kept him from obtaining a permanent post. Public taste changed and his teaching began to fall off. Except for occasional successes—his opera, *Le Nozze di Figaro* (*The Marriage of Figaro*) (1786) and the *Singspiel, Die Zauberflöte* (*The Magic Flute*) (1791)—the last ten years of his life were spent, for the most part, in poverty.

In 1788 he gave up public performances, relying on a meager income from teaching and loans from various friends to sustain himself and his family. In spite of these troubles he continued to compose, but his health began to decline. When he died in 1791 at the age of thirty-five, he was buried in an unmarked grave in a part of the cemetery reserved for paupers.

His Work

Unlike the meticulous Haydn, who kept a chronological list of all his compositions, Mozart never bothered to organize his musical papers in any fully consistent fashion. In the nineteenth century, Ludwig von Köchel compiled a roughly chronological listing of Mozart's music (numbering up to 626). This catalogue, along with substantial revisions and additions by later musicologists, remains in use today.

The most recent edition of Köchel's catalogue, in which the number of each piece is preceded by the initial "K," includes twenty-one stage works, twenty-seven concert arias, fifteen Masses, over fifty symphonies, twenty-five piano concertos, twelve violin concertos, some fourteen concertos for other instruments, twenty-six string quartets, seventeen piano sonatas, forty-two violin sonatas, and numerous works for miscellaneous chamber-sized ensembles.

Religious music   Mozart composed almost all of his church music at the beginning of his career, when he was working in Salzburg. His two greatest choral works, unfortunately, were left incomplete. The first of these was the gigantic Mass in C Minor (1782), intended as an offering of thanks for his marriage to Constanze. The second is also his last work, the Requiem in D Minor. In 1791 Mozart accepted a commission to write this work on behalf of a nobleman who wished to remain anonymous. Mozart died before the work was finished. At the request of Mozart's widow Franz Süssmayr, one of the composer's pupils, finished the piece.

Opera   Mozart's operas are the only eighteenth-century works in this genre to have remained consistently in general repertory. For the most part, they fall into one of three categories: (1) Italian *opera seria*, including *Mitridate* (1770), *Idomeneo* (1781), and *The Clemency of Titus* (1791); (2) comic Italian opera, including *The Marriage of Figaro* (1786) and *Cosi Fan Tutte* (1790); and (3) German *Singspiel*, including *The Abduction from the Seraglio* (1782). Two of Mozart's most popular and significant operas resist such classification. *Don Giovanni* (1787), subtitled "humorous drama," vacillates between high comedy and genuine tragedy in following the career of the legendary Don Juan. *The Magic Flute* (1791), though cast in the form of a German *Singspiel* with intermittent spoken dialogue, might better be considered a morality play bound up in a fairy-tale setting. In many ways *Don Giovanni* may be regarded as the greatest of the eighteenth-century Italian operas; *The Magic Flute* may be considered the first German opera and one of the greatest.

Instrumental music   The amazing fluency with which Mozart composed his operas is also evident in his instrumental music. He was able to carry around finished compositions in his head, once remarking that "the committing to paper is done quickly enough. For everything is already finished, and it rarely differs on paper from what it was in my imagination."

Many of the twenty-five piano concertos were composed for Mozart's own use in his public performances. These concertos demonstrate many of Mozart's most progressive ideas. His string quartets, at first influenced by Haydn's, also reveal Mozart's mastery of musical forms.

His final three symphonies—Nos. 39, 40, and 41 (the *Jupiter Symphony*)—were composed during the summer of 1788. Nothing is known about the circumstances of their composition, but these three works stand among Mozart's finest contributions to instrumental music.

Symphony No. 40 in G Minor

Record 2 / Side 2

Example 12.1

Mozart's G-minor symphony follows the four-movement plan outlined earlier: fast-slow-medium-fast. It is scored for an orchestra consisting of flute, two oboes, two clarinets, two bassoons, two horns, and strings.

First Movement: *sonata-allegro form*

Exposition   The movement opens with a presentation of the first theme, which begins with two phrases having the same rhythmic pattern and, consequently, the same length.

Example 12.2

The phrases differ from one another in their *melodic contour* and *melodic activity*. Phrase 1 is melodically static for most of its life, dwelling on the two notes e♭ and d. It suddenly becomes active at the end as it leaps upward. Phrase 2, on the other hand, is melodically active at the beginning, based on a descending scale passage, and becomes melodically static in its last two notes, which are the same pitch. These paired phrases, and elements drawn from them (especially the rhythmic motive ♫ ♩), are crucial to the life and structure of the entire movement. As the theme begins, these phrases are sounded softly by the first and second violins, with the second violins playing an octave lower than the first. The violas, cellos, and basses play an accompaniment without melodic significance, and the woodwinds are silent. Consequently, the listener's attention is riveted on the pair of phrases located in the violins.

Both phrases are repeated one step lower. By this time the listener has come to expect repetitions of the rhythmic structure, melodic contour, and length of the two phrases, but Mozart introduces a new phrase, a surprise for the listener. This new phrase begins like Phrase 1, but continues in a different melodic contour and abandons the rhythmic pattern of 1 and 2. It does maintain the same phrase *length*, thus satisfying the listener's expectation to a degree.

Example 12.3

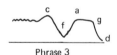

Phrase 3 is repeated, but this time it is extended and for the first time *phrase length* is altered, resulting in another surprise for the listener, who has come to expect the repetition of Phrase 3, and the familiar length of time. The woodwinds then enter and introduce a new melodic element, while the strings preserve the familiar rhythmic motive.

Example 12.4

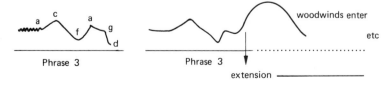

The new melodic element leads to a cadence in the dominant key of D.

After this interruption in the flow of melody, there is a return to the original paired phrases, which are played twice. Just as the listener becomes convinced that he is going to hear them repeated as they were before, there is a sudden entrance of new material—the bridge.

Example 12.5

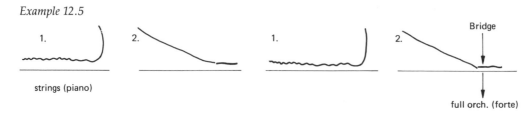

Example 12.6

Mozart has presented material in such a way as to make the listener expect its continuation. He then upsets this expectation by the introduction of new elements which, while different from the original material, preserve traces of it. He then satisfies the listener's expectations by a literal return to the original material, only to upset the listener again by the unpredictable appearance of the bridge, with an abrupt change of dynamics from piano to forte, with the entire orchestra participating.

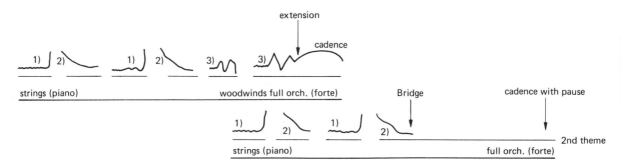

The bridge section is an extended modulation closing with a strong cadence on the dominant chord of the key in which the second theme will be stated. A pronounced pause follows, which clearly separates Theme 1 and the bridge from Theme 2. This marked differentiation of themes is typical of both Haydn and Mozart.

The second theme appears in the relative key of B flat major. It is a lyrical, expressive melody composed of phrases of unequal length and different contours. The second theme acts mainly as a foil to the first.

In the last section of Theme 2, before the closing material, Mozart utilizes elements of the first theme, notably the figure ♫♩ ♫♩, with both the original rhythmic and melodic patterns found at the beginning of Phrase 1. This last section is presented in dialogue fashion between the clarinet and the bassoon, then finally is stated and expanded in the high first violins, accompanied by a sudden change in dynamics from soft to loud. By this means of referring back to material that was so noticeable in Theme 1, Mozart adds a unity to this exposition over and above that contained in the procedure of sonata-allegro form. Indeed, the entire exposition is unified by the basic motive ♫ ♩.

The exposition is immediately repeated, providing the listener with the opportunity to become more familiar with the themes so that he may follow their destinies in the drama of the development section.

Development   As the development section begins, the violins present the paired phrases of the first theme in a variety of keys and at a variety of pitch levels. The material is restated in the course of modulation to new keys. The changes that occur in the melodic structure are the result of modulation.

Just as the third statement of the two phrases is finishing, Mozart adds a new developmental technique. Suddenly the phrases are stated not in the violins, but in the lower strings. They are then passed back and forth between the lower and upper strings. The upper strings provide contrapuntal material to the theme when it appears in the lower strings, and the lower strings play the same contrapuntal material when the theme passes back to the upper strings. The beginning of this passing back and forth technique is accompanied by a sudden and unexpected change from piano to forte.

Example 12.7

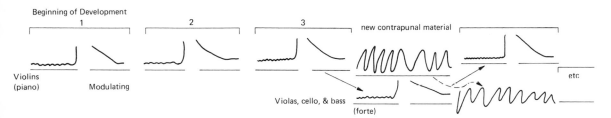

Here again, Mozart has established in the mind of the listener certain expectations and then created a surprise by doing something different. The listener now experiences the paired phrases in a new way.

This passing back and forth from high to low strings continues and the listener becomes accustomed to it and expects it to continue. Then, after the second statement of the phrases in the lower strings, the violins take up the phrases and a remarkable change takes place. After Phrase 1, Phrase 2 is begun. But instead of Phrase 2's static ending, there appears the sudden leap that ends Phrase 1. In other words, Mozart has combined the melodically active elements of each phrase into one new phrase:

Example 12.8

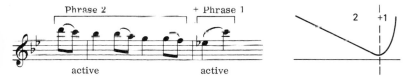

This is a new developmental technique, a *reduction* of the basic material from the exposition. The new phrase, a composite of the two original phrases, states material from both phrases in the same length of time formerly required to state the material of just *one* of the phrases.

After the combination of phrases is stated three times, it is followed by still another change. The polyphonic texture that began when the paired phrases were passed back and forth between the upper and lower strings and continued through the three statements of the composite phrase gives way to a return to a homophonic texture, in which the upper strings have a new version of the two phrases. This new version combines the *static* elements of the two phrases.

Example 12.9

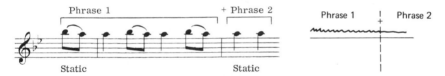

It represents a further reduction of the melodic material, but this time the reduction is not only one of length, but also of *melodic activity*.

The rest of the developmental section continues systematically to break down the material. Before the violins have concluded the second composite phrase, the flute and clarinets state a shortened version of it.

Example 12.10

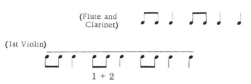

After this is stated several times, the woodwinds answer with a further shortening of the phrase.

Example 12.11

This figure is the shortest form of the material, and the rest of the development section exploits it by passing it back and forth between high and low strings. Finally, the flute and clarinets alternately state the figure, using it as a springboard to reintroduce gently the entire first theme as the violins begin the recapitulation.

Thus the "drama" of the development section ends as the melodic material, having been reduced to its smallest component, reappears in its original form.

Example 12.12

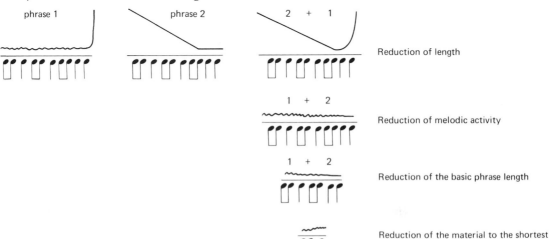

Recapitulation   The recapitulation opens with a statement of the first theme as it was heard in the exposition. A bridge passage, an extended form of the bridge in the exposition, leads to the second theme, again after a pause for the entire orchestra. The second theme appears in the tonic key of G minor.

Coda   A brief coda, based on the first phrase of the first theme, brings the movements to a close in the original key of G minor. Here again the appearance of Phrase 1 adds additional unity and structural solidity to the movement.

Second Movement: *andante*

The second movement generally conforms to the four-movement plan of the sonata: its key (E flat major) contrasts with the key of the first movement (G minor); it is slower in tempo and, to some extent, quieter and more lyrical than the first movement. It is somewhat unusual, however, because, unlike the second movement of many Classical symphonies, it is based on sonata-allegro form.

Exposition   The first theme consists of three parts (A, B, and C). Part A begins with imitative entrances—first in the violas, then in the second violins, and finally in the first violins, which end part A. The melodic material of B consists of short fragments separated by rests. These fragments are stated by the first and second violins duplicating each other an octave apart.

Both A and B are then repeated, with changes and additions. The repeat of A begins in the cellos and basses, moves to the violas, and is then finished by the second violins, while the first violins play a new, added melody. When B is restated, the first violins continue to play new material, while the B melody, originally played by the upper strings, is now played by the lower strings.

Example 12.13

The last measure of B is replaced by the beginning of C. It is built on a small figure (so small it is barely noticed) from the B part of the first theme: . As the movement continues, this small figure becomes more important.

The orchestra is brought to a full cadence and pause before the bridge is introduced. The bridge begins with a downward octave leap in which the higher note is played loudly (*forte*), the lower note is played softly (*piano*), and the rhythm is somewhat syncopated. But as it unfolds, the figure ♯♭ becomes the predominant element, stated by the strings, answered by the woodwinds, and cast into scalelike passages. This fragment "takes over" and is continued throughout the remaining part of the bridge by the woodwinds, while the strings play an expanded version of the imitative opening of the first theme.

The second theme begins with new and contrasting material, but soon the familiar figure is integrated into it (at the places marked with an "x" in the following notation).

Example 12.14

The figure is also present in the closing material of Theme 2. Indeed it is included in every part of this exposition—sometimes barely noticeable, sometimes dominating the material—tying together the entire exposition. Here again, Mozart has bound together the contrasting themes by carrying a common element through them all. The unity of the exposition becomes even more apparent when it is repeated.

Development   The development section is based on the opening rhythmic pattern of the first theme ♪♫♫| and the figure that played such a prominent part in the thematic material of the exposition ♬. These two ideas are presented consecutively first and then in combination, one played in the strings and the other in the woodwinds, and vice versa.

Recapitulation   In the recapitulation, Mozart again finds ingenious ways to upset the expectations of the listener. Parts A and B of the first theme are presented normally. When the theme is repeated, however, the end of part A is changed somewhat and is immediately followed not by part B, but by the beginning of the bridge. After this "premature" entrance of the bridge, part B appears. The bridge resumes and leads to the second theme, which is stated in the principal key of E♭. A closing section, based on the ♬ ♬ figure, ends the recapitulation. Mozart indicates that the entire development and recapitulation is to be repeated, resulting in the overall scheme: exposition, exposition, development, recapitulation, development, recapitulation.

This movement is evidence of the flexibility with which the forms of the Classical period were treated.

Third Movement: *minuet and trio*

This relatively simple movement, a stylized rendering of the old dance form, provides a contrast to the structural complexities of the other movements. It is cast in ABA form, with minuet (A), trio (B), repeat of minuet

(A). There are also internal repeats within the large sections. The overall structure of the minuet and trio can be diagrammed as:

A	B	A
Minuet	Trio	Minuet
a a b b	c c d d	a b
G minor	G major	G minor

Again, Mozart adds unity by including a suggestion of a in the b section and a full statement of c as part of the d section. Note that when the minuet reappears after the trio, the internal repeats are not observed.

Minuet   An opening A section in the key of G minor has phrases of unequal length: two three-measure phrases are followed by a five-measure phrase and a concluding phrase of three measures. This non-symmetrical device was favored by both Haydn and Mozart. The a section is repeated, and the b section, in the key of B flat, the relative major, begins with a melodic motive from the a section played by the lower strings and upper woodwinds, while the violins and bassoons introduce a new motive. The b section is also repeated. The minuet is characterized by two distinct rhythmic patterns: a syncopated rhythm that is used for the main melodic material, and a regular one-two-three rhythm in the bass.

Trio   The middle section is called a trio because it was originally a contrapuntal composition using three voice parts. In the Classical symphony it generally is not a three-voice texture but does use a smaller instrumental grouping than the minuet. This trio, in the key of G major, provides a lyrical contrast to the sturdy syncopated rhythm of the minuet.

The symphonies of Mozart and Haydn almost always maintain the third-movement minuet and trio, the slightest of the movements. Later, in the hands of Beethoven, the third movement of the symphony was transformed into a different kind of movement, one that assumed a weightier role in the four-movement plan.

Fourth Movement: *sonata-allegro form*

Exposition   The first theme consists of two melodic ideas: the triad of G minor played in a rapidly rising "rocket" figure, which is played *piano*, and a contrasting figure, which is played *forte*.

Example 12.15

After the theme is repeated several times, a new element adds dynamic contrast, moving from loud to soft. A bridge leads to a cadence and pause, and the second theme begins, played by reduced orchestra, first only the strings and then only the woodwinds. A closing, based on the bridge material, leads to a repetition of the exposition.

Development and Recapitulation   The "rocket" motive of theme 1 and an extensive modulation are the basis of the short development section. Passed from one section of the orchestra to another, the motive is treated polyphonically with overlapping entrances. Gradually it leads to a pronounced pause that separates the development from the recapitulation. Mozart intended that the entire development, recapitulation, and coda be repeated.

Summary

The G-minor symphony not only provides a superb example of Mozart's craft, but also illustrates general characteristics of the Classical style and the Classical symphony.

The four-movement plan of the sonata is followed; there is *no thematic relationship* among the movements; each movement is self-contained and none of the materials of one movement appears in any other movement. In terms of overall structure, the main unifying force is *key:* movements 1, 3, and 4 are in the common key of G minor, creating *tonal unity.*

Within individual movements, clarity and balance are probably the most pronounced stylistic features. Contrasting materials and sections are for the most part clearly and carefully set off from each other—often with the help of such musical devices changes in dynamics, cadences, and pauses—without the blurring of relationships we will encounter in later periods of music.

Mozart's symphony demonstrates the organizing power and wonderful flexibility of sonata-allegro form. Three of the work's four movements are organized by this formal procedure, all of them solid in design, yet completely different from each other in their expressive qualities.

Chamber Music

Even after the orchestra had emerged, music for smaller ensembles continued to thrive as wealthy patrons commissioned works to be performed in their salons for private audiences.

The multimovement sonata structure that we encountered in the symphony was also used in chamber music for a wide variety of instrumental combinations. The string quartet, consisting of a first and second violin, a viola, and a cello, became, in the Classical era, the most important chamber music medium. Its popularity continued well into the twentieth century in the works of Bartok, Hindemith, and others.

Franz Joseph Haydn was the first great master of string quartet composition, which occupied him throughout most of his long and creative life.

Haydn (1732–1809)

Culver Pictures, Inc.

Franz Joseph Haydn was born in Rohrau, a small Austrian village located near the Hungarian border southeast of Vienna. His parents, both of peasant stock, seemed to have encouraged their son's musical ability and entrusted his earliest musical training to a relative, Johann Franck, a schoolteacher and choirmaster in the nearby town of Hainburg. At age six, Haydn was already singing in Franck's church choir and had begun playing the clavier and violin.

In 1740, the composer and choirmaster at St. Stephen's Cathedral in Vienna stopped in Hainburg to recruit singers for his choir. Impressed with Haydn's voice, he arranged to take the young boy back with him to Vienna.

For the next nine years Haydn immersed himself in the routine of a Catholic choirboy. He received a smattering of elementary education at St. Stephen's choir school and continued with violin and voice lessons, but his training in composition and theory was erratic and largely self-taught. In 1749, when his voice began to break, Haydn was abruptly dismissed and turned out into the street.

The following years were hard ones. At first Haydn made his living teaching clavier by day and playing in street bands and serenading parties by night. His reputation as a teacher and vocal accompanist, however, gradually spread, and he started serious composition. In 1759 he was appointed *Kapellmeister* and chamber composer to a Bohemian nobleman, Count Morzin. He composed his first symphonies for the count's small orchestra.

In 1760 Haydn married Maria Anna Keller, but the marriage, which lasted forty years, was a tragic mistake. They were incompatible in temperament, and she was incapable of bearing children.

The unhappy marriage was offset by his appointment in 1761 as assistant music director to Prince Paul Anton Esterhazy, head of one of the most powerful and wealthy Hungarian noble families. Haydn's contract stipulated that he was to compose whatever music was required of him (which would become the property of his patron), to keep the musical instruments in good repair, to train singers, and to supervise the conduct of all of the musicians.

Despite the rigid and burdensome requirements of his contract, Haydn enjoyed his work and was to say later, "My prince was pleased with all my work, I was commended, and as conductor of an orchestra I could make experiments, observe what strengthened and what weakened an effect and thereupon improve, substitute, omit, and try new things; I was cut off from the world, there was no one around to mislead and harass me, and so I was forced to become original."

Haydn remained in the employ of the Esterhazy family for almost thirty years, serving first Prince Paul Anton and then his brother, Prince

Nikolaus. Despite his isolation at their country estate, his fame gradually spread throughout Europe. He was able to fulfill commissions from publishers and other individuals all over the Continent. When Prince Nikolaus died in 1790, Haydn was retained as nominal *Kapellmeister* for the Esterhazy family, but he was now independent. Moving to Vienna, he resumed his friendship with Mozart and gave lessons to a young, rising composer named Ludwig van Beethoven. He made two successful trips to London (1791–1792, 1794–1795), where he conducted a number of his own symphonies, written on commission for the well-known impressario Johann Salomon. After his second London visit, he ceased writing symphonies, turning instead to the composition of Masses and oratorios. After 1800 his health began to fail, and he lived in secluded retirement. He died in 1809 at the age of seventy-seven.

His Work

The great majority of Haydn's work was composed during his service to the Esterhazy princes. The biweekly concerts and opera performances at Esterhaz, Prince Nikolaus' country estate, engendered a prodigious flow of instrumental and vocal music. Most of Haydn's 104 symphonies were written for the small but excellent Esterhazy orchestra.

Symphonies   The symphonies form a remarkably complete record of Haydn's development as a composer, ranging in unbroken continuity from his earliest crude, somewhat ephemeral, efforts to the rich and masterful works of the 1780s and 1790s. Many of the more popular symphonies bear nicknames: the *Horn Signal* (No. 31, 1765); the *Farewell* (No. 45, 1772); the *Surprise* (No. 94, 1791); and the *Drumroll* (No. 103, 1795) are but a few. His greatest works in this genre are the last twelve symphonies, called the *London* symphonies, which were written for his two London visits.

Chamber Music   While many of Haydn's experiments with musical form were carried out in the symphonies, his chamber music, particularly the string quartets, was equally significant in his development as a composer. In his eighty-four quartets, Haydn laid down many of the fundamental principles that were taken up by younger composers such as Mozart and Beethoven. The six works making up Opus 20 (the *Sun Quartets*, 1772) are among his masterworks in this genre. The later sets of Opus 33 (*The Scherzos* or *Russian Quartets*, 1781) and Opus 50 (1787) represent still further advances in Haydn's musical development.

Other chamber works include more than twenty *divertimenti* (light, "diversionary" pieces written in a simple, popular style) for miscellaneous wind ensembles, thirty-one piano trios, eight sonatas for violin and piano, and some 126 trios for viola, cello, and baryton (an obsolete string instrument about the size of a cello which Prince Nikolaus enjoyed playing). Of some sixty sonatas written for piano, fifty-two survive.

Though he was a good string player, Haydn did not consider himself a virtuoso performer. Consequently, his solo concertos are few. They include four for violin, one for cello, two for horn, the well-known trumpet concerto, and five for keyboard instruments. A good many concertos have

Figure 12.3 Haydn, at the piano, spent many of his most productive years composing for and conducting the small but excellent orchestra of the Esterhazy princes. His isolation on the Hungarian estate was, as Haydn later recalled, a strong force for originality. (The Bettmann Archive)

been lost, and still others attributed to Haydn have not yet been authenticated as coming from his hand.

Opera   Opera was a highly important part of musical activity at the Esterhazy palace, and Haydn was for a long time quite proud of his more than twenty stage works. The Austrian Empress, Maria Theresa, reputedly said, "If I want to hear a good opera, I go to Esterhaz." When Haydn became familiar with Mozart's incomparable genius for opera composing, however, he realized that his own works were of limited and transitory importance. Today they are all but forgotten.

Masses and Oratorios   Haydn's Masses and oratorios present a different story. The last six of his twelve Masses, composed between 1796 and 1802, are his crowning achievement as a church composer—works of old age demonstrating a mastery of form and technique accumulated over more than fifty years of composing. Several of them—*Missa in Tempore Belli (Mass in Time of War)* (1796), the *Missa in Angustiis (Nelson Mass)* (1798), and the *Harmoniemesse* ("Wind-band" Mass, 1802)—rank among Haydn's masterworks. Stimulated by Handel's oratorios, some of which he had heard during his London visits, Haydn produced two of his own. Titled *The Creation* (1796–1798) and *The Seasons* (1798–1801), they have remained in concert repertoire to this day. Contemporary with these major vocal works was Haydn's gift to the Austrian people, the national anthem, *Gott erhalte Franze den Kaiser (God Save the Emperor, Franz*, better known as the *Austrian Hymn*). He wrote it on his own initiative as a patriotic gesture when Napoleon's armies invaded Austrian territory in 1796. During the French bombardment of Vienna in 1809, he played it to comfort himself. It was the last music he heard before he died.

String Quartet Opus 33, No. 3 (The Bird)

Record 3/Side 1

Haydn developed the string quartet from an eighteenth-century form called the *divertimento*. He built on the earlier form, giving it more substance and scoring it for two violins, a viola, and a cello. His eighty quartets, written over the course of his creative lifetime, evolved slowly into a sophisticated form. Together they constitute one of the most important bodies of chamber music literature.

The quartets of Haydn's Opus 33 are collectively known as *Gli Scherzi (The Scherzos)* because Haydn uses the more rapid scherzo rather than the minuet and trio. They are also known as the *Russian Quartets* because they were dedicated to the Russian Grand Duke Pavel Petrovitch, who visited Vienna in 1781. Number 3 of this set became known as *The Bird*, owing to the birdlike trills and ornaments in the first, second, and fourth movements.

Example 12.16

"Bird" motive

First Movement

Exposition   The clarity and balance that we encountered in the music of Mozart are again evident here in the clearly separated, repeated phrases, the sudden contrast and extension of one phrase, and the use of dynamics to reinforce structure. These techniques are all important elements in the Classical style.

The "bird" ornaments heard in the first theme provide a unifying element throughout the first movement, stressing the tight unity among the contrasting sections.

The first theme begins with soft, short, repeated notes in the second violin and viola. Against this background, the first violin enters with the main melodic material, dwelling on a long and repeated note that crescendos to more active movement. The cello enters to help climax the crescendo, and the phrase ends with the first violin playing a rapid downward figure. After a pause the phrase is repeated at a different pitch level and in a different key. After another pause the phrase appears to begin to repeat (the second violin and viola play the beginning notes) but the first violin takes up a different melody that returns to the original key of C major. The cello enters to begin the second part of the theme, which ends in a cadence and another pause.

Example 12.17

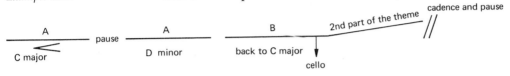

Characteristically, the bridge between Themes 1 and 2 uses elements from Theme 1. The second theme makes abundant use of the ornamental ("bird") element of the first theme. The exposition closes with material derived from the very end of the bridge. The entire exposition is then repeated.

Development   Although relatively short, the development section draws from all three stages of the exposition and is extremely interesting. It begins with a statement of the A phrase of Theme 1. Then elements of Theme 2 and the bridge are combined, after which Theme 2 is stated first in the high strings, then in the low strings. Elements from Theme 1 and the closing material are briefly combined and led into successive statements of the ornamental notes at rising pitch levels. The rising feeling is helped along by a crescendo leading to two long chords that leave the listener in a state of animated suspense. The suspense is quieted by an apparent return to Theme 1, but the return turns out to be false. Instead, it leads to a development of the bridge that ends in a genuine recapitulation.

Recapitulation   The recapitulation is rather standard except that the second part of Theme 1 is omitted. After the entire development and recapitulation are repeated, there is a coda consisting of (1) an exploitation of the "bird" ornament, (2) a fragment of the closing material, (3) a crescendo and cadence, and (4) a complete statement of the A phrase of Theme 1. The movement ends in the original key of C major.

Second Movement

The six quartets of Opus 33 depart from sonata structure in two respects. First, the minuet and trio movement is replaced by the scherzo and trio. Second, the positions of the second and third movements are reversed: the scherzo and trio is second and the slow, lyrical movement is third.

This scherzo movement is a wonderful example of Haydn's ability to use instrumental range, color, and articulation and musical texture, dynamics, and form for expressive purposes. The movement has a three-part scherzo-trio-scherzo structure, with the sections set off from each other by obvious cadences and pauses. The contrast between them is marked. The scherzo employs all four instruments in a low register and homophonic texture. It is dark, smooth, sustained, and thick. The trio is reduced to two violins playing in the higher part of their ranges, within a polyphonic texture using staccato articulation. It is light, bright, thin, and brittle, employing ornamental trills reminiscent of the first movement.

Example 12.18

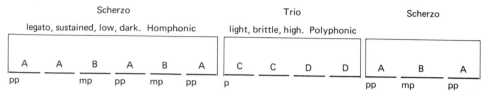

The formal scheme with its repeated return to A places a great deal of structural and expressive weight on that section of music—so much so that the A section and its qualities tend to dominate the movement. The B section serves as a mild contrast to A, and both C and D intensify the character of A by providing a greater contrast to it, thereby underlining its qualities upon its return.

Third Movement

The slow third movement is a theme and variations. The first violin, which spins out the long theme, is clearly the prominent instrument. The theme is lyrical, almost aria-like in its melodic arches and contours. In contrast to Bach's melodies, with their long linear contours, Haydn's are comprised of short fragments. In the two variations, the harmonic and tonal settings remain largely as they were in the theme, but the shape of the melody is subjected to modifications and alterations. Those sections that are preserved are given extensive variation, mostly through the addition of decorative notes, creating a much more florid melodic line. Throughout the entire movement the first violin is a solo instrument and the other three strings maintain a secondary, accompanying function.

Fourth Movement

The last movement of the quartet is an intriguing example of Haydn's sense of humor in music. The melodies are jocular, the tempo is very fast, and the texture is light. A series of tricks and surprises manipulate the mind of the listener up to the concluding measures.

Technically it combines the rondo principle of alternating themes with the development and recapitulation of sonata-allegro procedures. The rondo was frequently used in the last movement of a composition to bring it to a joyful or playful conclusion.

In Haydn's final movement there is a gay, bouncy two-part theme in C major; the second part combines materials of the first with the "bird" figure of the first movement. After both parts are repeated, the theme ends with a pause. The second theme begins without a bridge passage. The B theme, also in two parts, is in A minor. The first part is repeated, and the second develops material from the first theme. Toward the end of the section the rhythmic material that began theme A is passed back and forth among the instruments. The obvious intent of this is to suggest the return of theme A, but the listener is kept in suspense as to *when* it will return. The suspense increases when the rhythmic figure is shortened to a two-note version, the dynamic level changes suddenly from forte to piano, and a dominant chord is outlined which cries for resolution to the tonic. At this point, when the listener is convinced the music will plunge into the A theme, there is instead a sudden, unexpected pause, after which the theme finally does enter (Example 12.19).

Example 12.19

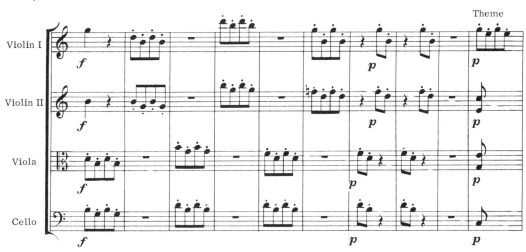

This "trickery," involving the reappearance of theme A, is again evident later in the movement. After the restatement of themes A and B, another developmental section occurs that leads back to A. This presentation of the theme ends in a cadence and a pause. But after this convincing ending, Haydn launches into a coda beginning with the two-note "bird" motive and moving to the more active rhythmic material from the A theme. A feeling of conclusion is created by the increase of activity as all four instruments play the rhythmic material. The crescendo pushes forward, but instead of ending, Haydn stops not on the expected C major chord but on a chord in a different key. The chord is full of suspense and implies anything but a conclusion. After a pause, which intensifies the suspense, there is a drive to a forceful cadence in the tonic C major, and, apparently, the long-delayed ending. But this is followed by yet another section, played very softly, to give us an extra unexpected ending, a kind of final chuckle from the composer.

The Concerto

During the Baroque era, the word "concerto" referred to both the concerto grosso and the concerto for solo instrument with accompaniment. Bach's Brandenburg Concerto No. 5 and Vivaldi's descriptive solo concertos *The Seasons* are good examples of the two types.

In the Classical era, composers continued to develop the solo concerto. The violin and piano were the favored solo instruments but concertos were also written for such other instruments as the cello, trumpet, French horn, and clarinet.

Although it differs from the symphony and the string quartet, the Classical concerto is an example of the sonata ideal. Unlike the others, which have four movements, the concerto has three movements in a fast-slow-fast sequence. The minuet and trio is not usually included.

Other differences are evident in the individual movements. First, each movement has an additional section called the *cadenza*. Played by the solo instrument alone, it draws on elements of the main thematic materials of the movement. The cadenza has the quality of an improvised, virtuoso performance. In the early Classical period, cadenzas were indeed improvised by the soloists, but later composers wrote cadenzas for their concertos. Second, sonata-allegro movements are altered for the interplay of the solo instrument with the orchestral ensemble. Instead of one repeated exposition there is a *double exposition*. In the first exposition the material is set forth by the orchestra alone. The solo instrument then presents the material of the second exposition while the orchestra assumes a secondary role. Thus, the exposition takes the following form:

orchestra alone			solo instrument and orchestra		
A	bridge	B	A	bridge	B

The exposition is then followed by a development section involving both solo instrument and orchestra. The movement concludes with a recapitulation, based upon the second exposition, a cadenza, and closing material.

A	bridge	B	cadenza	closing material

In his more than fifty concertos, Mozart established the form and style of the Classical concerto. As a group they are among the most enduring legacies of the Classical period, and many of them remain standard items in the concert repertoire. Mozart wrote most of his concertos for the piano or violin, but he also wrote for such solo instruments as clarinet, flute, and bassoon. His concertos for this latter group still rank among the outstanding solo works for these instruments.

Violin Concerto No. 5 in A Major

In 1775, when he was nineteen years old, Mozart composed three violin concertos, in G major, D major, and A major. The A-major violin concerto is one of the most frequently performed of Mozart's works. In it he combined his clarity of expression and mastery of formal procedure with his knowledge of the violin. The work is scored for solo violin and an orchestra consisting of two oboes, two horns, and strings.

First Movement

Record 3/Side 1

The first movement is in sonata-allegro form, in the tonic key of A major. Although it adheres to the double exposition scheme in principle, it departs from it in important and interesting details. The orchestral exposition includes the normal contrasting themes

Example 12.20

Example 12.21

Example 12.22   separated by a bridge and ending with a closing section and a pause.

But then a short adagio section for solo violin and orchestra serves as a *slow introduction* to the second exposition. This slow section ends with another pause and the second exposition (allegro) begins, but not in accordance with the "normal" plan outlined above. Rather, several interesting variations follow, involving both themes and the bridge of the first exposition.

The melodic material of theme A of the first exposition is again stated by the first violins of the orchestra over which the solo violin plays a new and markedly different melody.

Example 12.23

In addition, this section is considerably longer than it was in the first exposition.

The bridge of the second exposition is quite different from the one in the first. Its melodic significance almost achieves the stature of a theme in its own right.

Example 12.24

The second theme, drawn from the first exposition, is expanded at the beginning and at the end by the addition of new thematic material.

	B	
new	original	new
------------------------	————————————	------------------------

Example 12.25

etc.

Example 12.26

etc.

The development section features the solo violin with very sparse orchestral accompaniment. The melodic content of the development is essentially new material. The section ends with the solo violin, joined by the first violins, playing material from the first bridge. The recapitulation is a mixture of the two expositions, with emphasis on the second. A cadenza, which appears before the closing material, climaxes the conclusion of the movement.

The flexibility with which an expert composer such as Mozart could manipulate formal procedures is nowhere more evident in the early Classical era than in this movement.

Second Movement

The design of the second movement is less important than its quality as an outpouring of lyrical beauty. Written in the contrasting key of E major (the key of the dominant), it displays in a slow tempo the broad outlines of sonata-allegro scheme. Its essence is in the soaring, arching melodies, long, spun-out melodic lines, and graceful ornamentations. The "singing" quality of the solo violin dominates the movement, which again includes a cadenza immediately before its conclusion.

Third Movement

The last movement is, somewhat like the first, a curiosity. The third movement of a concerto was usually a rondo, with variations built around a recurring melody. But instead of a fast rondo or sonata-allegro movement, we have a rondo for which Mozart indicates *"tempo di menuetto"* (in the tempo of a minuet). Actually, the movement is a mixture of the *minuet* (present in the tempo and styling of its first section), *sonata-allegro* procedure (employed in the modulating bridge and the "hint" of a recapitulation, and the *rondo* with its repeated return of the first section alternating with contrasting sections).

The movement's commanding structural feature is the repeated return of theme A, each time in the same key of A major. The A theme is the element of continuity and unity. Other melodic sections provide fascinating contrasts in melodic and rhythmic design, in key, and even in meter and tempo.

The minuet theme falls into four sections: The initial phrase (1) played by the solo violin with light accompaniment is followed by a partial repeat of the same material (2) by the first violins as the dynamic level suddenly rises to forte. This repeat of the phrase ends somewhat differently.

Example 12.27

The solo violin then plays a new phrase (3) followed by an almost flippant concluding measure (4), which provides the cadence and pause to signify the end of a major formal section.

Example 12.28

A genuine bridge follows, which modulates to E major for the appearance of the first contrasting section (B), which is introduced by the figure

Example 12.29

and a pause.

At the conclusion of each of the contrasting sections B, C, D and at the end of a repeat of B there is a new cadenza. Each of the four cadenzas is different, but all four allow virtuoso performances while serving the structural function of transitions back to the A theme. As the A theme reappears, it undergoes some changes. These changes involve compression and variation either of the melody or of the accompaniment. But the A theme is clearly recognizable at each of its appearances and thus performs a unifying function.

Of all the sections, D shows the greatest degree of contrast. It is changed not only in material, but also in meter (from triple to double) and in tempo (from the stately minuetto to allegro). These modifications intensify the return of the familiar and contrasting melodic section A, reinforcing A's unifying effect.

The A-major violin concerto is without question one of Mozart's most interesting and appealing masterpieces in the concerto form. Indeed, it is a crowning work of the Classical period.

Summary

Instrumental music arrived at a new level of maturity during the Classical period. Instruments were improved greatly in their ranges and technical capabilities, and composers began to score their works for standard groupings. Larger groups evolved into the orchestra, with an increased number and variety of instruments. Because of the social customs of the day, chamber music also flourished and encouraged sophisticated compositions in which each player performed an individual part.

Sonata-allegro form and the multimovement structure became the main basis for music composed in the early Classical period. The two great masters of the Classical era—Haydn and Mozart—developed and refined sonata-allegro form in their symphonies, string quartets, and concertos.

chapter 13

The Classical era was essentially a period of instrumental music. The new instrumental style and forms became the area of greatest concentration for the major composers of the time. Vocal music occupied a position of secondary importance. The lieder (songs) written by Haydn, Mozart, and Beethoven are considered a relatively secondary part of their

Classical Vocal Music

compositional efforts. The operas composed by Haydn to entertain the guests at Esterhazy have vanished into history, and Beethoven's opera, *Fidelio*, represents his entire achievement in this form.

However, the age was not without significant and lasting achievements in the area of vocal music. Specifically, some of the large choral works of Mozart, Haydn, and Beethoven and many of Mozart's operas made lasting contributions to the body of vocal literature.

Of the three giants of the Classical era, Haydn contributed the largest number of compositions to the choral music repertoire. Two of his oratorios, *The Creation* and *The Seasons*, are still widely performed; together with his Masses, they constitute his most important contribution to vocal music.

Missa in Angustiis (Nelson Mass)

Record 3/Side 2

Haydn's *Missa in Angustiis* (*Mass in Time of Peril*) is one of the choral masterpieces of the Viennese Classical period. Better known as the *Nelson Mass*, it was written in 1789 during the naval Battle of the Nile. When Lord Nelson visited Eisenstadt Castle in 1800, this Mass was among the works performed in his honor.

The orchestration of Haydn's Masses varied from work to work according to the instruments and players available to him at the time. The

Nelson Mass is scored for a comparatively small orchestra consisting of three trumpets, timpani, organ, and strings, together with four solo voices (SATB) and four-part chorus (SATB). The organ is used alternately as a continuo instrument merely filling in chords, a carryover from Baroque practice, and as an ensemble or solo instrument.

The text is divided into six main sections and five subdivisions:

Kyrie	*Credo*	*Sanctus*
Gloria	*Et incarnatus*	*Benedictus*
Qui tollis	*Et resurrexit*	*Agnus Dei*
Quoniam tu solus		*Dona nobis*

Each of the individual subdivisions of the text occupies an entire movement, so this setting of the Mass consists of eleven movements.

Kyrie

The prevalence of sonata-allegro procedure in instrumental music has been well established in the previous chapter, but its organizing force was by no means confined to instrumental music. The first movement of the *Nelson Mass* is an example of how the sonata-allegro principle was applied to choral composition.

The first theme, in D minor, is characterized by short, emphatic pronouncements by the chorus on the text *Kyrie eleison* ("Lord have mercy"). The trumpets and timpani sound a prominent figure (𝅘𝅥𝅮𝅘𝅥𝅮), which alternates with sharp chords in the strings. The organ, meanwhile, plays sustained continuo chords.

The second theme is dominated by the soprano solo voice, singing elaborate virtuoso passages, quite instrumental in character.

Example 13.1

Chri - ste e - lei - son, e - lei - son

Ky-ri-e e-lei-son

The light texture, the *piano* dynamic level, the key change (to the relative F major), and the concentration on the individual voice are a marked contrast to the driving force of the first theme.

The prominent elements of the development are sung by the chorus. The solo part from the second theme is now played by the violins. Imitative entrances in the chorus lead to a climax where all four parts come together. The drive that results from these insistent overlapping entrances of the voices is enhanced by constant modulation.

The key returns to D minor for the recapitulation. Here the second theme resembles the original theme in texture, dynamics, and the relationship of the solo soprano voice to the orchestra, but new melodic material is involved.

The coda ends with the entire orchestra hammering out the rhythmic figure (𝅘𝅥𝅮𝅘𝅥𝅮) on which the movement began.

Gloria, Qui tollis, and Quoniam tu solus

Although the second, third, and fourth movements each appear to be self-contained, they are actually parts of one three-movement complex.

The driving tension and restlessness that characterized the *Kyrie* are immediately dispelled at the striking beginning of the *Gloria*. The important thematic material of the A section, on the text *"Gloria in excelsis deo"* ("Glory to God in the highest"), is introduced in dialogue fashion between the soprano soloist and the chorus.

Example 13.2

The dynamic level drops to *piano* for the contrasting B section, *"et in terra pax hominibus"* ("and on earth peace to men"). The emphasis is on the solo tenor and bass parts, whose imitative entrances grow into a moving, expressive duet.

The chorus enters in unison octaves in the C section, loudly proclaiming *"laudamus te"* ("we adore Thee"), and the section builds to an attenuated ending on *"glorificamus te"* ("we glorify Thee").

A kind of development begins with successive statements of the A melody, utilizing new words and modulating into different keys. It opens with the solo alto, who is answered by the soprano, and then, more fully, by the chorus. After expanded statements of B by the solo voices, the chorus brings the movement to a rather abrupt close, without the expected return of the A theme.

The slow, quiet *Qui tollis* movement is, structurally, a straightforward example of alternating themes. The solo bass has the dominant part, often paired with the first violins. Frequently the bass voice and first violins answer each other in a back-and-forth manner. The organ is used as a solo instrument in conjunction with the choral entrances, and while the choral entrances are expressive in themselves, they also constitute a considerable "surprise" element in the movement. It is impossible to anticipate either when they will occur or whether they will occur softly in unison or loudly in full harmony on statements of *miserere nobis* and *deprecationem nostram*.

The *Qui tollis* has no real conclusion, but ends instead on a chord of suspense, the dominant. Its resolution comes in the opening measures of the *Quoniam tu solus* movement, which, in addition, returns to the melody from the *Gloria*. Thus the lack of conclusion in the preceding movement, coupled with the reappearance of the original theme of the *Gloria*, acts as a powerful unifying element in the three-movement complex.

Example 13.3

After the solo and choral statements of the A theme, a quiet transition section on the words *"cum sancto spiritu"* ("with the holy spirit"), leads to a long, vigorous fugue. The coda, which uses material from the *Gloria* movement, creates further unity and builds to one of Haydn's brilliant and exhilarating endings on

A-men A - men!

Credo

The *Credo* is divided into three parts, which constitute the fifth, sixth, and seventh movements. The fifth movement, which begins with *Credo in unum Deum"* ("I believe in one God"), is a two-part canon. The sopranos and tenors sing the first part against the altos and basses on the second. The tempo is fast, and there is a driving rhythm throughout, with much activity in the orchestra.

In contrast to the fifth movement, the sixth, *Et incarnatus* ("and was incarnate"), is slow and quiet. The pervading feeling is one of lyricism and melodic grace. The first theme is stated in turn by the orchestra, the solo soprano, and the chorus. The concluding section includes an interesting example of a fragmented phrase when the chorus reenters on the *pianissimo "et sepultus est"* ("and was buried").

et se - pul - tus est

A concluding coda adds weight and finality to the movement's mood of despair.

The seventh movement, *Et resurrexit tertia die* ("and on the third day He arose"), burst forth *forte*, in a fast tempo, and with great musical activity to convey the atmosphere of triumph and resurrection. This movement is particularly interesting for the abundance of technical devices that Haydn has employed to organize it: imitative entrances are used to build momentum; homophonic texture and choral declamation set off the meaning of the text, and striking differences in dynamics and pitch contrast the *vivos* ("living") with the *mortuos* ("dead"). Haydn further organizes the movement by introducing each section with a prominent exclamation of *Et* by the chorus:

> *Et . . . et in spiritum sanctum*
> *Et . . . et unam sanctam catholicam*
> *Et . . . et vitam venturi saeculi*

The brilliant final *Amen* section triumphantly culminates the movement and brings to a close the long *Credo* text.

Sanctus and Benedictus

The eight and ninth movements consist of five subsections:

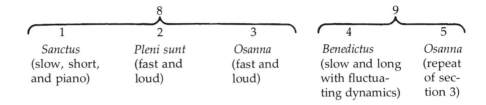

1	2	3	4	5
Sanctus (slow, short, and piano)	*Pleni sunt* (fast and loud)	*Osanna* (fast and loud)	*Benedictus* (slow and long with fluctuating dynamics)	*Osanna* (repeat of section 3)

The *Sanctus* is a slow introductory section, ending on a dominant chord which is resolved by the energetic entrance of the *Pleni sunt*, an allegro choral section with an active orchestral background. This section merges without a break into the *Osanna*. In fact, the *Osanna* is not recognized as a separate section until it returns without the *Pleni sunt* at the end of the next movement.

The *Benedictus*, which follows, is very much like the sonata-allegro movement of a concerto. It is a fascinating piece of music in its own right, with a double exposition (the first in the orchestra, the second in the solo soprano and chorus), a short development section, a genuine recapitulation, and a dramatic coda. The *Benedictus* has no conclusion; it stops on a dominant chord, followed by a pause. The resulting suspense is dispelled when the *Osanna* returns, bringing the entire complex to a stirring and convincing ending.

Agnus Dei and *Dona nobis*

The concluding movements of the *Nelson Mass* are a tribute to Haydn's skill and ingenuity in constructing a brilliant ending. The quietest section of the entire Mass, the *Agnus Dei*, is the only movement that does not include the chorus, trumpets, or timpani. Adagio in tempo and lyrical in expression, it is the perfect foil for the loud and buoyant finale.

Here again we encounter two movements that are harmonically linked. The *Agnus Dei* ends on a long dominant chord that implies resolution to the tonic of B minor. But instead of beginning in the expected key, the new movement jolts the listener by opening in the key of D major, the principal key of the Mass.

The *Dona nobis* is a fast, loud, choral fugue set against intense orchestral activity. The imitative entrances of the soprano, alto, tenor, and bass are followed by a jocular, homophonic section in the chorus, while the violins play a kind of chirp in the background. This lightheartedness turns into flippant gaiety near the end, when there is a sudden and unexpected halt, followed by a pause, then a resumption of the very quiet statements of *"Dona nobis pacem"* ("grant us Thy peace") by the chorus with interjections of the chirping figure by violins.

Example 13.4

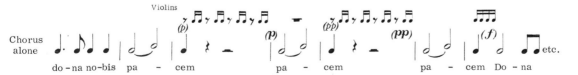

Finally, there is an energetic push to a brilliant ending.

It is interesting to note that the next-to-last movement, the *Agnus Dei*, actually completes the text of the Ordinary of the Mass. But an ending in the quiet, subdued atmosphere of this movement would not have been readily accepted by the aesthetic dictates of the time, which required a joyous and vigorous finale. Haydn thus built a final movement on the last three words of the *Agnus Dei* text—*"Dona nobis pacem"*—which could satisfy the expectation of popular taste.

One of the great choral masterpieces of the Viennese Classical period, the *Nelson Mass* continues to enjoy a favored position in today's choral repertoire. It and Haydn's other Masses, as well as Mass settings by Mozart and Beethoven, represent the Classical treatment of the Mass text that was first set to music in the medieval period, thrived in the Renaissance, and continued to interest composers in all periods of music history, including Bach in the Baroque era, Schubert in the nineteenth century, and Stravinsky in the twentieth.

The History of Opera

Music and drama have been closely associated ever since the beginning of civilization. Ancient Greek drama included music, as did the liturgical plays of the Middle Ages. In the sixteenth century, actors began to perform musical interludes between the acts of plays. These *intermezzi* led to the development of a new form which combined music and dramatics.

The first operas were composed in Florence and consisted mostly of simple melodies and harmonies. The book, or *libretto*, usually centered on a mythological or historical subject. Occasionally, comic characters were included. The great Baroque composer Claudio Monteverdi used more expressive melodies, richer harmonies, and fuller orchestras in his operas. In *Orfeo* (1607) he introduced a variety of innovative elements, including solos, choruses, and orchestrally accompanied dances.

In 1637, when the first public opera house opened in Venice, the center of operatic activity moved there. Venetian-style operas were popular throughout Europe (except in France, which had its own type of opera, based on earlier court ballets and dramatic tragedies).

As opera developed, songlike arias and duets were introduced to provide contrast to the recitatives. The more dramatically static arias usually expressed a character's feeling or reactions to a situation.

Like comedy and tragedy, opera evolved in two forms. While *opera seria* were based on serious plots, lighter versions, called *opera buffa*, were developed around comic plots. During the eighteenth century, opera buffa rose in importance, and some of its elements began to penetrate the mainstream of operatic convention. The most important of these was the ensemble finale, in which all the characters were on stage and singing at the end. Opera buffa was also the first genre to exploit the bass voice, particularly in comic roles. Gradually, the plots and characters of the two operatic styles began to merge, with even the lightest operas containing some serious or even tragic episodes.

As opera developed, its conventions became more rigid. The dramatic elements were subordinated to the supremacy of the singers who demanded extra arias and elaborately ornamented those they performed. Recitatives were strictly alternated with arias in da capo (ABA) outline.

Christoph W. Gluck (1714–1787), a German composer who had studied in Italy, led the reform movement to restore simplicity and natural expression to opera. In his operas, including *Alceste* (1767), *Iphigenie en Aulide* (1774), and *Iphigenie en Tauride* (1779), the music and other elements were integrated to serve the overall dramatic unity.

Although they show some influences of the work of Gluck, Mozart's operas reveal a basic disparity; for him, the drama did not dominate, but rather served the supreme element, the music. Mozart's diverse training and broad outlook made him equally comfortable with Italian opera seria and opera buffa, and their German counterpart, *Singspiel*.

Le Nozze di Figaro (The Marriage of Figaro)

Record 3/Side 2

Mozart's first *opera buffa,* with its lively, amusing libretto and delightful solo and ensemble music, is the epitome of the genre. Mozart read over one hundred librettos before he found his collaborator, Lorenzo da Ponte, who was willing to translate Beaumarchais' play from the French into Italian and adapt the story to the specifications of the composer. The choice of the language was important since, even in German-speaking countries, audiences preferred to see operas performed in Italian. *The Marriage of Figaro* was first produced at the Burgtheater in Vienna in 1786.

Beaumarchais' original play was a political satire, but da Ponte removed the political references, leaving a very human and natural comedy. The plot is complex, involving several pairs of lovers, intrigues between servants and their masters, a case of mistaken identity, and a few unlikely coincidences. The plot revolves around the efforts of a servant (Figaro) to outwit his master (Count Almaviva). This theme was a favorite convention of the period, and Mozart applies it with humor and skill. (Since there are several complications and subplots, it is important to have a libretto in hand while listening to the music.)

The Plot

Figaro, a valet to Count Almaviva, is preparing to marry Susanna, the countess' chambermaid. Figaro has borrowed a large sum from Marcellina, the old castle housekeeper, promising to repay the money by a certain date or marry her if he defaults. The count has designs on Susanna and tries to seduce her, but she tells Figaro and the countess, and together they scheme to frustrate the count's plans.

Since Susanna will not yield to him, the count decides to take Marcellina's side in the financial dispute and force Figaro to marry her. This plot is foiled by the discovery that Marcellina and her advocate, Dr. Bartolo, are actually Figaro's long-lost parents, from whom he was kidnapped as an infant.

Meanwhile, Susanna and the countess have been conniving; their trick involves a case of mistaken identity. Susanna promises to meet the count in the garden that night, but it is the countess, disguised as Susanna, who actually keeps the appointment. Figaro learns of the meeting and thinks that Susanna is deceiving him. The count is caught red-handed by his wife, confesses his attempted infidelity, and begs forgiveness, which she grants laughingly. Figaro marries Susanna.

Figure 13.1   Mozart's first opera buffa, The Marriage of Figaro *was the epitome of its genre. Its lively, natural comedy, three-dimensional characters, and compelling music have made it a favorite for two hundred years. (RCA Records)*

The Music

The Marriage of Figaro is more profound than the usual opera buffa because both the composer and the librettist could create characters with the emotions of three-dimensional people. This is done not only in the solo arias, but in the ensemble numbers as well. In an operatic ensemble it is possible to have each character singing different words and displaying different emotions while singing with the others; in other words, everyone can think and react simultaneously, without waiting to take turns, as is necessary in spoken drama. This is often done in the finale used to end opera buffa.

In Classical opera the orchestra was subordinate to the voices, but had its own elaborate and lively idiom. Mozart made full use of the opportunity to develop motives in the traditional symphonic manner. The opera orchestra also helps with characterization, particularly in accompanied recitatives, where the moods are dramatic and change quickly. In this way the orchestra can be used to hint at action that is supposedly taking place offstage and can contradict a character's words and expose his true feelings.

By examining one scene of *The Marriage of Figaro*, we will be able to see Mozart's use of musical devices to further the dramatic action and the characterization. At the beginning of Act III, Susanna and the Countess arrange for Susanna to meet the count that night. Their dialogue, and the subsequent conversation between the count and Susanna, are in secco recitative. In the duet that follows, the count rejoices at Susanna's agreement to meet him, while she (in an aside to the audience) asks forgiveness for her lie. Each one has distinctive music, so that it is quite clear that they are singing about two different things.

The next recitative ends with Susanna mentioning to Figaro, as they leave, that he has won his case. The count overhears her remark and sings a recitative expressing his fury and plotting to force Figaro to marry Marcellina. This recitative is accompanied by the full orchestra and includes many sudden changes of key, tempo, and dynamics. It leads to an aria by the count in which he explains how jealous he is of his happy servant Figaro, how he will get revenge, and how happy the thought of revenge makes him. The aria is in two large sections; the second section is faster than the first and is repeated with an extended and ornamented cadence. The style of the accompaniment changes frequently, to reflect the count's different thoughts.

As the count finishes, he meets the judge, who has just upheld Marcellina's right to repayment or marriage. Figaro mentions that he cannot get married without his parents' consent, and he has not been able to locate them, since he was kidnapped as a child. He describes the circumstances, and Marcellina and Dr. Bartolo realize that he is their child. This dramatic action is covered quickly in recitative, and then a large ensemble begins: the reunited family rejoices together ("beloved son," "beloved parents").

Susanna enters, sees Figaro embracing Marcellina, and misunderstands the situation. During the next section, a sextet, Susanna and the count both rage furiously, with a jagged, dotted musical line,

Example 13.5

Fre -mo,Sma-nio dal fu - ro - re

while Figaro and his parents calmly note that Susanna's jealousy is a sure sign of her love. The judge joins the count, making the balance in the sextet even—three against three. Finally Susanna listens to their explanation that Marcellina is Figaro's mother. Scarcely believing it, she questions each one of them in turn: *"Sua madre?"* Each one answers *"Sua madre!"* and the pitch level rises with each statement. The same device is used when Dr. Bartolo is introduced as Figaro's father.

The sextet ends with all characterssinging, but the balance has changed from three and three to four and two, since Susanna has changed sides and is no longer angry. The two groups have almost identical texts:

Susanna, Marcellina, Bartolo, Figaro:	**Count, Don Curzio**
Al doce contento	*Al fiero tormento*
di questo momento	*di questo momento*
quest' anima appena	*quest' anima appena*
resister or sa.	*resister or sa.*

The musical setting makes their different feelings perfectly clear. The happy four sing smoothly and lyrically, with Susanna (the highest soprano) expressing her joy with an ornamented musical line. The count and the judge sing another jagged, dotted line to express their anger. At the end, where both groups have identical words, the different meanings are expressed by the speed of the notes: the angry men sing much faster than the others.

Example 13.6

In the fourth and final act, the count is caught in the garden by his wife, everyone is forgiven, and the action culminates in the marriage of Figaro.

Summary

Haydn's *Missa in Angustiis,* popularly known as the *Nelson Mass,* was written in 1789 during the naval Battle of the Nile. It is scored for a small orchestra of trumpets, timpani, organ, and strings, with four solo voices and a four-part chorus. Throughout the six main sections, comprising eleven movements, Haydn's great musical genius is allowed full play. The listener is carried from themes of driving force to adagio passages of light texture, from exhilarating and dynamic movements to slow and expressive sections. Considered a masterpiece, this work is a favorite in contemporary choral repertoires.

One of Mozart's most famous comic operas is *The Marriage of Figaro,* produced in Vienna in 1786. Adapted from a play by Beaumarchais, the plot involves a servant (Figaro) and his efforts to outwit his master (Count Almaviva) who is pursuing Figaro's betrothed, the chambermaid Susanna. Intrigue, coincidence, and mistaken identity highlight the complex action. The opera contains an amusing libretto and delightful solo and ensemble music, featuring realistic characters and the skillful use of orchestral devices to enhance the characterization.

chapter 14

The Music of Beethoven

Probably no single composer has influenced the course of musical events more than Ludwig van Beethoven. His evolving style had a profound effect on the musicians of his time, and the music he left to the world has continued to influence musicians and to have great public appeal. In 1970, concert halls around the world presented programs of his music to commemorate the 200th anniversary of his birth in 1770. Although he is considered a representative of the Classical era, Beethoven in many ways was a precursor of Romanticism. His life bridged two centuries almost equally, and his spirit seemed more in tune with the cataclysm that followed the French Revolution than with the contentment of the Age of Reason. While he injected a new freedom into the Classical forms, Beethoven continued to adhere to them. His great contribution was to carry forward the tradition of Mozart and Haydn, building on the structures they had developed and elevating them to new heights of power and expressiveness.

Beethoven (1770–1827)

The Bettmann Archive

Ludwig van Beethoven was born in the Rhineland city of Bonn, the son of a singer in the Electoral Court chapel. His musical education was taken over by his father, who hoped to make his boy into a child prodigy like Mozart. Though never fulfilling his father's hope, young Beethoven did learn piano and violin quickly. He received instruction from several musicians at the court, and by the age of twelve he was substituting at the chapel organ. In 1784 he was appointed to a permanent position as assistant organist and had already begun to make his mark as an improviser at the piano. After his mother died in 1787, his father's alcoholism grew worse, and Beethoven's home life became increasingly less bearable.

The year 1790 marked a turning point in the young composer's career. Haydn, passing through Bonn on his way to London, urged the Elector to send Beethoven to Vienna for further study. Two years later at the age of twenty-two, Beethoven moved to Vienna, where he remained the rest of his life. At first he studied composition with Haydn; but unsatisfied with the older man's methods, he turned to other composers for instruction. Though he was a frequent performer at musical evenings held by prominent Viennese nobility, Beethoven did not play in public until 1795, when he performed one of his early piano concertos.

Unlike Mozart, his popularity with both the general public and the aristocracy of Vienna never declined; and unlike Haydn, he never had to endure the rigors of the eighteenth-century system of musical patronage. Though he may have yearned at times for the prestige and outward security of a court position, he remained proudly and fiercely independent throughout his life. During most of his career he was able to count on annual stipends from a small circle of aristocratic friends and admirers. He seemed to enjoy moving about in the upper echelons of Viennese society, remarking that "it is good to mingle with aristocrats, but one must know how to impress them." He was one of the first composers to demand and obtain an equal footing with this aristocracy solely on the basis of his genius. It was his fortune to come upon the world in a time of rapidly changing values and increasing social mobility. The emerging middle-class audience and the growth of public concerts provided ample opportunities for performance of his music. The rising demand for his works enabled him to live off the sale of his music to publishers.

During the first years of the nineteenth century, when Beethoven seemed to be approaching the height of his career, he became aware of a growing deafness. He became deeply depressed when he realized that his career as a performer would end. In a moving letter to his two brothers, written from the small town of Heiligenstadt outside Vienna, to be read after his death, Beethoven confessed:

Figure 14.2   Beethoven se-cluded himself outside Vi-enna in Heiligenstadt, when he realized he was growing deaf. (The Bettmann Ar-chive)

My misfortune pains me doubly, in as much as it leads to my being misjudged. For me there can be no relaxation in human society, no refined conversations, no mutual confidences: I must live quite alone and may creep into society only as often as sheer necessity demands; I must live like an outcast. If I appear in com-pany I am overcome by a burning anxiety, a fear that I am running the risk of letting people notice my condition. . . . . Such experiences almost made me de-spair, and I was on the point of putting an end to my life — The only thing that held me back was my art. For indeed it seemed to me impossible to leave this world before I had produced all the works that I felt the urge to compose, and thus I have dragged on this miserable existence.*

After his affliction became painfully obvious, he gave up conducting and playing in public. His principal means of communication became a notebook in which his few visitors were invited to write their remarks. As he withdrew into his art, his works became more complex, more abstract, and more incomprehensible to his fellow musicians. He never married, and when total deafness set in after 1820, he became almost a recluse. Beethoven died in 1827 at the age of fifty-seven.

*Emily Anderson (ed. and transl.), *The Letters of Beethoven*, 3 vols. (New York: St. Martin's, 1961), Vol. 3, p. 1352.

Figure 14.3 Beethoven, at fifty-three, had become a total recluse because of his deafness. Some of his most important and far-reaching work was completed in these last years of personal turmoil. (Culver Pictures, Inc.)

His Work

In comparison to the production of Mozart and Haydn, Beethoven's works seem surprisingly few. This is partly due to his method of composing. Mozart never lacked musical inspiration, and ideas flowed from his hand with miraculous ease; Haydn confessed to the necessity of resorting to prayer at difficult moments, but he kept to a regular schedule of composition. Beethoven, however, had to struggle. Ideas did not come easily, and he filled innumerable pages with slowly evolving sketches. Even his finished compositions were continually rewritten and revised. The second reason for limited production was his attitude toward composition. He regarded music, above all, as art, and he generally took on only those commissions that he personally wished to fulfill.

If his works took longer to write than was usual at the time, they were also more substantial, both in content and length. His works include nine symphonies; nine concert overtures; five piano concertos; one violin concerto; sixteen string quartets; ten sonatas for violin and piano; five sonatas for cello and piano; thirty-eight sonatas for solo piano; twenty-one sets of variations for piano; one opera, *Fidelio*; an oratorio, *Christus am Ölberg (Christ on the Mount of Olives)*; *Choral Fantasia* for piano, chorus, and orchestra; and two Masses, one in C major, the other, entitled the *Missa Solemnis,* in D major.

Most musical scholars divide Beethoven's career into three periods: the first extending to about 1802, the second extending to 1814, and the last ending with his death in 1827. The first period was a time of assimilation of the Classical tradition of Mozart and Haydn and includes the string quartets of Opus 18 (1798–1800), the First Symphony (1799), and his first three piano sonatas.

The second period was perhaps the happiest of his life; it was certainly the most productive. During it he wrote masterpiece after masterpiece: seven more symphonies, including the gigantic *Eroica* (No. 3, 1803) and the Fifth (1805); the *Rasoumovsky Quartets* of Opus 59 (1806); his opera *Fidelio* (with no less than three versions appearing from 1805 through 1814); and the *Waldstein* and *Appassionata* piano sonatas of 1804.

Figure 14.4   The manuscript for Egmont *shows signs of the struggle and painstaking reworking that marked Beethoven's composing sessions. Although ideas did not come easily, their thorough development has acclaimed him one of the masters of Western music.*

His last style period, a time of great personal troubles, was less productive, but in many ways it was the most important of the three. It culminated in his monumental Ninth Symphony (1823), the equally immense *Missa Solemnis* (completed in 1824), and increasingly abstract late quartets and piano sonatas. In these works he developed many of the musical ideas that influenced the coming Romantic movement. The innovations they contained in form and harmonic structure were not fully understood or appreciated until almost half a century after his death.

Elements of His Style

Beethoven's music shows evidence of several general stylistic characteristics. One that is immediately apparent is size. His works tend to be much longer than those of Haydn or Mozart.

Another striking characteristic is the prevalence of the developmental process. Beethoven lengthened the development section of sonata-allegro form, giving it a weight equal to that of the exposition and recapitulation, and used development in other parts of the movement, especially in the *coda*. In many of his works the coda is not a short, tacked-on ending but is extended into a second development section, sometimes followed by a second coda that acts as a genuine coda, i.e., a short, concluding section.

In general, Beethoven adhered to the schemes of separate, self-contained movements, unrelated thematically. But there are exceptions: the Sixth Symphony (the *Pastoral*) has five movements, and there is no break between the last two. And the Fifth Symphony, which we shall analyze below, was a striking departure from the principle of thematic independence among the movements.

Within the four-movement scheme, he radically transformed the *third* movement. The short, stately minuet and trio was replaced by a scherzo and trio movement of an entirely different character. Swift of tempo, and fully proportioned in its length, Beethoven's scherzi are the equal of the other movements, performing an important structural and expressive role in the overall scheme of the work.

His music is characterized by an intense, dramatic profile of fluctuating dynamics. Frequently he used special dynamic effects, such as a crescendo that is not allowed to climax, but is aborted by a sudden change to pianissimo. He also used long crescendos for structural and expressive purposes. A crescendo slowly builds momentum and energy culminating in the appearance of an important event, such as the beginning of the recapitulation. Under these circumstances, the beginning of the recapitulation would also serve as a climactic ending of the development section.

Beethoven was ingenious in the use of *silence*. In his music, silence functions both as a structural element, separating sections, and as an expressive element, building suspense.

The qualities that we have outlined here are characteristic of Beethoven's work in general. Other, more specific, qualities can be delineated in his orchestral works.

Orchestral Style

Beethoven's orchestral sound is more powerful and dramatic than that of Mozart or Haydn. This increased intensity was the result of both an expansion of the orchestra and a change in the ways in which the instruments were used. More players were added to the string section, and two horns (sometimes four), two trumpets, and timpani were included as standard parts of the orchestral ensemble. The normal woodwind section was comprised of two flutes, two oboes, two clarinets, and two bassoons. For extra color and power, Beethoven occasionally added piccolo, contrabassoon, and three trombones. The trumpets, horns, and trombones assumed a greater role than they had previously and the timpani was no longer a mere adjunct to the trumpets, but was used independently, even as a solo instrument.

Working with this expanded orchestra, Beethoven made important contributions to the craft of *orchestration*, the utilization of instruments for expressive and structural purposes. In this area he greatly influenced later composers in the Romantic era for whom orchestration became a major component of musical composition.

The increased dimensions, extended use of development, advanced exploitation of dynamics, employment of suspense-building devices, and powerful use of an expanded orchestra are among the most important stylistic features of Beethoven's symphonies. Beginning with the Third and culminating in the Ninth, they revolutionized orchestral writing and playing. Together they constitute a series of enduring masterpieces.

Symphony No. 5 in C Minor

Record 3/Side 2;
Record 4/Side 1

Beethoven's Fifth Symphony, which he began in 1804, was first performed in Vienna in December, 1808. It is probably the most popular of Beethoven's symphonies, not only for its terse and memorable themes, but also for its unity.

First Movement

The first movement of the symphony is an excellent example of Beethoven's skill at building a large structure out of a small motive, in this case .

Example 14.1

Its stark and forceful announcement, played by all strings and clarinets, stands at the beginning of the movement.

After these two statements, there is a change to *piano* as the motive is used to create the initial phrase of the first theme, in the principal key of C minor.

Example 14.2

The theme is soon abruptly driven to a dramatic halt by a crescendo, leading to three loud, separated chords. The last chord lingers on a long-held note in the first violin, creating a feeling of suspense that is dispelled when the full orchestra, fortissimo, hammers out the motive. This dramatic and isolated statement of the motive draws attention to it, interrupting the flow of the theme. With another extreme change, from full orchestra playing fortissimo to strings playing piano, the theme is resumed, building on the motive.

Example 14.3

Shortly after the resumption of the theme, several important features of Beethoven's style appear. The intensity increases, underlined by the gradual addition of instruments, stepped-up rhythmic activity, and climbing pitch level, all combining in a mighty crescendo that envelops the bridge and culminates in two sharp chords separated by silence and followed by silence, dramatically setting off the appearance of the second theme.

The second theme, in E flat major, is launched by the four-note motive announced by the horns.

Example 14.4

The second theme continues with a lyrical legato melody in the first violins and the woodwinds. The basic motive is still present as a kind of punctuation in the lower strings.

Example 14.5

As the rhythmic activity of the theme increases, the basic motive reasserts itself, commanding full attention in the closing material ending the exposition, which is then repeated.

Example 14.6

The first phase of the development concentrates on the basic motive, in a manner similar to Theme 1, gradually leading to the winds and strings answering each other.

The second phase of development begins with the opening phrase of theme two and turns it into one of the most intense examples of suspense building in the history of musical composition. After the violins state the phrase twice, each time followed by rhythmic punctuations in the winds and lower strings, the phrase

is transferred to the winds, where it is played fortissimo in a shortened form. The strings answer with the two long notes of the phrase, and the winds and strings continue to alternate this two-note pattern.

Example 14.7

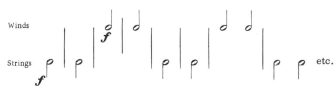

This stretch of music creates the atmosphere of suspense and expectation that is intensified when the dynamic level is progressively lowered through a diminuendo (>) and the musical material is reduced to one chord.

Example 14.8

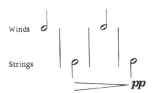

There is no "theme," no "motive," only the seemingly endless answering back and forth on this barest of fragments. Finally there is a jolting, forte entrance of

and it would appear that the suspense is ended, but the music immediately reverts to softly alternating winds and strings. Again the listener is caught in the atmosphere of suspense, finally to be ended with another entrance of the basic motive that now is used as a driving force that crescendos into a climactic

Here Beethoven shows complete mastery of form and structure—the simple four-note motive and its rhythm acquire an awesome impact as he develops it. Its reappearance constitutes the climactic ending of this development and at the same time the beginning of the recapitulation.

The recapitulation is quite straightforward, with the addition of a short oboe solo and minor changes in orchestration. But the closing material does not end the movement. Instead, there is a long coda, which is actually a new development section treating the basic motive, followed by the lyrical first phrase of the second theme. This becomes the new driving element which builds to yet another climactic statement of the opening figure in Example 14.8. There is then a short second coda based on the first theme and a crescendo to a final appearance of the basic motive.

Second Movement

Superficially, the second movement follows the Classical style: it is in a contrasting key (A flat major) and meter (3/8); it is slower in tempo (andante con moto) and, at least in the beginning, establishes a lyrical, relaxed atmosphere in relation to the first movement.

It is a theme and variations, with a two-part theme containing several distinctive contrasting elements. The first part begins with a lyrical, flowing melody played by violas and cellos, followed by a contrasting phrase initiated by the woodwinds. The second half of the theme is dominated by a loud phrase, played by horns and trumpets in C major. It is followed by a soft, suspenseful ending that leads into the first variation.

In the first variation, only the viola-cello melody is varied. With minor changes in the accompaniment, the rest of the theme is merely repeated in its original form. The second variation begins with an intensification of the first variation of the viola-cello melody.

Example 14.9

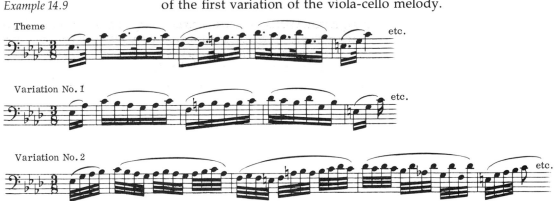

At this point the movement appears to consist of a clear theme and variations, and a listener expects to hear the entire theme a number of times, varied each time in a new way. But after the beginning of the second "variation," the theme never again appears intact, either in varied or original form. Only parts of it are used.

The music that follows is more characteristic of development than of variation. Fragments as well as whole phrases of the theme are manipulated in a variety of ways. Modulation, change of tempo, fluctuating dynamics, crescendos climaxing in the dramatic appearance of part of the theme are all used in the building of the movement. The movement closes with a return to the "woodwind" phrase followed by a coda based on the viola-cello theme. This movement is yet another testimony to Beethoven's preoccupation with and mastery of the developmental process.

Third Movement

The scherzo and trio movements of Beethoven's symphonies were a radical departure from the minuet and trio of the symphonies of Haydn and Mozart. This particular scherzo is thematically linked to the first movement through the prominent use of the basic motive (♫♩). The movement is not self-contained, but leads directly into the last movement without a break. Further, it is a fascinating example of how dynamics and orchestration influence musical structure.

Like the minuet and trio, the scherzo and trio has a three-part structure: scherzo-trio-scherzo. It, too, is in the key of the first movement, but the similarities end there.

The first scherzo alternates two contrasting ideas: a quiet, brooding, mysterious section (A) with a faltering, "stop-and-go" quality is followed by the loud, vigorous, driving thrust of the second theme (B), which is based on the familiar motive:

Example 14.10

Example 14.11

The trio shifts to C major and begins with a short section that is immediately repeated. After the two stumbling beginnings,

the second section of the trio continues with imitative entrance material in the strings that is eventually taken up by the entire orchestra, culminating in forte pronouncements of the motive (see B above).

The section is repeated, beginning forte, but as it continues it becomes not louder but softer. Instead of the gradual accumulation of instruments and crescendo, there is a diminuendo and a thinning of orchestral sound until only cellos and basses are left for the quiet return to the scherzo (A).

In the repeat of the scherzo, the themes no longer contrast dynamically; both are now pianissimo. The ♫♩ motive, originally so loud and bold as played by the horns, is now subdued as it is shared by the clarinet and pizzicato first violins. By reducing the dynamic level and subduing the orchestration throughout the entire repeat of the scherzo, Beethoven has profoundly changed the character of the music and created an atmosphere of almost excruciating restraint and expectation.

The scherzo does not "end" but turns into one of those suspense-ridden stretches of music of which Beethoven was a master. Here he uses a technique called *pedal point*, in which a long tone is maintained in the bass against changing harmonies in other parts. In this case, the timpani continually plays the note C. Over this pedal point, a long melodic arch, gradually unfolds, played by the first violins, first in fragments, and then as a continuous rising line pulling against the timpani roll. Higher and higher this line pulls, eventually joined by the rest of the orchestra on a long dominant chord and a crescendo that climaxes with breathtaking force in the triumphant and stirring C major melody that begins the last movement. The third and fourth movements are thus united with dramatic effect.

Example 14.12

Fourth Movement

The last movement is fast and is in the key of C major rather than making the expected return to C minor. Beethoven tended to end large works brilliantly in major keys. To provide greater color and strength to the movement, he added a piccolo, contrabassoon, and three trombones to the orchestration.

It is a sonata-allegro movement with three themes. Two of them draw upon the basic motive of the first movement for part of their material. In theme 1 the motive is one of many parts

Example 14.13

but in theme 2 the motive constitutes the primary melodic and rhythmic substance.

Example 14.14

The motive is not used in theme 3, although later in the movement the material from this theme is used in association with the motive.

Example 14.15

The bridge between themes 1 and 2 is exceptionally long, and its melodic importance rivals the themes themselves.

Example 14.16

It is stated first in the winds and horns and then expanded in the high strings with the ♫ motive introduced as a secondary accompanying figure. The bridge modulates from C to G major, ending with repetitions of the motive as it leads to the second theme.

The overall organization of the exposition may be diagrammed as:

Theme 1	long	Theme 2	short	Theme 3	closing
	bridge		bridge		
C major	⟶	G major	⟶	G major	⟶	G major

There is no break between the third theme and the closing. After the repeat of the exposition, the closing material flows into the development section—indeed with almost no indication of where one ends and the other begins.

The development section makes forceful use of the orchestra with emphasis on winds and brass, extended use of dynamics, and modulation. It first concentrates on theme 2, then combines elements of theme 2 with the rhythm of the beginning of theme 1. This fragment of theme 1 becomes the driving force, leading to a very loud fanfare-like section, introducing a remarkable phase of development. At the end of the fanfare, the first violin continues playing a repeated note in a diminuendo that leads to a direct quote from the *third* movement, in C minor and 3/4 meter and based on the basic motive. Using this quote, the development builds through a long crescendo to the recapitulation. Here we have a quote from the third movement culminating in the recapitulation of the fourth movement, similar to the use of material at the end of the third movement which ushered in the beginning of the fourth. And again, because of the way in which it is approached, the first theme of the fourth movement produces a "victorious" effect.

The recapitulation proceeds in a normal fashion until we come to the closing material after theme 3. Instead of an ending, a long coda ensues. Beginning very much like the original development, it concentrates on theme 1. It builds to the six sharp, individual chords separated by rests in the style of an ending. But at this point Beethoven suddenly launches another phase of development, this time centering on the long bridge. The reappearance of the bridge is a startling surprise after the false ending. It is the material used for an exhilarating increase in tempo leading to a whirlwind ending, built on the third theme and the basic motive.

Example 14.17

First in the strings, then with winds added, the first phrase of theme 3 is repeated many times at breakneck speed. It steadily builds momentum and climaxes in the trumpet announcement of the opening theme.

What follows is without question one of the longest and most emphatic endings in music history—bringing to a close one of the most remarkable compositions of all time.

Piano Sonata, Opus 57 (Appassionata)

Another portion of Beethoven's major work was focused on his compositions for the piano. Two of his greatest sonatas, the *Waldstein* (Opus 53) and the *Appassionata* (Opus 57), were both written in 1804, the year he began work on his Fifth Symphony. Both were works for solo piano, but unlike Classical chamber compositions, they were not intended for performance before a few listeners in a small room. Rather they are "symphonic" in proportion and suitable for the concert hall.

The capabilities of the piano had developed considerably since the time of Mozart. Improvements were due primarily to the addition of metal braces to the frame, permitting thicker strings to be stretched under greater tension. The resulting sound gave the piano a much greater dynamic range and brilliance.

The *Appassionata Sonata* is convincing evidence of the degree to which Beethoven exploited the effects that could be obtained from this improved instrument. He fully understood how rich and powerful the sound of the piano could become in the hands of a skilled performer.

The sonata maintained the three-movement plan—fast, slow, fast—without the characteristic break between the second and third movements.

First Movement

The first movement, in the key of F minor, is in sonata-allegro form. Here Beethoven makes use of the pitch range of the keyboard from very low to very high. The utilization of these extremes was one of the ways in which Beethoven expanded the style of keyboard music.

Example 14.18

Example 14.19

Example 14.20

Two stretches of music in this movement are very much like *cadenzas*. One ends the development and introduces the recapitulation, and the second ends the recapitulation and introduces the allegro finale. The closing coda is a tour de force for the virtuoso pianist, as it races at breakneck speed and with fortissimo dynamics. The theme is doubled in octaves and sounded in the most brilliant register of the piano. In a gesture typical of Beethoven, it then progresses from its point of climax to one of repose. In the last measures, the dynamic level drops from fortissimo to pianissimo to triple piano. The theme is sent soaring to the heights of the keyboard, then plummeting to a final whispered cadence five octaves below.

Second Movement

The second movement is a lyrical theme and variations in D flat major. In this movement Beethoven demonstrates his skill at exploiting the lower range of the piano and creating striking effects by the juxtaposition of high and low sections. The initial somber theme is stated in the rich and sonorous lower register of the keyboard. The theme is in two parts, each of which is repeated.

The first variation preserves the theme's contour but alters the rhythm. The right hand transforms the legato articulation into short, detached notes. The left hand, meanwhile, syncopates the rhythm of the theme, so that notes now appear slightly after the beat.

The second variation returns to the smooth legato of the opening, with the right hand playing chordal figures while the left hand retains the original bass line with slight rhythmic alterations. The material in both hands has been transposed one octave higher than in the original, thus creating a lighter, less massive texture.

In the first two variations the repetition structure of the theme is retained, but in the final variation this is no longer the case. Beethoven uses a motive based on the opening of the theme as a superstructure around which he weaves rapid chordal and scale figurations; here again we witness his exploration of development possibilities.

The magic that sometimes results from the juxtaposition of high and low registers emanates from the last simple statement of the theme at the close of the movement. The first three chords of the phrase are low, the next high and this continued alternation gives the theme a new dimension. The movement does not end, but after a final statement of thematic material, merges directly into the third movement.

Third Movement

The last movement is in sonata-allegro form. But here the distribution among the various thematic elements is obscured. Indeed the three major sections of the form—the exposition, development, and recapitulation—are not clearly set off from each other.

After a brief introductory section, an arching sixteenth-note passage enters.

Example 14.21

This passage, or some variant of it, seems omnipresent throughout the entire movement. The movement sounds like a continuous development of this material, with other thematic elements embedded within or grafted onto it. The movement ends with a presto finale in a climax of overwhelming brilliance and excitement.

Concerto No. 3 in C Minor

The capabilities of the piano so forcefully evident in the *Appassionata Sonata* were also utilized by Beethoven in his five piano concertos. In them he combined the virtuoso aspects of the solo instrument with the dynamic and expressive capabilities of the symphony orchestra. The first three, composed during his early years in Vienna, were written for his own needs as a concert pianist.

Sketches for Beethoven's Concerto No. 3 in C Minor have been found dating back to 1797. The work was finished in December of 1800, and first performed, with the composer at the piano, in Vienna in April of 1803. It has a three-movement structure of fast-slow-fast, and is scored for the standard Beethoven orchestra.

First Movement

The opening movement, in the key of C minor, makes use of the sonata-allegro scheme with a double exposition.

Marked *allegro con brio* (fast with vigor), the movement contains the brilliant piano writing we have seen in the sonata—fast scale and trill passages, sweeps throughout the range of the keyboard, and employment of extreme pitch registers. For a good part of the movement, particularly in the development, the orchestra states the important thematic ideas while the piano plays cadenza-like material. The cadenza, which divides the two sections of the coda, takes on added importance and weight as it rhapsodically improvises on and develops the themes. The orchestra joins the piano as it rises to the flourishes of the fortissimo ending.

Second Movement

Again illustrating his willingness to use unusual key combinations, Beethoven cast the second movement in the distant key of E major. The structure takes the form of a theme and variations. The theme is typical of Beethoven—rhapsodic, expressive, and highly ornamented. The variations that follow assume the character of freely invented improvisations. The orchestra has been reduced to flutes, bassoons, horns, and muted strings, and the dynamic level rarely rises above piano.

Third Movement

The third movement is a spirited rondo, with the orchestra restored to its original strength. The rondo theme is announced first by the piano alone and then taken up by the orchestra. Between statements of the main thematic material, the piano plays brilliant interpolations, sometimes developing elements of the theme, sometimes freely invented figurations. The rondo theme returns following the first cadenza and is again interrupted by brilliant passages from the soloist. After the second solo cadenza, Beethoven dramatically introduces the surprise elements characteristic of the closing moments of a rondo: the meter shifts from 2/4 to 6/8, the tempo from *allegro* (fast) to *presto* (very fast), the key from C minor to C major, and the thematic material changes to a rhythmically and melodically altered version of the initial rondo.

In the final measures, the solo and tutti sections alternate in abrupt changes of dynamics, and the movement ends in a fortissimo burst by the full orchestra.

Summary

In his symphonies, sonatas, and concertos, Ludwig van Beethoven expanded nearly every aspect of Classical composition. He lengthened the coda, development, and bridge sections; increased the size and volume of the orchestra; replaced the minuet with the scherzo; and introduced a variety of surprise elements to suit his expressive purposes.

With the piano's new concert hall proportions, Beethoven made wide use of the instrument's lyric and virtuoso capabilities. His melodic themes alternated with brilliant improvisations utilizing the full range of the keyboard.

The grace, sophistication, and lucidity of Mozart and the good-natured humor of Haydn did not retain the same focal positions. Beethoven shook the earth and music was never the same again. In the next chapters we will see how his strength and power directly affected the composers of the Romantic era.

**Part IV
Suggested
Listening**

Beethoven, Ludwig van

Symphony No. 3 in E-Flat, Op. 55 (Eroica). Initially titled "Bonaparte" (Beethoven withdrew the title in anger at Napoleon's self-proclamation as Emperor), this was the first of Beethoven's truly revolutionary works. In place of the usual slow movement it has a funeral march with contrasting major and minor sections; the minuet is replaced by one of the composer's earliest orchestral scherzo movements; and the finale is a complex set of variations.

Symphony No. 9 in D Minor, Op. 125. Perhaps the greatest symphony ever composed, this work remained a source of inspiration to subsequent composers throughout the nineteenth century. Its most striking innovation is the choral finale on Schiller's *Ode to Joy;* the three preceding movements are on an equally grand scale: the second is an immense scherzo built around a single rhythmic motif, and the third is a set of variations on a double theme.

Haydn, Franz Joseph

Symphony No. 45 in F-Sharp Minor (Farewell).   One of Haydn's most dramatic and unorthodox symphonies, this work illustrates his style at its most romantic and imaginative extreme. The opening movement introduces, by way of experiment, an extended new theme in place of the regular development; and in the final movement, the tempo suddenly changes from presto to adagio and the instruments drop out one by one, leaving only two violins to conclude the work.

Mozart, Wolfgang Amadeus

Die Zauberflöte (The Magic Flute).   If *The Marriage of Figaro* may be considered the culmination of eighteenth-century Italian comic opera, *The Magic Flute* stands as the first masterpiece of German romantic opera.

Symphony No. 41 in C Major, K. 551 (Jupiter).   The "Jupiter" is particularly famous for its closing movement in which several thematic ideas are used as subjects for short fugal sections and then are combined together in the coda.

Title page by Ludwig Richter for Robert Schumann's Songs for the Young.

Plate 11.   John Constable's Stoke-by-Nayland illustrates the artist's belief in accurately representing nature. Largely unappreciated in his own time, Constable's mastery of lighting changes and weather now make him one of the greatest of Romantic artists. (Courtesy the Art Institute of Chicago, Mr. and Mrs. W. W. Kimball Collection)

Plate 12. Eugène Delacroix's Liberty Leading the People commemorates the French revolutionaries' storming of the barricades.
Delacroix's emphasis of color and emotion over classical form was itself a revolutionary break with tradition. Louvre Museum, Paris.
(Courtesy Photographie Giraudon, Lauros)

Plate 13.   Claude Monet's La Gare de Saint-Lazare attempts to convey what the eye actually sees rather than what the mind knows is there. For Monet, as for the other Impressionists, one of the most important subjects of painting was light. Louvre Museum, Paris. (Courtesy Photographie Giraudon, Lauros)

Plate 14. Paul Cézanne's concern was with restoring to the canvas the viewer's sense of space and solidity in the subject matter. Rocks in the Forest exemplifies his distortion of natural shapes and disinterest in traditional perspective in order to convey this psychological impression. (Courtesy The Metropolitan Museum of Art, Bequest of Mrs. H. O. Havemeyer, 1929. The H. O. Havemeyer Collection.)

part V Music of the Romantic Era

The Romantic era was an age of revolution. Rising out of the social and political upheavals that followed the French Revolution, Romanticism dominated the arts of the nineteenth century. The eighteenth-century ideal of the perfection of man through reason was not totally forgotten, but the emphasis shifted from the individual to society as a whole, and from philosophy to science and technology.

The Arts of the Romantic Era

In technology, a number of inventions contributed to man's material well-being: the railroad and steamship sped his travel on land and sea; the telegraph and telephone provided long-distance communication; the elevator and skyscraper facilitated the growth of cities; and the discovery of pasteurization and theories of evolution ushered in a new era in science. Social reformers sought other methods for improving the way man lived. Labor unions organized to accomplish industrial reforms. Communism and socialism offered alternatives to existing ideologies.

The most progress was made by those who had already achieved economic security: the large and still-growing middle class. The working class still suffered from poverty, slums, epidemics, and exploitation. But toward the middle of the century, governments and individuals made large-scale efforts to improve these conditions through public housing, city and town planning efforts, sanitation laws, mass education, and the beginnings of the "welfare state." There was an optimistic feeling that a scientific approach would gradually eliminate society's ills.

This optimism was mixed with a high moral purpose and was expressed in a tone of self-righteousness that is perhaps the least attractive aspect of the nineteenth century. Standards of behavior and taste were set by the middle class, who believed that things *were* good if they somehow expressed "goodness." People were expected to follow rules of etiquette; spontaneity and frank expression of feelings were frowned upon in polite society.

These attitudes inevitably influenced the arts, especially since the only sizable market left for artists was the middle class. The middle class demanded that the arts represent the high moral values they had set for themselves: courage, honesty, piety, and patriotism. Artists, therefore, painted large numbers of historical, mythological, and scriptural scenes that today remain unseen and forgotten in museum basements. This art is called *academic*, because it reflected the values of the official academies that supported it. It also reflected the high standard of technical skill of the academic artists.

In music it was the age of the virtuoso soloist. Great pianists and violinists, such as Franz Liszt and Nicolo Paganini, became internationally known celebrities drawing large audiences as they played music which they wrote to show off their dazzling techniques.

The orchestra grew in size, variety, and versatility as composers explored its coloristic possibilities. Nationalism became an important force in music, particularly in Russia and other countries that did not have strong musical traditions. The Romantic influence in literature and the arts gave increased impetus to opera and program music.

Techniques of painting and sculpture advanced to the point that any competent student could learn and apply some of these techniques of perspective, composition, copying, and modeling so that, superficially at least, his work imitated an old master's. Also during this time, new research into history and archaeology provided a more accurate picture of the clothing, houses, and utensils of ancient times, permitting reconstructions of amazing accuracy.

Other artists, however, parted company with the academicians and blazed trails of their own. In general, the history of nineteenth-century painting is their story. For the first time, a sharp break occurred between those who created art for society and those who created art "for art's sake." For the most part, the latter were rejected by critics, patrons, and academic artists; indeed, the notion of the artist starving in a garret—dramatized by Puccini in the opera *La Bohème*—originated at this time. Today such artists as Courbet, Manet, Monet, Renoir, Degas, Van Gogh, Gauguin, Seurat, and Cézanne are considered the visionaries of nineteenth-century art. Similarly, such composers as Wagner, Bruckner, Franck, and Fauré, sometimes neglected in their own time, now appear among the giants of nineteenth-century music. Curiously, the society that respected courage and honesty as ethical ideals did not recognize these qualities in artists who, like the great scientists, discovered new insights into man and nature.

As early as 1836, the great English landscape painter John Constable (1776–1837) described the polarity of nineteenth-century art when he stated that painting "is *scientific* as well as *poetic*." By scientific, Constable meant that nature should be accurately pictured. Constable painted what he saw; unlike painters who drew their inspiration, color schemes, and compositions from old masters, Constable went to the countryside where he made sketches of meadows, trees, and clouds that he later reworked in his studio (Plate 11). Today it is possible to visit that part of

Figure 15.1 William Turner often used nature as a vehicle for his own fantasy. Paintings like Snowstorm: Steamboat Off a Harbour's Mouth *offer vivid impressions of nature's power and turmoil. (The Tate Gallery, London)*

England where Constable sketched and recognize not only the landscape but also the quality of light that he captured.

The same can scarcely be said for Constable's countryman and contemporary, William Turner (1775–1851). For Turner, landscapes and seascapes were points of departure for fantasy. In his *Steamer in Snowstorm*, a storm at sea becomes a painted veil of cloud, snow, smoke, and water blown together by a wind whose force can almost be felt (Figure 15.1).

Both Constable and Turner strongly influenced the most revolutionary painter of the early nineteenth century, the Frenchman Eugene Delacroix (1799–1863). Delacroix rejected the academic notion that artists should imitate Greek and Roman models; he was not even particularly concerned with accurate draftsmanship, believing that color was far more important. A work of art, Delacroix felt, should overwhelm the viewer, forcing him to feel the emotion that inspired the artist. Delacroix's musical parallel was the French composer Hector Berlioz, who revolutionized music by enormously enlarging the size of the orchestra and, more important, by creating a rich musical texture never before heard. To commemorate the French Revolution, Delacroix depicted the citizens of Paris storming the barricades in a painting that ignores realism. In it, Delacroix combines the allegorical figure of Liberty carrying the Tricolor and the revolutionaries carrying their muskets (Plate 12). He was concerned with what the poet and critic Baudelaire called "the heroism of modern life. . . ."

The French painter Gustave Courbet (1819–1877) went further than Delacroix and chose his subject matter from the everyday life of laborers and peasants, giving his working-class models a heroic quality similar to Caravaggio's (see Chapter 8). In his painting *Bonjour, Monsieur Courbet*, the artist depicts himself as a laborer with his painting materials strapped to his back as he goes out to a day of sketching in the country. But the deference shown to him by the two other men in the painting indicates that Courbet also thought of himself as an aristocrat (Figure 15.2).

Realism was manifested not only in painting. Novelists such as Charles Dickens in England and Emile Zola in France wrote about the

Figure 15.2 In Bonjour, Monsieur Courbet, *Gustave Courbet depicted himself as a laborer-artist on his way to his sketching site. Courbet's controversial choice of working-class models introduced new realism to the Romantic Era. (Fabre Museum, Giraudon)*

brutalized life of the working class; and Georges Bizet's opera *Carmen* does not deal with mythological beings or aristocrats, but with a girl who works in a cigarette factory.

More than the devotion of artists to realism influenced the choice of subject matter. Nineteenth-century physicists made discoveries about the nature of light and vision, and a number of painters began applying these scientific discoveries to their work. The first was Edouard Manet (1832–1883). Since the Renaissance, painters had given their works the feeling of roundness and solidity by carefully grading light and shadow;

Figure 15.3 Edouard Manet's use of harsh contrast in The Balcony *underscored his observations that sunlight obviates most subtle gradations of lighting. His technique also deemphasized the traditional importance of perspective. (Louvre Museum, Giraudon)*

Manet realized that in sunlight such gradations are not perceived, but that we see objects in harsh contrasts of light and dark. In depicting the quality of natural light, Manet played down perspective, another traditional pillar of painting, and emphasized the flat surface of the canvas itself.

These innovations were carried a step further by the Impressionists. They painted landscapes, flowers, portraits, still lifes, and scenes of everyday life. But to heighten the realistic effect, they concentrated on producing an overall impression of what the eye sees, rather than what the mind knows is there. In a sense, their real subject was light. Abandoning their studios to paint out-of-doors, they carefully noted how sunlight illuminates a subject, and duplicated this effect by breaking up the surface into tiny flecks of paint. So eager was Claude Monet (1840–1928) to capture the precise quality of illumination, that he set up a dozen different canvases when he painted a haystack or a church facade and moved from one to another as the light changed during the course of the day, starting the same round of canvases the next day.

Art critics, accustomed to the platitudes of academic painters, viewed Impressionism with total hostility, calling the painters madmen, frauds, amateurs. By the end of the century, however, the public came to appreciate the beauty of Impressionist painting. The Impressionists had demonstrated that exalted historical, religious, or patriotic themes do not necessarily constitute the most important subject for good art and that the real subject matter of painting is color and form. In turn, composers began realizing that program music—that is, music that tries to tell a story—is a dead end.

Great as the Impressionist achievement was, later artists sought still newer means to attain the feeling of visual excitement they wanted to communicate. Vincent Van Gogh (1835–1890), the greatest Dutch painter since the seventeenth century, rejected fidelity to nature and, by distorting shapes, combining colors dramatically, and applying paint to canvas in frenzied daubs, he endowed with vitality such objects as an old pair of shoes, a chair, and his own unprepossessing face. Paul Gauguin (1848–1903) rejected traditional art (along with Western civilization) and sought inspiration from Japanese art and the natives of Tahiti, among whom he lived. In his paintings, large areas of bright, flat color and sinuous line combine to convey a feeling of overpowering sensuality.

A less instinctive, more scientific approach was taken by Georges Seurat (1859–1891). Instead of mixing colors on his palette, Seurat applied tiny dots of pure color to the canvas (a method called *pointillism*), expecting that they would combine in the mind of the viewer and still retain their intensity.

All these artists have one trait in common; they were interested in the surface appearance of things. Paul Cézanne (1839–1901), while sympathetic to Impressionism, felt it could not convey the solidity one senses when looking at a mountain, a tree, or even an apple. His achievement was to recreate this sense of the mass of objects in paintings (Plate 14). To do so, he freely distorted natural shapes and ignored the rules of perspective. While retaining the intense color of the Impressionists, Cézanne realized the goal Constable had set for painting a half century before—that it should be both scientific and poetic.

Figure 15.4   The legendary Gauguin rejected Western tradition in favor of South Seas inspiration and subjects, as in The Moon and the Earth. *His use of flat, bright color and sinuous line lend a sensuous feeling to his works. (Paul Gauguin.* The Moon and the Earth *(Hina Te Fatou). 1893. Oil on burlap, 45 × 24 1/2". Collection, The Museum of Modern Art, New York. Lillie P. Bliss Collection.)*

chapter 16

The Romantic period in music is roughly congruent with the nineteenth century. In some respects, it was a logical extension of the principles established during the Classical era. In other respects, however, it represented a fundamental departure from those principles. Even within the outlines of

Song and Piano Music

the basic structures of the Classical period—the sonata, sonata-allegro form, theme and variations—formal balance and lucidity of structure gave way to spontaneity, to emotional depth and richness, much of which was foreshadowed in the works of Beethoven. In addition, the Romantic era saw the classical forms abandoned altogether by some composers. Instead, there was a heavy reliance on literature, nature, the pictorial, and the supernatural as sources for musical inspiration and as frameworks for musical forms.

Romantic composers made some of their most remarkable achievements in harmony and tone color, and the harmonic vocabulary became increasingly rich during the nineteenth century. Chromatic harmonies, modulations to distant keys, complicated chords, all tended to blur the outlines of the tonal system of major and minor keys. Harmony became a means of expression rather than merely an element of musical structure. The Romantic interest in tone color is shown by the phenomenal growth of the orchestra during this period. For the first time, instrumental color was regarded as an important element of music, on a par with melody, harmony, and rhythm. Instruments were improved, new ones were invented, new combinations were discovered, and the art of

Figure 16.1 The Romantic period witnessed tremendous popularity for the short piano piece. The social intimacy created by this smaller musical form is illustrated by this drawing of Schubert playing for his friends at the home of Josef von Spaum. (The Bettmann Archive)

orchestration became a prime preoccupation for many composers of the age.

The Romantic period is often described as the age of the art song and the short piano piece, since these two genres constitute some of the most interesting musical literature of the nineteenth century. This fascination with the smaller forms is one of the two major aspects of the Romantic spirit; the other aspect centered upon the larger forms, which offered greater scope in which to expand and develop.

These small pieces had an intimate quality, as though the composer were speaking directly to a small group of friends. [The media that seemed most suitable to them were the piano and the solo voice.]

Lieder

The art song is a musical setting of a poem for solo voice and piano, and the German words *lied* and *lieder* (plural) became the standard terms for this type of song. The lied became an important musical genre in the work of major composers early in the nineteenth century.

In the mid-eighteenth century the lied had been a simple song with keyboard accompaniment. It was strophic in structure, each verse having the same musical setting. The text was treated syllabically (one note for each syllable) and the accompaniment served merely to support the singing voice.

Toward the end of the eighteenth century, the *ballad* became popular in Germany. Its length, quality of dramatic adventure, and the alternation between narration and dialogue required greater musical resources than the strophic procedure offered. Hence the ballads were *through-composed.* Each section of the text had its own music that contrasted with the music preceding and following.

The lied became exceptionally popular in the early Romantic period and attracted the greatest composers of the time. The earliest and, in many respects, the most important of these composers was Franz Schubert.

Schubert (1797–1828)

The Bettmann Archive

In many ways the circumstances of Franz Peter Schubert's life were the very essence of the romantic's view of an artist's condition. During his brief and troubled lifetime, Schubert lived in poverty and was unrecognized, except by a small circle of friends; only after his death was his genius more widely acknowledged. He was born in a suburb northwest of Vienna, the fourth surviving son of an industrious and pious schoolmaster. His formal musical training, never very systematic, began with violin lessons from his father and piano instruction from an older brother.

In 1808, at the age of eleven, Schubert obtained a place in the choir of the Imperial Court Chapel and was thereby privileged to attend the *Stadt-Konvict* (City Seminary), one of Vienna's most prestigious boarding schools. In addition to his regular studies and music lessons, he became a violinist in the school orchestra, later assuming the duties of conductor on various occasions. The numerous works he composed during these years at the *Konvict* include songs, overtures, religious works, an operetta, and six string quartets. His first symphony was written in 1813, the year in which he left the *Konvict,* and his first Mass was successfully performed in 1814.

After leaving the *Konvict,* Schubert returned home to live, first attending a training college for primary school teachers and then teaching at his father's school. The regimen of the classroom was not suited to his temperament, and he applied for the musical directorship of the new State Normal School at Laivach (now Ljubljana in Yugoslavia) in 1816, but was turned down. Unable to find any other permanent employment at that time, he resolved to earn his living by taking music students, selling his compositions, and writing for the theater. In 1817 he moved to Vienna.

During the early 1820s, performances of Schubert's solo songs and vocal quartets for male voices aroused considerable public interest, and his name became widely known throughout Vienna. Two of his operettas were produced with moderate success, and a number of songs and piano works were published. These successes were offset by his continuing inability to obtain a salaried position. In 1822, a serious illness, probably syphilis, necessitated a stay in the hospital and a prolonged period of recuperation. The following year, *Rosamunde,* a play with incidental musical by Schubert, failed dismally, closing after only two performances. It was his last work for the theater.

The last four years of his life were a continual battle against ill health and poverty. Though his music, particularly the songs, continued to draw high praise from fellow musicians, including Beethoven, it was not until 1828 that a public concert of his works was given. He was unable to live on the pitifully small income from his music publications, but he continued to compose at a feverish pace. Despite his weakening health, he seemed at the height of his creative power. In the fall of 1828 he became ill with what was diagnosed as typhoid fever and died on November 19, at the age of thirty-one. His last wish, to be buried near Beethoven, was granted, and on his tombstone was written: "The art of music here entombed a rich possession but even far fairer hopes."

His Works

During the seventeen years between 1811, when he was 14, and 1828, the year of his death, Schubert composed about 1000 works. They include 9 symphonies, 50 chamber works and piano sonatas, a large number of short piano pieces, several operas and operettas, six Masses and about 25 other religious works, nearly 100 choral compositions, and more than 600 songs.

Schubert never chose to extend his famous Symphony No. 8 in B Minor beyond the original two movements, which he finished in 1822. Nicknamed "The Unfinished," the work was first performed in 1865, 43 years after his death.

He is best known, however, for his abundant body of lieder. The lieder use a wide variety of poetry, drawing on leading poets of his time, Goethe and Schiller among them. In addition to settings of individual poems, Schubert wrote two song *cycles* (series of songs that tell a story), *Die schöne Müllerin (The Maid of the Mill,* 1923), and *Die Winterreise (Winter Journey,* 1827).

Schubert employed both the strophic (which he used with considerable flexibility) and through-composed forms with great imagination. His songs also reflected the supremacy of the poem as the generating force. The shape and quality of the melodic line, the choice of harmonic progressions, the rhythmic character of the work, and the entire structure were fashioned to serve the poem. And the piano accompaniment, now no longer a mere harmonic background for the voice, joined with the voice, virtually as a full partner, bringing to musical life the essence of the poem.

Gretchen am Spinnrade

One of the finest examples of the use of the piano is found in *Gretchen am Spinnrade (Gretchen at the Spinning Wheel).* Gretchen, who in Goethe's play has fallen in love with Faust, sings as she sits at her spinning wheel. Her thoughts, with rising emotion, dwell on her lover.

GRETCHEN AM SPINNRADE
(Goethe, *Faust*)

Meine Ruh ist hin,
Mein Herz ist schwer;
Ich finde sie nimmer
Und nimmermehr.

Wo ich ihn nicht hab;
Ist mir das Grab,
Die ganze Welt
Ist mir vergällt.

Mein armer Kopf
Ist mir verrückt,
Mein armer Sinn
Ist mir zerstückt.

Meine Ruh ist hin,
Mein Herz ist schwer,
Ich finde sie nimmer
Und nimmermehr.

Nach ihm nur schau' ich
Zum Fenster hinaus,
Nach ihm nur geh' ich
Aus dem Haus.

Sein hoher Gang,
Sein' edle Gestalt,
Seines Mundes Lächeln,
Seiner Augen Gewalt,

Und seiner Rede
Zauberfluss.
Sein Händedruck,
Und ach, sein Kuss!

Meine Ruh ist hin,
Mein Herz ist schwer,
Ich finde sie nimmer
Und nimmermehr.

Mein Busen drängt
Sich nach ihm hin!
Ach dürft' ich fassen
Und halten ihn,

Und küssen ihn,
So wie ich wollt',
An seinen Küssen
Vergehen sollt'!

Meine Ruh ist hin,
Mein Herz ist schwer. . .

GRETCHEN AT THE SPINNING
WHEEL*

My peace is gone,
my heart is heavy;
never, never again
Will I find rest.

Where I am not with him
I am in my grave,
the whole world
turns to bitter gall.

My poor head
is in a whirl,
my poor thoughts
are all distracted.

My peace is gone,
my heart is heavy;
never, never again
Will I find rest.

I seek only him when I look
out of the window,
I seek only him when I leave
the house.

His noble gait,
his fine stature,
the smile of his lips,
the power of his eyes,

and the magic flow
of his speech,
the pressure of his hand,
and oh, his kiss!

My peace is gone,
my heart is heavy;
never, never again
Will I find rest.

My bosom yearns
towards him.
If only I could seize him
and hold him

and kiss him
to my heart's content—
under his kisses
I should die!

My peace is gone.
My heart is heavy. . . .

*S. S. Prawer, ed. and transl., *The Penguin Book of Lieder* (Middlesex, England: Penguin Books Ltd., 1964), pp. 33–34.

The piano accompaniment, which represents the spinning wheel, mirrors her growing agitation. As Gretchen conjures up her lover, a running sixteenth-note figure (the sound of the wheel) intensifies and gradually accelerates. As the voice rises higher and higher, the sound of the whirling wheel crescendos, stops, and Gretchen cries out *"und ach—sein Kuss!"* ("and oh, his kiss"). Gretchen sits transfixed by her passion, as does the listener.

It is not the voice but the piano that tells us that Gretchen returns to her senses. The spinning motive in the piano (pianissimo) makes two faltering starts; then with the third, the song is in motion again, with the spinning reintroducing the voice on *"Meine Ruh ist hin"* ("My peace is gone").

The words *Meine Ruh ist hin* and their melody begin each verse and act as a unifying element throughout the song. Gretchen repeats these words once more at the end of the song in a sigh of resignation. As the sound of her voice fades away, the whirring of the piano's spinning motive closes the piece as it began it.

Die Forelle

The Romantic view of nature is evident in *Die Forelle (The Trout)*, one of Schubert's shorter lieder. The poem concerns the struggle between a fish and a fisherman; typically, the Romantic poet's sympathy lies with the fish.

DIE FORELLE	THE TROUT*
In einem Bächlein helle,	*In a bright little stream,*
Da schoss in froher Eil'	*in joyous haste,*
Die launische Forelle	*a playful trout*
Vorüber wie ein Pfeil.	*flashed past me like an arrow.*
Ich stand an dem Gestade	*I stood by the shore*
Und sah in süsser Ruh	*and in sweet contentment I watched*
Des muntern Fischleins Bade	*the little fish bathing*
Im klaren Bächlein zu.	*in the clear stream.*
Ein Fischer mit der Rute	*A fisherman with his rod*
Wohl an dem Ufer stand,	*stood on the bank*
Und sah's mit kaltem Blute,	*and coldly watched*
Wie sich das Fischlein wand.	*the trout's windings.*
So lang' dem Wasser Helle,	*So long as the water*
So dacht ich, nicht gebricht,	*—I thought—remains clear,*
So fängt er die Forelle	*he will not catch the trout*
Mit seiner Angel nicht.	*with his line.*
Doch endlich ward dem Diebe	*But at last the thief*
Die Zeit zu lang. Er macht'	*grew impatient. He*
Das Bächlein tückisch trübe,	*treacherously dulled the clear stream,*
Und eh' ich es gedacht,	*and before I could think it*
So zuckte seine Rute,	*his rod quivered*

*S. S. Prawer, ed. and transl., *The Penguin Book of Lieder* (Middlesex, England: Penguin Books Ltd., 1964), pp. 37–38.

Das Fischlein zappelt' d'ran,	*and the fish was struggling on his hook.*
Und ich mit regem Blute *Sah die Betrogne an.*	*I felt the blood stir within me* *as I looked at the cheated trout.*

In form *Die Forelle* is almost strophic. The first two verses have identical music: a simple melody, with a very simple harmonic background. The accompaniment makes use of a short, rising figure that seems to sparkle and babble like a brook, conveying a mood of cheerful calm.

The third verse of the poem is much more excited, as the fish is caught. Schubert echoes this change of mood by putting aside the strophic form. The new melody is backed by a more agitated, more chromatic accompaniment. For the last two lines of the song, however, Schubert returns to the original melody and accompaniment. Although the text of the poem does not repeat the opening lines, the reappearance of the first melody rounds out the form of the song. Some years later, Schubert used this song as a basis for a set of variations in the Quintet in A Major (Op. 114), the famous "Trout" Quintet.

Erlkönig

Record 4/Side 2

While two of the Romantic period's favorite themes, nature and painful love, occupy *Die Forelle* and *Gretchen am Spinnrade*, the supernatural is involved in Schubert's setting of *Erlkönig (King of the Elves)*. The poem, a ballad by Goethe, tells the story of a father riding on horseback holding his son. As they hurry through the windy night, the boy imagines that the *Erlkönig* (the symbol of death) appears and tries to entice the son to follow him into death.

ERLKÖNIG (Goethe)	KING OF THE ELVES[*]
Wer reitet so spät durch Nacht und Wind?	*Who rides so late through the night and the wind?*
Es ist der Vater mit seinem Kind;	*It is the father with his child.*
Er hat den Knaben wohl in dem Arm	*He holds the boy in his arm, grasps*
Er fasst ihn sicher, er hält ihn warm.	*him securely, keeps him warm.*
"Mein Sohn, was birgst du so bang dein Gesicht?"	*"My son, why do you hide your face so anxiously?"*
"Siehst, Vater, du den Erlkönig nicht? Den Erlenkönig mit Kron' und Schweif?"	*"Father, do you not see the Elf-King? The Elf-King with his crown and train?"*
"Mein Sohn, es ist ein Nebelstreif."	*"My son, it is only a streak of mist."*
"Du liebes Kind, komm, geh' mit mir! Gar schöne Spiele spiel' ich mit dir; Manch' bunte Blumen sind an dem Strand,	*"Darling child, come away with me! I will play fine games with you. Many gay flowers grow by the shore:*

[*]S. S. Prawer, ed. and transl., *The Penguin Book of Lieder* (Middlesex, England: Penguin Books Ltd., 1964), pp. 34–35.

Meine Mutter hat manch' gülden Gewand.''	*my mother has many golden robes.''*
''Mein Vater, mein Vater, und hörest du nicht,	*''Father, father, do you not hear*
Was Erlenkönig mir leise verspricht?''	*what the Elf-King softly promises me?''*
''Sei ruhig, bleibe ruhig, mein Kind:	*''Be calm, dear child, be calm—*
In dürren Blättern säuselt der Wind.''	*the wind is rustling in the dry leaves.''*
''Willst, feiner Knabe, du mit mir gehn?	*''You beautiful boy, will you come with me?*
Meine Töchter sollen dich warten schön;	*My daughters will wait upon you.*
Meine Töchter führen den nächtlichen Reihn'	*My daughters will lead the nightly round,*
Und wiegen und tanzen und singen dich ein.''	*they will rock you, dance to you, sing you to sleep.''*
''Mein Vater, mein Vater, und siehst du nicht dort	*''Father, father do you not see the Elf-King's daughters there, in that dark place?''*
Erlkönigs Töchter am düstern Ort?''	
''Mein Sohn, mein Sohn, ich seh' es genau:	*''My son, my son, I see it clearly:*
Es scheinen die alten Weiden so grau.''	*it is the grey gleam of the old willow-trees.''*
''Ich liebe dich, mich reizt deine schöne Gestalt;	*''I love you, your beauty allures me,*
Und bist du nicht willig, so brauch' ich Gewalt.''	*and if you do not come willingly, I shall use force.''*
''Mein Vater, mein Vater, jetzt fasst er mich an!	*''Father, father, now he is seizing me!*
Erlkönig hat mir ein Leid's gethan!''—	*The Elf-King has hurt me!''—*
Dem Vater grauset's, er reitet geschwind	*Fear grips the father, he rides swiftly,*
Er hält in den Armen das ächzende Kind,	*holding the moaning child in his arms;*
Erreicht den Hof mit Müh' und Not;	*with effort and toil he reaches the house—*
In seinen Armen das Kind —	*the child in his arms —*
war tot.	*was dead*

Actually the poem has four separate characters: the narrator who introduces and closes the song, the frightened child, the frantic father, and the sinister *Erlkönig*, all sung by one voice with piano accompaniment.

As in *Gretchen am Spinnrade*, the piano is a crucial element in the song. It sets the atmosphere at the beginning: the wild wind, the galloping horse, and the anxiety of the father.

Example 16.1

The triplet figure in the right hand occurs in various forms throughout, sustaining the highly charged atmosphere until the final moments of the song. The figure in the left hand appears periodically to indicate the running horse and to unify the piece musically.

Schubert portrays the characters and sets them off from each other by a number of devices, particularly by manipulating the piano accompaniment. Whenever the *Erlkönig* enters, for example, the dynamic level drops to pianissimo, the piano accompaniment changes, and the vocal line becomes smooth and alluring.

Schubert reflects the son's mounting terror by repeating the same melodic material each time he cries out to his father at successively higher pitch levels. An upward leap on *"Mein Sohn"* and *"Sei ruhig"* marks the father's utterances that act as modulatory bridges linking the passages of child and *Erlkönig*.

The father's final statement ends with the strong drop of the interval of a fifth doubled by the left hand of the piano. The same figure recurs as the *Erlkönig* utters his last words as he seizes the boy,

Example 16.2

Example 16.3   and is repeated once more in the boy's cry as he is taken in death.

The last verse shows Schubert's sense of drama and the manipulation of the song's elements to heighten the emotional impact. The piano is silent as the narrator sings "the child in his arms," a single chord sounds, increasing the feeling of suspense, and the narrator concludes "was dead."

Other Lieder Composers

In addition to Schubert, both Brahms and Schumann wrote memorable lieder. But Brahms remains better known for his instrumental work, which will be discussed in the next chapter. Schumann, who will be considered later in this chapter as a composer of piano music, deserves no less recognition for his songs. Although he lacked Schubert's Classical qualities—serenity, poise, a perfect sense of balance—he more than compensated with his exceptional gift for creating an emotional union between poetry and music.

The Piano

The favorite instrument of the Romantic age, the piano, ideally suited the dual personality of the period: the intimate, delicate side as well as the brilliant flashy one. The popularity and importance of the piano stemmed indirectly from Beethoven, who had written a great deal of excellent and demanding music for it. During the nineteenth century the piano became a universal instrument.

The huge and varied literature for piano produced during the Romantic period falls into two broad categories; one consists of short, intimate, lyric pieces, similar in scope and feeling to lieder, while the other includes the larger, more brilliant exhibition pieces written for virtuoso performers. As one might expect, the outstanding lieder composer, Franz Schubert, was also a master of the small lyric piano piece. These little pieces, which he called either *impromptus* or *moments musicaux*, are miniature gems. Each is characterized by its distinctive mood, with Schubert's inimitable correlation of form and musical content. These works became models for many later composers.

Another composer who excelled in this genre was Felix Mendelssohn (1809–1847). Mendelssohn will be discussed in a later chapter as a composer of traditionally oriented orchestral music, but he was also a virtuoso pianist and composer for his instrument. His conservative Classical bent led him to continue writing in the traditional forms, and he wrote two concertos and three sonatas for the piano. But his most popular piano pieces were written in the small, songlike form introduced by Schubert. Mendelssohn called his collection *Songs Without Words,* a title that indicates his awareness of the close link between this type of piano piece and the lied of the same period.

The other aspect of Romantic music—the grandiose, flashy, exhibitionist side of the style—became an increasingly important element of the rapidly growing literature for the piano. Virtuosity impressed the Romantic audience and dozens of second-rate (and worse) composers began pouring out compositions for this market. Much of this music was shallow and meaningless, offering only a display of technical prowess.

However, three important composers—Robert Schumann, Frederic

Chopin, and Franz Liszt—realized the piano was capable of much more. Although each man responded in his own way, they all shared a common belief in the potential of the instrument. The pieces they wrote are so well tailored to the piano that it is virtually impossible to arrange them satisfactorily for any other medium.

Robert Schumann spent his early years composing primarily for the piano. Alternating between visionary dreams, moodiness, and exultation, his music expresses the contradictions and tensions inherent in Romanticism.

Schumann (1810–1856)

The Bettmann Archive

Robert Schumann was born in Germany in the Saxon town of Zwickau. His father, a bookseller, recognized his son's talent and arranged for piano lessons when the boy was seven. Schumann began to compose soon after, but his interest in music was paralleled by a fascination with literature. With his father's encouragement, he read widely, particularly Goethe and Byron, and wrote poetry and a novel.

The year 1826 was a doubly tragic one: his elder sister committed suicide at the age of nineteen, and shortly afterward his father died. Schumann's mother persuaded him to take up law, and to please her he enrolled at the University of Leipzig. But "chilly jurisprudence, with its ice-cold definitions" repelled Schumann, who gained his mother's permission to devote himself to music.

By 1830 he was taking lessons from Leipzig's well-known pianist Friedrich Wieck, with whom he also boarded. His dreams of becoming a piano virtuoso, however, were cut short by a permanent injury to his right hand caused by a gadget he had rigged in hopes of improving his fingering technique. Accepting the disaster with philosophical detachment, he threw all his energies into composition and the writing of music criticism.

During the decade of the 1830s, Schumann developed steadily as a composer and critic. His compositions, primarily for piano, received favorable attention and a number of them were published. In 1834, with a small group of friends, he founded the highly influential *Neue Zeitschrift für Musik (New Journal for Music)*. As editor from 1835 to 1844, he strongly espoused progressive musical art, attacking with great fervor the shallow *salon* music and insipid Italianate stage productions then in vogue. Through his many articles and essays, often signed with fanciful pseudonyms, Schumann helped shape the taste of the nineteenth century. He was among the first to acknowledge the genius of both Chopin and Brahms.

In 1835 he fell in love with Clara Wieck, the daughter of his former piano teacher, who was then sixteen. Their marriage was opposed by her father, who wanted her to marry someone wealthy enough to support her own career as a concert pianist. They finally married, without her father's consent, in 1840. The years immediately following the marriage were among Schumann's happiest, and his joy was reflected in his composition. In 1840 he devoted himself almost exclusively to composing more than 130 songs; in the next year he completed his first two symphonies; and in 1842 he turned to writing chamber music.

In 1843 he joined the faculty of Mendelssohn's newly founded conservatory at Leipzig, but his career, up to now so promising, was threatened by a mental breakdown. He resigned from the conservatory, moving first to Dresden and then to Düsseldorff. There his mental condition became worse; he threw himself into the Rhine, and after being saved from drowning, was confined to an asylum near Bonn. He died there, at the age of forty-six, leaving behind his wife and seven children.

His Work

With Chopin and Liszt, Schumann was one of the creators of modern piano technique. Almost all of his most popular and greatest works for piano date from his early years as a composer, up to 1840. They range from miniature character pieces, whose titles place them wholly within the Romantic aesthetic—*Papillons (Butterflies)*, *Carnaval*, *Kinderscenen (Scenes from Childhood)*—to large, classically oriented works such as the three piano sonatas, the Fantasy in C Minor, the Symphonic Etudes, and the Piano Concerto in A Minor.

As a symphonist, Schumann is frequently criticized for his weakness as an orchestrator and his failure to achieve unity of large-scale form. Of his four symphonies, the Symphony No. 1 in B-flat Major (*Spring*, 1840), is perhaps the most spontaneous and Romantic in spirit.

It was as a miniaturist that Schumann's lyric gifts, his mastery of detail, and his poetic imagination show themselves to best advantage. If these qualities are somewhat obscured in his symphonies, they find their best expression in his songs. His great cycles of 1840—*Myrthen (Myrtle)*, *Frauenliebe und Leben (Woman's Love and Life)*, and *Dichterliebe (Poet's Love)*—rank with those of Schubert as the greatest of nineteenth-century song cycles.

His chamber music, much of which was written in 1842 after he had thoroughly studied the quartets of Haydn and Mozart, includes three string quartets, three trios, a piano quartet, and a piano quintet. Of the choral music, most of which is neglected today, *Das Paradies und die Peri* (1843) and *Scenes from Goethe's Faust* (1849–1853) are his most important compositions. Schumann's one opera, *Genoveva* (1848), was not a success.

Schumann was well aware of the conflicting aspects of Romanticism, and the same conflicts were reflected in his own personality. He often wrote about imaginary characters who represented the two contrasting outlooks: Florestan, the impulsive revolutionary, and Eusebius, a moody, introspective dreamer. In his writings, these two characters often engage in spirited debates, and in his music it is often possible to weigh the influence of these two sides of Schumann's nature.

Much of Schumann's music was poetically inspired; the pieces and collections have titles that suggest the sources of their inspiration.

Schumann's style is very free and flexible, almost kaleidoscopic, with rapid alternations between the Romantic extremes of intimacy and brilliance. There is never any attempt to overwhelm the listener with virtuoso displays; the technical difficulties in the music serve the cause of the poetic inspiration.

Fantasiestücke (Fantasy Pieces), Op. 12

Schumann considered the *Fantasiestücke* to be among his best compositions. This set of eight short pieces represents a constant interchange between the two mythological characters, Florestan and Eusebius; for the first four pieces, they alternate, while the last four include elements of both within each piece. The first, second, seventh, and eighth pieces from the *Fantasiestücke* illustrate Schumann's freedom of content, form, and style.

Des Abends (The Evening)   This movement embodies the reflective character of Eusebius, with the picture of a peaceful, undisturbed evening, and might well be termed monochromatic, illustrating a single mood with great economy of means. The work is in six sections, each of which begins with a descending melodic line:

Example 16.4

The same accompaniment is used throughout the piece. The sections are quite similar, even though the piece modulates several times. The dynamic level remains soft throughout.

Aufschwung (Soaring)   In sharp contrast to the opening piece, this one is fast, loud, and enthusiastic, mirroring the character of the youthful Florestan. The work is in ternary form (ABA), with each A section further subdivided into an aba form of its own (Schumann was very partial to ternary form). The a section alternates between hammering chords with a melody beneath them and a smoother descending theme. The b section, which follows, is more quiet, longer, and much more lyric. The a theme then returns briefly. The B section has no such distinct formal outlines; it modulates freely, with many changes of dynamics and tempo. A long crescendo leads to the return of the A section.

Traumes Wirren (Dream Visions)   This short and lively piece is monopolized by lighthearted Florestan; the moody Eusebius emerges only in the short B part of the ternary (ABA) form. The A section is light and fast, requiring considerable pianistic technique. The B section is slower, sustained, chromatic, and lower in pitch.

Ende vom Lied (End of the Song)   In a letter to his intended bride, Clara Wieck, Schumann explained that this piece pictured a wedding (probably theirs), with all the good spirits that usually attend such an event. The piece is again in ternary (ABA) form, and the exuberant Florestan predominates. But in the coda, Eusebius takes over, as the composer's happy thoughts change to despair at his fear of losing his beloved. The A section is marchlike, while the B portion is livelier, with more dancelike rhythms and more dynamic contrasts; the return of the A section is somewhat abbreviated. The coda utilizes some melodic material from the A section, and this poignant concluding section is soft, low in pitch, and very sustained.

Chopin (1810–1849)

The Bettmann Archive

Frederic Chopin was one of the most creative and original composers in the history of music. Almost none of his mature works relies on traditional devices or forms; he created an entirely new musical idiom. His style is unique and easy to identify; every phrase is characteristically his. Chopin's art is inescapably linked to the sonority of the piano, the only possible means of expression for him. Chopin suffered neither the privation and neglect that Schubert experienced nor the corroding mental illness that tormented Schumann. But although his life was marked by fame and the friendship of some of the greatest artists of the time, it ended in a mortal illness and an early death. When he died at the age of thirty-nine, he left behind him a literature for the piano unequaled before or since, and his critics, borrowing a character from Shakespeare, dubbed him the "Ariel of the piano." He followed no national school of Romanticism, and one can be no more specific than to call him a European composer.

Chopin was born near Warsaw on February 22, 1810, of a French father and a Polish mother. His father, Nicolas, had come to Poland to teach French to the sons of the Polish nobility, and it was in these surroundings that young Frederic received his formal education. He studied piano at the Warsaw School of Music, showing an early talent for the instrument. He gave his first public concert at the age of seven. By the age of fifteen, he had already published some compositions, and by nineteen he had achieved eminence in both composition and performance. He traveled widely through Europe and was received enthusiastically wherever he played. So cordial was the reception at Chopin's first concert in Paris, in 1831, that he decided to make that city his home and never again returned to Poland.

The public and his peers immediately recognized his genius, and he was in constant demand as a teacher and performer. He played frequently in Parisian salons, which had become the meeting places of the artists, musicians, and writers devoted to the New Romanticism. His circle of friends included Victor Hugo, Balzac, Alexandre Dumas, Liszt, Berlioz, Schumann, and the painter Delacroix. Reviewing some of Chopin's works, Schumann wrote of him that he was the "boldest and proudest poetic spirit of the time." His admirers were legion and he was the recipient of almost fanatic acclaim.

Among the influential members of Parisian artistic society was a woman novelist, Mme. Aurore Dudevant, who wrote under the name of George Sand. Through Liszt, Chopin met George Sand in 1837, when he was twenty-eight and she was thirty-four. It was a relationship that was to have a profound effect on his life, and though happy at first, their relationship became increasingly bitter. By the time Chopin developed tuberculosis in 1847, their affair had deteriorated completely.

In 1848, with the full knowledge that he was in failing health, Chopin traveled to England and Scotland, where he stayed for seven months. There his concerts and strenuous activities sapped his fast-ebbing strength. Heartbroken over the bitterness that accompanied the conclusion of his affair with George Sand, his energies exhausted, he returned to Paris, where he spent his remaining months. The funeral following his death on October 17, 1849, was attended by the elite of Paris society, artists as well as aristocrats; only Mme. Sand was absent from among the mourners. As a final gesture to his homeland, he wished his heart to be returned to Poland, while his body was buried between Cherubini and Bellini in Père Lachaise Cemetery in Paris.

His Work

Chopin wrote almost exclusively for the piano. His only major works that include orchestra are the Piano Concertos in F Minor and E Minor (Warsaw, 1830), written when he was twenty. Although these early works are weak in structure and tedious in orchestration, they still appear in concert repertoire. A third piano concerto was begun, but all that survives is an *Allegro de Concert* (Op. 46, 1841) that was put together from older material.

The bulk of Chopin's music falls into one of three categories. The first consists of technical studies or *Études*, two collections of twelve each, published in 1833 and 1837, and three without opus numbers. Each of the études presents a single technical problem and usually develops a single musical motive. In many ways they summarize Chopin's conception of the technical possibilities of the piano. But they are more than mere exercises; they are also a series of miniature, abstract tone poems.

The second category consists of works composed in small, intimate forms, including twenty-four preludes, nineteen nocturnes, two impromptus, and numerous waltzes, polonaises, and mazurkas. The influence of Polish melodies and rhythms on Chopin's style is most clearly demonstrated in the polonaises and mazurkas. These are Polish national dances in triple meter, with Slavic rhythmic patterns and folklike melodies. The simple dance forms are frequently expanded into fantasies and tone poems. Chopin's most intimate pieces are the nocturnes and waltzes. The nocturnes were character pieces of melancholy moods with expressive melodies sounding over an arpeggiated accompaniment.

The third category consists of works written in relatively large, free form. It includes four scherzos, five ballades, and six fantasies. The ballades and scherzos demonstrate Chopin's ability to work within large-scale forms. He was apparently the first to employ the term *ballade* for an instrumental piece. All of his ballades are in 6/4 or 6/8 meter, and Chopin borrowed freely from the existing sonata-allegro, rondo, and song forms to create this new and epic genre. Good examples of these large-form works are the Ballade No. 1 in G Minor (Op. 23, 1831) and the Ballade No. 2 in F Major (Op. 38, 1836–1839). Chopin adopted the scherzo, which consisted of a piece in 3/4 meter moving at a rapid tempo, from Beethoven.

In addition to these three main categories, Chopin composed three sonatas of which only one (in B Minor, Op. 58, 1844) ranks as an important work. It is significant that none of Chopin's pieces, contrary to the prevailing fashion of the time, bears a fanciful, Romantic title. Chopin, a master at creating expressive atmosphere and mood, resisted programmatic tone painting in his pieces.

Two other pieces stand in a category by themselves: the Fantaisie in F Minor (Op. 49, 1840–1841) and the *Polonaise Fantaisie* (Op. 61, 1845–1846). These two pieces are among Chopin's most monumental works.

There are no real precedents for Chopin's works; his style is personal and Romantic, completely opposed to the Classical world. They depend on no large standard forms and exhibit little sense of structure and balance. His music is whimsical and arbitrary, elegant and enchanting. Beautiful melodies and sparkling harmonies weave forms to suit themselves. There is considerable repetition in his works, often with just a touch of ornamentation to add interest to the repeat. Chopin's pieces give the illusion of being improvised (something every Romantic composer longed to be able to do), but actually they are carefully and consciously constructed.

Although Chopin was a revolutionary force in Romantic music, he was never bizarre or exhibitionistic. His music expresses sentiments ranging from melancholy to exaltation, but he avoids empty virtuosity. The subtle qualities of his music are enhanced by the use of a performance technique called *rubato* in which the melody is permitted to forge ahead or lag behind very slightly, while the accompaniment maintains a steady beat.

Ballade No. 1 in G Minor (Op. 23)

Record 4/Side 2

This ballade, one of Chopin's larger works, is essentially a dramatic narrative for piano. The title indicates the composer's intention, since the term *ballade* originally meant a long narrative poem. Although there is no specific story underlying this composition, the feeling of narration is strongly implied by the sections in different tempos, linked by ritards and accelerations, and by the free use of rubato.

The repetition of three themes forms the structure of the ballade. Chopin deliberately obscures the form by interspersing beautiful and lengthy episodes, transitions, and a coda between the repetitions of themes. The emphasis on nonstructural material, as well as the absence of pauses between the sections, reinforces the sense of continuity and the apparently free-flowing and evolving character of the work.

The ballade opens with a short, improvisatory introduction; the subsequent first theme is a waltzlike melody

Example 16.5

in the minor mode. A long transition section builds to a climax, and then subsides to a quiet imitation of horn calls. Theme 2, in a major key, is soft and lyrical, with an accompaniment of slowly arpeggiated chords in the left hand.

Example 16.6

Theme 3 follows immediately, still very soft but in somewhat faster note values and with a triplet figure in the melody.

Example 16.7

Theme 1 returns, this time over a pedal point and is stated much more dramatically; there are several sudden changes of dynamics. Eventually it builds up to a *forte* restatement of theme 2, with full chords in both hands. A very long episode follows, with brilliant passage work and modulations; a long descending scale leads into another restatement of theme 2, still *forte,* and with a faster-moving accompaniment than before. Theme 3 follows again, this time *forte,* but grows quieter and introduces the final and abbreviated return of theme 1, again over a pedal point. The coda of this ballade is long, fast, and full of scales and arpeggios, utilizing the exceptionally wide range of the piano.

Piano Music of Liszt

The third of the major Romantic composers who focused on compositions for the piano was Franz Liszt (1811–1886). An important and innovative composer of descriptive orchestral music, he was also a significant force in the creation of a new style for the piano.

Almost all of Liszt's compositions for the piano come from his early compositional years, until about 1840. During this period he not only wrote original works for the piano, but also transcribed operas and symphonies for the instrument. Through his attempts to find piano sonorities that could stand in place of orchestral colors, he discovered sounds in the instrument, a whole new world of sounds which no one had ever imagined were possible.

Liszt was an important innovator in the area of style as well as sonority. He acknowledged the originality of Chopin's style, but saw that it would not serve as the basis for a new general approach; it was too personal and intimate to be adopted by other composers. Instead, he took a more dramatic or rhetorical direction, exploiting the orchestral possibilities of the instrument. Liszt fought the rising tide of empty virtuosity with his own meaningful virtuosity, no less exciting or dramatic but intimately bound up with the content and structure of his works.

Summary

During the Romantic period the carefully measured controls of Classicism gave way to spontaneity. The Romantic movement sought a fusion of all art forms and a union of man with nature. In music, the Romantic style was characterized by a concentration on the lyrical and melodic aspects of a work. The carefully constructed forms of the Classical period were freely manipulated by Romantic composers.

The German lied became exceptionally popular in the early Romantic period and attracted the greatest composers of the time. In many ways the most important composer in this genre was Franz Schubert, who wrote more than 600 songs in his brief lifetime.

The piano, which was ideally suited to both the intimate and brilliant aspects of Romanticism, was the favorite instrument of the period. The literature produced for the piano consisted of two main types: short, lyric pieces, similar in scope and feeling to the lieder, and larger exhibition pieces written for virtuoso performers. Three composers in particular realized the capabilities of the piano and developed a new type of literature for it.

Robert Schumann wrote works ranging from miniature character pieces to large, classically oriented sonatas and concertos. His style was free and flexible, alternating between the Romantic extremes of intimacy and brilliance.

Frederic Chopin wrote almost exclusively for the piano. His work falls into three main categories consisting of études, intimate forms, and large, free forms. With their rhapsodic melodies, his pieces often give the illusion of being improvised, but were actually very carefully constructed.

Franz Liszt, who transcribed a large number of operas and symphonies for the piano, discovered new ways of exploiting the orchestral possibilities of the instrument. In his compositions he fought the empty virtuosity of the period with a brand of virtuosity of his own.

chapter 17

Throughout the Romantic period, the orchestra grew in size, variety of color, and versatility. This growth, first seen in the symphonies of Beethoven, culminated in the huge proportions needed for the tone poems of Richard Strauss. Composers primarily responsible for the growth of the orchestra, such as Berlioz and Liszt, had little interest in

The Romantic Traditionalists

chamber music. They found the string quartet and other chamber groupings far too limited for their purposes. With its amazing fund of tone colors and dynamic gradations, the orchestra was the ideal vehicle for them. At the same time they discarded the Classical symphony, with its formal procedures. However, a stream of Classical tradition continued to flow through the Romantic period.

Some Romantic composers cultivated and expanded the traditional forms in both orchestral and chamber music. In so doing, they utilized elements from two periods of music history. Though essentially Classical in broad design, their works were richly endowed with romantic harmonies, color, dynamics, theme constructions, and orchestration. The leading composers in this group were Franz Schubert, Felix Mendelssohn, and Johannes Brahms.

The Symphony

The Romantic symphony grew in the shadow of Beethoven's symphonic writing. Beethoven's music affected virtually all the early Romantic composers, some by his use of the orchestra, others by his expansion of form. Early in the Romantic period, the symphonic writing of Franz Schubert was influenced first by Haydn and Mozart and finally by Beethoven. Schubert's gift for lyrical melody and his propensity for

249

chromatic harmonies constantly threatened to subvert the purely structural aspect of his symphonic writing. But his last two symphonies, the *Unfinished Symphony* (1822) and the big C Major (1828) take their place along with those of Beethoven in the repertoire.

If Schubert was the outstanding symphonist of the beginning of the Romantic period, Johannes Brahms deserves that honor for the latter part of the century.

Brahms occupies a unique place in the history of the Romantic movement. Although he was much admired by his Romantic contemporaries, he disagreed with the Romantic notion that the literary and pictorial arts should be fused with music. He had no argument with the style of his fellow composers, only with the nonmusical sources of their inspiration. Instead of following the dominant trend of his time, he looked back to Beethoven and the older forms of the Classical era.

Brahms (1833–1897)

The Bettmann Archive

Born and raised in Hamburg, Johannes Brahms received his earliest musical training from his father, a double-bass player. The family was not wealthy and at an early age Brahms had to contribute to the family income by playing the piano in local taverns. At the age of twenty he met the famed Hungarian violinist Eduard Reményi and toured Germany as Reményi's accompanist. On one of his tours, his first attempts at composition were heard by Joseph Joachim, the foremost violin virtuoso of the time. Through Joachim, Brahms was introduced to Franz Liszt and Robert Schumann, who were both greatly impressed by the young composer. Schumann, always eager to do what he could to advance the career of young promising composers, wrote a laudatory article heralding Brahms as the coming genius of German music.

Schumann and his wife, Clara, welcomed Brahms into their home. After Schumann suffered his mental collapse, the devoted friendship of Brahms enabled Clara to survive the tragedy of her husband's illness. Their friendship grew to love even though she was fourteen years Brahms' senior. When Schumann died in a Bonn asylum, Brahms was at Clara's side. After Schumann's death, however, the passion subsided into a lifelong friendship and Brahms never married Clara Schumann.

In his thirties, Brahms took several posts in various German towns, conducting and organizing choral groups and music societies. He spent much of his time in Vienna, finally settling there in 1878. His reputation as a composer grew to international proportions, and in 1877 Cambridge University offered him the degree of Doctor of Music. He declined, being reluctant to make the long journey, but he accepted a similar honor from the University of Breslau, acknowledging it by writing the celebrated *Academic Festival Overture,* which is based in large part on popular German student songs.

Brahms was not a controversial figure, as so many of his contemporaries were, and he had no personal enemies. Yet in his dealings with others his characteristic charm could give way to the most acerbic sarcasm. To one musician who was trying to maneuver Brahms into paying him a compliment, he said, "Yes, you have talent, but very little." But when the daughter of Johann Strauss presented him with her fan so that he might autograph it, he wrote the first few measures of Strauss' *Blue Danube Waltz* and signed it, "Not, alas, by Johannes Brahms."

Brahms remained a bachelor all his life, living simply and composing methodically. He enjoyed the respect and admiration of his peers, inspiring the noted conductor Hans von Bulow to coin his famous phrase, "the Three B's of Music," which placed Brahms as a descendant of the genius of Bach and Beethoven. After his death, his fame grew as many societies were founded to publish and perform his works. In the concert repertoire, Brahms' symphonies occupy a place second only to that of his acknowledged master, Beethoven.

His Work

Record 4/Side 2

With the exception of opera and the romantic tone poem, Brahms composed in all the familiar instrumental and choral idioms of the nineteenth century. He was a careful composer, closely supervising publication of his works.

Brahms did not attempt to compose symphonies until quite late in his life. His first symphony (C minor) took him twenty-one years to write and was not finished until 1876. Three others followed during the next nine years: No. 2 (in D major, 1877), No. 3 (in F major, 1883) and No. 4 (in E minor, 1884–1885). These works remain as some of the most frequently performed symphonies in modern times.

Brahms deliberately delayed symphonic composition until late in life, but his mastery of symphonic style was developed through the composition of serenades, concertos, and overtures. His first orchestral composition was a Serenade in D Major (1857–1858), followed by his first piano concerto (in D Minor, 1858). His other concertos include the renowned Violin Concerto in D Major (1878), the second piano concerto (in B-flat major, 1878–1881), and the Double Concerto in A Minor for violin and cello (1887). His overtures include the *Academic Festival Overture* (1880) and the *Tragic Overture* (1880–1881). Falling into none of these categories is the very popular and masterful *Variations on a Theme by Haydn* (1873).

Choral music, both sacred and secular, attracted Brahms throughout his career. His *Ein Deutsches Requiem* (*A German Requiem,* 1857–1868) ranks as one of the choral masterpieces of the nineteenth century, but it was by no means his only large-scale work for chorus and orchestra. Others include a cantata, rinaldo (1863–1868), *Schicksalslied* (*Song of Destiny,* 1871) and *Nänie* (1880–1881). Smaller works include a cappella choruses for various voice combinations, motets, canons, part songs, and psalm settings, many employing various types of instrumental accompaniment. One of the most popular of these works is the *Liebeslieder Walzer (Lovesong Waltzes,* 1868–1869) for piano, four hands, and either mixed solo quartet or chorus.

Brahms' contributions to chamber music repertory were the most substantial of all nineteenth-century composers after Beethoven. They include three trios for violin, cello, and piano, three piano quartets, a piano quintet, two cello sonatas, three violin sonatas, two clarinet sonatas, three string quartets, and two string quintets. Brahms' piano works reveal a mastery of contrapuntal texture and reflect his own conception of pianistic technique and virtuosity. Among them are variations on themes by Schumann, Paganini, and Handel, three sonatas, and a number of ballades, rhapsodies, fantasies, and intermezzi.

His Symphonic Style

Brahms retained the traditional four-movement structure of the late Classical symphony: fast–slow–scherzo-like–fast. In many ways his style is a direct outgrowth of the symphonic style of Beethoven: he continued to expand sonata-allegro form, enlarge the orchestra, and use dynamics and sonorities as structural elements.

Brahms' use of sonata-allegro form involves some changes, primarily in the treatment of the bridge section and the coda. The bridge becomes much more important; its material often sounds like a genuine theme, and it is often difficult to distinguish between the bridge and second theme on first hearing. The first and second themes are still contrasted in the Classical manner, but there is often no noticeable separation (such as a rest) between them.

The beginning of the recapitulation is sometimes obscure because Brahms tends to lead into it unobtrusively; it is frequently characterized by reorchestration of the exposition material, a device Beethoven used. The coda is extended, as in Beethoven's works, and used as a second development section. In contrast to Beethoven, however, Brahms often ends movements very quietly.

One of Brahms' favorite structural devices is to build new themes out of short motives taken from earlier material. This brings an additional element of unity to a movement, beyond that provided by sonata-allegro form. In his Second Symphony, he carries the unification process one step further; the first and last movements are linked by their common use of a basic three-note motive. This is an unusual procedure for a symphony, although Beethoven had done it with the ♪♪♪ ♩ motive in his Fifth Symphony. Brahms often incorporates the motive into themes in a subtle way, and it appears in many rhythmic variations.

Brahms uses a slightly larger orchestra than Beethoven, with still more important roles given to the lower strings, winds, and brasses. The violas and cellos are often assigned to lyrical themes, as in the second movement of Beethoven's Fifth Symphony. Brahms' orchestra includes four French horns, which are given important parts. Trombones continue to be part of the orchestra, and a tuba is added. The timpani are often treated independently, and even have solo passages. Although Brahms' orchestra is large by Classical standards, it is conservative in comparison with the huge ensembles used by more radical Romantic composers such as Hector Berlioz and Richard Wagner.

Symphony No. 2 in D Major

Exposition   The first theme is divided between two groups of instruments. It begins with the basic three-note motive in the cellos and basses, and continues with additional material, first in the horns and bassoons and then in the upper winds.

First Movement: *allegro non troppo (sonata-allegro form)*

Example 17.1

It is typical of Brahms to dispense a theme among several instruments or instrumental groups. Their instrumental colors become part of the theme, and thus the theme can be effectively varied by changing its instrumentation. After a descending arpeggio in the strings, isolated statements of the basic motive and an elongated version of it

Example 17.2

lead directly to the bridge. In the bridge the basic motive is incorporated into a melodic phrase, which is heard first in the violins. Later the time values of the motive are cut in half

Example 17.3

and a modulatory section leads to the second theme.

The second theme has two distinct components, arranged in ABA form. The A section is a long, lyrical melody, introduced by the lower strings. The B part of the theme begins with a loud, jagged, syncopated idea, followed by another rhythmic variation of the basic motive. After a lengthy section in which the accent is displaced, and the second beat sounds as if it is the first, the A theme is restated by the strings with a highly decorative flute accompaniment. A short closing section completes the exposition. Although Brahms intended the exposition to be repeated, most conductors today ignore his intentions.

Development   The development section opens with the basic three-note motive in the low strings and the remainder of the first theme in the horns, as was done in the exposition. The motive is answered by a new phrase from the oboe. This new idea is taken from the horn part, and it is the inversion (upside-down version) of the basic motive. Soon the original second half of the first theme, is brought into play, as it was in

the exposition, and builds to a fortissimo climax. The trombones inter-
rupt with overlapping statements of the basic motive, which is taken up
by other instruments. After another Beethovenian climax, the melodic
bridge material returns in the winds, and is answered by yet another
new idea from the oboe, again using the basic motive. For a period of
time, all these themes are interwoven. Then, with a change of dynamics
from fortissimo to piano, a false recapitulation begins (with theme 1 in
the horns and trumpets), followed immediately by the bridge material.
This builds to another climax, which is resolved by a descending scale
leading into the true recapitulation.

Recapitulation   The beginning of the recapitulation is not very obvious, since Brahms has disguised it by reorchestration. The first theme
returns in the oboes instead of the horns, accompanied by the bridge
material in the viola, and the bridge material is not used to make a
transition to the second theme. Rather, the second theme group is introduced by a series of descending arpeggios, a timpani roll, and a short
pause. The second theme is again in ABA form; the first A section has
flutes and clarinets added above it. The B section of the theme, with its
jagged, syncopated pattern, followed by a version of the basic motive, is
restated quite literally. Following the return of the A section, a series of
descending scales and a deceptive cadence lead to the coda.

Coda   The coda of this movement includes two new themes (built
from earlier material) and ends with what might be described as a disin-
tegration rather than a climax. The first new theme is a long solo for the
French horn (one of the favorite instruments of the Romantic period),
built from the inversion of the basic motive. Next, the violins introduce
another new theme that is related to theme 1, while the cellos and basses
play the basic motive. This builds to a climax and subsides to a quiet
version of the basic motive at double speed. A rapid crescendo leads to
the final climax, and then the movement disintegrates. After isolated
statements of thematic fragments and the basic motive, getting softer
and softer, the winds sustain a final chord.

Second Movement: *adagio non troppo*

This movement is not in any of the traditional forms; it has a very
definite structure of its own, combining features of several formal procedures, without strictly adhering to any of them. Basically, the movement consists of a number of themes, some of which are developed,
most of which are recapitulated. The multiplicity of themes and the
occurrence of a false recapitulation tend to blur the formal outlines of the
movement.
     The movement opens with theme A, a slow, lyric melody played by
the cellos. This theme has three sections, which are later treated
separately. After the initial statement, the flutes and violins restate the
first two sections, and the horn begins the B theme. This new motive is
treated contrapuntally, with entrances heard in the oboe, flute, and cello

parts. Then the section drives toward a cadence with imitative entries of a figure based on A_2. The following C section, with a prevailing off-beat triplet pattern, is remotely related to the first part of A; it ends abruptly, and the D section begins.

The rising triplet theme of the D section is introduced by the strings, and then taken up by the winds:

Example 17.4

This is the most steadily driving section of the movement, pushing its material into immediate development. The section builds to a loud climax, which is followed by several soft statements of the opening triplet figure of the D material. After another climactic build-up, and more isolated thematic fragments, a false recapitulation begins. What seems like a restatement of the first part of theme A is really only more development of it. The oboe states it first, and then the flute and horn try it in a different key; the triplet figure continues in the accompaniment.

The real recapitulation of A is carefully disguised; the theme is hidden in an ornamental triplet pattern in the violin part. Only the last section of the theme is presented in its original, undecorated form. The recapitulation of the B section has the theme in the flutes and horns, and is then somewhat altered in the lower strings; an ornamented version of A_2 follows. The C section never appears in the recapitulation. The D theme is stated once, after a stumbling beginning, and then disintegrates. The short coda rounds out the form by returning to the A material, with triplets in the horns and timpani. The movement ends quietly.

Third Movement: *allegretto grazioso—presto ma non assai*

With this movement Brahms has written a cross between the minuet and trio of the earlier Classical symphony and the Beethovenian scherzo that developed from it. This is a light, graceful movement, basically in triple meter, and very sectionalized. It is organized into a five-part alternating form ABACA, and the large sections are clearly distinguished by changes in meter and tempo. Several of the individual sections can also be divided into aba subsections. Almost all the musical material is derived from the opening theme.

Fourth Movement: *allegro con spirito* (sonata-allegro form)

One of the most confident and jubilant movements Brahms ever wrote, the final movement of the Second Symphony, bears almost no traces of the heavy resignation that marks most of his music. This movement even ends with a crashing, bravura finale in the best Beethovenian tradition.

The usual sonata-allegro form is followed in this movement, and the contrast between the two themes is particularly notable. The first, although quiet, is brisk and sparkling, while the second theme is a lyrical, expressive melody, played at a slower tempo. Though they sound quite different, both themes are based on the original three-note motive that opened the symphony. By relating the first and last movements of the symphony this way, Brahms provided an uncommon degree of unity to the entire work. This desire to make a four-movement structure into a single entity is typical of much Romantic music.

The statement of the first theme is followed by a very long bridge (in which some development takes place), leading to the second theme. This theme is accompanied by a figure derived from the basic motive. The closing section of the exposition is also very developmental, with many sudden changes of dynamics.

The development section opens with a restatement of theme 1, and most of the development is based on this theme. Several changes of tempo occur, and the section ends slowly and softly. The recapitulation begins with a sudden resumption of the original tempo and proceeds through abbreviated versions of the first theme and bridge. The second theme is louder and more emphatic than it had been originally. A long coda, containing more development of both themes, ends with a great crashing finale, climaxed by a stirring marchlike trumpet and trombone version of the once-lyrical second theme.

Other Romantic Symphonists

Anton Bruckner (1824–1896), an Austrian composer and organist, joined Brahms in the effort to retain Classical forms within an expanded harmonic and structural framework. Bruckner was a simple and very religious man, deeply involved with Catholic mysticism. Symphonic in technique, his three Masses are of sufficient caliber to rank Bruckner as the most important church composer of the late nineteenth century.

Bruckner's nine symphonies show his kinship to Classical tradition in their formal design, but their exceptional length and weighty orchestration mark them as Romantic works. Wagner was one of Bruckner's idols, and Bruckner's emphasis on chromatic tones and shifting tonalities shows Wagner's influence. Bruckner, in turn, influenced later composers in his native Vienna, with Mahler and Schoenberg being the most prominent examples.

The Austrian composer and conductor Gustav Mahler (1860–1911) wrote huge, complex works in a characteristically late Romantic idiom. His nine completed symphonies are in the traditional format with separate movements, although many programmatic and operatic elements can be observed. In four of the symphonies there are parts for voices as well as instruments. Mahler's symphonies encompass the gamut of emotions, from ecstasy to depression and horror. He tried to make each symphony a complete world in itself, with all types of themes and techniques, ranging from the semipopular to the most sophisticated.

These large-scale works are unified, to some extent, by the use of recurring themes and motives.

Mahler is also famous for his songs and song cycles; the *Kindertotenlieder* (*Songs on the Death of Children*, 1902) and *Das Lied von der Erde* (*The Song of the Earth*, 1908) are particularly outstanding. Themes from the songs are often quoted in the symphonic works. Mahler's last works—the Ninth Symphony, the unfinished Tenth, and *Das Lied von der Erde* —are in a simpler, more contrapuntal style than his earlier compositions. They also show a much weaker sense of tonality and thus point toward the important developments of Schoenberg and the Viennese school in the early twentieth century.

The Concerto

The concerto for solo instrument and orchestra presented the same basic problem to the Romantic composers as did the symphony: although the external form of the concerto continued to be popular, the internal logic was missing. Most Romantic concertos lacked the balance between soloist and orchestra that was typical of Mozart's concertos, or the dynamic give-and-take between them that characterized Beethoven's. The majority of Romantic concertos were either pleasant pieces or bombastic tirades, intended only to demonstrate the soloist's virtuosity.

Because the Romantic period was fascinated with exhibitions of virtuosity, composers wrote very difficult solo parts in their concertos. There was a steady growth of virtuoso technique, particularly on the piano and the violin, all through the nineteenth century. This virtuosity was begun by Beethoven, whose works were considerably more difficult to play than Mozart's. It was spurred on by the arrival of Nicolo Paganini (1782–1840) on the European concert stage in 1820; this phenomenal Italian violinist astounded and enchanted all who heard him. Unfortunately, many second-rate Romantic composers mistook virtuosity for content; thus many Romantic "exhibition pieces" exist which are nothing but empty, meaningless fireworks.

However, the master composers of the period used virtuosity as an adjunct to lyric and expressive writing. Robert Schumann, Johannes Brahms, and Felix Mendelssohn wrote outstanding concertos during the Romantic period. Schumann's Piano Concerto in A Minor (Op. 54) is a beautiful and original piece. His unalterably Romantic spirit led him to dissolve the Classical concept of the concerto as a struggle between two opposing forces. Schumann's piano and orchestra thus support and help each other in a free and poetic way.

The other two Romantic composers who wrote successful concertos (both for violin and orchestra) were closely allied with the Classical tradition. Brahms' concerto is a direct descendant of Beethoven's great violin concerto, while Mendelssohn's contains qualities derived from Mozart and Beethoven. Both Brahms and Mendelssohn had close emotional ties to Classical precepts, which enabled them to work within the traditional concerto framework, but to invest it with their own personal styles, most often Romantic in flavor.

Mendelssohn(1809–1847)

New York Public Library

Unlike most of the great composers of his generation, Felix Mendelssohn-Bartholdy not only achieved artistic success but also lived a life of relative ease and financial security. Born into a wealthy and cultured Jewish family—his father was a banker, his grandfather a distinguished philosopher—he and his brother and two sisters were brought up as Christians. His precocious talent was quickly recognized, and his mother began teaching him piano when he was very young. After the family moved to Berlin from Hamburg in 1812, his formal training was entrusted to Carl Zelter, an eminent composer, teacher, and head of the famous *Singakademie*.

Mendelssohn's parents both loved music, and chamber ensembles frequently performed in their home. The young boy's earliest compositions were played by these instrumentalists, and by 1821 he had composed trios, quartets, sonatas, and operettas. His debut as a concert pianist had been made even earlier—in 1818—and he mastered both violin and viola while still in his teens. The first striking demonstration of his genius as a composer was the overture to Shakespeare's *A Midsummer Night's Dream*, written in 1826 when he was seventeen. Three years later he made his mark as a conductor when he revived J. S. Bach's *St. Matthew Passion*. This performance of the Passion, a great triumph for Mendelssohn, was the first given since Bach's death almost eighty years earlier and began a widescale revival of Bach's music.

Early in the 1830s, Mendelssohn traveled extensively throughout Europe. He conducted his concert overture *Fingal's Cave (The Hebrides)* in London and met Hector Berlioz in Italy. Returning to Berlin in 1833, Mendelssohn decided to seek a permanent post and applied for the then vacant directorship of the *Singakademie*. He was turned down—one of his few failures—but in the same year he was asked to become town musical director at Düsseldorf. Two years later, in 1835, he accepted an offer to become conductor of the famous *Gewandhaus* Orchestra in Leipzig.

In 1837 Mendelssohn married Cécile Jeanrenaud, the daughter of a French Protestant clergyman. In 1841 they moved to Berlin where, at the request of Kaiser Freidrich Wilhelm IV, Mendelssohn took charge of the music division of the newly established Academy of Arts. The position did not require close supervision and he was able to develop his plans for a conservatory at Leipzig. In 1843 the conservatory opened with a distinguished faculty in residence, and several years later Mendelssohn moved his family back to Leipzig.

Though his health began to deteriorate after 1846, Mendelssohn continued to work heavily. The death of his elder sister, to whom he was deeply attached, was a major tragedy, and he never recovered from the shock. Falling into a severe depression, he soon became bedridden and died in Leipzig at the age of thirty-eight.

His Work

Despite his relatively short life, Mendelssohn produced many works, ranging from large-scale symphonies and oratorios to intimate chamber works and leider. His first published symphony (in C Minor, 1824) was actually the thirteenth he had written. Of the four symphonies that still remain, one–apparently influenced by Beethoven's Ninth–is for chorus and orchestra, entitled *Lobgesang* (*Hymn of Praise*, 1840). The others are descriptive: No. 3 (*Scottish*, 1830–1842), No. 4 (*Italian*, 1833), and No. 5 (*Reformation*, 1830–1842.) His concert overtures also reveal a programmatic inspiration; they include *A Midsummer Night's Dream* (1826), *Calm Sea and Prosperous Voyage* (1830–1832), and the overture to Victor Hugo's play *Ruy Blas* (1839).

Along with these major orchestral works, Mendelssohn composed many chamber pieces, including six string quartets, two piano quartets, four violin sonatas, two cello sonatas, and an octet for strings (Op. 20, 1825) the latter being one of his most original and delightful works.

Mendelssohn's long-standing appreciation of Bach's music shows up in his several collections of preludes and fugues for piano. The bulk of his piano music, however, consists of short character pieces in a highly Romantic vein. The most popular of these are the eight collections of *Songs Without Words*, published between 1829 and 1845. His finest large-scale work for piano is the *Variations Sérieuses* (Op. 54, 1841).

Mendelssohn's virtuosity as a pianist naturally affected his concertos and other lengthy works for piano and orchestra. Aside from two piano concertos (No. 1, 1831; No. 2, 1837), he composed a *Capriccio Brillante* (1832) and a *Rondo Brillante* (1834), both showpieces of decidedly lesser significance. One of his greatest concertos, however, is the Violin Concerto in E Minor (Op. 64, 1844).

Though he composed a great many church choruses and an equally substantial number of art songs, Mendelssohn's reputation as a vocal composer rests on his two oratorios, *St. Paul* (1836) and *Elijah* (1846). In them, Mendelssohn incorporated elements of Bach's Passion style and Handelian oratorio form. They are generally considered the most successful nineteenth-century works of their kind.

Many of Mendelssohn's later works, composed in the 1840s, appear to be somewhat uninspired and lacking in the imaginative, original qualities so evident in his early overtures. In one work, however, he fully recaptured the magical verve of the *Midsummer Night's Dream* overture: The incidental music he wrote for the same play in 1842, including the famous "Wedding March," stands as a fitting companion to his youthful masterpiece.

Violin Concerto in E Minor (Op. 64)

Record 5/Side 1

Mendelssohn's violin concerto retains the three-movement structure of the Classical concerto, with two minor deviations: there is no definite break between the first and second movements, and the last allegro has a short introductory allegretto non troppo section. The work is scored for solo violin and an orchestra composed of two each of flutes, oboes, clarinets, bassoons, horns, trumpets, and timpani, and the usual string sections.

The solo part is quite difficult and demanding, especially when compared to the violin part of Mozart's Violin Concerto in A Major. The part frequently goes very high (where it is especially difficult to play in tune) and requires outstanding technique.

First Movement: *allegro molto appassionato* (sonata-allegro form)

Exposition   This movement lacks the double exposition common to most concertos. Instead, the solo violin enters at the beginning, and makes the first statement of theme 1. The opening measures of the theme contain two contrasting ideas, the first built of leaps from one chord tone to the next and the second a smooth descending figure:

Example 17.5

These two fragments are developed separately later in the movement.

A series of short virtuoso passages for the soloist, some of them unaccompanied, leads to the orchestral statement of theme 1, and then to the bridge. The bridge material—an angular and chromatic descending line—is stated first by the orchestral violins and oboes, and then, an octave higher, by the soloist. The solo part evolves into a long virtuoso passage of arpeggios, scales, and double stops, which modulates to prepare the entry of the second theme in G major (the relative major of E minor).

The orchestration is reduced for the introduction of the second theme, which is played by clarinets and flutes, while the solo violin sustains a long, low pedal point. Then the roles are reversed—the violin takes the melody and the winds accompany the violin. The violin extends the theme into a long soaring melody, ending on a very high note.

Development   In the development section the first theme and the bridge material are exploited fully, while the second theme is completely ignored. The section opens with the soloist's statement of the first theme in B major, and the orchestra then elaborates, first on the second fragment of it, then on the first. Meanwhile the solo violin performs acrobatics. The bridge material is reintroduced and stated at several different pitch levels, and the ensemble then returns to its previous occupation—the violin performs technical stunts, accompanied by development of the first fragment of theme 1. Mendelssohn ends this section with a crashing orchestral chord, and when the dust settles, the soloist is discovered already in the midst of the cadenza.

The cadenza for this movement, written out by Mendelssohn, forms an integral part of the work. It overlaps into the surrounding orchestral parts—an example of the Romantic urge to obliterate the formal distinction between sections. The violinist plays a series of arpeggios, ending with a long one that rises to a high note; this happens three times, with the last note higher each time. After a series of trills on fragments that recall theme 1, the violin proceeds to a long series of fast arpeggios, becoming softer and softer. Finally, as the soloist continued this pattern, the orchestra comes in quietly with the recapitulation of the first theme played by the flute, oboe, and first violins.

Recapitulation   The orchestra performs the entire recapitulation of the first theme while the violinist continues his cadenzalike arpeggios. He stops when the bridge material is introduced by the orchestra, and enters again with a descending passage that modulates from E minor to E major. The second theme is recapitulated in this key, again with a reduced orchestration. The section ends with the violin's extension of theme 2 into a long lyric melody.

Coda   This movement has an extensive coda, containing more development of the first theme, and then a Beethovenian rush to the end, combining bridge material and fragments of the first theme. Most of this development is handled by the orchestra, while the soloist continues to weave his virtuosic technical acrobatics around the thematic material. The movement ends with a loud orchestral cadence; with almost no break, a long note in the bassoon links the first and second movements.

Second Movement: *andante*

The slow movement is in alternating form, ABA, with a coda; its key, C major, is somewhat unusual, since it is neither the relative major nor the dominant of E minor, the principal key of the concerto. The bassoon link from the first movement is expanded into a brief orchestral introduction, but the movement proper begins with the entrance of the solo violin.

The violin is totally dominant in the A section, singing a long, sustained melody in a very high range. The accompaniment is provided by the strings, with occasional punctuation by the winds. The section ends with a cadential closing trill, and the brasses enter to herald the beginning of the B section.

Compared to the A section, the B section of this movement is quite long. It modulates into several keys, and develops some of its material. It opens with a theme stated by the orchestral violins, cellos, and oboes. The second violins and violas play an accompaniment figure that alternates rapidly between two notes:

Example 17.6

After this orchestral statement of the theme, the soloist enters and plays both the theme and the accompaniment simultaneously. Soon the orchestra takes over the accompaniment figure, and the soloist plays the theme in octaves. Eventually the thematic material is reduced to short fragments, and a descending chromatic solo passage leads to the return of the A section.

The violin repeats its arching melody, but with a different background. After the climax of the melody, the violin drops down to its low register, and the accompaniment reverts to what it had been in the first A section. This leads directly into the coda, which consists of a series of sequential passages by the solo violin, accompanied only by winds, almost to the cadence.

Third Movement: *allegretto non troppo—allegro molto vivace* (introduction and sonata-allegro form)

Introduction   The use of a short, slow section to introduce a movement in sonata form was a frequent occurrence in the Classical period, and Mendelssohn uses it in this concerto. The allegretto non troppo section, for solo violin and strings, also serves the purpose of modulating from the C major cadence of the second movement to the key of E major.

Exposition   The beginning of the allegro molto vivace section also has an introductory function. The brasses, bassoons, and timpani make emphatic rhythmic statements, which are answered by the soloist with fast-rising arpeggios. Then the violinist quietly introduces the first theme, a fast, scherzo-like motive with a very light accompaniment.

Example 17.7

The solo part becomes very florid as the orchestra takes the theme and begins to fragment it; the bridge material is derived directly from the material of theme 1. Finally a long, rising scale by the solo violin introduces the second theme.

This second theme has two distinct halves, clearly separated by a sharp change in dynamics (a Beethovenian technique). The first phrase is a bouncy, somewhat jerky figure, played loudly (ff); the second phrase is piano and is almost identical with theme 1.

Example 17.8

This dynamic contrast is emphasized by the orchestration: the entire orchestra states the first half of the theme, but only the first violin section answers with the second half. After the solo violin takes its turn at the second theme, a short closing section leads to the development section.

Development   The development section begins with orchestral exploitation of the first half of the second theme, modulating through several keys while the soloist embellishes it with rapid scales and arpeggios. Soon the violin introduces theme 1, in its entirety—but it is a false recapitulation, for the theme is in the key of G major. The orchestra elaborates on this theme, and the violin joins in, gradually developing the idea into cadenza-like material, although the accompaniment never drops out. A long, scale passage by the soloist introduces the recapitulation.

Recapitulation The recapitulation of this movement is somewhat abbreviated. It moves quickly from the first theme to the second, with its alternation of orchestra and soloist and its sharp dynamic contrasts. A closing section elaborates on the material of the first half of the second theme, while the violinist plays excited arpeggios and chords. A big orchestral climax leads to the coda, beginning with a series of trills by the solo violin. The coda builds in intensity to a grand conclusion. This is really an ending of the finale type, even though there is no increase of tempo.

Mendelssohn's violin concerto has become one of the four or five most popular works for the instrument, taking its place in the repertoire alongside those of Mozart, Beethoven, Brahms, and Tchaikovsky.

Chamber Music

The outstanding composers of chamber music during the Romantic period were, again, the three composers with the closest ties to the Classical spirit: Schubert, Mendelssohn, and Brahms.

Although most of the chamber music of the period followed the Classical outlines laid down by Mozart, Haydn, and Beethoven, it was also colored by the new Romantic interest in sonority. Romantic composers formed new, unusual groupings, many of which combined instruments from two different families.

Some chamber music of the Romantic era approached symphonic proportions. The number of players was still small, but the composer treated the ensemble more like a small orchestra than a chamber group. There was an increase in the number of works written for five to eight performers, and a corresponding decrease in the number of quartets composed. Many chamber works included the favorite Romantic instrument, the piano. Its addition made possible an expansion of sonority without a major increase in the number of performers.

Chamber Music of Schubert and Mendelssohn

Franz Schubert wrote a considerable amount of chamber music, much of it for the enjoyment of his friends rather than for the public. His chamber music style, like his symphonic style, displays a Romantic gift for lyric melody and a love of interesting patches of color and harmony; nevertheless, he managed to contain his Romantic leanings within the traditional forms.

The so-called *Trout Quintet* (Op. 114) contains one movement of variations on Schubert's *Die Forelle*. The quintet is scored for the rather unusual combination of piano, violin, viola, cello, and double bass (one of the very few chamber works that includes the double bass). The whole quintet has a light flavor, in marked contrast to the serious tone of the string quartet that contains variations on his song, *Der Tod und das Mädchen (Death and the Maiden)*.

Schubert's other outstanding chamber works include a magnificent string quintet (for the usual string quartet plus one additional cello), and an octet that mixes strings and winds (string quartet, double bass, clarinet, horns, and bassoon).

Felix Mendelssohn's chamber music is not as interesting as his symphonic writing. His themes are lyrical, sometimes even elegant, but his development of them is often merely repetitious. The majority of his works are for string ensembles without piano; his craftsmanship is particularly evident in his Octet for Strings.

Chamber Music of Brahms

In terms of both quality and quantity, Brahms was the greatest chamber music composer of the Romantic era—a worthy successor to Beethoven in every respect. His innate understanding of Classical forms enabled him to use them freely, without lapsing into the rhapsodic and somewhat unorganized idiom characteristic of so many Romantic composers.

Brahms was a careful and disciplined composer, and frequently revised his earlier works. He was particularly fascinated with instrumental colors, and experimented to find the precise combination to suit each of his works. For example, his Piano Quintet in F Minor (Op. 34A) was originally composed for string quintet (with two cellos); next he rearranged it for two pianos, and finally satisfied himself with the combination of the two types of sounds in the piano quintet version.

Many of Brahms' chamber works employ unusual combinations of instruments. In his Trio in E-flat (Op. 40), he combines piano, violin, and waldhorn (the valveless predecessor of the French horn); this produces a very sonorous, Romantic sound, but poses a difficult problem for the composer. A theme that sounds natural on one kind of instrument (a violin, for example) often sounds contrived and unnatural on another (like a horn, or a piano). Brahms was able to create themes that suited all three of the different families represented in this delightful trio. The same problem was also faced and solved in his beautiful Clarinet Quintet (Op. 115).

Sextet in B-Flat Major (Op. 18)

This work, the first of two by Brahms for the combination of two violins, two violas, and two cellos, is a marvelous union of Romantic lyricism with Classical poise and balance. The instrumentation is rich and sonorous and exemplifies Brahms' interest in the lyric capabilities of the lower strings. The themes are as beautiful as any he ever wrote, and the formal structure is impeccable.

The four movements are in the traditional forms; the first allegro ma non troppo is in sonata-allegro form; the second movement, andante, ma moderato, is a set of variations on an original theme strongly suggestive of Hungarian gypsy music; the third is a buoyant Beethovenian scherzo and trio; and the final movement is a large rondo (alternating form: ABACA coda).

Many aspects of Brahms' symphonic style also appear in this sextet. In fact, his chamber works approach symphonic conception and proportions. In the first movement, the bridge and coda sections are very extensive. The variations of the second movement are both melodic and harmonic—in some sections the melody is not present in any form, but the underlying harmonic structure remains intact.

Perhaps the most significant aspect of this sextet is how it uses the colors available from the six stringed instruments. Brahms beautifully exploits the almost infinite number of groupings of the six instruments. Frequently, he has two or more instruments double the same part, in unison or in octaves, to enrich the sound.

A few examples of the groupings Brahms selected illustrate his sensitivity to color. The first movement opens with three instruments: one viola and both cellos. The melody is in the first cello part, while the normally higher viola plays a lower accompanying part. Since one cello is playing high in its range, the other low, the two sound like two completely different instruments. The theme is restated by a violin and viola in octaves, while the other violin and one of the cellos play the accompaniment figure in octaves, and the second cello provides the bass.

In other memorable combinations, some instruments play pizzicato while others continue to use their bows. The unearthly sound of the fifth variation in the second movement, where only the four highest instruments are playing, is followed by the cello duet in the next section. Brahms also makes use of his favorite trick of dividing a theme between two different groups of instruments; for example, in the last return of the A section of the rondo, three high and three low instruments play alternate measures of the theme.

Summary

A stream of Classical thought continued to flow through the Romantic period. Although some Romantic composers discarded the Classical forms, another group cultivated and expanded them in both orchestral and chamber music settings. The leading composers in this group were Franz Schubert, Felix Mendelssohn, and Johannes Brahms.

Nearly all of the early Romantic composers were influenced by Beethoven, either by his use of orchestra or by his expansion of form. In his four symphonies, Brahms retained the traditional four-movement structure of the late Classical symphony: fast–slow–scherzo-like–fast. He continued to expand sonata-allegro form, to enlarge the orchestra, and define structures by means of dynamics and sonorities.

Because Romantic audiences were fascinated by exhibitions of virtuosity, composers wrote difficult solo parts for their concertos. Many second-rate composers of the period substituted virtuosity for content and wrote meaningless "exhibition pieces." Other composers, however, used virtuosity as an adjunct to lyric and expressive writing.

Brahms and Mendelssohn each wrote a concerto for violin and orchestra. Brahms' descends directly from Beethoven, while Mendelssohn's contains qualities derived from both Mozart and Beethoven. Both composers worked within the traditional concerto framework, but filled it with their own personal styles, which were often quite romantic in conception.

Although most of the chamber music of the Romantic period followed the outlines laid down by Mozart, Haydn, and Beethoven, it was also colored by the Romantic interest in sonority. In chamber music, romantic composers formed new and unusual groupings, many of which combined instruments from two different families, as in the case of Schubert's octet for strings and winds.

chapter 18

While Brahms and other Romantic composers of a traditional bent were expanding and enriching the methods and forms established earlier, many of his contemporaries sought different methods of musical organization. New modes of expression were needed for their artistic purposes, particularly in relation to the creation of pieces of major proportions. These composers derived much of their inspi-

Program Music

ration from nonmusical idioms. The poem, a visual object, natural phenomena, provided not only the general suggestive impulses but, to varying extents, were considered the dominating ideas of particular pieces of music, determining shape and form. The use of the nonmusical idea as the basis of the musical structure thus became a primary force in the development of romantic music. The technique allowed for considerable variation in the degree of dependence on the external idea: if it was used only in a general way, the music is *descriptive* of the idea. But often the relationship was much more direct: the composer had a detailed plan, frequently a *story*, in mind, and the music was correlated with it as closely as possible. Such a work is known as *programmatic*, or *program, music.*

Neither the principle nor the techniques of program and descriptive music were invented during the Romantic period. In fact, they extend far back into the music of the Medieval and Renaissance eras. We have already mentioned *Le Chant des Oiseaux* by Clément Jannequin (ca. 1485–ca. 1560) in which the singers imitate bird calls. In the Baroque period, Antonio Vivaldi (1653–1713) depicted the scenes and activities of each season of the year in his violin concerto *The Four Seasons.*

267

Johann Sebastian Bach contributed to the genre of program music with his *Capriccio on the Departure of a Beloved Brother* (1704), a set of descriptive movements for solo harpsichord. Beethoven's Sixth Symphony, the *Pastoral Symphony*, has descriptive titles attached to each of the five movements. They depict country scenes: "Merrymaking of the Peasants," "Storm," "Thankful Feelings after the Storm," and so forth. Certain natural effects, like bird calls and thunderstorms, are portrayed very clearly.

With all these early examples of programmatic techniques, why is the Romantic period always singled out as the age of program music? There is a very good reason: Romantic composers substituted the device of the nonmusical program for formal musical organization. The earlier composers, by contrast, had used programmatic technique in conjunction with their usual formal patterns. Beethoven's Sixth Symphony is essentially Classical in outline, with sonata-allegro movements, a scherzo— all the usual forms. The programmatic elements are subordinate to these forms. In fact, Beethoven warned that the descriptive titles were not to be taken too literally; the music was to be an "expression of feeling rather than a depiction of events."

Some Romantic composers, particularly those more oriented toward Classical forms, continued to use the techniques of program music in this subordinate way. Mendelssohn is a prime example; several of his symphonies are descriptive, but they are still coherently constructed along Classical lines. His *Italian Symphony* (1833) and *Scotch Symphony* (1842) are generalized landscape paintings. The former includes images of the sunny, vibrant south, with peasant dances and chanting pilgrims; the latter depicts the gray and somber north, using the heroic ballads of the area and the swirl of bagpipes. Here the relation of music to the extramusical element is general.

Berlioz (1803–1869)

The Bettmann Archive

The more radical Romantic composers used programmatic techniques in a very direct and dramatic way. Among the most radical was Hector Berlioz, whose compositions centered on the grand forms of opera, oratorio, the symphony, and the Mass. For several of his larger works Berlioz supplied detailed programs. His *Symphonie Fantastique* (1830) is a powerful musical drama in five movements, based on the following program:

Introduction

A young musician of extraordinary sensibility and abundant imagination, in the depths of despair because of hopeless love, has poisoned himself with opium. The drug is too feeble to kill him but plunges him into a heavy sleep accompanied by weird visions. His sensations, emotions, and memories, as they pass through his affected mind, are transformed into musical images and ideas. The

Record 5/Side 2

beloved one herself becomes to him a melody, a recurrent theme (idée fixe) which haunts him continually.

I. Reveries. Passions

First he remembers that weariness of the soul, that indefinable longing, that somber melancholia, and those objectless joys which he experienced before meeting his beloved. Then, the volcanic love with which she at once inspired him, his delirious suffering, his return to tenderness, his religious consolations.

II. A Ball

At a ball, in the midst of a noisy, brilliant fête, he finds his beloved again.

III. In the country

On a summer evening in the country, he hears two herders calling each other with their shepherd melodies. The pastoral duet in such surroundings, the gentle rustle of the trees softly swayed by the wind, some reasons for hope which had come to his knowledge recently — all unite to fill his heart with a rare tranquility and lend brighter colors to his fancies. But his beloved appears anew, spasms contract his heart, and he is filled with dark premonition. What if she proved faithless? Only one of the shepherds resumes his rustic tune. The sun sets. Far away there is rumbling thunder — solitude — silence.

IV. March to the Scaffold

He dreams he has killed his loved one, that he is condemned to death and led to his execution. A march, now gloomy and ferocious, now solemn and brilliant, accompanies the procession. Noisy outbursts are followed without pause by the heavy sound of measured footsteps. Finally, like a last thought of love, the idée fixe *appears for a moment, to be cut off by the fall of the axe.*

V. Dream of a Witches' Sabbath

He sees himself at a Witches' Sabbath surrounded by a fearful crowd of specters, sorcerers, and monsters of every kind, united for his burial. Unearthly sounds, groans, shrieks of laughter, distant cries, to which others seem to respond! The melody of his beloved is heard, but it has lost its character of nobility and reserve. Instead, it is now an ignoble dance tune, trivial and grotesque. It is she who comes to the Sabbath! A shout of joy greets her arrival. She joins the diabolical orgy. The funeral knell, burlesque of the Dies Irae. Dance of the Witches. The dance and the Dies Irae combined.*

Berlioz felt that the audience did not have to be aware of the program; he intended the musical work to be self-sufficient. However, the program does serve to introduce the music, and explains the situation that inspired each movement.

The *Symphonie Fantastique* was revolutionary in its use of a single motive to link all the movements; this so-called *idée fixe* represents the hero's image of his beloved and recurs in various transformations throughout the piece. The work's real unity, however, comes from the steady development of the dramatic idea through all five movements rather than from any carefully worked out details of musical construction.

*Translation from Hector Berlioz, *Symphonie Fantastique* (New York: Edition Eulenburg, Inc.), p. iii.

Berlioz was a master of orchestration. He experimented extensively with individual instruments and with their combinations, and in 1844 he wrote his treatise, the first comprehensive text on the subject. He used a huge orchestra, and devised many unusual combinations of instruments. His rich romantic imagination and inventiveness are evident in practically every measure of the *Symphonie Fantastique* and greatly influenced later composers such as Debussy and Stravinsky.

Liszt (1811–1886)

The Bettmann Archive

Franz Liszt was another important composer of Romantic program music. He considered the music and its program as parallel works of art, evoking the same feelings in different media.

Next to his good friend and admirer, Hector Berlioz, Liszt stands as the supreme romantic of the nineteenth century. As a virtuoso pianist, a renowned lover, and a friend and supporter of almost all the great composers of his time, Liszt embodied what subsequent generations have come to consider as the Romantic ideal.

Born in Hungary, the son of a steward of the Esterhazy family, he began his instruction on the piano at the age of six. Following a number of successful concert appearances as a boy, a group of Hungarian nobles offered an annual stipend over a six-year period to further his musical training. In 1821 his family moved to Vienna, where Liszt took lessons from the famous teacher Carl Czerny and studied theory with Antonio Salieri. His public appearances were so successful that his father took him to Paris. There he continued to develop his piano technique on his own, studied composition under Anton Reicha, and began a series of extended concert tours. After the death of his father in 1827, Liszt settled permanently in Paris. In 1831, after attending a recital by the virtuoso Italian violinist Nicolo Paganini, he determined to adapt Paganini's virtuosic techniques to the piano. From Paganini, more than anyone else, he derived his style of showmanship.

Though flamboyant in personality and performance, his mannerisms never outshone his musicianship. As a pianist he held firmly to the idea that the interpreter's duty was to reveal the innermost intention of the composer, and his understanding of Beethoven's piano works was no less intimate than it was of Chopin's compositions.

During the 1830s he carried on a love affair with the Countess Marie d'Agoult and settled with her in Switzerland. (One of the three children born to them, Cosima, later married Richard Wagner.) In 1848 he found a firm position, as court music director at Weimar, from which to promote the "new music" of such composers as Berlioz and Wagner. At Weimar he started his second great love affair, with the Princess Carolyne von Sayn-Wittgenstein, who was also his secretary. In 1859, feeling a call to the priesthood, he settled in Rome and took minor orders, and in 1866 Pope Pius IX conferred on him the title of Abbé. After 1870 he divided his time between Rome, Weimar, and Budapest, surrounded always by a throng of friends, students, and admirers. He died in Bayreuth during the Wagner festival of 1886.

His Work

As an orchestral composer Liszt's greatest achievement was his development of a type of program music called the symphonic *tone poem*. He composed fourteen of them, mostly at Weimar. They include *Tasso* (first version, 1849; revised version, 1854), *Les Préludes* (1854), *Orpheus* (1854), *Mazeppa* (1854), and *Hamlet* (1858). Only one, *Les Préludes*, remains in the standard concert repertory today.

The tone poems demonstrate Liszt's intense preoccupation with developing new harmonic idioms. His monumental *Faust Symphony* (1857), based on Goethe's epic work, in many ways catalogues Liszt's experiments in building new harmonic structures and melodic progressions.

Liszt's other important works for orchestra include a symphony based on Dante's *Divina Commedia* (1867) and the very popular *Mephisto Waltzes* (the first in 1860, the second in 1880). For piano and orchestra Liszt wrote two concertos (No. 1 in 1849, revised 1853; No. 2 in 1848, revised 1856–1861) and a paraphrase on the chant *Dies Irae*, *Totentanz* (Dance of Death, 1849; revised 1853–1859).

The vocal works include three large-scale Masses for chorus and orchestra, a Requiem, a number of psalm settings, and three oratorios, *The Legend of St. Elisabeth*, *Christus*, and *Stanislaus*.

Liszt's piano music includes an enormous variety of forms and styles: transcriptions of orchestral works, variations on well-known symphonic and operatic themes, brilliant showpieces, technical studies, and impressionistic tone poems. Liszt published a large number of technical studies, some of which are intended for concert performance and others that are designed as pedagogical exercises. Among these are three *Études de Concert* (1848), six studies (1851) transcribed from Paganini's solo violin caprices including *La Campanella*, and twelve *Études d'Exécution Transcendante* (1851), including *Mazeppa*.

Some of Liszt's finest and most advanced compositions are found in his collections of tone poems for piano: three books of the *Album d'un Voyageur* (1835–1836), *Consolations* (1849–1850), *Harmonies Poétiques et Religieuses* (1845–1852), and three series of *Années de Pèlerinage* (compiled between 1848 and 1877). One of his most significant large-scale piano works is the one-movement *Sonata in B Minor* (1853), in which four themes are worked out and transformed in a free, rhapsodic manner.

In addition to his original compositions, Liszt transcribed a large number of orchestral and operatic works for piano and performed his transcriptions on his concert tours. In an age that lacked radio, television, and recording mechanisms, Liszt's concerts brought otherwise unavailable music to large segments of the public. His transcriptions included selections from all of Wagner's major operas, Weber's *Der Freischutz*, Verdi's *Rigoletto* and *Aida*, complete versions of all of

Beethoven's symphonies, Berlioz's *Symphonie Fantastique* and *Harold in Italy*, overtures by Weber, Rossini, and Berlioz, and his own orchestral tone poems. In converting orchestral works to the piano Liszt not only fulfilled an educational service to his audiences but also greatly widened his own perception of the full potential of the instrument. There is no doubt that the experience gained in writing these transcriptions enabled him to make significant advances in piano technique and composition.

Liszt called many of his orchestral works symphonic poems rather than symphonies. Also called tone poems, they are single-movement works, relatively short, and very free in form. They have descriptive titles, although they derive their basic coherence from purely musical elements. In this sense Liszt's concept of program music is closer to Beethoven's than to Berlioz's. Liszt often builds a piece by deriving the melodies and even the accompaniment figures from a very simple motive. This is genuine symphonic development, although accomplished outside the context of the Classical forms.

Les Préludes

Record 5/Side 2

The best known of Liszt's symphonic poems, *Les Préludes* (1854), is actually not a descriptive or programmatic piece at all. Liszt originally wrote it as the orchestral overture to a choral work but later decided to publish it separately. Looking for a suitable program, he was struck by the parallel construction of one of Alphonse de Lamartine's *Meditations Poétiques*. He translated it freely and adopted it as the program for his composition.

PRÉLUDES

What is our life but a series of Preludes to that unknown song, the first solemn note of which is sounded by Death? The enchanted dawn of every existence is heralded by Love, yet in whose destiny are not the first throbs of happiness interrupted by storms whose violent blasts dissipate his fond illusions, consuming his altar with fatal fire? And where is to be found the cruelly bruised soul, that having become the sport of one of these tempests does not seek oblivion in the sweet quiet of rural life? Nevertheless, man seldom resigns himself to the beneficent calm which at first chained him to Nature's bosom. No sooner does the trumpet sound the alarm, than he runs to the post of danger, be the war what it may that summons him to its ranks. For there he will find again in the struggle complete self-realization and the full possession of his forces.

Liszt composed *Les Préludes* for a full, Romantic orchestra—flutes, oboes, clarinets, bassoons, four horns, trumpets, trombones, tuba, timpani (three drums), harp, and strings. For the finale (the section analogous to the call to battle), a side drum, cymbals, and a bass drum are added. The manner in which the orchestra is used is typically Romantic: the winds are often used as solo instruments; the French horn, a favorite Romantic instrument, is particularly prominent; fluctuations in tempo and dynamics occur frequently.

Example 18.1

The stages of life mentioned in the poem correspond to the sections of Liszt's piece. It opens with a brief introduction, built on a three-note motive that will later be used in the construction of most of the themes

Example 18.2

in the composition. The opening is slow and tentative. The motive gradually expands by enlarging its second interval

Example 18.3

and eventually leads to the first theme. It is an expansive and majestic melody, vaguely related to the opening motive. The accompanying figure includes a direct statement of the motive.

Example 18.4

The next section, parallel to the mention of love in the poem, contains two themes. The first

is introduced by the low strings and then is treated as a horn solo in another key. The opening motive is quite prominent in this theme. The second theme (played by the four horns, and the violas divided into four sections) has the notes of the motive spaced out, with other material in between.

Example 18.5

x indicates the notes of the basic motive.

Eventually these two themes are used simultaneously.

In the section of the piece corresponding to the storm, rushing chromatic patterns are interlaced with brief statements of the basic motive. Frequent changes of tempo increase the sense of agitation. As the storm subsides, the first love theme returns and leads to a section corresponding to the "sweet calm of rural life." The beginning of this lovely section, with its pastoral theme,

Example 18.6

features the woodwinds. Soon the strings join in and the second love theme is added to the pastoral tune.

A gradual increase in tempo, dynamics, and intensity leads to the climactic finale, the call to battle (a procedure similar to that used by Beethoven at the end of the last movement of his Fifth Symphony). The final section opens with a martial transformation of the first love theme sounded by the horns and trumpets.

Example 18.7

Figure 18.3   Franz Liszt at the piano. Among his listening friends are some of the great artistic figures of the nineteenth century: (l. to r.) Musset, Victor Hugo, George Sand, Berlioz, Rossini, and Countess D'Agoult.

A bridge leads to a marchlike variation of the second love theme, with drums and cymbals added to the rest of the orchestra. Eventually the section returns to the majestic first theme, accompanied by the basic motive, and the piece comes to a vigorous conclusion.

Although some modern listeners find *Les Préludes* excessively melodramatic, Liszt's contemporaries had no such feeling. His symphonic poems, well designed and effectively scored, had considerable influence on the subsequent course of orchestral music.

Descriptive music, of the general type initiated by Liszt, became popular throughout Europe. Many pieces were intended to convey impressions of particular places; an outstanding example is the cycle of six symphonic poems entitled *Ma Vlast (My Fatherland,* 1874–1879) by the Czech composer Bedřich Smetana (1824–1884). The best known of these six is *Vltava (The Moldau).*

A different approach to descriptive music in found in *Pictures at an Exhibition* (1874) by the Russian composer Modest Moussorgsky (1839–1881). This set of ten descriptive piano pieces and several interludes is based on the works of a painter and sculptor friend of the composer. The images portrayed include a dwarf, a medieval castle, a Polish oxcart, and the Great Gates of Kiev in Russia. Several orchestral arrangements of these pieces have been made, the best known of which is by the French composer Maurice Ravel.

Strauss (1864–1949)

The Bettmann Archive

Although the late Romantic composer Richard Strauss lived nearly half way through the twentieth century, the bulk of his tone poems were written in the nineteenth century. In these works the influences of both the detailed and realistic descriptions of Berlioz, as well as the less specific descriptions of Liszt, are felt. Thus, *Tod und Verklärung (Death and Transfiguration,* 1889) and *Also sprach Zarathustra (Thus Spake Zarathustra,* 1896) have general, philosophical programs, while the comic *Till Eulenspiegels lustige Streiche (Till Eulenspiegel's Merry Pranks,* 1895) and *Don Quixote* (1897) have more specific programs.

Strauss was a skilled composer, a virtuoso at writing effectively for large orchestra. Although his thematic inventions were rarely profound, they were always fresh and uninhibited. A practical musician, Strauss realized that he was not innovative enough to follow in Liszt's steps, with essentially programless tone poems. He, therefore, chose to continue the detailed realism of Berlioz, but incorporated some of the supreme musicianship that marks Liszt's works.

A knowledge of the program is essential to the understanding of a Strauss tone poem. The explanations and comments are an integral part of the work and help give it coherence. Strauss used his detailed programs to solve the problem of unification that plagued the later Romantic composers; it is a nonmusical solution, but it works. Of course, it is impossible actually to depict an object or event in musical language, but when the listener knows the composer's intention in advance, he can recognize and appreciate the effort when it occurs.

Don Quixote (Op. 35)

The program of Richard Strauss' tone poem *Don Quixote* (1897) is taken from the great Spanish satirical novel of the same title, written in the early seventeenth century by Miguel de Cervantes. Don Quixote is a gentle, dignified, and rather simpleminded old man who becomes slightly addled by reading books about the Age of Chivalry. He decides that he must become a knight, seeking adventure and revenging wrongs.

Strauss selected a series of episodes from Cervantes' tale and depicted them in a set of ten freely constructed variations on two themes, which represent Don Quixote and his squire, Sancho Panza. These musical characterizations are enhanced by assigning particular instruments to each man. A solo cello portrays Quixote, described as "The Knight of the Sorrowful Countenance"; Sancho Panza is depicted by a solo viola, with occasional help from the bass clarinet and tenor tuba.

The variations on these two themes are not as strict as those encountered in earlier music; no attempt is made to preserve the structure or the harmonic pattern of the themes. In fact, it might be more accurate to consider these "fantastic variations" (as Strauss himself subtitled them) as short episodes or rhapsodies on the themes, transformed to suit the particular adventures the composer selected.

A brief summary of the program is as follows:

VAR. I. Don Quixote mistakes a windmill for a giant and attacks it; he is dumped from his horse.

VAR. II. Mistaking a herd of sheep for an enemy army, Quixote manages to kill several before the shepherd stones him.

VAR. III. Quixote's sentimentality and Panza's practical nature are contrasted in conversation between the knight and his squire.

VAR. IV. Quixote encounters a procession of pilgrims, attacks them, and is routed; they continue on their way.

VAR. V. Standing watch by his weapons at night, Quixote dreams of his lady love, Dulcinea.

VAR. VI. Quixote and Panza meet three village girls; Panza tries to persuade his knight that one of them is Dulcinea, but Quixote is not fooled.

VAR. VII. The adventurers imagine a ride through the air as they sit blindfolded on a wooden horse.

VAR. VIII. Finding an oarless boat, they embark and capsize.

VAR. IX. Mistaking two Benedictine monks for evil magicians, Quixote puts them to flight.

VAR. X. Quixote is defeated in a duel with another knight, and returns home in humiliation.

EPILOGUE. Don Quixote's mind clears, and he meditates over his imagined adventures; death comes, and he faces it in a noble and dignified manner.

The work opens with a long introduction that represents Don Quixote's longing for adventure, his confusion caused by reading too many books about knighthood, and his "ideal woman," Dulcinea. Then the principal themes are presented: first the would-be knight, then his squire.

Example 18.8

Don Quixote

Sancho Panza

The most outstanding aspect of *Don Quixote* is the manner in which Strauss uses the orchestra to obtain specific effects. The large orchestra includes a number of unusual instruments, such as the bass clarinet, tenor tuba, contrabassoon, and even a barrel-shaped "wind machine," designed to imitate the sound of the wind. In Variation II, brass instruments with mutes clearly depict the bleating sounds of the sheep. The pilgrims in Variation IV are represented by a slow march, played in octaves by the brasses. The march starts very softly and grows louder to indicate the approach of the procession. Don Quixote's theme is heard briefly but soon disappears; the pilgrims' theme marches on and dies away in the distance.

Richard Strauss represents a logical extension of Romantic orchestration and programmatic techniques. He adopted Berlioz's ideas about realism in music and pushed them to their limit; his use of the orchestra for dramatic and special effects was brilliant. Although Strauss never claimed to be one of the most gifted composers of his age, he was certainly one of the most effective.

Summary

Because they chose to abandon the Classical forms, Romantic composers were forced to find new ways of unifying their larger works. A favorite method was to use a nonmusical idea for inspiration. If the idea was used in a general way (to depict a place, a feeling, or a time of year, for instance), the music was called descriptive. If it was used in a specific way, following a detailed plan or story, the music was said to be programmatic.

Although Beethoven used programmatic elements in his music, he cautioned his listeners that the music was to be "an expression of feelings rather than a depiction." The more traditional Romantic composers followed his lead in subordinating the nonmusical idea. Mendelssohn, in particular, wrote symphonies that were called descriptive but that were clearly unified within their Classical structure.

The more radical Romantic composers used the programmatic technique in a different way. Hector Berlioz, a master of orchestration, supplied detailed programs with several of his larger works. These works derived their real unity from the development of a dramatic idea from one movement to the next. Although the programs explained the situation that inspired each piece, Berlioz did not feel that a knowledge of the text was essential to the understanding of the work.

Franz Liszt wrote single-movement works in a new and relatively free form, which he devised. Called symphonic tone poems, they bore descriptive titles and differed from Berlioz's program music in that their basic coherence sprang from purely musical elements.

Richard Strauss combined influences from both Berlioz and Liszt in his tone poems, written in the latter years of the century. Unlike either of his predecessors, however, Strauss depended heavily on the text to unify his works. The explanations and comments are integral parts of his tone poems, helping to give them coherence.

chapter 19

During the later part of the Romantic era, nationalism in music became an important force. There had been some stylistic differences in the music of different nations ever since the early fifteenth century. In the seventeenth century,

Nationalism

France and Italy had taken the lead in dominating the European musical scene. Germany became an important force by about 1750 and assumed the dominant position in music at the beginning of the nineteenth century. But the Classical style, as determined by Haydn, Mozart, and Beethoven, had no distinctive national characteristics—it was international and cosmopolitan.

As a result of the Romantic movement's fascination with exotic and primitive cultures, there was a growing interest in folk music during the nineteenth century. German folk songs were assimilated into the general style, but this was nothing really new; composers from Haydn to Brahms had used folklike melodies comfortably and naturally. Many of the best-known Romantic composers borrowed folk elements for exotic touches; Liszt and Chopin, for example, used Hungarian and Polish tunes in their works.

The most important and obvious effect of the nationalistic movement took place in countries that did not have strong musical traditions of their own. Before the nineteenth century, countries such as Russia, Bohemia, the Scandinavian countries, and the United States had been musically dependent on the leaders of European culture, particularly Germany and Italy. They had imported their music, and the musicians to perform it.

During the Romantic era, self-conscious and even aggressive nationalistic feeling flared up in both literary and musical circles. The reaction took different forms in different countries, although there were some common features. They ranged from the use of national subjects for operas and symphonic poems, and the occasional quoting of folk music material, to more general traits, such as the adoption of characteristic national idioms (in melody, harmony, rhythm, form, and tonal color) into the mainstream of Germany's Romantic musical language.

Many important nationalistic composers were not founders of schools of composition, but were isolated figures. The whole nationalistic movement was rather short-lived, soon coming to terms with the prevailing currents of the more strongly established European cultures. Nevertheless, in its brief tenure nationalism enriched the central musical language with new idioms and procedures.

Russia

Russia is the classic example of a nation that was suddenly exposed to Western civilization and became culturally dependent before first having a chance to find its own national voice. Prior to the reign of Peter the Great (1672–1725), Russia was isolated from the West; Peter forced Western customs and ideas on his people and eliminated national traditions. This pressure created the beginnings of a cultural division between the liberal, Western-oriented aristocracy and the more traditional, conservative masses. The split was reflected almost immediately in Russian literature and gradually appeared in music also.

European music was introduced to Russia late in the seventeenth century, and Italian opera was particularly popular at the Imperial Court. Music was definitely a luxury in Russia, imported for the upper classes and monopolized by foreigners. But in the nineteenth century, a new sense of national pride began to grow, demanding that there be something "Russian" about the music produced for Russian consumption. At about this time, the first significant Russian composer, Glinka, appeared.

Glinka (1804–1857)

Although Michael Glinka studied with German and Italian musicians, he became closely associated with the members of a nationalistic literary movement in St. Petersburg. At their urging, he wrote a "national opera," which he filled with the spirit and melody of the Russian people. His opera, *A Life for the Tsar*, was first performed in 1836. Russia had a vast supply of folk music and liturgical chant (for the Orthodox church), and Glinka was one of the first to draw on these resources.

After a few years, even the fashionable aristocracy came to accept the fact that Glinka's new opera represented the first stage of a truly Russian art music. His second effort *Russlan and Ludmilla* (1842), however, was not so well received—an unfortunate circumstance, since it is actually a better work.

The Bettmann Archive

The Split between Nationalists and Cosmopolitans

About the time of Glinka's death the Russian musical world divided into two camps. Some Russian composers wanted to be completely independent of the West, writing Russian music addressed to Russians only. Others were convinced that Slavic culture had reached a dead end and should be abandoned for the cosmopolitan culture of Western Europe. This split was paralleled in literary circles in which the novelist Dostoyevsky (1821–1881) was a leading nationalist, while Turgenev (1818–1883) represented the more conservative faction.

Since the composers of the conservative school were writing in the "international" German Romantic style, their music soon became known to Western audiences and has remained popular in the concert repertoire to this day. The music of the nationalistic group, which was directed almost exclusively to Russian audiences, remains less well known to us. Also, the composers who adopted the Western tradition had good examples and teachers available to them, but the nationalists had very little to guide them except the work of Glinka.

The "Mighty Five"

The leaders of the nationalistic school of composition in Russia, who professed to have no interest in the music of the West, were a strange group. Known as the "Mighty Five," they were not professional musicians, except for the leader and teacher of the others, Mili Balakirev (1837–1910). The rest were professionally employed in other fields: Alexander Borodin (1834–1887) was a chemistry professor at a medical school, César Cui (1835–1918) was a military engineer, Modest Moussorgsky (1839–1881), an army officer, and Nikolai Rimsky-Korsakov (1844–1908), a naval officer.

Despite the impressive name given to their group, most of them were not first-rate composers. Balakirev and Cui were uninspired salon composers, writing pallid imitations of French pieces. Borodin and Rimsky-Korsakov were much more significant composers. However, their musical training was basically Western-oriented, and they were able to assert their nationalism only through the use of Russian subject matter. Borodin's best works are an opera, *Prince Igor* (1890), and a symphonic sketch, *In the Steppes of Central Asia*. The music for the Broadway musical *Kismet* is taken from his work. Rimsky-Korsakov, who disguised his poverty of invention with opulent and overwhelming orchestrations, is best known for his orchestral tone poem *Scheherazade* (1888) and for "Song of India" from his opera *Sadko* (1898).

Modest Moussorgsky is often considered to be the founder of modern musical naturalism and realism. The outstanding composer of the Russian nationalist school, he understood the spirit of the Russian people and portrayed it with feeling and intensity. In his greatest work, the opera *Boris Godunov* (1874), the realism is evident on all levels. In the area of small detail, his vocal lines follow the accents of natural speech, and his portrayal of crowd scenes is very effective. On a deeper level, he expresses musically the deep and often verbally inexpressible passions that rage in men's souls. The story centers on an alleged murder by the Tsar Boris, who reigned from 1598 to 1605. The opera describes Boris' mental anguish resulting from his guilt, and the greed of an ambitious pretender to capture the throne. The real heroes of the opera are the Russian people, who must suffer because of the struggle for their land. Moussorgsky has expressed their suffering in a musical folk drama that is the greatest musico-dramatic masterpiece of Eastern Europe.

The Cosmopolitan School

The cosmopolitan Russian group deliberately wrote in the prevailing German Romantic style, with very little sense of the nationalist elements that surrounded them. Most of these composers were well-trained professionals, not amateurs like the nationalists. Among them, the most important were Alexander Serov (1820–1871), Anton Rubinstein (1829–1894), and Peter Ilyich Tchaikovsky (1840–1893).

The most outstanding member of the cosmopolitan school was Peter Ilyich Tchaikovsky. Although a contemporary of the "Mighty Five," he stood outside their sphere of influence, taking his inspiration from traditional Western European music. He was the first Russian composer to gain an international reputation.

Tchaikovsky (1840–1893)

New York Public Library

Born in Votkinsk, in a remote province of Russia, Peter Ilyich Tchaikovsky received his earliest musical training from a French governess. When he was ten his family moved to St. Petersburg, where he was enrolled in a school of jurisprudence. Upon graduation at the age of nineteen he became a government clerk, but soon decided to pursue a musical career. Although he had shown no signs of genius either as a pianist or as a composer, he was accepted at the age of twenty-one to the newly established St. Petersburg Conservatory. He began serious composition under Anton Rubinstein, the institution's founder and the most eminent pianist and composer in Russia.

He graduated in 1865, winning a gold medal for a cantata based not on a Russian subject but significantly, a German one—Schiller's *Hymn to Joy*. The following year he became a professor of harmony at the Moscow Conservatory, a position he was to hold for twelve years. His early works, which include overtures, string quartets, and a programmatic symphony, demonstrate little of the individual style that marked his later achievements. He widened his experience, however, through frequent trips abroad.

In 1876, after returning from the first Bayreuth Festival, Tchaikovsky acquired the support of an unusual benefactress, Nedezhda von Meck, a widow who had inherited an immense fortune. After learning through a third party that the composer was in financial need, she commissioned several works at large fees. She arranged to pay him a fixed annuity so that he could devote himself completely to composition. Their relationship, lasting thirteen years, was carried on entirely by letter. They agreed never to meet, and except for several accidental encounters in public places, the bargain was kept.

In 1877 Tchaikovsky married Antonia Milyukova, a conservatory student. The marriage was a disastrous failure, and after an attempt at suicide by plunging into the Moscow River, he arranged a legal separation. With the financial help of Mme. von Meck, he then embarked on a trip to Italy, Paris, and Vienna.

Despite an increasing tendency toward melancholic depression, Tchaikovsky remained a highly productive composer. His Fourth and Fifth Symphonies (1877 and 1888) and the ballets *Swan Lake* (1876) and *The Sleeping Beauty* (1889) were soon performed all over Europe. By the 1880s he had reached the height of his career. Suddenly, for reasons that have never been fully explained, Mme. von Meck withdrew her support and friendship. Though her action was a severe blow to his pride, Tchaikovsky was by now able to afford the financial loss, and his capacity for work remained undiminished. During 1891 and 1892, he undertook several concert tours in America, Poland, and Germany. When he went to St. Petersburg in 1893 to conduct the premiere of his Sixth Symphony, the *Pathétique*, he fell ill and died, a victim of the cholera epidemic that had been raging in the city.

His Work

Tchaikovsky's best-known works are his last three symphonies, his three ballets, his two symphonic fantasies, his violin concerto, and his first piano concerto. He composed his first three symphonies between 1866 and 1875. The fourth was completed in 1877, the fifth in 1888, and the sixth (the *Pathétique*) in 1893.

His ballets—*Swan Lake* (1875–1876), *The Sleeping Beauty* (1888–1889), and *The Nutcracker* (1891–1892)—remain among the most celebrated works of their kind, and the orchestral suites drawn from them are basic items in present-day concert repertoire as well.

Tchaikovsky's ten most successful tone poems are the overture-fantasia *Romeo and Juliet* (1869) and the fantasia *Francesca da Rimini* (1876).

Of Tchaikovsky's ten works for solo instrument with orchestra, the most popular with performers and audiences alike are the Piano Concerto No. 1 in B-flat Minor (1875) and the Violin Concerto in D (1878). Of his ten operas, the only two that continue to be performed regularly are *Eugene Onegin* (1877–1878) and *The Queen of Spades* (1890). Few of his chamber works or choral pieces are heard today but many works for piano remain perennial favorites, among them *Barcarolle*, *Troika*, and *Song Without Words*. *None But the Lonely Heart* is the most familiar of the more than one hundred songs written throughout his career.

Although Tchaikovsky followed traditional procedures in his symphonies, his main efforts were directed at creating beautiful melodies and brilliantly orchestrated textures. The Fourth Symphony has an elaborate program wedged into the traditional symphonic format. Tchaikovsky's Fifth Symphony uses a theme linking the four movements, much as Beethoven and Brahms had done in the symphonies previously studied.

Symphony No. 6 in B minor (Pathétique)

Record 6/Side 1

Tchaikovsky's last symphony is certainly his most masterful and the most popular today. The composer described it as a programmatic symphony, although he never revealed the program, and to this day it remains unknown. The title *Pathétique* was suggested by the composer's brother, as a substitute for the composer's original idea of *Program Symphony*. The most unusual formal aspect of the symphony is that it ends with a slow movement, rather than with a loud and triumphant allegro.

Tchaikovsky wrote for the typically huge Romantic orchestra: three flutes (one of which occasionally changes to piccolo), two oboes, two clarinets, two bassoons, four horns, two trumpets, three trombones, tuba, timpani (three drums), and strings. The strings often divide to form extra sections and thicker texture. The orchestration is typically Romantic, with considerable emphasis on winds and especially on the French horn. The strings are used in extremely high registers, and frequently double each other in several octaves. The tempo fluctuates considerably throughout coupled with sudden changes of dynamics.

First Movement: *adagio—allegro non troppo*

Although there are two well-defined themes in this opening movement, and the development is in fairly good symphonic style, the music tends to "sprawl" and it is not easy to find the outlines of a sonata-allegro form. After an opening adagio, the first theme is presented, consisting of two short phrases.

Example 19.1

A long transition follows, and finally muted strings introduce the second theme. This lyrical melody is one of Tchaikovsky's most beautiful and memorable.

Example 19.2

The theme is stated several times, with transitional material between the statements.

The development begins after a solo clarinet plays the opening of the second theme very softly. The first theme builds to a climax and then subsides to the point where only the double basses are playing. This is followed by a section in which the upper strings play off the beat (although the total effect sounds as though they are on the beat and the winds are off). This leads back to a further development of the first theme and finally to its recapitulation.

The second theme is not developed, but this is not surprising, for a beautiful melody can seldom be dismantled into little fragments. It has too much individuality as a whole to be chopped up successfully. In contrast, the first theme was built of small, clearly defined motives, which served admirably as development material.

The recapitulation, when it finally arrives, is not at all similar to the original statement of the theme; only the theme itself reappears. This time the strings and winds alternate, each with one fragment of the theme at a time. After a long transition, in which the brasses are prominent, the second theme returns; it is stated first by the strings and then repeated by solo clarinet, as in the exposition. A very short coda concludes the movement.

Second Movement: *allegro con grazia*

This lovely waltzlike movement is written in an unusual meter: 5/4. It flows very smoothly and naturally—which is difficult to achieve in one of the so-called irregular meters. As if to compensate for the lack of formal clarity in the first movement, this one is in a clear-cut ternary form with coda. In fact, each section is also in a ternary form of its own, so the entire movement can be analyzed as:

A	B		A	coda
aabbaa¹	ccdd	transition	aabbaa¹	a²c¹

Example 19.3 The opening melody, a, is presented by the cello section.

It involves extensive repetition of phrases, as do many of Tchaikovsky's melodies. The entire theme is repeated by the winds, and then the whole opening section is repeated literally. The theme of the b subsection has the same rhythmic pattern as the original theme, and also passes from strings to winds. The return to a theme is marked by a complete reorchestration: the winds play the melody in octaves, while the strings play fast pizzicato scales. The strings start to repeat this theme, but soon transform it into a short closing section; the rising scale pattern of the opening theme (without the triplet figure) is heard in the brasses.

The central section of the movement is marked "sweetly and mournfully"; it is performed entirely over a pedal point, played by the double basses, timpani, and sometimes bassoons. The thematic material of the c and d themes are again identical rhythmically.

Example 19.4

C Theme

D Theme

The final repeat of c is replaced by a transition section in which the strings play the rhythmic pattern of theme c, while the winds play the opening motive of theme a in alternate measures. Finally the strings join the winds with the a theme, and this leads to the return of the A section.

The return is almost a literal repeat of the original a section; there are some very slight changes in the orchestration, but otherwise they are identical, including their closing sections. The short coda opens with the rising scale figure (related to theme a) and then moves to fragments of theme c. Portions of the two principal themes alternate quietly as the movement ends.

Third Movement: *allegro molto vivace*

This scherzo-like march is approximately in sonata-allegro form, but with two very interesting deviations. There are the usual two themes, but the exposition (and recapitulation) treat them in ternary fashion. Thus we have a theme 1–theme 2–theme 1 pattern for each of these sections. The development section is fairly standard but the unusual feature is that a large portion of it is also used as the introduction to the movement. This introductory section consists of an extensive develop-ment of a simple motive:

Example 19.5

The exposition is ternary and, probably because the second theme is really nothing but a short motive, repeated four times.

Example 19.6

A return to the first theme is necessary to balance the section.

The introduction is now quoted verbatim as the first part of a de-velopment section. It is followed by a stretto treatment of the motive of theme 1, played first by the brasses and winds and then also by the strings. A series of frantically rushing scales precedes the recapitulation, which follows the same ternary format as the exposition. Another un-usual feature is the key scheme—the recapitulation does not return to the original E major of the first theme but to G major. The recapitulation is reorchestrated, with the opening statement using the entire orchestra playing sforzando. The finale of this movement is quite exciting, and includes several more statements of the motive of the first theme. The brass instruments are featured, along with bass drum and cymbals.

Fourth Movement: *adagio lamentoso*

This slow final movement, with its brooding Romantic closing, troubled the composer as he was writing it; at one point he thought he might want to replace it after the first performance. Since he died only eight days after the symphony's premiere, however, no changes were ever made. After his death, the public was profoundly impressed with the movement, which many claimed was Tchaikovsky's prophecy of his own death.

No clearly defined form is found in the construction of this move-ment. The overwhelming feeling of resignation is emphasized by the phrases that seem to die before they are really completed. Eventually a

Example 19.7

tentative melody emerges. In Tchaikovsky's inimitable manner, it is simple, repetitive, and, in context, quite beautiful.

The melody becomes more assertive; it is played an octave higher, with a countermelody in the winds.

The strings and brasses treat the melody as a dialogue, which culminates in an intense section of descending scales. The theme is then fragmented, with pauses between each statement. The opening material is recalled, and leads to another climax, which falls off suddenly. A single stroke of a gong, accompanied very softly by trombones and tuba, introduces the closing section: a quiet statement of the melody, in dialogue again—first between the upper and lower strings, and then between the two halves of the cello section. The movement ends very softly, with only the cellos and double basses playing.

Other Nations

The highly distinctive nature of Russian folk music and Slavic culture made the nationalist movement there very obvious. But Russia was not the only country in which nationalistic forces brought about a revolution in the musical scene. However, the effect of nationalism was not quite so marked in other nations because of their historic closeness to the mainstream of Romantic music.

Bohemia

Bohemia (an area which is now part of Czechoslovakia) had been an Austrian colony for centuries, and thus had always been in touch with the mainstream of European music. Many fine musicians were produced in this region, but until the Romantic era no distinctively Czech national style had developed. Even when a nationalist movement did arise, no extreme effort was made to avoid Western influence.

The two composers who led in the formation of a national style were Bedřich Smetana (1824–1884) and Antonín Dvořák (1841–1904). Both were fully trained in traditional methods: Smetana's style was closely related to Liszt's, while Dvořák's was much closer to that of Brahms.

Smetana (1824–1884)

Regarded as the founder of the Czech national school, Bedřich Smetana was a composer dedicated to merging the spirit of Bohemian folk music with the innovations of the European musical pioneers of his day. A gifted pianist from childhood, Smetana performed the works of the classical masters. His traditional orientation was supplanted, however, when on a visit to Prague, he had the opportunity to hear Liszt and

The Bettmann Archive

Berlioz. Smetana came to share with these men not only a fascination with progressive musical ideas but a spirit of nationalism, to which his dream of a Bohemia free from Austrian rule responded.

During the year of the revolution, 1848, Smetana opened a school of music in Prague; but by 1856 he had abandoned this enterprise and traveled to Sweden. There he worked as a teacher and conducted a concert society. After six years Smetana again returned to his homeland, this time finding the oppressive atmosphere of the war years gone, and a new and dynamic liberalism in the air. Soon after his return, a Czech national theater for opera, plays, and ballet was established. Smetana used the occasion to begin work on an opera in the Czech language.

During the next twenty years, the composer produced ten operas, each encompassing patriotic themes. His first, entitled *The Brandenburgers in Bohemia*, was performed in 1866, followed in the same year by one of his most famous operas, *The Bartered Bride*. In this opera, Smetana told of a village romance and recounted the comic antics of local Bohemian peasants. The success of both these works marked the beginning of the Czech national school of music.

Smetana continued to write operas, some celebrating the legendary past of his country, such as in *Dalibor and Libussa*; others explored the French comic tradition, such as in *The Two Widows*. Then, in 1874, the composer suddenly became deaf. One might have expected an end to his spiralling career, but instead, Smetana continued to compose. During the next five years, he wrote his famous cycle of symphonic poems, *Ma Vlast* (*My Country*, 1879). These six works celebrated his country's legendary past, the rivers and hillsides and great Bohemian historical moments. One of the most famous works in this cycle is called *Vlatova* or *Moldau*. It traces the course of the river Moldau from its source through the countryside, past great castles and a wedding feast.

Later in his career, Smetana again turned to opera, producing such works as *The Kiss* (1876), *The Secret* (1878), and *The Devil's Wall* (1882). But this enormous emotional and physical outpouring took its toll; Smetana became a victim of mental illness. The composer ended his days, six years later, in an asylum for the insane.

Throughout his work, Smetana's indebtedness to European composers is evident. His comic operas suggest Mozart, his heroic legendary operas are reminiscent of Wagner, and these and his symphonic poems show the influence of Berlioz and Liszt. But in all his music—opera, symphonic poems, chamber works, choral works, and piano polkas and dances—the Czech national voice is ever present. Though he did not borrow or invent folk melodies, the liveliness and spontaneity of his works are representative of the national vigor and identity of his country. So, too, the subject matter of his works often suggest his ties to his homeland.

Bedřich Smetana did not abandon the grandiose form of composition that his Western European musical heritage had given him, but he did skillfully temper its formal structures and harmonies with a gentle and casual treatment of his own and with a lyrical, folklike liveliness. These qualities gave the Czech people a national repertoire in celebration of their country's own unique spirit.

Dvořák (1841–1904)

The Bettmann Archive

The desire to establish a distinctive Czech national school was the ambition of yet another Bohemian composer, Antonín Dvořák. Born in a small village near Prague, Dvořák journeyed there at the age of sixteen to study music and to become a master of the German classical tradition. Yet this man, who was one day to establish Czech prominence in the areas of symphony and chamber music, found musical recognition elusive for many years.

The Prague public first became aware of Dvořák with the performance of his patriotic choral work *Hymnus* in 1873. This success prompted a grant from the Austrian ministry of fine arts, which supplied the composer with a small income. However, it was the patronage of Brahms, whom he met a year later, that thrust him into musical prominence. In 1878, Brahms persuaded a German music publisher to print the composer's *Moravian Duets* and *Slavonic Dances*. This accomplishment allowed Dvořák to spend the 1880s touring Europe conducting his own work, and eventually he was able to attain the position of professor of composition at the Prague Conservatory.

Dvořák's career ultimately brought him to America. Here he served from 1892 to 1895 as artistic director of the National Conservatory of Music in New York. Dvořák returned to his own country to accept the directorship of the Prague Conservatory in 1901. He died three years later at the age of sixty-three.

Dvořák's versatility is reflected in his legacy of concertos for violin, cello, and piano; in his fourteen string quartets; in his four great oratorios; his five symphonic poems; his famous cantata, *The Spectre's Bride* (1884); his four piano trios and two quintets; and his no less than eleven operas and nine symphonies, among a multitude of other works.

Dvořák was most prolific in his production of operas. Throughout his lifetime he labored to compose a work equal in prominence to those of his Bohemian compatriot, Smetana. However, few of his operatic works achieved this goal, although three—*The Devil and Kate* (1899), *Russalka* (1901), and *Armida* (1904)—are considered notable.

Dvořák's greatest contribution was in the art of the symphony. The most famous of his works in this form was his *Fifth Symphony* (1893), written during his visit to the United States. Subtitled "From the New World," the *New World Symphony*, as it is popularly called, combined the structure of the traditional German symphony with the melodies of the American Negro spiritual.

First Movement   Following the traditional exposition–development–recapitulation structure of the sonata form, this movement is striking for its subtle incorporation of the familiar American spiritual *Swing Low, Sweet Chariot*.

Second Movement   Here again, Dvořák turned to the American folk song for inspiration. Using a simple ABA pattern, the first section is an adaptation and elaboration of the melody *Going Home*. This is followed by a thematic restatement from the first movement, which serves as contrast. The final section concludes the pattern with a repetition of the A section melody, *Going Home*.

Third Movement   This scherzo section, said to resemble the dance of the American Indian, is a playful and lively movement. It is included in the tradition of Beethoven, and in fact has much in common with the scherzo of Beethoven's *Ninth Symphony*. To integrate this movement into the body of the symphony, the section concludes with the restatement of the themes of the first movement.

Fourth Movement   This fiery and rapid movement merges the themes of the earlier parts, and in so doing brings unity to the work.

In all his compositions, including symphonies, opera, chamber music, and piano duets, Dvořák reflected his nationalist impulse to create a unique Czech musical style. While devoted to the musical traditions of German classicism, his sensitivity to the Czech folk idiom is evident in his spontaneous use of melody and in the adaptation of native music in his work.

Norway

Grieg (1843–1907)

The Bettmann Archive

Perhaps the best-known Scandinavian composer of his century, Edvard Greig was a passionate exponent of Norwegian nationalism throughout his lifetime. Born in Bergen, his early musical education was in the German Romantic tradition at Leipzig and later at Copenhagen, where he studied under Gade, a successor of Mendelssohn. But as he strove to become an accomplished pianist, conductor, and composer, Grieg also grew more and more fervently committed to his country's movement toward independence from Sweden, and this patriotic fervor gave a special inspiration to his music.

Greig's nationalism found its musical expression in the lyricism borrowed from the folk music of his country. In the songs, piano miniatures, and dances that make up much of his musical legacy, there is always the air of native Norwegian music. This was also true of his large-scale works, particularly his masterpiece, the Piano Concerto in A Minor (1868), a work written when the composer was only twenty-five years of age.

But Grieg was never quite comfortable with the grand symphonic forms of composition. His larger works, in the traditional forms, seem artificial, lacking unity or sense of structure, and their nationalistic character seems imposed and unnatural. Grieg's love of simple folk melodies was far more compatible with the more intimate compositional forms. Among these are his most important and best-known works, including the *Peet Gynt Suite* (1876), consisting of incidental music written for Ibsen's play; *The Holberg Suite*, a collection of songs composed to honor the eighteenth-century Norwegian playwright, Ludvig Holberg; and *The Last Spring*, a song which he later arranged for string orchestra. These works, as well as his ten collections of *Lyric Pieces* for the piano, two *Norwegian Dances*, four *Symphonic Dances* for orchestra, and other pieces, brought him much success at the turn of the century.

In all of his works, Grieg incorporated into his music not only the national folk music that was an expression of his patriotism but many national idioms, including drone basses, cross-rhythms (for example, combinations of 3/4 and 6/8), and many other features of modal melody and harmony, that would later influence other composers. Edvard Grieg lived to see his hopes for Norwegian independence fulfilled and to see his efforts go far toward the establishment of a national musical style in Norway.

Finland

Finland's leading composer, Jean Sibelius (1865–1957), can be considered nationalistic only in certain respects. He was deeply involved with the national literature of Finland, particularly the national epic, the *Kalevala*. He chose texts from it to set as songs, and it provided subjects for many of his symphonic poems, including the familiar *Finlandia*. (One of the themes from *Finlandia* was chosen as the national anthem of Finland.) Sibelius does not quote or imitate folk songs in his works, and shows no real nationalistic traits except in his choice of texts and subject matter.

England

The same can be said for the most prominent of the late Romantic composers in England, Sir Edward Elgar (1857–1934). He used subjects related to national legend or art in his choral work *The Banner of St. George* (1897) and the symphonic poem *Falstaff* (1913). But there is no use of English folk songs in his works and his writing has no characteristically English traits. His style is unique and personal, full of color, exuberance, and emotion. Elgar's best-known works are his oratorio *The Dream of Gerontius* (1900) and the orchestral *Enigma Variations* (1899). His *Pomp and Circumstance* is widely played at graduation ceremonies.

United States

As we will discuss in Chapter 26, music in the United States was dominated by the German Romantic tradition. Toward the end of the nineteenth century a few composers tried to incorporate native materials into their compositions. One of the most notable was Edward Mac-Dowell (1861–1908), who used Amercan Indian melodies in his Second Orchestral Suite *(Indian Suite)* of 1896.

Summary

Nationalism was most evident in countries that did not have strong musical traditions of their own.

Russia, in particular, began to produce music in a unique national idiom. Michael Glinka drew from his country's vast supply of folk music and liturgical chant to write the opera, *A Life for the Tsar,* first performed in 1836. A group of Glinka's successors comprised a nationalistic school known as the "Mighty Five." The outstanding members of this group were Alexander Borodin, Nikolai Rimsky-Korsakov, and Modest Moussorgsky. Moussorgsky, composer of the opera *Boris Godunov,* is often considered to be the founder of modern musical naturalism.

While the "Mighty Five" looked to their homeland for inspiration, another group of Russian composers looked outside their country to the prevailing traditions of Western European music. The outstanding member of this cosmopolitan school, Peter Ilyich Tchaikovsky, was the first Russian composer to gain an international reputation.

The forces of nationalism were also felt in other European countries and in the United States. A national style developed in Bohemia through the efforts of Bedřich Smetana and Antonín Dvořák. Edvard Grieg sought to establish a national style in Norway and Jean Sibelius wrote music based on the national literature of Finland.

chapter 20

Virtually every major composer of the Romantic period wrote some type of choral music. From small, fairly simple homophonic part songs to colossal works involving soloists,

Romantic Choral Music

massive choruses, and immense orchestral forces, choral music occupied an important place in the music of the time. The quality of the large chorus with its lush sound was particularly well suited to the Romantic style with its concentration on sonority and color.

Schubert

Franz Schubert's most important contributions to choral music are embodied in his settings of the Mass. While still in his teens, Schubert wrote four Masses, the best of which is the short and modest setting in G major. The Mass in E-flat Major (No. 6) was written in the last year of his life and has much merit, but its predecessor in A-flat major is Schubert's choral masterpiece. Written over a period of several years (1819–1822), it is a work of major proportions, requiring approximately fifty minutes for its performance. It is scored for four soloists (SATB), chorus, and the typical Romantic orchestra. The solo parts are of only secondary importance, the chorus and orchestra having the major roles. All the way from the harmonically rich *Kyrie* through the concluding *Dona nobis pacem*, the work is one of flowing beauty.

Mendelssohn

In June of 1845, the Committee of the Birmingham (England) Music Festivals invited Felix Mendelssohn to conduct the Festival of 1846 and to compose a major work for the occasion. Mendelssohn declined to conduct, but he agreed to compose; the result was the oratorio *Elias*

(Elijah), his most important choral work. Immediately popular, it assumed a place in the choral music of England ranking with Handel's *Messiah* and *The Creation* by Haydn.

Elijah is a full-fledged oratorio with a dramatic plot brought to life by a roster of soloists, an extensively employed chorus, and a full orchestra. The writing is quite dramatic, with an intensive emphasis on pictorial settings illustrating the influence of Handel's style as shown in his *Israel in Egypt*.

Today, *Elijah* is still well known, not through complete performances of the entire work but from its most memorable movements such as the bass aria "It is enough," "If with all your hearts" for tenor, the chorus "He, watching over Israel," and the concluding "and then shall your light break forth as the morning breaketh."

Berlioz

In 1846, the same year that *Elijah* had its first performance, Hector Berlioz conducted the premier of his dramatic legend or *opera de concert*, *The Damnation of Faust*. This work, along with the *Requiem* (*Grande Messe des Morts*, 1837) and the *Te Deum* (1855), are representative of the colossal Romantic choral style. The forces involved are gigantic. The *Requiem* calls for 210 voices, a large orchestra, and four brass bands positioned in various locations and representing the calls to the Last Judgment. The *Te Deum* requires two choruses of 100 singers each, 600 children's voices and an orchestra of 150 players. These and other works such as the *Funeral and Triumphal Symphony* and *Romeo and Juliet*, a dramatic symphony with choruses, are typical of Berlioz's grandiose style and similar to that found in his *Symphonie Fantastique*.

Another side of Berlioz's musical nature is found in *L'Enfance du Christ* (*The Childhood of Christ*, Op. 25, 1850–1854). Quite unlike the works referred to above, this piece requires modest choral and orchestral forces and is characterized by lyricism rather than stirring bombastic power.

Called a Sacred Trilogy, its three parts are entitled *Le Songe D'Hérode* (*Herod's Dream*), *La Fuite en Egypt* (*The Flight into Egypt*), and *L'arrivé à Saïs* (*The Arrival at Saïs*). By far the most effective of the three parts is the central section, which includes the lovely chorus in which the shepherds bid farewell as the Holy Family prepares to flee from the wrath of Herod.

Brahms

Johannes Brahms composed some of the most enduring choral music of the Romantic period. He wrote for a wide variety of choral combinations and in diverse styles. Brahms composed several large works for chorus and orchestra, some with several soloists. Among these are the cantata *Rinaldo* (Op. 50); the incomparable *Schicksalslied* (*Song of Destiny*, Op. 54) for chorus and orchestra; and *Triumphlied* (*Song of Triumph*, Op. 55). The most important of his large-scale choral compositions was one of his early works, *Ein Deutsches Requiem* (*A German Requiem*, Op. 45). It was composed over a period of eleven years and was finished in 1868 when Brahms was thirty-five. It not only preceded much of his other choral writing, but was written a full eight years before his first symphony.

Ein Deutsches Requiem (A German Requiem, Op. 45)

Record 4/Side 2

Unlike the Requiems of Mozart, Berlioz, Verdi, and later Fauré, Brahms' setting does not employ the traditional Latin text, which is actually a Mass for the Dead (Missa pro defunctis). Rather, it is a setting of non-liturgical German texts which Brahms selected from the Lutheran Bible. A comparison of the Brahms text with the Roman Catholic liturgy shows a marked difference in intention and feeling: the Latin text prays for the soul of the dead, while Brahms' text is designed to console the living.

The opening words of the two texts confirm this:

Roman Catholic Text	**Brahms Text**
(Missa pro defunctis)	*(Ein Deutsches Requiem)*
Requiem aeternam dona eis Domine	*Selig sind, die da Leid tragen,*
(Give them eternal rest, O Lord)	*denn sie sollen getröstet werden*
	(Blessed are they that mourn, for they shall be comforted)

Brahms' entire composition conveys this pervasive feeling of consolation in both the text and the music.

The work consists of seven movements and is scored for chorus, soprano, and baritone soloists and a large orchestra. The chorus and orchestra participate in all seven movements, although the orchestration varies somewhat from movement to movement. The role of the soloists is minimal, with the baritone appearing in the third and sixth movements and the soprano appearing only in the fifth.

First Movement

I

Selig sind, die da Leid tragen,
  denn sie sollen getröstet werden.

Blessed are they that mourn,
  for they shall be comforted.

MATTHEW V, 4

Die mit Tränen säen, werden mit
  Freuden ernten.
Sie gehen hin und weinen und
  tragen edlen Samen, und
  kommen mit Freuden und
  bringen ihre Garben.

They that sow in tears shall reap
  in joy.
They that go forth and weep,
  bearing precious seed, shall come
  again with rejoicing, bringing
  their sheaves with them.

PSALM 126, 5–6

This movement is an excellent example of Brahms' sensitive use of the orchestra; the instruments create a dark, somber tone quality that reflects the mood of the text. Brahms achieved this effect by omitting the high, bright sound of the violins and by dividing the lower strings into several parts: violas into two sections and the cellos into three.

The work begins with a short orchestral introduction in which the upper cello and viola parts enter imitatively with an expressive melodic fragment over a repeated tone in the bass (pedal point):

Example 20.1

This and the following choral section serve as principal unifying elements, which recur in the middle and at the end of the movement.

The contrasting section is built on the text beginning *"Die mit Tranen"*; it expresses the tears (*Tränen*) with a falling melodic line, then climaxes at *"werden mit Freuden"* with a joyful rising motive and comes to a quiet conclusion at *"ernten."* The music of the opening section returns, and the chorus takes up the imitative entries with the words *"Sie gehen hin und weinen."*

After a short stretch of new material, the music set to *"werden mit Freuden"* returns, now with the text *"kommen mit Freuden."* Then the opening material is restated in its entirety, with the first two lines of text also repeated. A short coda, which decreases in intensity and volume, ends the movement.

Example 20.2

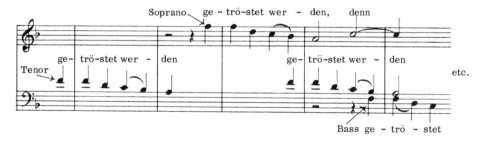

This section has greater significance than might appear, since Brahms repeats it almost literally at the end of the seventh movement, thus unifying the entire Requiem.

Second Movement

II

Denn alles Fleisch ist wie Gras und alle Herrlichkeit des Menschen wie des Grases Blumen.	*For all flesh is as grass, and all the glory of man as the flower of grass.*
Das Gras ist verdorret und die Blume abgefallen.	*The grass withers, and the flower falls away.*

I PETER I, 24

So seid nun geduldig, lieben Brüder, bis auf die Zukunft des Herrn.	*Now therefore be patient, dear brethren, until the coming of the Lord.*

Siehe, ein Ackermann wartet auf die köstliche Frucht der Erde und ist geduldig darüber, bis er empfange den Morgenregen und Abendregen.	Behold, the farmer waits for the precious fruit of the earth and is patient over it until it receives the early and the late rain.
	JAMES V, 7
Aber des Herrn Wort bleibet in Ewigkeit.	But the word of the Lord endures forever.
	I PETER I, 25
Die Erlöseten des Herrn werden wieder kommen, und gen Zion kommen mit Jauchzen; ewige Freude wird über ihrem Haupt sein;	The ransomed of the Lord shall return and come to Zion with rejoicing, everlasting joy shall be upon their heads;
Freude und Wonne werden sie ergreifen und Schmerz und Seufzen wird weg mussen.	Joy and gladness shall they obtain, and sorrow and sighing shall flee away.
	ISAIAH XXXV, 10

This movement calls for the full orchestra. The tempo is slow and the opening has the character of a funeral march. The upper strings are muted, maintaining the subdued tone of the first movement.

Example 20.3   The instrumental introduction is constructed of two quiet motives: first

Example 20.4   and then

The orchestra repeats these two sections while the lower choral parts (ATB) enter with a soft and somber setting of the words *"Denn alles Fleisch"*

Example 20.5

changing to *"Das Gras ist verdorret"* when the orchestra reaches the B motive. An orchestral bridge follows, based on the A material, which incorporates a prolonged, steady crescendo to the return of the A and B motives again. This time the full orchestra and chorus are involved, starting loudly, but with a decrescendo to the B, and then remaining quiet to the end of the section.

In the succeeding section based on the text *"So seid nun geduldig,"* the tempo is somewhat faster and the choral and string statement is echoed by the winds. The section ends with the same text that began it; and after a short transition provided by the horns, the beginning of the piece returns and the entire march section is repeated.

A sudden and startling contrast takes place at the words *Aber des Herrn Wort*, leading to a fast section with a fugal treatment of the text *Die Erlöseten des Herrn*, based on a very jagged and jumping theme:

Example 20.6

After a contrasting section with many sudden changes of dynamics, the fugue subject returns in stretto—first in the winds, then in the chorus, strings, and brasses; it builds to a huge climax at the words *"kommen mit Jauchzen."* The coda, marked *"Tranquillo,"* is in sharp contrast to the frenzy of the preceding section. The fugue subject is heard again in the orchestra, while the chorus repeatedly sings *"ewige Freude."* The movement dies away, ending with a series of soft, descending scales in the orchestra.

Third Movement

III

Herr, lehre doch mich, dass ein Ende mit mir haben muss, und mein Leben ein Ziel hat, und ich davon muss.	*Lord, make me to know my end, and what is the measure of my days, that I may know how frail I am.*
Siehe, meine Tage sind eine Hand breit vor dir, und mein Leben ist wie nichts vor dir.	*Behold, my days are as a hand-breadth to Thee, and my lifetime is as nothing before Thee.*
Ach wie gar nichts sind alle Menschen, die doch so sicher leben.	*Surely, mankind walks in a vain show, their best state is vanity.*
Sie gehen daher wie ein Schemen, und machen ihnen viel vergebliche Unruhe, sie sammeln und wissen nicht wer es kriegen wird.	*Mankind goes about like a shadow, and they are disquieted in vain, they heap up riches and know not who will gather them.*
Nun Herr, wess soll ich mich trösten? Ich hoffe auf dich.	*Now Lord, for what do I wait? My hope is in Thee.*

PSALM 39, 4–7

Der Gerechten Seelen sind in Gottes Hand und keine Qual rühret sie an.	*The righteous souls are in God's hand, and no pain shall afflict them.*

WISDOM OF SOLOMON III, 1

This movement, which includes the first appearance of the baritone soloist, is divided into three major sections. The first two are related, both musically (they are in the same key, D minor, with common thematic material) and textually (both consider man's frailty); the third section is very different, expressing confidence in God's mercy with a joyous fugue in D major on an entirely new subject.

The first section is in aba form; each of these subsections consists of a statement by the soloist and the repetition of the statement by the chorus. The soprano section repeats the melody sung by the baritone, while the lower parts of the chorus provide harmonization. The orchestral parts vary in activity and importance, sometimes merely reinforcing the chorus, but other times adding important thematic material.

The second large section, which begins at *"Ach, wie gar nichts,"* is in triple meter rather than the duple meter of the first section. The baritone begins again, with the motive from the first section heard in the active wind accompaniment. After a very short orchestral interlude, the soloist continues with *"Sie gehen daher,"* which has melodic material quite reminiscent of the theme at the beginning of the movement; meanwhile the orchestra continues to state the motive from the opening section. Then the chorus makes an abbreviated restatement of *"Ach, wie gar nichts,"* and the section ends with a huge climactic succession of entrances of *"Nun, Herr."* Once more Brahms displays his tendency toward a quiet ending after a strong climax: the last choral statement of *"wess soll ich mich trösten?"* has a thinner texture (just the winds), and the dynamic level is reduced to piano.

The third and last section of the movement is introduced by soaring melodic lines of the chorus at the words *"Ich hoffe auf dich,"* sung over a pedal point on A. At the words *"Der Gerechten Seelen sind in Gottes Hand,"* the pedal changes to D, and a gigantic fugue begins, with the subject stated first by the tenor section:

Example 20.7

Der Ge-rech-ten See-len sind in_ Got-tes Hand und kei-ne Qual rüh - ret sie an,

This loud and driving choral fugue is accompanied by orchestral parts that are faster and even more excited; finally the excitement is caught by the soprano section, which joins the violins in a long melismatic passage:

Example 20.8

und Kei - ne   Qual _____   etc.

The movement ends with a huge crescendo, expressing the faith and hope mentioned in the text.

Fourth Movement

IV

Wie lieblich sind deine Wohnungen,	*How lovely is thy dwelling place,*
Herr Zebaoth!	*O Lord of Hosts!*
Meine Seele verlanget und sehnet	*My soul longs and faints*
sich nach den Vorhöfen des Herrn;	*for the courts of the Lord;*
mein Leib und Seele freuen sich	*my body and soul rejoice*
in dem lebendigen Gott.	*in the living God.*
Wohl denen, die in deinem Hause	*Blessed are those who dwell in thy*
wohnen, die loben dich immerdar.	*house, praising Thee evermore.*

PSALM 84, 1, 2, 4

This serene and sunny movement is in obvious contrast to the exuberance of the previous one. The winds play an important role in the orchestration, often echoing the choral parts. The movement is also characterized by a frequent sense of rise and fall with melodies ascending and descending.

At the words *"die loben dich immerdar,"* the homophonic texture is abandoned and a fugal section begins, with the subject in the soprano and a countersubject in the bass.

Example 20.9

After building to a climax, with considerable syncopation in the accompanying string parts, the section comes to a quiet ending. The coda that follows contains the opening material in the orchestral parts, but the chorus has a new figure.

Fifth Movement

V

Ihr habt nun Traurigkeit	*You now have sorrow,*
aber ich will euch wieder sehen	*but I will see you again*
und euer Herz soll sich freuen	*and your hearts will rejoice*
und euer Freude soll niemand	*and no one will take your joy*
von euch nehmen.	*from you.*

JOHN VXI, 22

Sehet mich an: Ich habe eine	*Look upon me: for a little time*
kleine Zeit Muhe und Arbeit	*sorrow and labor were mine,*
gehabt und habe grossen Trost	*and now I have found comfort.*
funden.	

ECCLESIASTICUS LI, 27

Ich will euch trösten, wie Einen
seine Mutter tröstet.

I will comfort you, as one whom
his mother comforts.

ISAIAH LXVI, 13

The solo soprano part plays a dominant role in this movement, the only one in which it appears. The part is full of long lyric phrases, punctuated by orchestral accompaniment and choral comment, the music for which is actually derived from the solo material. The wind instruments are particularly important, with many solo passages throughout the movement, while the strings have more of the routine accompaniment, such as the doubling of the chorus.

The text for solo is in ABA form, and the musical structure approximates an ABA outline, although the return of the A material is not at all literal.

Sixth Movement

VI

Denn wir haben hier keine bleibende
Stadt, sondern die zukünftige
suchen wir.

For here we have no lasting
city, but we seek that which
is to come.

HEBREWS XIII, 14

Siehe, ich sage euch ein Geheimnis:
Wir werden nicht alle entschlafen,
wir werden aber alle verwandelt
werden; und dasselbige plötzlich,
in einem Augenblick, zu der
Zeit der letzten Posaune.
Denn es wird die Posaune schallen,
und die Toten werden auferstehen
unverweslich, und wir werden
verwandelt werden.
Dann wird erfüllet werden das Wort,
das geschrieben steht: Der Tod
ist verschlungen in dem Sieg.
Tod, wo ist dein Stachel?
Hölle, wo ist dein Sieg?

Behold, I tell you a mystery:
We shall not all sleep,
but we shall all be changed
in a moment, in the twinkling
of an eye, at the time
of the last trumpet. [trombone]*
For the trumpet shall sound,
and the dead shall be raised
incorruptible, and we shall
be changed.
Then shall come to pass the saying
that is written: Death
is swallowed up in victory.
Death, where is thy sting?
Hell, where is thy victory?

I CORINTHIANS XV, 51–55

Herr, du bist würdig zu nehmen
Preis und Ehre und Kraft,
den du hast alle Dinge geschaffen,
und durch deinen Willen haben sie
das Wesen und sind geschaffen.

Lord, Thou art worthy to receive
glory and honor and power,
for Thou hast made all things,
and by thy will they were given
substance and were created.

REVELATIONS IV, 11

In many respects, this is the most dramatic movement of the entire work. It is characterized by extreme contrasts and driving climaxes, and its power is intensified by its position between the gentle fifth movement and the quiet, consoling seventh.

*In German, the "last trumpet" is a trombone (*Posaune* and not *Trompete*).

The movement consists of three large sections; the first two involve the solo baritone, while the third is a huge choral fugue. The first section is moderate in tempo (andante) and subdued in dynamics (pp); the texture is thin, with the upper strings muted and the cellos and basses playing pizzicato.

The second section begins with the solo baritone announcing *"Siehe, ich sage euch ein Geheimnis"*: *"Wir werden nicht alle entschlafen."* The melodic activity of the last word is reduced while the winds introduce a contrasting phrase.

Example 20.10

The chorus repeats the text on static chords; the strings play the baritone's original melody, which is again answered by the winds. The alternations (between baritone and chorus, strings and winds) continue during the phrase *"wir werden aber alle verwandelt werden."*

The baritone's next phrase, *"und dasselbige,"* still quiet and slow, marks the beginning of a drive to an engulfing climax at the end of the section. The momentum begins to pick up with the appearance of the original baritone melody at double speed in the violins and then flutes.

Example 20.11

A gradual crescendo in the lower strings carries it as far as the word *"Augenblick."* After an abrupt pause, the soloist begins alone with the text *"zu der Zeit der letzten Posaune"*; he is joined, appropriately enough, by the trombones and tuba. The tempo begins to accelerate, along with a gradual crescendo (*poco a poco*—little by little), and the chorus takes over from the soloist. The full orchestra joins in for a fortissimo climax on *"Po-sau- -ne."* As the tempo continues to increase, the strings begin a rapid rising and falling tremolo figure, while the winds punctuate with short chords. This leads directly into the second large section of the movement.

The rushing string figure continues into the next section, which is marked Vivace and is in triple meter. The chorus, singing *"Denn es wird die Posaune,"* is supported by the winds, brasses, and timpani. The choral parts are a mixture of straightforward declamation, tightly woven legato lines, and sharp stinging exclamations, all very loud.

This driving passage is interrupted by the baritone's final appearance; over a soft orchestral background, he sings *"Dann wird erfüllet,"* with melodic material reminiscent of his earlier passage, *"Siehe, ich sage euch."* His last word is engulfed by a resumption of the furious string passage work, which leads to a repetition of the material that opened the section, this time with the words *"Der Tod ist verschlungen."*

This section is extended beyond the repeat, concentrating on the contrast between the two phrases *"Tod, wo ist dein Stachel?"* with its very short, hard notes and *"Hölle, wo ist dein Sieg?"* which is very lush and legato. The accompaniment in the string section also differs for these two phrases. Gradually the emphasis shifts to the single word *"wo"*

wo ---- wo ------ wo ----------
Wo ist dein Sieg?

All the forces come together to emphasize these words, and the climax leads into the final section.

Brahms ends the movement with a long and triumphant fugue in C major. In general, the fugal voices are doubled by wind instruments, while the strings play accompaniments and countersubjects. The fugue subject is a broad, majestic statement, while the countersubjects are lighter and faster-moving.

Example 20.12

As a contrast to the emphatic quality of the fugal opening, the section *"Denn du hast"* is very soft and legato; this material occurs several times during the course of the fugue. Further contrast is provided by the homophonic setting that is sometimes given to the text *"zu nehmen Preis und Ehre und Kraft."*

Perhaps more than any other, this movement demonstrates Brahms' unique ability to combine Classical design—its carefully balanced and contrasting elements—with the expressive qualities of the Romantic spirit.

Seventh Movement

VII

Selig sind die Toten, die in dem Herrn sterben, von nun an. Ja der Geist spricht, dass sie ruhen von ihrer Arbeit; denn ihre Werke folgen ihnen nach.	*Blessed are the dead who die in the Lord from henceforth. Yea, saith the Spirit, that they may rest from their labors; for their deeds do follow them.*

REVELATIONS XIV, 13

The final movement of the Requiem marks a return to the spirit of the first movement, and to much of its musical material as well. Brahms has unified the entire work by linking the outer movements both textually and musically.

This movement is in ABA form with a coda; the first theme of the A section, *"Selig sind,"* is drawn almost directly from the coda of the first movement, where it was used for the words *"getröstet werden."*

Example 20.13

Se - lig sind die To - ten, die in dem Her-ren ster - ben von nun an, von nun an.

The B section begins with *"Ja, der Geist spricht,"* which is set for low voices singing in octaves, with trombones and horns; this leads to a tender section with the text *"dass sie ruhen,"* in which the winds play a very active part in the imitation. The material of the B section is then repeated, although in a somewhat abbreviated fashion, leading to a return of the opening material.

The opening theme is stated only once this time (by the tenor section), and the choral section is again repeated. The coda begins with a phrase in the alto and tenor sections that recalls the beginning of the return to original material from the first movement. It comes again, this time in another key, and leads directly into a literal restatement of the entire coda of the opening movement.

Ein Deutsches Requiem, like the great sacred choral works by Schütz and Bach in the Baroque period, was inspired by a deep concern for the state of man's soul; the more humanistic orientation of the Romantic age led Brahms to direct his words to the mourners rather than to the deceased. The texts of consolation and hope that he chose have an eloquent beauty of their own, and his music enhances this beauty still more.

Summary

In the Romantic period, instrumental music constituted the bulk of music literature, and opera and lieder were the predominant vocal genres. Nevertheless, virtually every major composer of the period wrote choral music in some form. The large chorus, with its lush sound, was particularly well suited to the Romantic style, which concentrated on sonority and color.

Franz Schubert's most important contributions to choral music are embodied in his settings of the Mass. Felix Mendelssohn's best-known choral work is his oratorio *Elijah,* which he composed for the Birmingham (England) Music Festival of 1846. Hector Berlioz's choral compositions include a gigantic *Requiem* that calls for 210 voices, a large orchestra, and four brass bands.

Some of the most enduring choral music of the Romantic period was written by Johannes Brahms. The most significant of his large-scale choral compositions is *A German Requiem*, which he composed over a period of eleven years. Its greatness rests not only on its mastery of technique, but also on its intensely personal and direct human communication.

chapter 21

Romantic Opera

Opera was one of the most important musical genres of the Romantic period. In the eighteenth century each of the three leading countries of musical Europe—France, Italy, and Germany—had its own operatic style. These national styles became even more distinct during the Romantic period.

French Opera

During the first half of the Romantic era, Paris was the operatic capital of Europe. Beginning in about 1820, with the rise of a large and influential middle class, a new type of opera developed. Called *grand opera*, it concentrated on the spectacular elements of the production, replete with crowd scenes, ballets, choruses, and fantastic scenery. The integrity of the drama and the music was often sacrificed for these special effects. Giacomo Meyerbeer (1791–1864), a German composer who had studied and worked extensively in Italy before coming to France, introduced grand opera to Paris with such operas as *Les Huguenots* (1836) and *Le Prophète* (1849). One of the best grand operas of the early Romantic period was *Guillaume Tell* (*William Tell*, 1829) by an Italian, Gioacchino Rossini.

Although grand opera received the lion's share of Parisian attention, the less pretentious *opéra comique* continued to be popular. The distinguishing feature of opéra comique was its use of spoken dialogue rather than sung recitative. Both the music and the plot tended to be simpler than in grand opera. Despite the word "comique," many operas in this form had serious plots.

Later in the nineteenth century, a new form developed as a compromise between the overwhelming spectacle of grand opera and the lightness of opéra comique. Called *lyric opera*, it evolved from the more serious type of opéra comique. Using plots taken from Romantic drama or fantasy, these works relied primarily on the beauty of their melodies. One of the finest lyric operas of the period, Charles Gounod's *Faust* (1859), was based on the first part of Goethe's famous play.

Toward the end of the century a new literary movement, opposed to Romanticism, developed in France. Called *naturalism*, it avoided all stylized gestures and portrayed brute force and immorality freely. At the same time an interest in exotic settings arose, particularly in France.

Georges Bizet (1838–1875) introduced naturalism to opera in his masterpiece *Carmen* (1875). The story of this fiery gypsy girl suggests both the exotic and the natural. The melodic and rhythmic vitality of the music and Bizet's brilliant orchestration effectively enhance and complement the dramatic action.

Bizet (1838–1875)

The Bettmann Archive

Born and brought up in Paris, Georges Bizet entered the Paris Conservatory at the age of ten, and by seventeen he had written his first symphony. His work revealed such talent and ingenuity that he was awarded the *Prix de Rome*, enabling him to study at the Italian capital. Unfortunately, this brilliant beginning was soon clouded by the cold reception of his audiences, who were startled and offended by the boldness of his realism and the starkness of the emotions displayed in his early operatic works.

Following his youthful compositions, Bizet created three operas: *The Pearl Fishers* (1863), *The Fair Maid of Perth* (1867), and *Djamileh* (1872). Of the three, only *The Fair Maid of Perth* was well received, but Bizet's skill in orchestration and musical structure began to build his reputation. Success came in 1872 when he composed the incidental music for *L'Arlesienne*, a piece filled with exotic harmonies and bold orchestration. This won him an offer to do an opera based on a libretto adapted from Prosper Mérimee's novel of a fiery gypsy girl.

The realism of the libretto, dealing as it did with earthy figures and driving passion, was a perfect vehicle for Bizet's imagination and love of folk melodies. He undertook the assignment, and the opera, entitled *Carmen*, was produced in 1875. The subject scandalized the audience, and the themes of desire, hate, and love proved too bold for its time. The touch of scandal that surrounded it, however, kept the opera running for several months, and Bizet was subsequently offered a contract for his next work.

But the opera's reception was a great blow to the composer, and emotionally exhausted by so many months and years of work, he was stricken by a heart attack and died. At the age of thirty-eight he had created the greatest French opera of his century and one of the best-loved operas in the world. His inspired vocal ensembles, his use of the orchestra to comment on the action on stage, his pounding rhythms, his masterly scoring, and his eminently singable melodies combined to assure him musical immortality. Five years after its unfavorable reception in Paris, *Carmen* returned to that city and was received with great enthusiasm.

Carmen

The story of *Carmen* revolves around the conflicts of four individuals: Carmen, the fickle and seductive gypsy girl employed in a cigarette factory; Don José, a soldier victimized by his own obsessive love; Micaela, the good and faithful childhood sweetheart of José; and Escamillo, the romantic bullfighter who captures Carmen's affections. Set in Spain, the action moves swiftly and probingly through the passions of love, desire, hate, and jealousy, until its tragic conclusion.

Act I The Prelude begins with a curious combination of themes. Juxtaposed are the melodies of the bullring at Seville, a lively, exciting passage that will be repeated in the final scene. This is followed by the famous melody of the Toreador Song:

Example 21.1

The final theme is the haunting motive of Fate, an ominous phrase that arises frequently and forebodingly throughout the work:

Example 21.2

The first scene is set in a town square at the moment of the changing of the guard. Don José and another officer enter, accompanied by a group of urchins. It is noon and the women who work in the cigarette factory pour into the square; with them is Carmen. As she enters, the Fate motive is played, but rhythmically altered; and Carmen's entrance is enhanced by the Habanera, a song performed to a tango rhythm. Noticing José and prodded by his failure to notice her, Carmen throws a flower to him. As he picks it up, the Fate motive is again sounded. Carmen no sooner returns to work when an argument ensues between her and another woman. When Carmen attempts to strike her, she is arrested and placed in the custody of José. As he escorts her to jail, it is not long, however, before Carmen has persuaded José to assist her in escaping.

Act II The second act opens in a tavern, where Carmen is entertaining the soldiers with song and dance. She is the focus of attention, especially from Escamillo, who enters to the opening strains of the Toreador Song. But Carmen is waiting for José, who has been newly released from jail for aiding her escape. His arrival is occasioned by a dance by Carmen. But when he arises to return to the barracks, Carmen taunts him for putting duty first. In response, he draws her flower from his coat and sings of his love for her. Now certain of her power over him, Carmen invites him to join the smugglers. His refusal is interrupted by an officer in his regiment who orders him away from Carmen. Jose attacks him, and his fate is determined. As a deserter, lawlessness is his only alternative, and the smugglers welcome him with a rousing finale.

Act III   In their mountain hideout, Carmen has already grown bored with José and they quarrel. As the orchestra plays the Fate motive, Carmen joins her gypsy friends to read their fortunes. The famous Card Trio ensues; Carmen draws the ace of spades, the card of death, announcing her fate. Shortly thereafter, Micaela arrives to tell José that his mother is dying. She sings her famous aria:

Example 21.3

As José leaves with her, the motive of Fate is heard again.

Act IV   The curtain rises to reveal a scene outside the arena. A crowd has gathered to cheer the bullfighters as they march in to the fanfare of the Overture. Among them is Escamillo with the adoring Carmen on his arm. As Escamillo enters the ring, José accosts her and begs her to go away with him. She refuses in a violent encounter, and he stabs her. The Toreador Song evolves into the Fate motive as José falls to his knees beside the body of the woman he loved.

Italian Opera

By the nineteenth century, opera was virtually the only important musical form being cultivated in Italy. The distinctions between opera seria and opera buffa were still maintained, although both felt the influence of French grand opera. The orchestra began to play a more important and colorful role and the chorus was also used more effectively.

Rossini, Donizetti, and Bellini

The most outstanding Italian opera composer of the early part of the nineteenth century was Gioacchino Rossini (1792–1862). His sense of melody and effective staging made him an instant success. Opera buffa seemed to be a natural outlet for his talents, and *Il Barbiere di Siviglia (The Barber of Seville*, 1816) ranks with Mozart's *Nozze di Figaro (Marriage of Figaro)* as a supreme example of Italian comic opera. As with Mozart's work, the skillful treatment of ensembles and the exposition of comic situations and characters make *The Barber of Seville* an exceptional opera.

In his thirty-two operas and oratorios Rossini sought to cultivate the art song to its highest possible level. Its function was to delight audiences with melodious and spontaneous music. This *bel canto* style, which emphasized beauty of sound, was also exemplified in the work of two of Rossini's contemporaries: Gaetano Donizetti (1797–1848), composer of some seventy operas, including *Lucia di Lammermoor* (1835); and Vincenzo Bellini (1801–1835), whose lyric and expressive style is particularly evident in his *La Sonnambula (The Sleepwalker*, 1831) and *Norma* (1831).

Verdi (1813–1901)

The Bettmann Archive

Born of a poor family in a little hamlet in Bussetto, Italy, Giuseppe Verdi began his musical training as the apprentice of the local church organist. His hard work and talent were rewarded with a stipend contributed by his town to enable the continuation of his studies at the Milan Conservatory. He was, however, subsequently turned down by the examiners, and through the financial aid of a friend continued his studies by means of private lessons.

At the age of 26, Verdi's first opera, *Oberto* (1839), was an instant success. To this musical triumph he added another, with the presentation of his third opera, *Nabucco*, in 1842. It was this work that brought him not only musical recognition, but national fame. The story of this opera dealt with the plight of the Jews in Babylon, but the parallel with the Milanese crusade for freedom from Austrian rule was so striking that Verdi was exalted as a patriot and champion of the Italian cause. His name soon became linked with the cry for independence, and his evident sympathies, as they were reflected in his works, brought the composer under suspicion of the police.

After producing a number of successful works, Verdi settled on a country estate in 1849. There he continued to pursue his political activities and produced, in succession, three of his most well-known works; *Rigoletto* (1851), *Il Trovatore* (1853), and *La Traviata* (1853). These productions are regarded as the culmination of his first creative period.

Years of intensive musical productivity followed, during which such memorable works as *Ballo in Maschera (The Masked Ball*, 1859), *La Forza del Destino (The Force of Destiny*, 1861), and *Don Carlos* (1867) were created. In 1872, Verdi's masterpiece of spectacular grand opera, *Aida*, was written. With its cohesive dramatic structure, wealth of melodic, harmonic, and orchestral color, and subtle characterizations, this work is regarded as the height of his second creative phase.

Following this triumph, Verdi did not produce another operatic work for sixteen years. Then, in 1893, *Otello*, an opera unlike any he had previously written, was performed in Milan. Regarded by many critics as the pinnacle of Italian tragic opera, its sense of continuity is unequaled in his earlier works and contains an orchestration that never obscures the voices. Verdi's last work, *Falstaff*, written in 1893, when the composer was nearly eighty years of age, is a comic opera and again one of the greatest of the genre. His very last compositions were the Four Sacred Pieces for Chorus, written three years before his death.

Verdi's mastery of the operatic form continued to grow and refine itself throughout his lifetime. Among his sources of inspiration were the literary classics of Shakespeare, Schiller, and Victor Hugo, and the lyrical and expressive styles of Rossini, Bellini, and Donizetti.

The development of Verdi's style is frequently discussed in contrast with that of his musical contemporary, Richard Wagner. While each of these composers brought romantic opera to its height in his native country, each did so by using quite different approaches. As Wagner explored the philosophical undertones in his librettos, Verdi rejected symbolism in favor of more realistic human drama. Though his plots are not so strictly ordered as Wagner's, spontaneity and a sense of dramatic effect gave his works great tragic expression, while unity was provided through logical musical development and recurring themes.

Verdi and Wagner also disagreed on the relative importance of the various elements of voice, plot, and orchestration. Wagner believed that the most important aspect of his work was the drama, with the music expressing or echoing the complexity of the deeper meanings of the theme. Verdi, on the other hand, emphasized the singer's part, placing the importance of melody over the role of the orchestra. Thus his singers rarely compete with the musical background.

Verdi's keen sense of drama, his command of emotional and even passionate expression, and his emphasis on the melodic line were aspects of his style that evolved as the composer matured. In *Otello*, for example, his control over the orchestra and the work of his librettists, as well as over the dramatic development of his plot, reached its height. The composer died in 1901, his reputation as the greatest composer of Italian opera in the nineteenth century ensured.

Aida

Aida was written at the request of the Khedive of Egypt to commemorate the opening of the Suez Canal. Set in Egypt during the reign of the Pharoahs, the opera reflects all the opulence and pageantry of that extravagant era. Written in 1870, the opera was first performed on Christmas Eve, 1871.

Act I   As the Prelude begins, a brief lyrical phrase is introduced. This is the short melody used to identify the heroine, Aida.

Example 21.4

The first act establishes the love triangle between Radames, the young captain of the guard; Amneris, daughter of the King of Egypt; and Aida, the Ethiopian slave of Amneris. In a trio, each sings of his secret feelings: Radames of his fear of interference from Amneris; Amneris of her jealousy of Aida; and Aida of her love for the young captain. The King and his entourage join the group just as a messenger announces that

Amonasro, leader of the Ethiopians, has launched an invasion of their city. Radames is proclaimed leader of the Egyptian army, and Amneris hands him the flag of battle, singing "Return victorious!" accompanied by the entire assembly. Aida is left alone to lament secretly because it is her father who leads the opposition.

Act II, Scene 1   In Amneris' lavish quarters, the princess is dressing while being entertained by her servants. Aida enters, and Amneris, scheming to find out if she loves Radames, falsely reports his death. Aida's response prompts her anger, and she threatens vengeance. Just then, the return of Radames is proclaimed by the sound of trumpets.

Scene 2   As a crowd gathers at the city gates to greet the triumphant Egyptian soldiers, the famous "Triumphal March" is played:

Example 21.5

This is the occasion of a lavish parade with great pageantry. At last Radames arrives, is crowned with laurel, and is granted any reward he desires. Seeing her father among the prisoners, Aida begs for mercy for her countrymen, and Radames responds by soliciting this as his reward. The King agrees to spare them, and bestows Radames with the hand of his daughter.

Act III   Amneris is brought to a temple at the banks of the Nile where she is to await her wedding day. As she leaves, Aida's theme is played, and Aida enters alone to meet Radames. She sings a song of lament for her country, "O patria mia," when her father arrives unexpectedly. He reminds her of the evils perpetrated by the Egyptians and of her own slavery, urging her to learn the Egyptians' road of attack against the Ethiopians' planned invasion. A reluctant Aida persuades Radames to flee with her to Ethiopia, and he tells her the road to avoid his soldiers. Suddenly Amonasro reveals himself, and Amneris appears at the temple entrance crying "Traitor!" Radames surrenders as Aida and her father flee.

Act IV, Scene 1   The Princess accosts Radames in the judgment hall and promises to save his life if he will forsake Aida. He refuses and is led away to hear his verdict: he will be buried alive.

Scene 2   In a subterranean vault below the temple, Radames awaits his death. Suddenly he discovers that Aida has hidden herself in the vault with him. As a chorus of priests and priestesses chant above, the lovers sing their final duet, a farewell, "O terra addio" (Farewell oh earth),

Example 21.6

and the stone is lowered to seal the vault.

The *Verismo* Movement

Toward the end of the nineteenth century, a movement toward naturalism and realism took place in Italian literature, following a similar movement in France. Called *verismo* (realism), it quickly penetrated Italian opera. Bizet's *Carmen* served as a model for the three Italian composers who led the movement: Giacomo Puccini (1858–1924), Ruggiero Leoncavallo (1858–1919), and Pietro Mascagni (1863–1945). Puccini, the most successful of the verismo composers, effectively united grand opera and realism.

Puccini (1858–1924)

Library of Congress

One of the most celebrated and successful of Italian opera composers, Giacomo Puccini was descended from a line of musicians that stretched back over five generations. His father, a theorist and director of the conservatory at Lucca, died when Puccini was only five, and so the boy's first lessons in singing and the organ were given by an uncle. During most of his childhood, Puccini showed only a modest talent for music; nevertheless, his mother insisted that he continue his studies, and by the age of sixteen he was composing in earnest—chiefly organ music for church services.

In 1880, Puccini obtained a scholarship from Queen Margherita to enter the Milan Conservatory. His most important teacher there was Amilcare Ponchielli, a well-known opera composer whose most notable work was *La Gioconda*. Once graduated from the Conservatory, he entered an opera competition with a work, *Le Villi (The Vampires,* 1884), based on a Slavonic legend. He failed to win the contest, but with Ponchielli's help the opera was produced in Milan on May 31, 1884. The success of the premiere persuaded the well-known publisher Giulio Ricordi to commission a second opera by Puccini. *Edgar,* as it was called, progressed slowly, and during this time Puccini ran off with Elvira Gemignani, the wife of a former schoolfriend (their marriage was not legalized until 1904). Owing largely to a poor libretto, *Edgar* (1884–1888) was not a success; however, Ricordi continued to support the composer, and both men worked over the book for the next work, *Manon Lescaut.* Its premiere, at the Teatro Regio in Turin on February 1, 1893, was an immense triumph.

While *Manon Lescaut* made Puccini famous in Italy, his next opera, *La Bohème (The Bohemians,* 1893–1896), brought him worldwide fame. He completed the work in his magnificent new villa next to Lake Massaciuccoli in northern Italy.

Puccini's only serious failure was, ironically, his favorite opera, *Madama Butterfly,* which opened in Milan on February 17, 1904. Despite the hisses and catcalls of the premiere, the work became quite popular outside Italy. In 1906, while in Paris for the first French production of *Butterfly,* Puccini received an invitation from the Metropolitan Opera in New York to attend performances of his operas taking place the following year. In New York, he found himself a celebrity; in between parties, shopping sprees, and sightseeing, he went to see a number of plays, one of which was *The Girl of the Golden West* by David Belasco. It became the basis for his next opera, *La Fanciulla del West.* Its premiere—which had been secured by the Metropolitan Opera—was one of the most glittering events of 1910, with Arturo Toscanini conducting and Enrico Caruso singing the lead male role. Although the work generated great enthusiasm at its premiere, it soon disappeared from both American and European stages, the only one of Puccini's major works to fall out of the general repertoire.

During World War I Puccini remained in Italy, working quietly on further operas. In 1921 he moved to Viareggio on the Adriatic and began working on his last opera, *Turandot.* It was left incomplete at his death. In 1923 he began suffering from what turned out to be cancer of the throat, and the following year he died of a heart attack. The task of finishing the final scenes of the work was entrusted to Franco Alfano, a distinguished younger composer. The opera was produced under Arturo Toscanini at La Scala, Milan, on April 25, 1926.

Puccini had a sure instinct for effective theater and a gift for creating rich and sensuous melodies. The opera that brought him international acclaim, *La Bohème,* is full of youthful ardor and enthusiasm but is also brutally realistic.

La Bohème

Record 6/Side 2

The Plot

The opera is set in the Latin Quarter of Paris (the artists' district on the Left Bank) in the 1830s. Rodolfo (a struggling young poet) and his friend Marcello (a painter) are freezing in their garret studio on Christmas Eve. Suddenly a friend enters with money, groceries, and firewood, and insists they all go out to celebrate. Rodolfo stays to finish an article he is writing but is interrupted by a knock at the door. The caller is Mimi, a neighbor, whose candle has blown out. She asks for a light, and he invites her in. She is ill and almost faints. When she feels strong enough to leave, they discover that her key is missing. As they search for it on the floor, their hands meet, and Rodolfo tells Mimi about his life and hopes. She describes her life as a maker of artificial flowers and her longing for spring and sunshine. Rodolfo declares his love and Mimi responds passionately. As the act ends, they leave to join his friends at the cafe.

The next act opens with a holiday crowd in the streets near the cafe. Marcello sees his old flame, Musetta, with a wealthy old codger in tow. She tries to attract Marcello's attention, embarrassing her escort and amusing the spectators. Finally she sings a provocative waltz and leaps into Marcello's eager arms.

Some months later, Rodolfo's jealousy has caused Mimi to leave him. She seeks out Marcello to ask his help and tells him of Rodolfo's unbearable behavior; Rodolfo arrives and Mimi hides. He starts to complain to Marcello of Mimi's flirting, but admits that he is actually in despair over her failing health. When Mimi's coughing reveals her presence, Rodolfo begs her to stay with him until spring, and she agrees.

The following fall, Rodolfo and Marcello are in the studio pretending to work, but actually thinking about their absent girls. Their fellow artists arrive for dinner and a hilarious evening begins. Musetta interrupts their gaiety, announcing that Mimi has collapsed on the stairs. They carry her in; all except Rodolfo leave to pawn their treasures to buy medical supplies. Rodolfo and Mimi recall their first meeting; their friends return and Mimi drifts off to sleep. She dies, and Rodolfo embraces her while the others weep.

The Music

Both the libretto and the musical setting of *La Bohème* are compact and economical, with much use of understatement. Puccini's style is essentially melodic, and the conversational aspect of his vocal writing is enhanced by two features: the scarcity of ornamentation and the lack of a sharp distinction between recitative and aria. The rhythm of the text is followed closely in the melody, and there are many short phrases and sentences, as are found in ordinary conversation. The orchestration is often simple and delicate, although quite effective.

The opera is carefully unified by cross-references from one scene to another which occur in both the libretto and in the music. For example, the first and last acts open with the same setting and cast—Rodolfo and Marcello in their studio; and much of the same music is used in the love scene in the first act as well as the recollection of it in the last act. Several other themes also recur at significant points throughout the opera.

One of the outstanding characteristics of Puccini's operatic writing is the skill with which he makes transitions from one mood and scene to the next. Where a lesser composer would finish one idea and separate it from the next by a rest, Puccini (like other great opera composers) knew how to make almost instantaneous shifts from one mood to another. One of the clearest instances of a masterful transition occurs at the end of Act II.

The scene is in the café where the four friends and Mimi are eating; Musetta and her new escort Alcindoro have entered, and Musetta is trying to attract Marcello's attention. He attempts to ignore her shouting and carrying on, but is secretly excited to know that she wants to return to him. The aria that she sings is a deliberate effort to see whether she can win his interest again. It is usually called "Musetta's Waltz," since Puccini directed that it be sung in a slow waltz tempo.

Example 21.7

Quan - do me'n vo'   quan-do m'en vo' so-let -ta per la   via la gen -te so-sta e mi - ra...

He also indicated many slight but expressive changes of tempo from one measure to the next. Several of the other characters comment on what she is saying in this aria; they continue as she finishes the waltz and

Figure 21.4 La Bohème brought Puccini worldwide fame. This 1910 performance at Berlin's Royal Opera House shows the Latin Quarter café where much of the opera's frivolity takes place. (The Bettmann Archive)

begins to argue with Alcindoro, who is protesting that she is embarrassing him.

Deciding to get rid of him, Musetta screams suddenly that her shoe is pinching her foot; she sends him off for a new pair. Following a rising chromatic scale, Marcello sings the theme of her waltz, while she continues to shout about her shoe and the others comment. Rodolfo and Mimi remark that she is quite attracted to Marcello, while the other two friends note that the whole scene is really very funny. This septet ends with Musetta and Marcello embracing as the orchestra takes over the waltz theme.

As the theme continues, the waiter brings the bill, and a marching drumbeat is heard in the distance. It is this overlap that makes the transition so effective, both musically and dramatically. As the friends discuss the bill and their lack of funds, the orchestra begins the march theme very softly

Example 21.8

A crowd gathers as the theme grows louder, trying to decide which direction the parade is coming from. This action continues while

Musetta takes their bill and has the waiter add it to Alcindoro's; the friends plan to melt into the crowd so that he will never find them.

As the military procession enters the stage, the crowd sings its comments on one pitch, in unison, while the orchestra repeats the march melody. The crowd falls in behind the soldiers as they leave, singing the march theme for the first time. Musetta has only one shoe, so the friends lift her to their shoulders and carry her off. While the crowd sings about the parade, they sing "Viva Musetta, the glory of the Latin Quarter!" The entire group marches offstage, and Alcindoro enters; he is given the bill and is dumbfounded.

German Opera

Unlike Italian opera, which built on past tradition, the Romantic opera that flourished in Germany was a new phenomenon, the result of experimentation and the effects of the Romantic movement in both literature and music. Its direct antecedent was the *Singspiel*, the national comic opera form with spoken dialogue that reached its artistic peak in Mozart's *The Abduction from the Seraglio* (1782). Through the influence of French opera, comic opera acquired many Romantic elements, without losing its national characteristics.

The composer who responded to a growing demand for genuinely "German" opera, was Carl Maria von Weber (1786–1826). A true Romanticist, he turned against the international style of the eighteenth century and built his own style on the legends and songs of the German people. His *Der Freischütz (The Freeshooter,* 1821) had features in common with French and Italian opera (particularly in musical style and form), but placed a new emphasis on the physical and spiritual background of the drama.

The typical German Romantic opera, such as *Der Freischütz,* had a libretto stressing the mood and setting of the drama. Nature was represented as a wild and mysterious force, and supernatural beings mixed freely with ordinary mortals. Human characters often symbolized supernatural forces of good and evil, the hero's victory meaning salvation or redemption. The orchestra played a major role in the music of the opera: harmony and orchestral color were important factors in dramatic expression, and recurrent themes were used to provide unity.

In the latter part of the nineteenth century, one of the most powerful personalities in the history of music emerged—Richard Wagner. German Romantic opera reached its highest point through his creation of the *music drama*. Wagner's harmonic idiom marked a turning point away from Classical tonality toward developments in chromaticism that extend to the present day.

Wagner concerned himself with nearly every aspect of nineteenth-century art: music, literature, poetry, drama, and stagecraft. He was influential not only as a reformer of opera but also as a music critic, writer on aesthetics, and political and social polemicist. While his accomplishments as a poet and playwright were overrated in his time, Wagner's impact on both the cultural and philosophical thought of nineteenth-century Europe was enormous.

Wagner (1813–1883)

The Bettmann Archive

Born in Leipzig, Richard Wagner was the son of a clerk in the city police court who died when his son was only six months old. His mother soon after married Ludwig Geyer, a gifted actor, playwright, and painter. It was rumored that Geyer was the composer's real father, and Wagner himself considered this likely. Wagner was a precocious child who showed an early interest in literature, writing a tragedy in the style of Shakespeare at the age of fourteen. His formal musical training was among the least systematic of the great nineteenth-century composers. He began piano lessons at age twelve, but never became a first-rate performer on any instrument. Like Berlioz, his great French contemporary, his music depended on the full resources of the orchestra.

Lack of adequate preparation did not prevent him from early attempts at composition. By 1832 several of his works—including two overtures and a symphony—had been publicly performed. The following year—at age twenty—he began his professional career, becoming chorus master for the Wurzburg theater. Positions at Magdeburg, Königsberg, and Riga followed in succession, and he began composing operas.

While in Königsberg, he married the actress Minna Planer and began work on an opera based on Bulwer-Lytton's historical novel, *Rienzi, Last of the Tribunes*. The years 1839 to 1842 were spent in Paris, where he tried vainly to gain a production of the work. His financial situation became desperate, partly because of his increasingly spendthrift ways, and the first serious breakdown in his marriage occurred.

Rienzi was finally accepted, not in Paris but in Dresden, Germany, and Wagner returned to Germany to supervise the production. The success of both *Rienzi* (1842) and his next opera, *Der Fliegende Holländer* (*The Flying Dutchman*, 1843), led to his appointment as conductor to the King of Saxony. For the next six years Wagner busied himself producing operas and writing two more himself: *Tannhäuser* (1842–1844) and *Lohengrin* (finished in 1848). Wagner's active participation in the revolutionary uprising of 1848 to 1849 forced him to flee to Switzerland.

While in exile, he turned to literary activity and wrote a number of essays, the most influential of which were *Das Kunstwerk der Zukunft* (*The Art-Work of the Future,* 1850) and *Oper und Drama* (*Opera and Drama,* 1851). In these he laid the foundations for his concept of music drama.

During his ten years in Switzerland, Wagner began putting his artistic theories into practice. By 1852 he had completed the poems of an epic cycle of four music dramas, entitled *Der Ring des Nibelungen* (*The Ring of the Nibelungs*). The music of the first two dramas—*Das Rheingold* (*The Rhine Gold*) and *Die Walküre* (*The Valkyrie*)—and part of the third—*Siegfried*—was completed by 1857. The tetralogy requires four separate days of three to five hours each for its performance.

The Ring of the Nibelung

In composing this work, Wagner was attempting to depict the corruption of modern society with its greed for money and power. Through the activities of giants, dwarfs, gods, and warriors, he symbolized the error of sacrificing love and compassion to the middle-class values of his day. Thus he portrayed the path of destruction brought about by the pursuit of a ring of gold forged by a race of dwarfs known as the Nibelungs.

The first opera in the series is *Das Rheingold* (*The Rhine Gold*). In this opera, Wagner tells of the theft of the gold from the river mermaids by the dwarfs. This deed, according to the composer, symbolized the renunciation of charity, love, and goodness; Wagner was criticizing the modern middle-class value on work, which he felt was emphasized to the detriment of emotion and human feelings. The dwarfs are in possession of the gold only briefly, as the gods steal it for themselves and mortgage it to a race of giants. Representing the establishment of nineteenth-century Germany, the gods and their king, Wotan, are examples of the height of corruption in the greed for money.

The second opera in the dramatic cycle, *Die Walküre (The Valkyrie)*, tells the story of Brunnhilde, a favorite daughter of Wotan, one of the goddesses called Valkyries (from which the title of this opera comes). Wotan instructs his daughter to oversee the punishment of a mortal who has eloped with the wife of another man. Sensing her father's preoccupation with obtaining the golden ring, Brunnhilde disobeys his orders and attempts to aid the couple. Forced to punish her disobedience, Wotan places her on a mountain ringed with fire, where she must sleep until rescued. Again the theme of renunciation of love for gold symbolizes the depravity of society and the corruption of its values.

The entire cycle was finished in 1874 with the composition of *Die Götterdämmerung (The Twilight of the Gods)*. In the intervening years, Wagner wrote two works that perhaps remain his most popular and frequently performed: *Tristan und Isolde* (1856–1859) and *Die Meistersinger von Nürnberg (The Mastersingers of Nuremberg,* 1862–1867).

However prolific his composing, Wagner experienced great difficulty in arranging performances of his works. Most were formidable in scale, requiring theatrical and musical resources beyond the means of even the largest opera houses. As he approached the age of fifty, he became discouraged. His debts continued to pile up, and he separated from his wife and even contemplated suicide.

Then in 1864 his fortunes changed. The new king of Bavaria, Ludwig II, a devoted admirer of Wagner's music, invited the composer to Munich with the promise of financial and artistic support. At this time, Wagner fell in love with Cosima von Bülow, the daughter of Franz Liszt and wife of one of Wagner's close associates. Cosima left her husband to join Wagner, completely devoting herself to his career. They were finally married in 1870, and together raised enough money to build an opera house devoted exclusively to producing his works. Located in the small Bavarian town of Bayreuth, the *Festspielhaus*, as it was called, was the scene of the first complete performance of the Ring cycle in 1876. One of the great artistic events of the century, this performance was the fulfillment of Wagner's life-long dream. He completed one more work,

Parsifal (1882), before illness forced him to travel to Italy in hope of regaining his health. He died, quite suddenly, in Venice on February 13, 1883.

His Work

Although his most significant works were his operas and music dramas, Wagner wrote a considerable amount of orchestral, choral, and solo vocal music, modeling his early symphonies and overtures largely after Beethoven's orchestral style. However, his most important instrumental piece is the *Siegfried Idyll*, a short work composed for Cosima's birthday celebration of December 25, 1870. His most outstanding vocal work is a collection of five settings of poems by Mathilde Wesendonk with whom Wagner had a passionate love affair in the late 1850s. Composed during 1857–1858, the collection is known today as the *Wesendonk Lieder*.

Wagner's early operas—*Die Feen (The Fairies,* 1833), *Das Liebesverbot (Love Prohibited,* 1836), and *Rienzi* (1842)—were written under the influence of Meyerbeer, Bellini, and Donizetti, the masters of grand opera whose works dominated the European opera houses of the early nineteenth century. With his next three operas—*Der Fliegende Holländer (The Flying Dutchman,* 1843), *Tannhäuser* (1843–1845), and *Lohengrin* (finished in 1848)—Wagner began his reform of operatic style and structure. These works represent a culmination of the German Romantic opera tradition that Wagner inherited from Carl Maria von Weber.

The reforming tendencies manifest in these three essentially Romantic operas become intensified in the Ring cycle. Wagner's plots (all of which were of his own creation rather than that of a librettist) now dealt with German mythology or historical legend. He developed a style of musical declamation that he termed *Sprechsingen* (singing speech) and gave the orchestra a role in the music drama fully equal in importance to that of the voice. Dramatic and musical unity were achieved by application of *Leitmotiven* (leading motives), or melodic fragments that represented specific characters, objects, or abstract concepts in the drama. These motives, sounded by both orchestra and singers, held the entire fabric of the drama together. Wagner's use of the *leitmotiv*, fitted into a flowing, flexible orchestral texture, attains its greatest development in *Tristan und Isolde.*

Wagner believed that a music drama should be a *Gesamtkunstwerk* (universal artwork) encompassing all the arts. The most important element should be drama, with the music serving to reinforce the dramatic expression. This concept was diametrically opposed to the one held by many earlier opera composers (Mozart, for example), who believed that the libretto should serve as a framework for the music.

Wagner wrote his librettos to include the philosophical issues that he considered to be of fundamental importance: the struggles between the forces of good and evil and between the physical and the spiritual, and the idea of redemption through unselfish love. Almost every scene and action in the Wagnerian work can be interpreted on two levels: first, at face value, and second, in terms of deeper and more symbolic meanings.

His Style

Wagner's basic principles, the organic unity of drama and music and the various levels of meaning, directly affected his musical style. The music is essentially continuous throughout each act rather than broken into separate recitatives and arias. Such continuity had been growing in nineteenth-century opera, but Wagner actually brought it to fruition.

The two levels of meaning of the drama are represented by the voices and the orchestra. The voices have the lesser role; through their actions and words, they explain the superficial meaning of the drama. The orchestra is used to express the inner meaning of the action, which the characters themselves often do not understand.

The expression of dramatic meaning by the orchestra requires the use of the leitmotiv, for which Wagner is famous (although he did not invent it). A leitmotiv associates a melodic fragment with a particular person, object, or idea; it is a kind of musical label that sounds every time its object appears in the drama. The technique is an extension of the use of recurring themes that had been found in the operas of Verdi, Puccini, and Weber; but Wagner's method of using them is much more consistent.

Leitmotivs are also used in a much more subtle way; as musical phrases, they can be varied or developed in the usual symphonic fashion. With every variation, and every change of context, they take on added shades of meaning. Wagner also uses them to suggest ideas to the audience. For example, the connection between two objects may be suggested by a similarity between their leitmotivs.

Although leitmotivs are woven into the orchestral fabric, they do not provide enough unification for works of such vast dimensions as Wagner's operas. Wagner, therefore, imposes formal structures on larger portions of the music dramas (such as whole acts), usually constructing them either in AAB or in ABA form. On such a large scale, forms are not obvious to the listener; nevertheless, they lend a feeling of balance and proportion to the work.

Tristan und Isolde

Record 6/Side 2

Wagner was at the height of his powers when he wrote *Tristan und Isolde.* As an outstanding example of his mature style, it has had great impact on several generations of composers. The complex web of leitmotivs is everpresent, but subordinated to a constant flow of emotions and inspired orchestral writing. The mood of tragic gloom is sustained by the extremely chromatic quality of the writing.

The Plot

The libretto is based on a medieval legend. The opera opens on shipboard, where the knight Tristan is escorting the Irish princess Isolde to Cornwall. There she is to marry his lord and uncle, King Marke. Isolde explains to her maid Brängane that she had met Tristan before; he had come to her, unknown and wounded, and she had healed him. When she later discovered that he had been the one who killed her fiancé in

Figure 21.6   This opening-act stage drawing for the first performance of Tristan und Isolde *in Bayreuth (1886) employs realistic shipboard scenery for the dramatic voyage to Cornwall. (The Bettmann Archive)*

Figure 21.7   The 1963 Bayreuth Festival production of Tristan und Isolde *used much more sparse and symbolic staging for Act I. Here, the mood of tragic gloom is visually set from the opening curtain. (Culver Pictures)*

combat, she became furious and tried to kill him. But when he looked in her eyes, she was unable to; she felt love instead. Isolde orders Brängane to prepare a death potion, so that she may kill Tristan and herself. They drink the potion and are condemned to a fate worse than death, for Brängane has substituted a love potion, and their attraction becomes an irresistible passion.

The second act opens in Isolde's garden, where she and Tristan plan to meet in secret that night; King Marke and the courtiers are off on a hunt. Brängane advises caution, but Isolde signals to her lover and he comes. Their long love scene is interrupted by the return of the hunting party, which includes Melot, a jealous knight who has warned King Marke about the affair. Marke questions Tristan, revealing that he married Isolde only to satisfy the people of his kingdom. Tristan does not defend his disloyalty, but asks Isolde if she will follow him to the "wondrous realm of night." She agrees; Tristan pretends to attack Melot, drops his guard, and permits himself to be seriously wounded.

The final act takes place at Tristan's ancestral castle in Brittany. His squire Kurvenal has sent for Isolde: the dying and delirious Tristan recalls their love and his longing. As she arrives, the dazed hero rips off his bandages and dies in her arms. King Marke, Melot, and the others arrive in a second ship, and Kurvenal and Melot kill each other. Marke forgives the unhappy lovers, and Isolde joins Tristan in death.

Such a simplified account of the plot gives no indication of the wealth of detail and symbolism with which Wagner has imbued it. The story actually represents a philosophy of life: an all-encompassing love inevitably leads to unsatisfied longing, then to death and a final transfiguration of two into one. This deeper level of meaning is symbolized by constant references to "day" and "night." Day is the world of conventional life and values, while Night is the inner world in which such a love exists. When Tristan asks Isolde to follow him to the "wonderous realm of night," he means the death in which their union can be complete.

Analysis of one scene from *Tristan und Isolde*, illustrates Wagner's use of the leitmotiv. In actual practice, it is difficult to label some of the motives. With slight variations, they seem to represent several different things. The opening passage of the opera is a case in point. The two motives here are often called Tristan and Isolde, or Grief and Desire. Together, they represent Yearning, or the Love Potion.

Example 21.9

Isolde or Desire

Tristan or Grief

Many basic emotions such as suffering, ecstasy, and desire are closely linked, and their motives are also related. Even the Day and Night motives are similar.

Example 21.10

In the last scene of the second act King Marke confronts the lovers, and Tristan is wounded. In addition to the motives mentioned above, several others will be encountered. Three come from the great love duet of the preceding scene; they represent Love's Peace, Love-Death, and Ecstasy.

Example 21.11

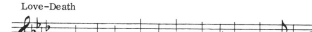

Example 21.12   The other two are associated with King Marke and his grief.

The scene begins at the very climax of the love duet. As the singers reach their final notes, the orchestra plays a loud and unexpected dissonant chord, Brängane screams, and Kurvenal shouts to Tristan to protect himself. Marke, Melot, and the courtiers enter. The music grows quiet as the two groups study each other. The Love-Death and Ecstasy themes are heard softly in the orchestra. They are followed by the Day theme, as Tristan sings *"Der öde Tag zum letzten Mal"* (The bleak day for the last time).

Marke, shattered, tells how deeply Tristan's betrayal affects him while the bass clarinet sounds his Grief motive. Tristan answers violently that this is all a bad dream; significantly, he calls it a day phantom, a morning vision, rather than a nightmare.

Marke, the innocent victim of fate, is a "day" person, with no control over his unhappy situation. Repeatedly he asks what he has done to deserve this. Marke can never know the answer to his question. At the same time, the orchestra answers the question for the audience by playing the Grief and Desire motive from the opening of the opera.

Tristan then asks Isolde if she will follow him; as he begins, the violins play the leitmotiv associated with Love's Peace. He describes the dark land to which they will go, in a lyric arioso passage. Isolde gives her assent in a similar section; he kisses her as the Ecstasy motive is heard. The infuriated Melot urges the King to defend his honor. Tristan challenges Melot, and finally lets himself be mortally wounded.

Another aspect of *Tristan und Isolde* that deserves special mention is Wagner's harmonic style, and particularly his use of chromaticism. Wagner continued to expand the chromatic idiom used by other Romantic composers (particularly Liszt in his symphonic poems). Wagner's use of the idiom in *Tristan* produced a new ambiguity of tonality through the constant shifting of key and the addition of nonchord tones to standard chord progressions. It is almost impossible to analyze this harmony in terms of the traditional system that had served from Bach to Beethoven. In its tonality, *Tristan* represents an important step toward the new systems of harmonic organization that evolved in the twentieth century.

Wagner's music in general, and *Tristan und Isolde* in particular, have been unusually influential. Wagner's harmonic style, continuous but irregular melodic writing, symphonic use of leitmotivs, and superb sense of orchestral color all influenced several generations of composers who followed him. He attained his ideal of the *Gesamtkunstwerk*, although his music had a force that his librettos did not. Since he intended that his music should serve the drama, it is ironic that today we sometimes hear the music alone performed in concerts, while the librettos could never stand alone as plays. But despite some errors in judgment, Wagner's accomplishments were truly outstanding, expressing the universal state of ecstasy toward which all Romantic artists had been striving.

Summary

During the early part of the Romantic era, Paris was the operatic capital of Europe. French opera concentrated on spectacular productions, featuring crowd scenes, ballets, choruses, and fantastic scenery. These grand operas, however, gradually gave way to lyric operas that emphasized Romantic plots and beautiful melodies. Toward the end of the century a naturalistic style developed, of which Georges Bizet's *Carmen* is a prime example.

In Italy, Gioacchino Rossini was the outstanding composer of the early part of the nineteenth century. His *Barber of Seville* is an excellent example of the Italian opera buffa. The dominant figure in Italian opera during the second half of the century was Giuseppe Verdi, who evolved a style that combined earthy, elemental emotions and clarity of expression. Toward the end of the century, a movement toward naturalism penetrated Italian opera. Called *verismo,* it is best exemplified in the works of Giacomo Puccini.

Romantic opera in Germany grew out of the *Singspiel,* the national comic opera form. The composer who established the genuinely Germanic style was Carl Maria von Weber. Typically, German operas represented nature as a wild and mysterious force and mixed supernatural beings with ordinary mortals in the plots. German opera reached its highest point in the works of Richard Wagner, who sought to write musical dramas that would encompass all the arts in a unified whole. To Wagner, the most important element was the drama, with the music relegated to serving the dramatic expression. The librettos, which he wrote himself, can be interpreted on two levels: first at face value, and second in terms of deeper and more symbolic meanings. Dramatic meanings were expressed by the use of leitmotivs, or melodic fragments associated with a particular person, object, or idea.

Part V
Suggested
Listening

Berlioz, Hector

Harold in Italy, Op. 16. This symphony in four movements is based on Lord Byron's *Childe Harolde,* with the solo viola as the main character.

Brahms, Johannes

Piano Quintet in F Minor, Op. 34. The four movements illustrate the juxtaposition of Brahms the lyricist with Brahms the contrapuntist.

Variations on a Theme of Haydn, Op. 56a. Originating as an Austrian pilgrim song which Haydn used and Brahms admired, the theme is the basis for a set of eight variations and a lengthy finale.

Chopin, Frederic

Etudes, Op. 25. The second set of twelve studies employing similar formal structure. Each is a study of a pianistic difficulty requiring a musical solution.

Moussorgsky, Modest

Pictures at an Exhibition. A series of ten pieces united by a *Promenade* which introduces the work. Composed after Moussorgsky was inspired by an exhibition of Victor Hartmann's paintings, it is available in piano and orchestral versions, orchestrated by Maurice Ravel.

Schubert, Franz

Die Winterreise. Twenty-four songs on the theme of loneliness which are musically united through rhythmic patterns and harmonic structures.

Title page by Picasso for Stravinsky's piano arrangement of
Ragtime. *(Courtesy SPADEM, French Reproduction Rights, Inc.)*

Plate 15.   Henri Matisse's Portrait of Mme. Matisse (Portrait with a Green Streak) exemplifies Expressionistic distortion of line and color in the service of rendering the artist's subjective impression. The Royal Museum of Fine Arts, Copenhagen. (Courtesy SPADEM, French Reproduction Rights, Inc.)

Plate 16.   Cubism was abstracted and purified by painters like Piet Mondrian, whose Broadway Boogie-Woogie combines only primary colors and right-angle forms. Much of Mondrian's work was limited to varied arrangements of squares and rectangles. (Mondrian, Piet; Broadway Boogie Woogie. 1942–43; Oil on canvas, 50 x 50"; Collection, The Museum of Modern Art, New York; Given anonymously.)

Plate 17.   Paint was dripped, flung, and poured onto this canvas to create Jackson Pollock's Number 27. The Abstract Expressionists believe that such methods will produce a painting just as revealing of the artist's personality as will the more conventional techniques. (Courtesy Whitney Museum of American Art, New York) ▶

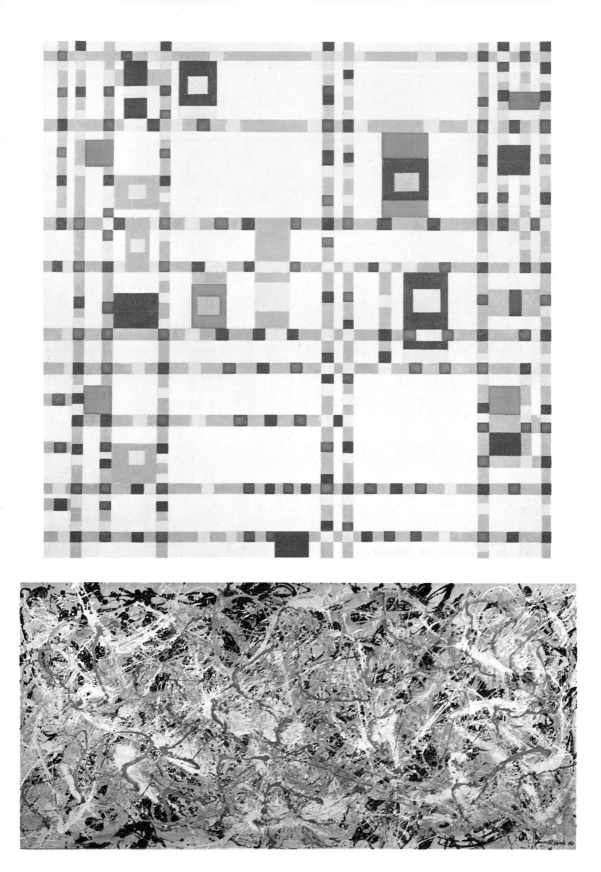

part VI   Music of the Twentieth Century

Never before the twentieth century was there a time of such varied experimentation in all the arts: in painting and sculpture, the depiction of actual objects was abandoned for pure color, line, and form; in literature, the novel and other traditional narrative forms were often discarded for free associa-

The Arts of the Twentieth Century

tion of words; in music, traditional harmony and tonality were rejected completely for atonality and serialism. The most important lesson twentieth-century artists learned from the avant-gardists of the nineteenth century seemed to be the necessity for total freedom of expression, even if it meant setting aside aesthetic standards that had persisted since the beginning of the Renaissance. In most cases, initial reaction to this break in tradition resulted in the alienation of the artist from society.

Gradually, however, public opinion changed. Many artists who had been called madmen half a century before became the respected old masters of modern art and literature: Pablo Picasso, Henri Matisse, Igor Stravinsky, Arnold Schoenberg, James Joyce, T.S. Eliot.

During the early years of the century, accepted ideas were challenged in many fields. Physicist Albert Einstein demonstrated that there was no clear distinction between matter and energy. Psychoanalyst Sigmund Freud posited that man's thoughts and actions were directed by unconscious fantasies and dreams. Anthropologists such as Sir James Frazier pointed out the parallels between the customs of Western civilization and those of so-called primitive societies. At the same time that those basic assumptions were being questioned, artists were also questioning the traditions of their own crafts.

333

Artists reflected their times in yet another important way. The twentieth century has been called the Century of the Common Man. Despite the violence of two world wars and countless riots and revolutions, there has persisted a belief in freedom and social opportunity for all. Furthermore, the twentieth century is characterized by the widely held belief that these goals can be realized through social action. With equal militancy, artists have demanded freedom for themselves, showing that individuality is still possible in a society of mass production and mass communication. Whereas artists of other eras accepted standards imposed by religion, monarchy, aristocracy, or the middle class, in the twentieth century they turned to themselves for their standards.

The desire of artists to express freely their attitudes toward themselves and the world is reflected in a major current of twentieth-century painting. Called Expressionism, it may be defined as art that takes as a starting point a realistic subject, such as a portrait, landscape, or still life, but distorts line and color to depict not so much the subject as the artist's subjective interpretation of it.

As early as 1905 several young artists—including Henry Matisse (1870–1954) and Georges Rouault (1871–1958)—exhibited their Expressionist paintings. Their distortion of form and arbitrary use of color (for its own sake, rather than to recreate reality) caused the critics to call them "Fauves," or wild beasts. Like the Impressionists a generation earlier, they proudly adopted this insulting remark as the name of their

Figure 22.1 The Spanish architect Antoni Gaudi rejected architectural tradition entirely by designing free-flowing, almost organic, buildings. The Casa Battló in Barcelona, for example, bears little resemblance to the classical symmetry of the past. (Antoni Gaudi. Casa Battlo. Barcelona, Spain. 1905–07. Photography, courtesy of The Museum of Modern Art, New York.)

movement, for it expressed their hostility to prevailing academic standards (Plate 15).

The Fauves had a strong influence on painters who used the distortion of line and color to express their alienation from middle-class society. A leading member of this group was the Russian Wassily Kandinsky (1866–1944), who sought to apply musical harmonies and tonalities to painting. Around 1910, Kandinsky took the drastic step of totally abandoning a recognizable image, pointing twentieth-century art in yet another direction.

Expressionism also left its mark on architecture. During the nineteenth century, architecture, like sculpture, was almost totally backward looking: churches were built in Gothic style and public buildings in Renaissance or Baroque style; private homes resembled Tudor manors or Italian villas. Totally rejecting such architectural academism, Antoni Gaudi (1852–1926), a Spanish architect, designed buildings of free-flowing, almost organic, forms. The square and functional style that dominated architecture in the twentieth century originated at the Bauhaus School in Germany. Obeying the dictum "form follows function," the Bauhaus architects abandoned the decorative ornamentation of the Victorian era. The director of the Bauhaus, Walter Gropius (1883–1969), designed a building for the school whose continuous glass surface became the model for many skyscrapers and even influenced the picture windows of suburban homes.

Figure 22.2 The functional form and glass walls of Walter Gropius' Bauhaus workshop wing (Dessau, Germany) have been absorbed into the architecture of today's skyscrapers and office buildings. (Walter Gropius. Bauhaus Building. Workshop Wing. Dessau, Germany, 1925–26. Photograph, courtesy of The Museum of Modern Art, New York.)

Figure 22.3   Pablo Picasso abstracted identifying elements of both men and violins in Man with a Violin, *an early example of Cubism. The artist's use of nearly three-dimensional geometrical forms gives the picture solidity and depth. (Philadelphia Museum of Art, Louise and Walter Arensberg Collection)*

Figure 22.4   Bird in Space, by Constantin Brancusi, is less an abstraction of a bird than a representation of flight. Brancusi's unexcelled craftsmanship and love of form heightened modern artists' consciousness of shape. (Constantin Brancusi. Bird in Space. (1928?) Bronze, unique cast, 54" high. Collection, The Museum of Modern Art, New York. Given anonymously.)

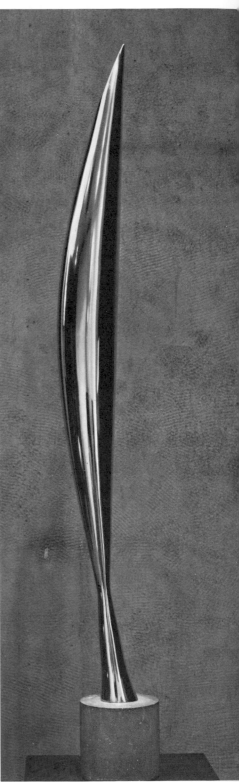

Figure 22.5   Using a characteristic theme, Henry Moore sculpted this Reclining Figure *to convey a sense of both the inner and outer space of his subject. Such concern with spatial void was a direct outgrowth of Cubism's new perspective. (Edith Reichmann)*

This geometrical style is closely related to the strongest current of twentieth-century painting, Cubism, conceived by one of the century's most inventive artists, Pablo Picasso (1881–1973). Cézanne had distorted the image to convey a sense of volume and space. About the year 1906, Picasso went even further, completely breaking up the surface of the painting into geometrical shapes that seem to advance and recede from the surface. Picasso's Cubist paintings have a sense of solidity and depth and at the same time retain a reference to actual objects. In *Man with a Violin*, we can recognize the figure and the instrument because Picasso has "abstracted" a few basic forms that all violins have in common (scrolls, strings, bridge, fingerboard) and all men have in common (ears,

chin, nose, mouth, shoulders, arms). By rearranging them, he depicts not a camera image of a man with a violin but the painter's idea of a man with a violin.

As a mode of painting, abstraction was widely adopted because it allowed painters and sculptors to deal with familiar objects without having to treat them realistically, recombining the elements into a work that finally must be seen as pure form and color.

Other painters developed and purified the geometric aspect of Cubism. The Dutch painter Piet Mondrian (1872–1944) limited much of his work to arrangements of squares and rectangles of gray, blue, yellow, red, or white, separated by black bands. With such simple elements, he achieved remarkable variety (Plate 16).

Cubist sculpture often leaned heavily on recognizable objects and most sculptors chose to work in more abstract styles. *Bird in Space*, by the Rumanian sculptor Constantin Brancusi (1876–1957), is not an abstraction of a bird so much as it is a rendering of the idea of flight. Traditionally, sculpture was concerned only with mass, or the space a piece of sculpture displaced; but after Cubist painters began showing a variety of views of an object simultaneously, sculptors considered another aspect of sculpture—void, or the space enclosed by a piece of sculpture. In the work of the British sculptor Henry Moore, born in 1898, voids, or "negative spaces," became integral parts of the sculpture.

While some artists distorted images of recognizable objects to heighten the viewer's emotional response, others devoted meticulous attention to painting objects that existed only in their fantasies. The depiction of fantasy is not new in art; it was frequently practiced by the Mannerists. In the twentieth century, fantasy became a dominant motif. A group of writers and artists—the Surrealists—formed a movement dedicated to externalizing fantasy. In 1924 they issued a manifesto advocating "pure psychic automatism . . . free from the exercise of reason and from any aesthetic or moral purpose." The Spanish Surrealist painter Joan Miró (b. 1893), for example, depicts in his *Dog Barking at the Moon* a nightmare landscape with whimsical figures that soon take on an eerie aspect.

The desire of the Surrealists to eliminate consciousness from the act of creation had its fulfillment in Abstract Expressionism, a method of painting that began in the United States in the late 1940s and soon spread to Europe. One of the originators of Abstract Expressionism, Jackson Pollock (1912–1956), developed a method of making huge works by pouring, spattering, and dripping paint onto the surface of his canvas (Plate 17). Here the act of painting is no longer dominated by the artist's fingertips holding and guiding a brush, but by the broader gesture of flinging paint; how it falls *is* the painting. Although the way the paint falls is determined by the motion of the artist's body, this, in turn, is determined by the artist's total person. Thus a painting made in this manner reflects the artist as accurately as if it had been carefully painted stroke by stroke.

Music in the twentieth century took two predominant courses. The first, led by such composers as Hindemith, Bartók, and Stravinsky, rejected traditional concepts of tonality and changed the way in which a tonal center was established and used. The second, led by Arnold Schoenberg, rejected tonality altogether and developed a revolutionary way of organizing music, called *serialism*.

chapter 23

The music of the twentieth century differs from earlier music so radically and in so many respects that it must be considered in a category of its own. One of the roots of the difference lies in the rejection of the traditional concept of functional tonality, which had dominated music for almost three hundred years. Functional tonality considered all notes and

The New Music

chords in their relationship to a single note, the central or *tonic* note of the key. Harmonic progressions away from and then back toward the tonic implied motion and rest, expectation and arrival. While much Romantic music strained the boundaries of functional tonality by the introduction of many more chromatic notes, most composers of the twentieth century have totally abandoned the assumptions on which the old tonal system was based.

Virtually all the formal structures developed during the Baroque, Classical, and Romantic periods depended on tonality as a major structural element. The fugue, sonata-allegro form, and even the Romantic tone poem were all based on certain assumptions about tonality that were shared by composer and listener alike.

Essentially only two paths were open to the composer who rejected the basic concepts of functional tonality. One was to reject any form of tonality whatsoever, to deny the importance of any one note over the others. This path was chosen by Arnold Schoenberg, who developed a system called *twelve-tone composition* or *serialism* to replace tonality as a structuring force. But other important composers chose a less radical course; they maintained the idea of tonal center or point of rest but significantly altered the methods by which the center is established and used. Composers in this category include Béla Bartók, Paul Hindemith, and Igor Stravinsky.

In addition to the changes in the element of tonality, twentieth-century music differs from the music of previous periods in two other important ways. The first is the increase in the amount and degree of *dissonance* used by most modern composers. Before the later part of the Romantic period, music was characterized by a certain relationship between consonance (the norm) and dissonance (the departure from the norm). Dissonant harmonies were expected to return to, or resolve into, consonance. In varying degrees and stylistic manifestations, this use of dissonance was true of the music of Palestrina, Bach, Mozart, Beethoven, and Brahms, as well as other Romantic composers.

The late Romantic styles of Wagner and Strauss placed more emphasis on dissonance. Dissonances were prolonged, and frequently a series of dissonances would occur before the ultimate resolution to a consonant harmony. Gradually this emphasis on dissonance increased to the point that in much twentieth-century music dissonance is used quite independently from consonance. The expected resolution of dissonance into consonance has been abandoned in much the same way that traditional tonality was discarded.

The harmonic structure of this music is characterized by dissonance rather than consonance. Harmonic progressions take place from dissonance to dissonance, with consonance used only incidentally, if at all. Actually, the music is heard as a series of dissonances, varying in their complexity or tension, from mild to exceedingly harsh.

From the Baroque to the post-Romantic period, chords had been built on intervals of the *third*. The tonic chord, for example, consisted of the first, third, and fifth tones of the scale, each a third apart. Other chords were constructed of the same intervals, but beginning on different tones of the scale.

As the interest in the possibilities of dissonance increased, new methods of chord construction were developed. More dissonant intervals were used as the basis for chord construction, resulting in a greater variety of "harmonic sonorities" than had existed before and more complex and harsher combinations than had been previously possible.

This greater degree of dissonance and the use of dissonance apart from consonance is a characteristic of "modern music" and is closely allied to the change in attitudes toward tonality.

The other change that marks twentieth-century music is its *rhythmic complexity*. In much modern music it is virtually impossible to ascertain any consistent metrical system, or even the actual beat.

Rhythmic complexity, harmonic dissonance, and an obscure or nonexistent tonal center, then, are three distinguishing characteristics of much twentieth-century music.

Bridging the Gap between Centuries

Toward the end of the nineteenth century the center of cultural activity in Europe was Paris. Several different musical styles were current; one was the cosmopolitan style, the basically German-Italian late Romantic style, strongly influenced by the monumental achievements of Richard Wagner. The leaders of this style of music in Paris were César Franck (1822–1890) and his pupils. In contrast to this pan-European style was the specifically French tradition, as cultivated by Camille Saint-Saëns (1835–1921), Jules Massenet (1842–1912), and Gabriel Fauré (1845–1924).

The underlying concept of this music was more Classical and orderly than Romantic and expressive. The music was subtle and understated, full of lyric melodies and carefully wrought details.

The musical culture of France was closely connected to the other arts, particularly painting and literature. One of the outstanding artistic movements of the turn of the century was Impressionism. Taking its name from a painting by Claude Monet entitled *Impression: Sunrise,* the title was adopted as a label for those artists who sought to capture the visual impression, rater than the literal reality, of their subject.

Though their work and methods were generally ridiculed by the critics, the Impressionists persisted in their exploration of the play of light and in their use of patches and dabs of color to build up an image. They also continued their habit of working out-of-doors and of utilizing bright afternoon light; mood and atmosphere and the richness of nature were among their major inspirations.

Though scorned in the 1870s, Impressionism began to achieve a measure of success and recognition in the 1880s. At the same time, the movement began to find parallel expression in the other art forms. Its counterpart in literature was Symbolism. Symbolist poets, among whom were Charles Baudelaire (1821–1867) and Arthur Rimbaud (1854–1891), attempted to achieve "musical" effects by manipulating the rhythm and sounds of words. The basic idea or emotion of each poem was suggested by clusters of images and metaphors.

Following the art and literary movements by some thirty or forty years, the Impressionist movement in music was similarly characterized by experimentation and by the rejection of past viewpoints. It too emphasized mood and atmosphere more than structure and celebrated the joys of nature. Impressionist music was soon recognizable by its fragile and decorative beauty, its sensuous tonal colors, its love of the subdued, its elegance, refinement, and beauty of sound. It cast off the more pompous, heavy, and serious quality of the German tradition. Again, France produced the most important composers of this school: Claude Debussy and Maurice Ravel.

Debussy (1862–1918)

The Bettmann Archive

The music of Claude Achille Debussy is programmatic, but in a very general way; there is no attempt to tell a story or express specific feelings. Rather, his music creates a "mood" or atmosphere to correspond wih its subject or program.

Debussy was born in Paris and was educated at the Paris Conservatory where he received traditional training in the cosmopolitan, late Romantic style. He absorbed it well enough to win the Prix de Rome at the age of twenty-two, but soon after he began to reject the Germanic tradition in general and Wagner's philosophy in particular.

Although Debussy's style is unique, many influences can be seen to have helped form it. Most important are the Romantic pianists Chopin and Liszt and composers in the French tradition. Paris was a center for Russian music, and Moussorgsky's idiom pointed Debussy in new directions. His interest in exotic music was stimulated by the Javanese orchestra (called a *gamelan*), which he heard at the Paris Exposition of 1889.

One of the strongest influences on Debussy's style was not musical at all, but literary; he was closely associated with a group of artists centered around Stéphane Mallarmé, the Symbolist poet. Through this connection Debussy became very interested in expressing the unique sounds and rhythmic patterns of the French language in music. French generally avoids strong accents, making use of vowels of different lengths for rhythm and stress. Debussy's choice of subject matter for many of his pieces also reflects his close association with this important literary movement.

His Work

Debussy's compositions for piano are among the most significant works for that instrument written during the present century. His early non-Impressionistic works include the *Suite bergamasque* (1893) and a suite *Pour le piano* (1901). His Quartet in G Minor for Strings (1893) left its first audience puzzled and critics complaining of an "orgy of modulations." A forerunner of Impressionism, it came to be recognized in the twentieth century as one of the most important string quartets since those of Brahms. The impressionistic style is fully evident in works published between 1903 and 1913: *Estampes* (*Engravings*), two collections of *Préludes*, and two of *Images*. Debussy's important orchestral works are all Impressionistic, beginning with the *Prélude à l'après-midi d'un faune* (*Prelude to the Afternoon of a Faun*, 1894), and continuing with the *Nocturnes* (1899) and *La Mer* (*The Sea*, 1905), a set of symphonic sketches.

Opera was one of Debussy's life-long interests, although he completed only one of the many projects he started. His operatic style was very much a reaction against Wagner's influence; the libretto of his *Pelléas et Mélisande* (1902) is taken from a Symbolist play, and the vague references and images of the text are matched by the strange harmonies and restrained colors of the music. Throughout the work the voices dominate over a continuous orchestral background. Debussy also wrote incidental music for a play and several sets of songs.

Debussy's Style and Its Influence

Debussy was the first European composer to break with the old system of tonality, and the new language he developed had a profound influence on almost every other composer of the twentieth century. His music is organized around sound patterns; he works with blocks of color and shifts from one to another very subtly. The harmonic basis of his music is entirely new, building on the symmetrical patterns of the whole-tone scale. Instead of relying on the traditional tonic-dominant-tonic sequence of harmonies, he often uses a series of chords built on adjacent degrees of the scale. These parallel chains of chords leave the piece without any clearly defined tonal center for extended periods, thus freeing other elements of the music to function as form-building devices, particularly rhythm, dynamics, texture, and instrumental timbre.

In one sense, of course, Debussy's style is clearly an offshoot of the Romantic movement; the emphasis on color and lack of interest in traditional forms and procedures are evidence of this, as are the literary associations of most of his works. But in another sense, Debussy represents the beginning of the new and radically different music of the twentieth century. His use of atonal harmonies took music into new and uncharted areas, and his free-associating forms and concentration on timbre influenced almost all later composers.

Prélude à l'après-midi d'un faune

Record 7/Side 1

This work was inspired by the Mallarmé poem *L'après-midi d'un faune*, published in 1876. Debussy first intended to write a dramatic work based on the poem but soon abandoned this operatic project for a smaller one; he described the *Prélude* as a "very free illustration of Mallarmé's beautiful poem." Without following the poet's intention exactly, Debussy portrays each of the scenes and evokes a suitable mood for each one.

This was Debussy's first orchestral work; he had not yet broken away completely from traditional ideas of form. The *Prélude* is very roughly in an AA'BA'' form although there is no literal repetition. In any event, the structure of the piece is much less important than its use of color and texture. The orchestration is somewhat unusual; the winds include three flutes, two oboes, one English horn, two clarinets, and two bassoons; there are four French horns, but the other brasses are omitted. Two harps, a pair of tiny antique cymbals, and the usual strings complete the orchestral forces. Virtually all thematic material is assigned to solo winds, primarily the flute and the oboe. The opening theme, which is heard in various transformations through most of the work, is a sensuous melody for unaccompanied flute:

Example 23.1

p doux et expressif

Example 23.2

The lyric theme of the middle section is introduced by all the winds in unison, with string accompaniment:

p expressif et très soutenu — *m.f*   *p*   *cre - scen - do*   *f*

The melodic material of the *Prélude* is very elaborate, and Debussy uses a combination of melodic and dynamic stress to build the climaxes of his piece. In line with his belief in the importance of the nonmelodic and harmonic elements of music, Debussy gives very detailed directions concerning subtle changes of tempo and dynamics. There are many dissonant chords, but they sound colorful and interesting rather than harsh. The harmonic structure and the rhythm are both somewhat vague and languid, as befits the subject matter of the piece.

Ravel (1875–1937)

Although there was no "Impressionist School" that followed Debussy, another French composer, Maurice Ravel (1875–1937), is often linked with him.

Born in Ciboure at the southern tip of France, Ravel was the son of a mining engineer whose futile dream was to become a musician. Having moved to Paris while Ravel was still an infant, his father encouraged his son's musical tendencies, and at the age of fourteen, enrolled him in the Paris Conservatory where Ravel studied for sixteen years under such masters as Fauré.

While in Paris, Ravel received support from a group of artists known as the "Apaches." Talented individuals from a number of artistic disciplines, this group recognized Ravel's gift for musical innovation and encouraged him in his composition efforts.

Except for the interruption of the First World War, which found the composer at the front lines driving an ambulance, Ravel's career continued its upward spiral. His works for the piano and voice, his chamber music, and his orchestral compositions had already gained him recognition as the foremost composer of his country. He proceeded with his work, interrupted by occasional tours of Europe, until 1928, when he left for the United States. Here he acquired a great admiration for American jazz and, upon returning to Paris, he began to patronize Parisian night clubs that featured this music.

Ravel continued to produce masterpieces until he died at the age of 62. A rare brain disease resulted in the slow loss of his speech and motor coordination; submitting to a dangerous operation, he never regained consciousness.

Ravel had much in common with Debussy. Philosophically, both composers agreed that music's goal was to serve a sensuous purpose, that the creation of beautiful sound was the ultimate aim. They also both considered themselves rebels against the music of German romanticism and the Wagnerian school. Together they shared an attraction to the medieval modes and to the novel scales produced by nationalist composers of other countries. The rhythms characteristic of Spanish dance music were also a mutual attraction, as were also the Oriental modes and colors.

But the similarities between the two composers can only be acknowledged to a limited extent. While Ravel made use of all the Impressionist devices, his compositional procedures were quite different in a number of ways from those of Debussy. There is less use of the whole-tone scale, and sparing use of dissonance in Ravel's work. His use of orchestral color is more brilliant and dynamic than Debussy's. For musical texture, he relied more on melodic lines rather than on the parallel blocks of sound which Debussy favored. Ravel also displayed a firmer sense of key and employed broader melodies, more distinct harmonic movement, and more driving rhythms than his predecessor.

Ravel created many compositions for the piano. The *Pavane pour une infante défunte* (*Pavane for a Dead Princess*, 1899), his *Jeux d'eaux* (*Fountains*, 1901), and *Miroirs* (1905) are examples of those that earned

Figure 23.2   Maurice Ravel combined the Impressionism of Debussy with a classical orientation toward form and balance. Ironically, the work for which he is most famous, Bolero, is much more primitive than his usual style. (The Bettmann Archive)

him the reputation of being one of the outstanding composers of piano music of the twentieth century.

Songs were also a source of fascination to Ravel, and he continued their composition until the end of his life. *Schéhérazade* (1903) is a song cycle for voice and orchestra. Ravel also succeeded in combining chamber music with voice, as in the *Trois Poèmes de Stéphane Mallarmé* (1913) and the sensuous *Chansons madécasses* (*Songs of Madagascar*, 1926).

Despite his popular repertoire of piano works, songs, and chamber music, Ravel is unquestionably best known for his orchestral works. His *Rapsodie espagnole* (*Spanish Rhapsody*, 1907) remains a favorite today. So, too, does his *Mother Goose Suite* (1912) for orchestra, adapted from his own piano composition. One of his most ambitious undertakings was *Daphnis et Chlöe* (1912), a ballet from which were taken two frequently performed orchestral suites. Two of his most enduring compositions are *La Valse* (1920) and *Boléro* (1928). In both, the artist made use of unusual elements. *La Valse* is notable for its unusual combination of traditional waltz rhythms and arresting and disturbing harmonic and textual elements. *Boléro*, drawing its inspiration from the Spanish dance of the same name, employs an uninterrupted crescendo and a repetitive single melody. To this great body of work must also be added the famous *Piano Concerto in G* (1931) and the *Concerto for the Left Hand* (1931), two virtuosic masterpieces.

In his later years, Ravel began to display a distinct and pervasive classicism in his music. The period from the close of World War I was one of attention to the clarification and simplification of his style. However, Ravel was not alone in his return to traditional forms, renewed emphasis on craftsmanship, and growing objectivity in music. These were, in fact, the hallmarks of a trend toward the earlier qualities of the classical spirit; they marked the beginning of the Neo-Classical movement.

Neo-Classicism

Although Ravel's Neo-Classicism grew out of his early association with Debussy, other French Neo-Classicists were strongly anti-Debussy, as well as anti-Wagner. A group of six composers formed around Erik Satie (1866–1925) and cultivated a lighter, more popular style. Their work created a new atmosphere, an acceptance of experimentation and a complete rejection of both the Romantic and Impressionistic traditions. The most important composers of this group were Arthur Honegger (1892–1955), Francis Poulenc (1899–1963), and Darius Milhaud (1882–1974).

Debussy's influence was not restricted to France by any means; it was felt in England, Spain, Italy, and America. England's most Impressionistic composer was Frederick Delius (1862–1934), a man of German extraction who spent much of his adult life in Paris. His style is lush and chromatic, with constantly shifting harmonies. His melodies, however, are rather simple, tonal, and even reminiscent of folk songs. In England, a country which had not been a significant force in music history for almost two hundred years, the twentieth century marked the beginning of a musical renaissance. A few composers early in the century, particularly Edward Elgar and Delius, had adopted the techniques and styles of the Continental mainstream, but it remained for Ralph Vaughan-Williams to use them in a uniquely English manner.

Ralph Vaughan-Williams (1872–1958) was influenced by Debussy's ambiguous tonalities and emphasis on sonorities. He studied orchestration with Ravel. But his interests also extended to English folk music, and to the music of the English Renaissance. Moreover, he felt that music was a democratic cultural phenomenon; it belonged to the common man and had to reflect his interests. The emphasis on choral music in Williams' early years is a part of the centuries-old tradition of choral singing in Great Britain.

The nationalistic aspect of Williams' music is not merely a matter of quoting folk songs; it is more a philosophical position that is indirectly expressed in the music. His symphonic style involves a nontraditional approach to tonality, but a generally romantic idiom. The nine symphonies and other large orchestral works are balanced by an extensive collection of vocal music. It ranges from simple folk-song settings to large operas, songs, and many choral works, including some with orchestral accompaniment. One of the finest of these is *Dona Nobis Pacem* (1936), a setting of texts by Walt Whitman, John Bright's "Angel of Death" speech, Latin liturgical prayer, and excerpts from the Old and New Testaments.

The most outstanding English composer today, Benjamin Britten (b. 1913), has also used voices extensively in his works. In fact, Britten is widely regarded as a great master at setting English texts to music. The language is awkward from a composer's point of view, but Britten handles it with consummate ease. His operas, particularly *Peter Grimes* (1945), are considered to be some of the best contemporary works in the traditional operatic format.

Britten's style shows influences from Stravinsky and Debussy, but bears an original stamp. Superficially, his music is rather simple and appealing, with a wide variety of forms and procedures and an essentially tonal harmonic language. But beneath the surface lie complex and carefully worked out structures that can be interpreted on several different levels.

Britten's *War Requiem* (1963) is an outstanding example of the elaborate forces that may be involved. This work entails the juxtaposition of the Latin text of the Mass for the Dead with English poems by Wilfred Owen, a young soldier-poet who wrote and died during World War I. This contrast is reflected in the orchestration, which calls for orchestra, chorus, boys' choir, and three soloists. The styles employed range from Gregorian chant to fugue to aria. The result is a highly dramatic work depicting the horror of war in a unique and very moving way.

Almost all of Britten's major works involve voices. Some are on a large scale—*Rejoice in the Lamb* (1943) and the *Spring Symphony* (1949), in addition to the *War Requiem* and the operas. The *Ceremony of Carols* (1942), a setting of medieval English Christmas texts for boys' choir and harp, is one of his best-known works. Britten has also made several contributions to the literature of the orchestrally accompanied song, including his *Serenade for Tenor, Horn, and Strings* (1943). He has also composed a small number of purely instrumental pieces, both orchestral and chamber.

A Spanish composer who first accepted Debussy's influence and later rejected it in favor of Neo-Classicism was Manuel de Falla (1876–1948). His earliest works were strongly nationalistic and employed the idioms of Andalusian folk music and dance very effectively. De Falla spent his last years in South America. His best-known works are *Noches en los jardines de España* (*Nights in the Gardens of Spain*, 1916) and a harpsichord concerto (1926); he also wrote several ballet and opera scores.

Impressionism also made its mark on an Italian composer, Ottorino Respighi (1879–1936), who studied with Rimsky-Korsakov in Russia before returning to his native land to teach and compose. Both instrumental and vocal music interested him; his most successful opera was *La Fiamma* (1934). He is best known today for his trilogy of nationalistically oriented symphonic poems: *Fontane di Roma* (*The Fountains of Rome*, 1917), *Pini di Roma* (*The Pines of Rome*, 1924), and *Feste Romane* (*Roman Festivals*, 1929).

In America, the composer most receptive to Debussy's ideas was Charles T. Griffes, who will be discussed in more detail in Chapter 26.

Some of the finest music of the period was produced by German-born Paul Hindemith. In addition to being a prolific composer, he was an exceptional performer on a variety of instruments, an eminent teacher of composition, and an important musical theorist. Like many composers of his time, he was concerned with the problems of musical organization. His systematic approach to these problems is embodied in his theoretical treatise *The Craft of Musical Composition*.

Hindemith (1895–1963)

The Bettmann Archive

Paul Hindemith was born in the town of Hanau, just outside Frankfurt. He began violin lessons at nine, branched out to learn other instruments, and was soon composing in a steady stream that was to make him among the most prolific of twentieth-century composers. At the Hoch Conservatory in Frankfurt he became close friends with the violin teacher Adolf Rebner, who helped him obtain a position as violinist in the Frankfurt Opera orchestra, which was conducted by Ludwig Rottenberg. In 1924, Hindemith married Rottenberg's daughter, Gertrude.

During his years with the opera orchestra, Hindemith gradually began to break with the highly chromatic styles of Wagner and Strauss. His song cycle *Das Marienleben (The Life of Mary,* 1923) was a landmark in his development as a composer, revealing a style devoid of Romantic traits. During the late 1920s he became interested in creating music that amateurs could not only listen to, but also play and sing. He began composing solo and chamber works, both instrumental and vocal, in a simple, melodically appealing style.

Following the performance of his large-scale opera *Cardillac* at Dresden in 1926, Hindemith's reputation as a composer spread throughout Germany. The following year he took a teaching position at the Berlin *Hochschule für Musik,* which he held until 1935.

With the nazification of Germany in the 1930s, Hindemith found himself under attack as a cultural Bolshevik and as an associate of Jewish musicians. When the performance of his opera *Mathis der Maler (Matthias the Painter,* 1932–1935) was banned in Germany, the premiere of this work took place in Zürich, Switzerland, in 1938.

In 1937 Hindemith made his first appearance in America and toured the country from 1938 to 1939. In 1940, when he was appointed to the music faculty of Yale University, he decided to settle in this country, becoming an American citizen six years later. He did not return to Germany until 1949, when he conducted the Berlin Philharmonic in a performance of his own works. In 1953 he moved back to Europe, teaching at the University of Zürich and conducting concerts throughout Germany and Austria. He died in Frankfurt on December 23, 1963, at the age of sixty-eight.

His Work

Hindemith wrote in virtually all traditional genres of composition and contributed important works to the twentieth-century repertory of almost all commonly played musical instruments. His ten operas, in addition to *Cardillac* and *Mathis der Maler,* include several early one-act works, a marionette opera, a children's opera, and another large-scale work, *Die Harmonie der Welt* (*Cosmic Harmony*, 1950–1957).

His vocal works include art song collections, a series of short solo cantatas, canons, and a number of madrigals composed toward the end of his career. His most important large-scale choral-orchestral work is *When Lilacs Last in the Dooryard Bloom'd* (1946), an American requiem with text from Walt Whitman.

The chamber music includes a series of works for miscellaneous ensembles, each entitled *Kammermusik* (seven in all), sonatas for solo instruments, seven string quartets, and a number of duets and trios. His most substantial contribution to piano literature is the cycle of twelve fugues, *Ludus tonalis* (1943), a twentieth-century counterpart to Bach's *Well-Tempered Clavier*.

Hindemith's best-known orchestral compositions are the symphony *Mathis der Maler*, based on his opera of the same name, and the *Symphonic Metamorphosis on Themes by Weber* (1944). He also wrote concertos for piano, clarinet, horn, cello, violin, and viola. Included among his works are several composed for dance, of which *The Four Temperaments* is probably the most frequently performed.

Hindemith's Style

In his early period, Hindemith's writing was very chromatic, almost atonal; his mature style evolved gradually in the 1920s. His approach to structure and tonality marks him as a traditionalist, although he operates within a chromatic framework. The texture of his music is most often contrapuntal, its linear aspect sometimes obscuring harmonic progression.

The system of tonality that Hindemith developed is based on the establishment of tonal centers—tones that serve as points of arrival or rest, but without the traditional concepts of key or major and minor modes—a system which enables the composer to exercise considerable control over the degree of dissonance he uses. Hindemith had hoped that this new system of tonality would serve as a universal musical language, for he felt it was based on natural acoustical principles and could accommodate itself to almost any style. In fact, this was not so; it served very well for Hindemith himself, but proved to be unsuitable for other styles.

Although his new synthesis of tonal procedures did not have the effect he had hoped for, Hindemith did exert considerable influence on the course of twentieth-century music. Probably his most important contribution was the reestablishment of a close working relationship between composers and performers. Since he himself was both, his feelings on the subject carried considerable weight. He tried to recapture the eighteenth-century (and earlier) situation in which composers wrote for specific occasions or for specific groups of performers. He idealized the days when almost all patrons and audiences were devoted amateur musicians themselves.

As a teacher of composition, Hindemith influenced a wide circle of younger men, both in this country and in Europe. During his years at Yale University he also exercised a profound influence in quite another direction. Hindemith was passionately interested in Medieval and Renaissance music and instruments, and the members of the Collegium Musicum which he directed at Yale constitute an important group of professional musicians performing and teaching early music in this country today.

Kleine Kammer-musik für fünf Bläser (Little Chamber Music for Five Winds), (Op. 24, No. 2)

This quintet from Hindemith's set of miscellaneous chamber works, written in 1922, is one of his most delightful pieces and illustrates the exuberance of his early style particularly well. It is written for the traditional wind quintet instrumentation: flute, oboe, clarinet, French horn, and bassoon. The five movements contrast clearly with each other. The two outer movements are the fastest and most complex structurally; the second and fourth are lighter; and the third is a lyric, slow movement.

Record 7/Side 1

First Movement: *Lustig*

Like most of Hindemith's writing, this movement has clearly recognizable melodic material, which is stated and even developed in a fairly traditional way. The first theme is presented by the clarinet

Example 23.3

while the horn, bassoon, and oboe accompany with a rhythmic motive taken from the theme: ♪♫ ♪. The theme is stated a second time by the oboe and then fragmented slightly; the flute joins in and after a few "mistaken" attempts presents the theme a third time.

The second theme, a more lyric melody, is introduced by the oboe, while the rhythmic accompaniment continues. The theme is repeated immediately by the flute and oboe together and followed by a series of arpeggio figures alternating between clarinet and flute. The clarinet states the second theme once more and begins to fragment it.

An arpeggio from the bassoon signals a return to the first theme, this time divided between the clarinet and the flute. The oboe restates the theme and the flute tries again to find it, this time breaking off into the arpeggio figure. Fragments of both themes and the arpeggio form a coda to end the movement.

Second Movement:
Walzer. Durchweg sehr leise

This lilting waltz is divided into several short sections; the overall form is AA'BCBA'' coda. The first theme is again introduced by the clarinet; the A' section is really just a "reorchestration"; the melody is given to the piccolo, which replaces the flute in this movement. The B section, featuring the oboe, is very short and serves to frame the more lyric C section, in which the French horn is prominent. After a literal repeat of B, another "orchestration" of A is introduced, which leads to a slower coda, which is composed of both new material and fragments of the B theme.

Third Movement:
Ruhig und einfach

This elegant, slow movement displays Hindemith's skill at spinning out long melodic lines; the form of the movement is a simple ABA' coda. The first theme is introduced by the flute and clarinet and then appears in the oboe and bassoon. After a pause the B section begins, first with just the accompaniment, consisting of ostinato patterns in the flute, clarinet, and horn. The expressive melody enters, played by the oboe the first time and then repeated by the oboe and bassoon together. A short transition leads back to the first section, which is presented in a slightly abbreviated version. The coda involves a combination of the first theme and ostinato accompaniment from the second section.

Fourth Movement:
Schnelle Viertel

Example 23.4

This light movement is based on a very simple plan: A short and pounding two-measure ritornello

alternates with short solos for each instrument in turn. The solo passages are very well suited to the particular instruments: the flute and clarinet have flowing arpeggios, the bassoon's line is somewhat lumbering, the oboe is dramatic, and the horn is expressive. However, everything happens so fast that the net effect is rather humorous.

Fifth Movement:
Sehr lebhaft

The form of this final movement is roughly that of a large arch: AB bridge CBA bridge coda. The three different sections are characterized largely by the rhythmic contours of their themes. The A theme is emphatic and presented with strong accents on the main beats by the entire ensemble. The B material is quite different: the upper parts are accented—but syncopated, off the beat—and set against a very regular bass line.

Example 23.5

Example 23.6

Example 23.7

After a transition of chromatic runs, a variation on the B material is presented; it is melodically different, but rhythmically related.

The bridge is made up of repeated groups of three notes and descending sequences. It leads to the C section, which is a soft and expressive flute solo, accompanied by ostinato patterns in the lower parts. After a short interlude, the C material is repeated, this time loudly. The B and A sections are restated almost literally, although in reverse order, and the bridge leads to a coda, which consists of fragments of both A and B material. The work ends with a very firm tonal cadence.

Bartók (1881–1945)

Culver Pictures

The most significant composer to emerge from Eastern Europe in the twentieth century was Béla Bartók. He was born in Hungary, the son of the director of a government agricultural school. His first piano lessons, begun at the age of five, were given by his mother. Following the death of his father in 1888, the family moved to Bratislava (now in Czechoslovakia), where Bartók began formal studies in music. While a student at Bratislava, he made his first public appearance as a composer and pianist in 1892, playing one of his own works, and formed a close friendship with Ernö Dohnányi, in later years one of Hungary's most noted pianists and composers.

In 1899, though admitted to the prestigious Vienna Conservatory, Bartók decided to follow Dohnányi to the Royal Academy of Music in Budapest. In Budapest he became strongly attracted to the music of Wagner and Richard Strauss. He also was caught up in the current nationalistic movement in politics, literature, and the arts then sweeping through Hungary. His first major composition, an immense orchestral tone poem entitled *Kossuth* (1903), commemorated the nationalist leader of the unsuccessful revolution of 1848. He became friends with Zoltán Kodály (1882–1967), the third member (with Dohnányi and Bartók himself) of the great trio of modern Hungarian composers.

Both Bartók and Kodály developed a strong interest in the problem of creating a national music and began collecting and analyzing Hungarian folk music. The earliest product of their research was a joint publication of arrangements of *Twenty Hungarian Folksongs* (1906). Bartók's interest in folk music began to have an immediate effect on his own work; side by side with the most current devices in composition appeared folk-derived rhythms and melodic patterns.

Following his graduation in 1902 from the Royal Academy, Bartók began a series of concert tours throughout major European cities which lasted for the next several years. During this period he became increasingly influenced by the French Impressionistic music of Debussy and his contemporaries. Bartók's own efforts at composition, however, did not seem to get off the ground during this period, and for a while he leaned toward a career as a concert pianist rather than as a composer.

In 1907 Bartók accepted an appointment as a piano teacher at the Budapest Academy, a post that he held for nearly thirty years. In 1909 he married Márta Ziegler, one of his pupils, and settled into a routine of teaching, composing, researching folk music, and making extensive concert tours. In 1923 he was divorced and married one of his piano students, Ditta Pásztory. They often toured together, playing works for two pianos, and in 1927 they came to America for a series of solo recitals and appearances with various orchestras.

The political turmoil of the late 1930s, brought on by the expansionist policies of Nazi Germany, convinced Bartók that he had to leave Hungary. In 1940 he emigrated to the United States, where he was soon given an appointment at Columbia University. While in New York, however, he developed leukemia and his health began declining seriously. He died in September, 1945.

His Work

Bartók was primarily an instrumental composer; with the exception of a large cantata, a small number of art songs, and collections of folk song arrangements, almost all his music falls into one of the following categories: music for solo piano, chamber music for strings (often with piano), concertos, orchestral works of various types, and stage works.

His works for piano range from technical studies and beginners' pieces through difficult recital pieces and concertos. His early piano music includes a rhapsody (1904), fourteen bagatelles (1908), and two elegies (1908). One of his earliest masterpieces is *Allegro barbaro* (1911), which demonstrates for the first time his assimilation of folk elements. His major contribution to piano pedagogy is the collection of 153 progressively graded pieces, published in six books as the *Mikrokosmos* (1926–1937).

Among his chamber works the most outstanding pieces are the six string quartets. This was the only musical form to hold Bartók's interest throughout his career, and the quartets rank among the finest contributions to the literature since the Viennese Classical period.

His ten concertos are all major works and most of them remain essential items in twentieth-century repertoire. They include three for piano; two for violin, of which the second (1937–1938) is a masterpiece that ranks with those of Beethoven, Mendelssohn, and Brahms; one for viola (1945), left unfinished at Bartók's death and later reconstructed; three rhapsodies, one for piano (1909), and two for violin (1928); and one for two pianos (1940).

Bartók's stage works include a one-act opera, *Bluebeard's Castle* (1911), with only two singing roles and a large orchestra; and two ballets, *The Wooden Prince* (1916) and *The Miraculous Mandarin* (1918–1919). His one major choral work, the *Cantata profana* (1930), based on a Hungarian legend, requires a double mixed chorus, tenor and baritone soloists, and a large orchestra.

Kossuth (1903), an orchestral tone poem and Bartók's first major work for orchestra, was highly acclaimed at performances in England and in Budapest. Following this success, Bartók brought out two suites for orchestra (1905, 1907) and three other orchestral works, all composed between 1908 and 1912. Other works for full orchestra were his *Dance Suite* (1923) and *Concerto for Orchestra* (1943), the latter being his orchestral masterpiece and one of the great works of this century. Two other popular works, both written for smaller forces, round out his orchestral music—*Music for String Instruments, Percussion, and Celeste* (1936) and the *Divertimento for String Orchestra* (1939).

Bartók's Style

Because of his interest in folk music, many people considered Bartók as a representative of a nationalistic school of composition. This is somewhat misleading because although he certainly went through a nationalistic phase in his youth, his mature works are part of the mainstream of European music. Throughout his life Bartók studied the folk music of Eastern Europe, and aside from the music of his native Hungary, he also worked on the music of Rumanian, Bulgarian, Slovakian, Turkish, and Serbo-Croatian peoples.

The effects of his studies on his own compositions were profound, especially in his approach to tonality. Most Eastern European folk music lies outside the traditional major-minor system, and Bartók realized the impossibility of using this material within the tonal system. He formed his own type of harmonic organization, one which could accommodate melodies not based on a major-minor tonality.

Bartók's studies also influenced his style of melodic writing, which sometimes has a folklike character. He rarely used actual folk songs in his compositions, but he understood how they were constructed and effectively imitated them.

Bartók's mature style is compact and economical. Often he derives his melodic material from just one or two very short motives used intensively throughout a composition. He structures large-scale pieces by using the same material in several movements. Bartók's writing is essentially contrapuntal; he thinks more in horizontal (melodic) than vertical (harmonic) terms. The harmonic organization of Bartók's music is freely chromatic and ranges from intense to relatively mild dissonances.

Traditional devices and forms are an important part of Bartók's style, and in this sense he can be called a Neo-Classicist. He employed fugue, canon, and other contrapuntal procedures and also made use of the sonata-allegro principle. These formal schemes were bent and altered to suit the occasion, however, since they were not being used within the tonal system for which they were originally designed.

Other aspects of earlier music that appear in Bartók's writing include the Baroque device of separating an ensemble into two antiphonal groups in order to make the contrapuntal lines more distinct. Bartók used this device in his outstanding *Music for Strings, Percussion, and Celesta* (1936). This work contains a very slow chromatic fugue, a dance-like sonata movement, and a furious rondo. It is unified by a motive that grows and expands from movement to movement. The instrumentation is quite unusual, although the use of percussion in small ensembles is characteristic of twentieth-century music.

Bartók's String Quartets

The six string quartets of Béla Bartók offer a concentrated picture of his development as a composer. They span a large portion of his creative life and represent an intensely personal contribution to the literature of the quartet. Bartók's attention to chamber music is characteristic of this century; most Romantic composers felt too limited and bound by this medium. Even Brahms, the most Classical of nineteenth-century composers, tended toward an orchestral sound in his chamber music and preferred to write for groups larger than the quartet.

Bartók's quartets are exceptional in the musical variety they encompass. There is no pattern or system apparent among them; each piece poses new problems and solves them in new ways. Each solution proves again the possibility of uniting simple melodic material with the most dissonant and chromatic harmony in a context that can make use of both traditional and new forms.

The First Quartet, composed in 1908, belongs to a transitional period in Bartók's stylistic development. It lacks the economy of his later works, and various influences on his style (Wagner, Brahms, and Debussy, in particular) are still close to the surface. The important principle of motivic development, however, is already apparent in this work, with a single four-note motive evolving gradually throughout. The main emphasis in this early quartet is melodic, and other aspects (rhythm, harmony, tonality) yield to it.

The Second Quartet (1917) is very different from the First in both mood and style. The chromatic harmonic idiom is much more pronounced and even includes some *bitonality* (simultaneous use of two different keys). The work has no real themes, only short motives that are developed continuously.

During the ten years that elapsed between the Second and Third Quartets, Bartók wrote some of his most abstract and almost atonal music. The Third Quartet (1927) is the shortest of the six and contains the most shockingly shrill sonorities. It is constructed as a single continuous movement, with four contrasting sections. For the first time a new and important principle of form is used in Bartók's work, a large-scale symmetry involving the entire work, with material shared by outer movements, which thus form an arch to frame a central section. This structure was characteristic of most of Bartók's works from 1927 to about 1936, culminating in *Music for Strings, Percussion, and Celesta.*

The Fourth Quartet, which followed the Third by only one year, is quite similar to it. The Fourth represents the peak of Bartók's constructional phase. Bartók pushes the principles of symmetry and motivic development almost to their outer limits. The work is in five movements and a double arch is formed by shared motivic material in the first and fifth movements and also in the second and fourth. The writing is very linear, and almost everything is derived from a single, six-note motive.

The Fifth Quartet, written in 1934, displays the same attention to formal symmetry but is not so tightly constructed in the area of motivic development. The thematic material is more folklike than in the Fourth Quartet, and the tonality is more clearly established.

The last quartet, the Sixth (1939), is in many ways the culmination of Bartók's life and work; it displays the ingenuity and self-discipline which are the hallmarks of his style.

String Quartet No. 6

Record 7/Side 1

The Sixth Quartet is marked by an exceptional variety of textures, sounds, rhythms, and forms. Rather than the archlike symmetry of the earlier quartets, Bartók organized this quartet around a central theme that introduces the first three movements and serves as the subject of the last movement. Bartók's exceptionally tight motivic development reinforces this cyclic procedure.

First Movement

Example 23.8

The quartet opens with the central theme played by the solo viola; it is marked *Mesto* (sad) and has a gloomy, searching effect.

After a short chordal introduction ending with a fermata, the tempo changes to *vivace* and the main part of the movement begins. It is in sonata-allegro form, with two contrasting themes. The basic material of theme 1 is presented first by the violin alone.

Example 23.9

These nine notes provide all the material for the first part of the piece, which consists of developmental use of the basic phrase. It is immediately broken into two motives, which are fragmented, inverted, and otherwise developed until a slight ritard introduces the second theme.

This second theme,

Example 23.10

played first by the violin over a pedal point in the lower instruments, has a mixture of unpredictable rhythms that give the music a folklike swing. The second theme is also characterized by fairly frequent changes in tempo. In the closing section that follows, Bartók refers to both themes by using short representative motives to suggest them, along with another ritard and diminuendo. With an abrupt change in tempo and dynamics (forte), the development section begins a restatement of the second part of the opening introduction, and immediately moves into development of the first and second themes. Bartók often expands his themes by adding a few more notes each time they occur. Early in the development section, the viola and cello add three notes to the first theme.

Example 23.11

Later, the cello lengthens it still more.

A false recapitulation, with theme 1 stated by the viola, precedes the real one, whose theme is in the violin.

The recapitulation of the first theme is shorter than it had been in the exposition, and the second theme is distributed among all four instruments. A coda, still using motivic material, relaxes gradually to a very soft and slow ending.

Second Movement

The *mesto* theme again introduces the body of the movement; this time a slightly expanded version is played by the cello while the other three instruments play a contrapuntal line in octaves. The second violin and viola play it tremolo, and all four instruments are muted.

Example 23.12

The thematic material for the main part of the movement, a march, is introduced softly by the second violin and taken up loudly by the ensemble in a very jagged dotted rhythm, with the instruments no longer muted. The march is essentially in ABA' form; the middle section is very expressive and rhapsodic, with the melody in the cello, very high in its range. Following a pseudo-cadenza for the entire ensemble, the dotted-rhythm march theme returns.

Third Movement

The introductory *mesto* theme is expanded here to a three-part setting, and again lengthened slightly. It leads directly to a wild, grotesque burletta (from the Italian word for joke), marked by grinding dissonances, violent contrasts, and humorous effects. There are many glissandos (slides) between notes, rapid alternation between pizzicato and playing with the bow, and some deliberately out-of-tune notes, to create a sort of musical smear. But the humor of this movement is largely ironic, and does not help to dispel the gloomy pall cast by the mesto theme.

The form of the burletta is also ABA' with a tender and lyrical middle section. It opens with a phrase that recalls the inversion of the first theme of the first movement and later brings in the second theme of that movement also. The return to the hammering burletta is played mostly in pizzicato. The coda that follows is bowed and refers occasionally to the material of the middle section.

Fourth Movement

The theme that has served as an introduction to the first three movements becomes the subject of the final movement. The despair of the *mesto* theme pervades the entire movement. The opening four-part statement of the theme, in imitation between the outer voices, is followed by fragmentation of its various parts. A soft and very slow restatement of the opening notes of the theme, accompanied by a static chord, leads to a coda, in which the two themes of the first movement are recalled. The movement ends, however, with the viola playing the *mesto* theme again, groping uncertainly as it had at the beginning. The final chords do not establish a clear tonality for the work; they accept rather than resolve the tension of dissonance. The cyclic unity provided by the constant return of both the *mesto* section and the themes of the first movement is balanced by the astonishing variety Bartók brings to this quartet. Many special effects are incorporated into the fabric of the work—the banjolike strumming of pizzicato chords, the special pizzicato in which the string is snapped onto the fingerboard, the slides and out-of-tune notes, the passages without vibrato—but variety is never used for its own sake; it always serves the more important overall design of the entire piece.

Stravinsky (1882–1971)

Arnold Newman

One of the most important figures in all of twentieth-century music first came to public attention in Paris. Igor Stravinsky is one of the greatest masters of modern music. His career, like that of his great Spanish contemporary Pablo Picasso, spans three generations; in their respective fields each played a dominant role in almost all significant trends of the first half of this century.

Stravinsky was born in a small Russian town on the Gulf of Finland near St. Petersburg, the third son of one of the most celebrated bass-baritone singers in the Imperial Opera. He began piano lessons at the age of nine, but his parents, though encouraging his piano studies, regarded his musical ability as a sideline and decided that he should study law at the University of St. Petersburg. At the university Stravinsky had the good fortune to make friends with the youngest son of Rimsky-Korsakov; he soon met the composer himself, then the leading figure in Russian music and one of the members of the "Mighty Five" circle of composers. By 1903 Stravinsky was studying orchestration with Rimsky-Korsakov. They became close friends and the elder composer acted as best man at Stravinsky's wedding to a cousin, Catherine Gabrielle, in 1906.

After completing his university studies in 1905, Stravinsky decided on a career as a composer. His earliest serious works were written under Rimsky-Korsakov's supervision. In 1909 he met Sergei Diaghilev, the impresario of the newly formed *Ballets Russes*, who commissioned the young composer to write music for a ballet based on an old Slavic legend. The work, entitled *L'Oiseau de feu (The Firebird)*, was premiered at the Paris Opera the following year. It was so successful that Stravinsky, almost overnight, became a celebrity in Western musical circles.

Two more ballets quickly followed: *Petrouchka* (1910–1911) and *Le Sacre du printemps (The Rite of Spring*, 1912–1913), the latter's premiere creating an unprecedented scandal in its use of novel orchestration and aggressive, barbaric rhythms. Undeterred by what proved to be only temporary criticism, Stravinsky kept up a continuous flow of composition. Until the outbreak of World War I he divided his time between Switzerland, Russia, and France. A member of the most distinguished musical and artistic circles in Europe, he came in close contact with Debussy, Ravel, de Falla, Jean Cocteau, and Picasso.

From the outbreak of the war until 1919 Stravinsky lived in Switzerland, and his compositional style showed a marked change from that of his earlier large-scale ballet scores. Most of his works written between 1913 and 1923—including three ballets, short piano pieces, songs, and chamber music—were scored for small instrumental ensembles of various types. His ballet *Pulcinella* (1919) and the Octet for Wind Instruments (1923) began his Neo-Classic period, which lasted until 1951.

Much of his time during the 1920s and 1930s was spent on tour through the principal cities of Europe and America. When World War II began, he settled in Hollywood, giving up his French citizenship (acquired after the Russian Revolution, when he became an expatriate), and became a naturalized American in 1945.

His Work

Taken as a whole, Stravinsky's work constitutes a unique variety of styles, genres, musical forms, and instrumental combinations. By and large, his most popular works continue to be the early Russian ballets, with their mixture of exotic tone coloring, complex orchestration, and striking, often barbaric-sounding, rhythmic patterns. Many of his later works demonstrate a far more austere style, clear—even dry—texture, and meticulous craftsmanship. Some show the influence of jazz; others are deliberately eclectic, harking back to Baroque or Classical models; and still others represent an attempt to strip music of any subjective or emotional appeal whatever.

In both numbers of works and quality of composition, Stravinsky ranks as a major composer for the stage. His eleven ballets include *Pulcinella* (1920), *Apollon Musagète (Apollo, Leader of the Muses,* 1928), *Le Baiser de la fée (The Fairy's Kiss,* 1928), *Jeux de cartes (Card Game,* 1937), and *Agon (Contest,* 1957). His four operas include two early comic works (both 1922), *Oedipus Rex* (1927) and *The Rake's Progress* (1951). Of his stage works the most popular is *L'Histoire du soldat (The Soldier's Tale,* 1928), scored for a chamber ensemble of seven instruments, "to be read, played, and danced."

The orchestral works include a number of suites drawn from full ballet scores, various light pieces for miscellaneous ensembles, and a few large-scale works. The most important of these are Symphonies of Wind Instruments (1920), Concerto for Two Pianos (1935), the Symphony in C (1940), and the Symphony in Three Movements (1945). Among the chamber works, a number of which are written for voice and miscellaneous instrumental groups, the best known are the Octet for Wind Instruments (1923) and *In Memoriam Dylan Thomas* (1954) for tenor, string quartet, and four trombones.

Stravinsky's first major choral work, and one of his undisputed masterpieces, was the *Symphony of Psalms* (1930) for chorus and orchestra, employing Latin versions of three psalms. His major liturgical work, the *Mass* (1948), was composed for mens' and boys' voices and ten instruments. Since the 1950s he has concentrated on vocal and choral music with orchestra or chamber ensemble. His choral music of this period makes use, in one form or another, of twelve-tone serial techniques. Among these are a cantata on four English Renaissance poems

(1951–1952) and an oratorio, *Canticum Sacrum (Sacred Song*, 1955–1956), composed for the city of Venice in honor of its patron, St. Mark.

Stravinsky's earliest works show some influence from Wagner, but even more from Rimsky-Korsakov and Debussy. The ballet scores that brought him public notice in Paris, *The Firebird* and *Petrouchka*, included stylized Russian and Eastern elements. Although both were exceptionally fine works, the first notable for its orchestration and delightfully varied repetitions and the second for its wit and strong rhythms, they did not quite prepare the musical world for the revolutionary violence of Stravinsky's next work.

Le Sacre du printemps (The Rite of Spring)

This third in the series of ballet scores, written by Stravinsky for Diaghilev's *Ballets Russes*, is subtitled *Pictures of Pagan Russia*. It depicts the cruelty of the primitive Russian peasants' rites to celebrate the coming of spring, culminating in the sacrifice of a young virgin, who dances herself to death while the tribal elders watch. The music is wild and primitive sounding, and the first performance (in Paris in 1913) turned into a genuine riot, with loud whistling and booing from the normally well-bred Paris audience.

The work is divided into two large parts, each of which includes several scenes; they are not really distinct movements, however, and are played without pause. The first half is called "The Kiss of the Earth"; after a slow introduction, the scenes are "Dance of the Adolescents," "Mime of Abduction," "Round Dance," "Mime of the Rival Cities," "Procession of the Priest," "The Kiss," and "Dance to the Earth." The second part, "The Great Sacrifice," also opens with a slow introduction, followed by "Secret Mime of the Girls," "Glorification of the Victim," "Invocation of Ancestors," "Dance of the Elders," and "Sacrificial Dance."

The orchestra for which Stravinsky composed *The Rite of Spring* is unusually large, calling for two piccolos, three flutes, alto flute, four oboes, two English horns, six clarinets of various sizes, four bassoons, two contrabassoons, eight French horns, five trumpets, one bass trumpet, three trombones, four tubas, a very large percussion section, and the usual strings. Stravinsky tends to use the instruments in blocks, keeping the string, wind, and brass sections fairly distinct. There are solos for almost every instrument, many of them in extremely high or low registers. The work is full of a variety of special effects, including some raucous slides and flutters.

The aspect of *The Rite of Spring* that most shocked its first audience, and has had the greatest impact on future generations of composers, was the rhythm. Stravinsky made a break with the traditional procedure of having the accents determined largely by the melodic and harmonic structure; the rhythm is very definitely a form-producing element in its own right in this work.

The new kind of rhythm that Stravinsky introduced here, especially in the "Glorification of the Victim" and the "Sacrificial Dance," is characterized by a rapid and rather mechanical mixture of two very short note values which are scattered in a completely irregular way, and the irregularity is emphasized by the appearance of strong accents, in unpredictable places.

Example 23.13

The effect is one of stumbling and produces considerable tension. This new kind of rhythm also appears in most of Stravinsky's later compositions, as well as in the works of many other later composers.

The melodic material of *The Rite of Spring* is not really used thematically; it is stated without ever being developed. Most of it appears in short fragments, with relentless ostinato accompaniments that prevent it from expanding to its full length and reaching a cadence. A folksong quality is evident in much of the melodic material, although, as far as we know, only the opening bassoon solo is taken from a genuine folk song.

Example 23.14

Stravinsky followed this monumental composition with a number of small-scale works for chamber groups of instruments and voices. He also wrote the last of his Russian-based works, *Les Noces*, a set of choral sketches describing a peasant wedding. Several characteristic features of Stravinsky's later use of tonality are present in his work from 1914–1917. A new kind of tonality is established, not based on the traditional functions (like the dominant-tonic relationship), by asserting by frequent repetition a particular pitch as a center of reference. Also evident is Stravinsky's technique of using several building blocks of ostinato patterns simultaneously; they overlap and produce shifting accents and conflicting rhythms.

Stravinsky's Neo-Classicism, usually dated from 1919, involves references to many older materials and styles, all transformed in his unique way. He has taken as subject matter almost everything from Renaissance music to jazz and used it as a basis for modern commentary and reinterpretation.

Symphonie de Psaumes (Symphony of Psalms)

Record 7/Side 1

Stravinsky's mature technique can be seen quite clearly in this work for chorus and orchestra, written for the fiftieth anniversary of the Boston Symphony Orchestra. The orchestration is rather unusual in that the violins and violas are omitted and two pianos and harp are used. The text is taken from Psalms 38, 39, and 150 and is sung in Latin. These Biblical excerpts form a sequence of prayer, testimony, and praise; the setting is divided into three corresponding parts, which are to be performed without pause.

LATIN (FROM THE VULGATE) | ENGLISH (FROM DOUAY-CONFRATERNITY)

No. 1: Psalm 38, verses 13–14.*

13. †*Exaudi orationem meam, Do-* | Hear my prayer, O Lord,
mine et deprecationem meam; | *and give ear to my cry;*
auribus percipe lacrimas meas. | *be not heedless of my tears.*
Ne sileas, quoniam advena ego | *For I am a guest with Thee,*
sum apud te,
et peregrinus, sicut omnes | *a sojourner, as were all my fathers.*
patres mei.

14. *Remitte mihi, ut refrigerer,* | *Turn from me, that I may recover,*
prius quam abeam et amplius | *before I go and am no more.*
non ero.

No. 2: Psalm 39, verses 2, 3, and 4.‡

2. *Expectans expectavi Dominum,* | *I hoped, I hoped in the Lord,*
et intendit mihi. | *and He stooped down to me.*

3. *Et exaudivit preces meas,* | *And He heard my cry,*
et eduxit me de lacu miseriae, | *and He drew me out of the pit of*
et de luto faecis. | *destruction, from the mire of the*
| *swamp.*

Et statuit super petram pedes | *And He set my feet upon a rock,*
meos,
et direxit gressus meos. | *and made firm my steps.*

4. *Et immisit in os meum* | *And He put a new song in my*
canticum novum, | *mouth,*
carmen Deo nostro. | *a hymn to our God.*
Videbunt multi, et timebunt, | *Many shall see, and they shall be*
| *filled with awe,*
et sperabunt in Domino. | *and they shall hope in the Lord.*

No. 3: Psalm 150, complete.

1. *Alleluia.* | *Alleluia.*
Laudate Dominum in sanctis | *Praise the Lord in His holy place,*
ejus;
Laudate eum in firmamento | *Praise Him in His majestic firma-*
virtutis ejus. | *ment.*

2. *Laudate eum in virtutibus ejus;* | *Praise Him because of His wonder-*
| *ful works;*
laudate eum secundum multitudi- | *praise Him because of His sublime*
nem magnitudinis ejus. | *majesty.*

*Psalm 38 in the Vulgate is Psalm 39 in the King James version.

†All numbers to the left of the Latin verses stand for verse numbers; the lines are given as they appear in the Vulgate.

‡Psalm 39 in the Vulgate is Psalm 40 in the King James version.

3. *Laudate eum in sono tubae,*   *Praise Him with the sound of trumpet,*

   laudate eum in psalterio et cithara.   *praise Him with harp and lyre.*

4. *Laudate eum in timpano et choro;*   *Praise Him with drum and dancing;*
laudate eum in cordis et organo.   *praise Him with stringed instruments and pipe.*

5. *Laudate eum in cymbalis bene-sonantibus;*   *Praise Him with sonorous cymbals;*

   laudate eum in cymbalis jubi-lationibus.   *praise Him with crashing cymbals.*

6. *Omnis spiritus laudet Domi-num!*   *Let everything that breathes praise the Lord!*
Alleluia.   *Alleluia.*

Part I

The first movement opens with an abrupt, widely spaced chord played by the entire orchestra. During the first part of this movement, the same chord is repeated five more times; it thus serves as an organizing force and also establishes a temporary tonality. Between the first few statements of the chord, rushing arpeggios treated as ostinato patterns are played by solo winds and then by the pianos.

Example 23.15

Example 23.16

The altos enter with a sustained line that alternates between two tones; the winds have much more active parts, with several different ostinato figures going simultaneously.

Example 23.17

The rest of the chorus joins in as the winds continue their patterns. After a very brief interlude, the altos and winds begin again. They are interrupted by the opening chord, and a new set of ostinatos begins, with the tenors singing *Ne sileas* on a single pitch. The section ends with a final jolt from the opening chord.

The second section opens with a familiar sound: active but repetitive parts in the winds, and slower, more lyric choral parts. The altos and basses begin at *Quoniam advena* in octaves and are soon joined by the rest of the chorus. When they reach the word *mei* the original type of orchestral background returns, as does the two-note theme, first as part of an alto-tenor duo, then in conflict between the sopranos and tenors.

Example 23.18

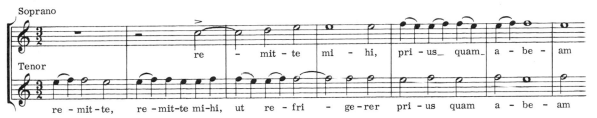

The ostinato patterns drop out for the last few measures of the movement.

Part II

Example 23.19

The second movement begins with a long, slow woodwind fugue; the subject is marked by a series of wide leaps.

Example 23.20

After a brief episode for flutes alone, a second fugue subject is introduced by the chorus.

During the exposition of this subject, fragments of the first one are still heard in the orchestra. The choral subject is used unaccompanied and in *stretti* (close overlapping entrances) at the words *Et statuit*. The orchestra returns with a few more fragments of the instrumental fugue subject, and then a dotted rhythm in the trombone part introduces a contrasting section.

The chorus parts are homophonic (chordal) from here to the end of the movement, although they are rhythmically almost as active as the orchestral parts. Fragments of the instrumental fugue subject are continued, first stated in a very jagged dotted rhythm, then broadly stated by the lower brasses. After building to a loud climax at *videbunt et timebunt*, a sudden decrease in volume to *piano* is introduced for the last words, *et sperabunt in Domino*. The chorus sings this phrase in octaves while a muted trumpet slowly plays the fragment of fugue theme and the cellos and basses play it twice as fast.

Part III

The last movement is considerably longer than either of the first two, and uses the setting of the word *Alleluia* as an organizational pillar. The entire first phrase, *Alleluia laudate Dominum*, is used again at the end of the movement, while the *Alleluia* alone serves as a major point of punctuation in the middle of it.

The opening section, with its slow-moving choral parts and instrumental ostinatos, is followed by a faster section for orchestra alone. It is characterized first by a repeated-note figure, always six notes, with the accent on the first. Gradually a rising triplet figure "takes over" (Stravinsky has said that it was inspired by a vision of Elijah's horse and chariot climbing the heavens). The section ends with a loud, crashing chord.

The next section, which begins with a soprano-alto duet, is somewhat calmer and is accompanied by short ostinato figures. After building to a climax, the six-note repeated pattern is reintroduced, this time sung to the words *Laudate Dominum*. This brief and very staccato interlude is followed by another slow section, with sustained vocal parts (starting with just the basses and gradually adding the other sections) and staccato wind ostinatos. This material builds to a huge climax, which is aborted as soft chords introduce the opening *Alleluia* again.

New ostinatos begin in the orchestra as the chorus sings *Laudate Dominum* with sharp accents on each syllable. A lively pattern is introduced by the harp and piano, and soon the chorus begins to interject the staccato repeated-note *Laudate Dominum* phrase, singing in block chords.

Example 23.21

The orchestral parts grow more and more active and eventually the rising-triplet pattern from earlier in the movement returns; the chorus drops out and the orchestra continues alone. After a chordal climax the six-note pattern is heard slowly and softly for the last time.

The chorus dominates the next section, which begins with imitative entries of a jagged yet lyric theme.

Example 23.22

It leads into the long and slow final section, where both voices and instruments chant hypnotically repetitive phrases. The work ends quietly with a literal restatement of the opening measures of the movement, and the words *Alleluia, laudate Dominum*.

Some of Stravinsky's music has a reputation for being "dry and unexpressive"; although this is a rather strong statement, it would certainly be valid to say that he goes out of his way to avoid anything that might seem like sentimentality. This leads him to some strange, even paradoxical, contrasts between the text and the music to which it is set. For example, he saves his most moving and poignant chord progression for the words "Praise Him upon the jubilant cymbals"; the praises of the finale are surrounded by a solemn processional and soft, awe-inspired *Alleluias*.

Stravinsky's Neo-Classical and "neo-tonal" style was dominant in Europe between the two world wars, although it was not the only one. An "atonal" technique was being developed in Vienna by Arnold Schoenberg and his followers. For many years these two approaches were considered opposites and completely irreconcilable. But in the postwar years almost everyone, including Stravinsky, adopted some form of Schoenberg's atonal procedure.

Prokofiev and Shostakovitch

A Russian composer whose development roughly paralleled that of Stravinsky was Sergei Prokofiev (1891–1953). His early works are very dissonant and rhythmically exciting—characteristics also associated with Stravinsky's early period, although the two men were working quite independently. Prokofiev lived abroad for many years, first in America, where his outstanding opera, *The Love for Three Oranges*, was premiered in 1921. During a subsequent stay in Paris, he wrote ballet scores for Diaghilev, as well as several symphonies and piano concertos.

Prokofiev returned to Russia in 1934, and worked at practical and propagandistic projects, including film scores, operas, and cantatas; he also continued to write symphonies, concertos, and sonatas. His music was frequently criticized by the Soviet regime, for reasons that are not totally clear to outsiders. He developed a very simple Neo-Classical idiom, using traditional forms and accompaniments, with a strongly tonal orientation. The lyric qualities of his mature works are superb.

Another Russian composer who has been even more deeply affected by the criticism of Soviet authorities is Dmitri Shostakovitch (b. 1906). His earliest works were Neo-Classical and tonal, but his ironic sense of humor led him to use more dissonance and a more vigorous idiom. His First Symphony is virtually a parody of a Classical symphony.

Shostakovitch's opera *Lady Macbeth of the Mtsensk District* (1930–32) was not received favorably, and he was attacked steadily until he evolved a new heroic style, first evident in his Fifth Symphony (1937).

Summary

The music of the twentieth century differs from earlier music in a radical way. Its three distinguishing features are rhythmic complexity, dissonance, and an obscure or nonexistent tonal center.

Around the turn of the century the musical culture of France was closely related to the other arts. Two of the dominant movements at the time were Impressionism in painting and Symbolism in literature. Both of these movements were influential in the development of Impressionism in music, a style that belongs almost exclusively to Claude Achille Debussy. Debussy's use of nontonal harmonies took music into new and unchartered areas, and his free-associating forms and concentration on timbre influenced almost all later composers.

Paul Hindemith, a German composer who immigrated to America, produced some of the finest music in the period between the world wars. Hindemith developed a system of tonality based on the establishment of tonal centers, but without the traditional concepts of major or minor keys.

Béla Bartók, the leading composer to come out of Eastern Europe, was profoundly influenced by the folk music of his native Hungary. Because most of this folk music lay outside the major-minor system, Bartók formed his own type of harmonic organization which could accommodate melodies outside the traditional system. His mature style is compact and economical. Often he derives his melodic material from one or two short motives and unifies large-scale pieces by using the same material in several movements.

One of the most important figures in all of twentieth-century music first came to public attention as a composer of ballet scores in Paris. But Igor Stravinsky, the Russian-born composer who lived in the United States until his death in 1971, wrote in a variety of styles and for a number of instrumental combinations. Between the world wars, his Neo-Classical and "neo-tonal" style was the dominant one in Europe. His career, like that of Pablo Picasso, spanned three generations, and he played an important role in almost all the significant trends of the first half of this century.

chapter 24

In the new kind of "tonality" used by many twentieth-century composers, the only alternative was to avoid the traditional concept of tonality completely. But the idea of the tonal center was such a fundamental one, in an architectural sense, that it could not simply be dropped. Rather, it had to be replaced by an organizing principle of equal strength and validity. The search for such an alternative was the life work of several Viennese composers early in this century. Their work took place at the same time that

Serialism

Stravinsky, Bartók, Hindemith, and others were expanding the idea of tonality. These two simultaneous developments outlined the course of musical composition for the first half of the century.

Schoenberg (1874–1951)

The composer who led the development of the atonal style was Arnold Schoenberg. At the start of his career he was closely allied with late German Romanticism, although he finished farther from it than almost any of his contemporaries. Together with two of his students, Alban Berg and Anton von Webern, Schoenberg took the fateful step of rejecting the concept of tonality completely, and wrote in what is called an *atonal* style. He later developed a new system of musical organization to replace tonality which involves setting the twelve chromatic tones in a chosen order, and then using them in various ways. This is called *serialism, twelve-tone* technique, or *dodecaphony*.

Almost single-handedly Arnold Schoenberg effected a radical and significant change in basic concepts of music. His development of the twelve-tone serial technique, which abandoned the principles of Classical tonality, opened the door to new methods of composing and new ways of constructing harmonic relationships. He viewed his new method of composing not as a dramatic, revolutionary gesture against the past but as a logical consequence of nineteenth-century chromatic developments in harmony. He developed his method over many years through a number of ever-more-radical compositions.

Schoenberg was born into a Viennese middle-class family; although his parents both loved music, neither provided much guidance in his early training. While in grammar school he studied the violin and cello and was soon composing and playing in chamber ensembles. An older friend, Alexander von Zemlinsky, who directed an amateur orchestral society, first interested him in serious musical study; and after working several years as a bank employee, Schoenberg decided in 1895 to embark on a musical career.

The two great influences on his early composition were the giants of late nineteenth-century German music: Brahms and Wagner. During the 1890s he wrote several string quartets and piano works and a small number of songs. In 1901 he married the sister of his friend, Mathilde von Zemlinsky. Shortly afterward he was engaged as a theater conductor in Berlin. There he became acquainted with Richard Strauss, who helped him obtain a teaching position and expressed great interest in his work. In 1903 Schoenberg returned to Vienna to teach musical composition. He became good friends with Gustav Mahler and, more importantly, took on as students two younger men, Alban Berg and Anton von Webern. Both pupils adopted Schoenberg's twelve-tone methods, developed them in their own individual ways, and were to influence decisively—along with their teacher—the future course of music.

During the first decade of the twentieth century, Schoenberg began turning away from the highly Romantic style of his earlier works and gradually developed his new twelve-tone method. While his name spread among composers and performers, public acclaim still eluded him. His first work to achieve fame was a song cycle, *Pierrot Lunaire* (*Moonstruck Pierrot*, 1912), which employed a half-sung, half-spoken technique called *Sprechstimme* (literally, "speech voice").

Schoenberg's growing reputation was interrupted by World War I, in which he served with the Austrian army, but soon after he was again active as a composer, lecturer on theory, and teacher. The 1920s marked a new direction, both in his composing and in his career. He went to Berlin in 1925 to teach composition at the State Academy of the Arts, taking with him his second wife, Gertrude Kolisch. (His first wife died in 1923.)

In 1933 Schoenberg's career again took another direction. With the advent of the Nazi party's assumption of power, he was dismissed from his post and he emigrated first to France, and then to the United States. His reputation as a teacher and as a "modernist" preceded him. After working in Boston and New York, he joined the faculty of U.C.L.A. He died in Los Angeles at the age of seventy-seven.

His Work

Schoenberg's work—amounting to fifty opus numbers, several early unpublished pieces, and three unfinished compositions—includes stage works, art songs, choral pieces, works for piano, a small number of orchestral compositions, and an extensive variety of chamber music.

His early works, up through the first years of the century, stand in the late German Romantic tradition of Wagner, Brahms, and Mahler. The tone poem, *Verklärte Nacht* (*Transfigured Night*, 1899), for string sextet and later revised for string orchestra, is perhaps his earliest significant work. His enormous choral-orchestral work, the *Gurrelieder* (*Songs of Gurre*, 1900–1901) and the symphonic tone poem *Pelleas und Melisande* (1902–1903) mark the high point of his postWagnerian manner of composition. From 1907 on, he wrote for smaller and more varied groups of instruments, and his style became more contrapuntal and chromatic. This change is seen in his second string quartet (Op. 10, 1907–1908), in the song cycle *Das Buch der hängenden Gärten* (*The Book of the Hanging Gardens*, 1908), based on poems of Stefan George, and in the Five Pieces for Orchestra (1909). Schoenberg's experimentation also extended to stage works: *Erwartung* (*Expectation*, 1909), a music drama for one performer; and *Die glückliche Hand* (*The Lucky Hand*, 1909–1913), a highly symbolic drama for solo, acting parts, and chorus. The most outstanding work of this period is *Pierrot Lunaire* (*Moonstruck Pierrot*, 1912), a song cycle for soloist and five instrumentalists. In 1913, he began his great unfinished oratorio, *Die Jakobsleiter* (*Jacob's Ladder*), in which the first twelve-tone row appears.

Schoenberg's twelve-tone technique is fully expressed in a series of solo and chamber works from the early 1920s: *Five Piano Pieces* (Op. 23, 1923), Serenade for Seven Instruments and Bass Voice (Op. 24, 1923), Suite for Piano (Op. 25, 1924), and Wind Quartet (Op. 26, 1924).

In 1928 Schoenberg completed what many regard as his greatest masterpiece, the *Variations for Orchestra* (Op. 31), his only work for full orchestra to employ twelve-tone technique. His most important works of the 1930s and 1940s are the Concerto for Violin and Orchestra (1936), the String Quartet No. 4 (1937), and the Concerto for Piano and Orchestra (1942). After he came to the United States he also composed a number of important works for chorus: *Kol Nidre* (1938), for speaker, chorus, and orchestra; *A Survivor from Warsaw* (1947), also for speaker, chorus, and orchestra; and the psalm setting, *De Profundis* (1950), for six-part chorus, his last work. His death left uncompleted his major opera, one of the great twentieth-century works in this genre, *Moses und Aron* (begun in 1931).

Schoenberg's earliest works were strongly influenced by Wagner, Brahms, and Strauss. He wrote in a late Romantic style, using many of the forms characteristic of the era. His symphonic poem *Pelleas und Melisande*, inspired by the Maeterlinck drama (which Debussy set as an opera at about the same time), and the symphonic cantata *Gurrelieder*, a gigantic and complex work for soloists, chorus, and orchestra, marked the end of his attempt to remain within the tonal establishment. Ironically, Schoenberg's most popular piece today, *Verklarte Nacht*, predates the establishment of his own revolutionary style.

Verklärte Nacht (Transfigured Night), Op. 4

This work for string sextet is definitely within the Wagnerian orbit. Although there is considerable chromaticism and dissonance, the work is in a tonally based idiom; the harmonic style is related to that of Wagner's *Tristan und Isolde*. The highly Romantic nature of *Transfigured Night* is evident both in Schoenberg's music and in the poem by Richard Dehmel that inspired it. This sextet represents the first significant extension of programmatic techniques into the realm of chamber music.

VERKLÄRTE NACHT *	TRANSFIGURED NIGHT
Zwei Menschen gehn durch kahlen, kalten Hain;	*Two people walk through the bare, cold woods;*
der Mond läuft mit, sie schaun hinein.	*the moon sails along, they gaze at it.*
Der Mond läuft über hohe Eichen,	*The moon sails over tall oaks,*
kein Wölkchen trübt das Himmelslicht,	*no cloudlet dims the heavenly light*
in das die schwarzen Zacken reichen.	*into which the black peaks reach.*
Die Stimme eines Weibes spricht:	*A woman's voice speaks:*
Ich trag ein Kind, un nit von Dir,	*I bear a child, and not from you,*
Ich geh in Sünde neben Dir.	*I walk in sin beside you.*
Ich hab mich schwer an mir vergangen.	*I sinned greatly against myself.*
Ich glaubte nicht mehr an ein Glück	*I believed no longer in good fortune*
und hatte doch ein schwer Verlangen	*and had yet a great desire*
nach Lebensinhalt, nach Mutterglück	*for a full life, for a mother's joy*
und Pflicht; da hab ich mich erfrecht,	*and duty; then I became shameless,*
da liess ich schaudernd mein Geschlecht	*then, horrified, I let my sex*
von einem fremden Mann umfangen,	*be taken by a stranger*
und hab mich noch dafür gesegnet.	*and even blessed myself for it.*
Nun hat das Leben sich gerächt:	*Now life has claimed its revenge:*
nun bin ich Dir, o Dir begegnet.	*now I have met you, you.*
Sie geht mit ungelenkem Schritt.	*She walks with awkward stride.*
Sie schaut empor; der Mond laüft mit.	*She gazes aloft; the moon sails along.*
Ihr dunkler Blick ertrinkt in Licht.	*Her dark glance drowns in the light.*
Die Stimme eines Mannes spricht:	*A man's voice speaks:*
Das Kind, das Du empfangen hast,	*Let the child that you have conceived*
sie Deiner Seele keine Last,	*be no burden on your soul,*
o sieh, wie klar das Weltall schimmert!	*oh look, how clear the universe shimmers!*
Es ist ein Glanz um Alles her,	*There is a glory around All here,*
Du treibst mit mir auf kaltem Meer,	*you drift with me upon a cold sea,*
doch eine eigne Wärme flimmert	*but a peculiar warmth flickers*
von Dir in mich, von mir in Dich.	*from you in me, from me in you.*
Die wird das fremde Kind verklären.	*It will transfigure the strange child.*
Du wirst es mir, von mir gebären;	*You will bear it to me, from me;*
Du hast den Glanz in mich gebracht,	*you have brought the glory into me,*
Du hast mich selbst zum Kind gemacht.	*you have made my self into a child.*
Er fasst sie um die starken Hüften.	*He holds her around her strong hips,*
Ihr Atem küsst sich in den Lüften.	*Their breath kisses in the air.*
Zwei Menschen gehn durch hohe, helle Nacht.	*Two people walk through high, shining night.*

*Based on the poem by Richard Dehmel, from his *Weib und Welt*.

The poem is divided into five sections, of which the first, third, and fifth are descriptive, while the second is the woman's passionate confession, and the fourth the man's warm and understanding reply. Schoenberg's music parallels this structure; like many late Romantic composers he uses a recurring theme to link the three descriptive sections. When this theme opens the work, it is somber and melancholy, with no accompaniment except a low pedal point.

Example 24.1

After a short transition, the second section begins; the woman's remorseful story is treated in an expressive section with many themes and episodes. One of the most tender melodies corresponds to the verse that describes her longing for maternal joy.

Example 24.2

After a passionate and restless episode, the third section begins with a quiet recitative by the first violin, which leads to the return of the original theme. This time the theme is fully harmonized and very forceful.

A series of high, shimmering chords introduces the fourth section, where a broad theme in the cello represents the man's comforting reply.

Example 24.3

An expressive duet between the violin and cello represents a dialogue between the man and the woman. The first theme is recalled briefly, and after several more episodes, the man's theme returns. It brings tranquility and introduces the final section. Eventually the original theme returns for the last time; no longer melancholy, it expresses the couple's happiness, which has transfigured the night.

It is interesting to compare *Transfigured Night* with the Sextet in B-flat Major for Strings (see Chapter 17) by Johannes Brahms. Of course, they represent opposite poles of the late Romantic style: the Brahms sextet is essentially Classical in form, while the Schoenberg is descriptive and structured to correspond to its program. They have an important feature in common, however; both tend to be symphonic in style. The rich instrumentation certainly has something to do with this, but so does the way the instruments are handled. In particular, the use of extremely high registers adds to the orchestral effect produced by the small chamber ensemble. Schoenberg, in fact, reorchestrated his sextet for string orchestra in 1917, and it is the revised version that has remained extraordinarily popular ever since.

Atonality and Expressionism

Beginning in about 1905, Schoenberg evolved a radically different style, one that was regarded by his contemporaries as quite revolutionary. Two different terms are often used to describe aspects of it. The first, *atonality*, refers to a systematic avoidance of any kind of tonal center. This is accomplished by avoiding simple, familiar chords, major or minor scales, and octave leaps. When these principles are combined with dissonance and a rapid succession of chords, the ear cannot find any stable point (tonic) to use as a center of reference. In this way the twelve tones of the chromatic scale are made equal, rather than seven "belonging" to the key of a piece, and five others "not belonging."

Schoenberg considered his new harmonic style to be a logical extension of tendencies already apparent in late German Romanticism. In the music of Wagner and Strauss, brief atonal passages can be found, although they are embedded in a tonal context. Schoenberg gradually increased the dissonance and chromaticism of his style until he eliminated them, in the sense that he negated their existence. When dissonance is no longer required to resolve to consonance, there is no dissonance. In the same way, if all twelve tones are equal, there is no major or minor norm, and no chromaticism outside that norm.

The second term used to describe Schoenberg's works in the period from 1905 to about 1912 is *Expressionism*. Borrowed from the field of art criticism, the term Expressionism or Expressionist refers to a school of German artists and dramatists who tried to represent the artist's innermost experience, using whatever means seemed suitable. The result is usually very intense and often revolutionary in method. Thus atonality in music is stylistically in the Expressionistic mode. The subject matter of Expressionism is modern man in his varied psychological states: isolated, irrational, rebellious, tense. There is no attempt to produce beautiful or realistic art, but only to penetrate and reveal inner feelings.

The problem that Schoenberg had to face, having abandoned tonality, was the loss of the form-building properties that the old system had provided. Without tonal centers and modulations, the traditional forms could not really exist. Without such simple but useful devices as the dominant-tonic chord progression, there was no harmonic guide to help distinguish a cadence from any other point in a phrase.

At first Schoenberg found only temporary solutions. He wrote short pieces and depended heavily on outside material (either literary or dramatic) to impose form on the music. This is a routine stopgap measure for a composer who has just discovered new materials but has not yet found out how to organize them. Debussy and Stravinsky did the same thing early in their careers.

The other techniques that unify a composition in the atonal style are motivic development and contrapuntal procedures, and Schoenberg makes full use of both. In fact, these devices had been a pronounced part of his personal idiom during his Romantic phase, but they became even more important as this style matured. Some of his works from this middle period are characterized by the dominance of a particular interval. Others contain canons and ostinato figures.

Schoenberg creates incredible variety within each piece of his music. Rarely is the same texture maintained for more than a single phrase. Instead, contrapuntal patches are interspersed with accompanied melody. Rhythm and dynamics are also subject to the same rapid variation. Two consecutive phrases are rarely equal in length. Schoenberg almost never uses literal repetition or any other formal symmetry, even when a repeated text in vocal music invites such treatment.

Schoenberg's music is difficult to understand because it is very compressed: changes occur with such rapidity that the unprepared listener is left behind. An excellent example of Schoenberg's Expressionistic and atonal style, with all its variety and complexity, is *Pierrot Lunaire* (1912), a setting of twenty-one surrealistic poems for vocalist, piano, flute, clarinet, violin, and cello. The singer (a woman) uses one of the composer's favorite techniques, called *Sprechstimme*, in which the part is half sung, half-spoken. The rhythms are indicated precisely, with approximate pitches. Each of the songs is orchestrated slightly differently, and Schoenberg's masterful contrapuntal technique is very evident.

Development of the Twelve-Tone Method

Schoenberg was very much aware of the limitations his free atonal style placed on him; he wanted to write longer pieces, but lacked a framework such as sonata-allegro form on which to build them. Tonality had been one means of making structural distinctions; in its absence, he needed to find a new technique to replace the formal differentiation tonal harmonies had provided. Form was very important to Schoenberg. He believed that some underlying organization was essential, no matter what radical changes took place in the harmonic idiom.

Gradually he evolved a system he described as a "method of composing with twelve tones that are related only with one another, not to a central tone: a tonic." The rudiments of this method are simple: the composer arranges the twelve pitches of the chromatic scale in a particular order. This is known as a *tone row*, or *series*, or *set*, for a specific piece. The row can be transposed to any pitch level, and used upside down (*inversion*), backward (*retrograde*), or upside down and backward *Example 24.4* (*retrograde inversion*).

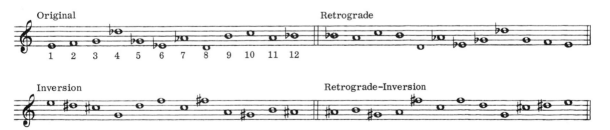

The notes of a given version of the row are all used before a new version is started; this insures that each of the twelve pitches has equal emphasis, and no tone becomes too prominent, assuming a central position.

The notes of the series (or any of its variations) are sometimes used in sequence, to form a melody or theme, and are used simultaneously in clusters to form chords. The system does not impose limits on rhythm, dynamics, or textures that the composer will choose, so it is not a mechanical music-producing method, as it might seem at first. A composer who writes with the serial technique is no more limited than one who chooses to write sonatas or fugues. The basic tone row provides some coherence, in the same way that tonal harmonies do; there is still room for an infinite amount of variety, limited only by the composer's inspiration.

It is not necessary to be able to analyze the technical construction of a serial piece in order to enjoy listening to it, but an example will clarify the most important premise of the method—that the various applications of the set are used to help define the form of the piece.

In one of Schoenberg's earliest twelve-tone pieces, the *Suite for Piano* (Op. 25, 1924), a minuet and trio offer clear illustration of the various uses of the row for formal distinctions. The entire trio follows:

Record 7/Side 2

Example 24.5

Trio from Suite, Op. 25

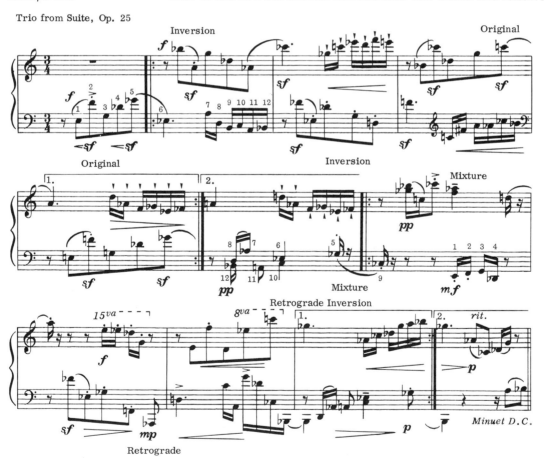

The basic tone row is the one given in the previous example, and its uses are marked on the score. The opening measures use the row as a melodic motive in a mirror-image canon between the two hands. This exposition is repeated, and then a transitional passage occurs. The row occurs in a jumbled order; it is not used motivically, but forms a new texture and prepares for the varied recapitulation that follows. The left hand introduces the backward version of the basic series, and the right hand inverts it again. This very condensed piece shows how a change in the texture and approach to the row can give form on a small scale; analogous techniques can be devised for larger structures.

Schoenberg had formulated his twelve-tone method by 1923, and he used it in most of his compositions thereafter. No longer tortured and Expressionistic, the works written in the 1920s have a marked air of confidence and playfulness. A traditional spirit is also evident. In a way, Schoenberg can now be called a Neo-Classicist. He uses forms resembling Classical ones (such as the minuet and trio in Op. 25), and contrasts his themes in a Classical manner, while continuing to write in a very dissonant idiom with serial techniques. This is quite different from Stravinsky's kind of Neo-Classicism, which used Classical ideas as a starting point for very original forms and thematic development.

Variations for Orchestra (Op. 31)

Record 7/Side 2

Example 24.6

Almost all of Schoenberg's serial compositions are for chamber ensembles. *Variations for Orchestra* is his only serial work for full orchestra. It is scored for a large ensemble with a full complement of winds, harp, celesta, mandolin, the usual strings, and a very extensive percussion section, including glockenspiel and xylophone. The piece consists of an introduction, a theme and nine variations, and a finale.

The basic series for this work is:

The introduction presents this series gradually in its opening measures; it is not used thematically yet, since that would anticipate the function of the theme section. After a slow beginning and a more emphatic central section, a quiet closing rounds it off. The trombone introduces a motive that will be heard occasionally throughout the piece.

Example 24.7

In the German system for naming notes, our B♭ is called B, and our B is called H—thus these four notes spell BACH. Johann Sebastian Bach used this motive as the subject of one of his organ fugues, and other composers have been intrigued by it since. In *Variations for Orchestra*, the BACH motive occurs in the last four notes of a transposition of the original row, and Schoenberg always treats it motivically in fairly long note values.

The theme section introduces the row as a theme; it is played by the cellos with a soft chordal accompaniment. What sounds like one long melody is actually the row, first in its original form, then in retrograde inversion, then in retrograde. At the end of the movement it is treated contrapuntally, with the cellos playing the original version while the violins play its inversion.

Example 24.8

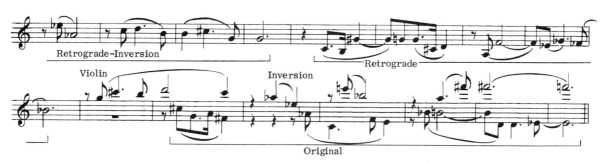

In the variations that follow, the row is always present in a melodic form, but it is not used with the same octaves or rhythms as in the theme, making it somewhat difficult to identify. Moreover, the entire row theme is not always the most important melodic material in each variation. Other motives also derived from the row are presented and developed; rhythmic ideas are elaborated; and varied instrumentations and contrapuntal textures are often the focus of attention. In a sense the conflict between the row as an underlying structural force (a substitute for tonality) and as thematic material is the basis of the piece.

One way to describe the variations is to locate the "theme" (meaning some continuous melodic variant of the basic series) and show how it is used. We can illustrate this most easily by giving the various rhythmic treatments of the theme in some of the variations.

Example 24.9

However, the piece is not designed so that the listener can follow the theme through each variation; so we must look further for the important aspect of each variation. Schoenberg writes so compactly that it is impossible to give more than a rough idea of the focus of each section.

VAR. I: The theme stays in the lowest bass instruments, with the full orchestra playing very short motives above.

VAR. II: The inversion of the theme is presented in canon by the violin and oboe. The texture is complicated by simultaneous canons on other subjects. The movement is scored very lightly, for only solo instruments, which helps clarify the complex contrapuntal texture. The BACH motive is heard in the trombone.

VAR. III: The theme is played mostly by the horns, but it is not particularly important. The first motivic material is a dotted arpeggio figure; a repeated-note group later turns out to be the central idea.

VAR. IV: The harp, celesta, and mandolin play the theme as an accompaniment to contrapuntal wind and string parts. The instrumental colors are quite unusual because of the choice of instruments.

VAR. V: The basses again have the theme, but attention focuses on the large leaps they make after each thematic note. These leaps are taken up by the other instruments and characterize the variation.

VAR. VI: The theme is hidden in the solo cello part, but the more interesting material is first in the clarinet, and then in the other winds.

VAR. VII: The piccolo, celesta, and glockenspiel play the theme in a very high register and entirely off the beat. The winds are featured again, and the rapid changes of instrumental color are notable. Toward the end of this rather long variation, the rhythmic patterns are quite exciting.

VAR. VIII: For the first time, the theme is not used melodically at the beginning of a variation. The texture provides the primary interest, with contrapuntal wind parts contrasted with rhythmic ostinatos in the strings. The theme appears in the flute and violin toward the end of the variation.

VAR. IX: The theme itself is the dominant feature of this variation. It is treated contrapuntally at the beginning, with short interludes between presentations; later only fragments of it are used.

FINALE: The BACH motive opens the last movement and proves to be of great importance. It is interspersed with various versions of the row theme and several other motives derived from row material. There are many changes of tempo and texture in this concluding movement.

By adopting the traditional theme-and-variations form, and bending it to suit the needs of his material, Schoenberg attempted to prove the universality of his techniques. The row as melodic material gradually becomes absorbed into the row as a structural principle.

Schoenberg and His Followers

Although Schoenberg's work received little favor during his own lifetime, he has had a major influence on contemporary composition. His revolutionary atonal style and twelve-tone method have been the subjects of great and often bitter controversy, but are recognized today as major intellectual achievements of the early twentieth century. Extensions of the serial technique are still being explored today, and virtually every major composer of the post-World War II era has written some works using serial techniques.

Much of the recent influence of Schoenberg's ideas has been transmitted through the music of two of his pupils and colleagues, Anton von Webern (1883–1945) and Alban Berg (1885–1935). Both men helped develop atonality and serial procedures, although they used them quite differently.

Berg is best known for his Expressionistic opera *Wozzeck* (1917–1921), an outstanding work that combines Classical forms, leitmotivs, *Sprechstimme*, and conventional singing with Berg's basically Romantic musical predisposition. In many other works Berg made use of Schoenberg's serial techniques, but often he chose rows that permitted him to use tonal-sounding chords and harmonic progressions. His music has a warmth that makes it more accessible than that of many other serial composers.

Schoenberg's other famous pupil, Webern, had a very different style of composition; he adopted atonality, but without any traces of Romanticism. Webern is noted for the economy and compactness of his works.

Figure 24.2 Anton von Webern deftly extended Schoenberg's atonal style with the economy and sensitivity of his compositions. Webern often divided a single melodic line among several instruments to create changes of timbre. (The Bettmann Archive)

His style is essentially contrapuntal and is marked by an exceptional sensitivity to color. Often a single melodic line may be divided among several instruments, each with only one or two notes at a time; the changes of timbre give the melody a new dimension.

Webern passed through the same stages of development as his teacher: chromaticism, free atonality, and serial organization. All his works are very short and sparse, and most are for small ensembles. His outstanding works include a symphony for nine instruments, a concerto, also for nine instruments, a string quartet, and a set of piano variations. He has also written several collections of solo songs and two cantatas.

Webern suffered the same lack of recognition as Schoenberg during his lifetime, but his music has been very influential since World War II. The lean character of his style and his isolation of the single note as a musical event, have captivated many recent composers, who have expanded the techniques of serialism to suit their own purposes.

Summary

The development of the atonal style was led by Arnold Schoenberg, a Viennese composer who emigrated first to Germany, then to France, and finally to the United States. Schoenberg rejected the concept of tonality completely, and devised a new system, ultimately called serialism, to organize his works.

Beginning in about 1905, Schoenberg evolved a style that systematically avoided any tonal center, thereby equalizing all twelve tones. As an organizing device, he depended heavily on literary or dramatic material, motivic development, and contrapuntal procedures. These were only temporary solutions, however, and could not be used successfully to organize longer pieces.

Tonality had provided a means of making structural distinctions. In its absence, Schoenberg found a method for arranging the twelve pitches of the chromatic scale in any fixed order, known as the *tone row, series,* or *set* for a specific piece.

The twelve notes of the series could be used in sequence, forming a melody or theme, or simultaneously in groups to form chords. Furthermore, the system did not impose limitations on rhythm, dynamics, or textures. As a result, the tone row provided coherence in the same way that tonal harmonies do, but still left room for an infinite amount of variety.

Schoenberg had formulated his twelve-tone method by 1923 and used it in most of his compositions. Although he received little recognition during his lifetime, he has been a major influence on contemporary composition. Extension of his techniques are still being explored, and virtually every major composer of the post-World War II era has written some music employing serial techniques.

Part VI Suggested Listening

Bartók, Béla

Mikrokosmos. A collection of piano pieces illustrating Bartók's compositional style from traditional nineteenth-century Hungarian harmonic structures and whole-tone scales to bitonality. Sets contain pieces ranging from the relatively simple to the fairly difficult.

Berg, Alban

Lulu. An uncompleted three-act opera illustrating the amalgamation of Wagnerian opera techniques with twelve-tone compositional techniques.

Debussy, Claude

Pelléas et Mélisande. Opera in five acts based on a medieval legend. It epitomizes the subtlety of Impressionism—each act is a continuum of musical narrative employing leitmotives.

Hindemith, Paul

Das Marienleben. A cycle of fifteen songs written to poems by Rainer Maria Rilke arranged into four groups. Each is organized metrically and tonally while contributing underlying ideas to a unified whole. Hindemith subjected the cycle to many revisions, finally publishing a completed revision in 1948.

Schoenberg, Arnold

Fantasy for Violin and Piano, Op. 47. A one-movement work. Exemplary of Schoenberg's work in America, it shows the extensions of a creative style within the twelve-tone idiom.

Stravinsky, Igor

Octet for Wind Instruments. A Neo-Classical work in two movements employing flute, clarinet, two bassoons, two trumpets, and two trombones. Evocative of concerto grosso form, it is contrapuntal in texture.

Illustration from Aaron Copeland's Billy the Kid, *Piano Solo Edition, by permission of Boosey & Hawkes, Inc.,
publisher.*

Plate 18.   John Singleton Copley was one of the few early American artists to achieve an international reputation. His Portrait of Paul Revere shows the insight into character and sculptural form for which he was known. (Courtesy Museum of Fine Arts, Boston. Gift of Joseph W., William B., and Edward H. R. Revere.)

Plate 19.   The Romantic style of Albert Pinkham Ryder's visionary landscapes foretold of twentieth-century Expressionistic developments. In
Siegfried and the Rhine Maidens, for example, Ryder conveyed emotion by
handling form and color very freely. (Courtesy National Gallery of Art,
Washington, Andrew Mellon Collection)

Plate 20. Artists like Charles Demuth applied many of
Cubism's techniques to the industrialized scenes of
America. My Egypt reflects a modified Cubistic concern for
form and geometric precision. (Courtesy Whitney Museum
of American Art, New York)

part VII Music in America

During the War of Independence, John Adams wrote that the Americans of his generation had to master the art of war so that the next generation would have freedom to develop agriculture and industry, in turn permitting their children to cultivate the fine arts. Adams' timetable for progress was more or less accurate if we accept as a standard

The Arts in America

for artistic maturity the creation of works that influence the artistic tradition of Western civilization. Maturity in literature was attained in the nineteenth century with Edgar Allan Poe, James Fenimore Cooper, and Walt Whitman. To a great extent, maturity in music came with jazz, which strongly influenced twentieth-century French music and, on the rebound, American symphonic music. In painting and sculpture, America did not develop a school of international significance until the mid-twentieth century with Abstract Expressionism, although discerning critics have long considered American movies a valid and powerful expression in the visual arts.

The reasons for this artistic lag are implicit in Adams' utilitarian order of priorities: independence, agriculture and industry, the arts. Although the colonies had grown and prospered for 150 years before the Revolutionary War, in Adams' time the United States was still largely unexplored wilderness. The energies of most Americans were necessarily devoted to survival in a hostile land. Settlements were isolated and communications slow; education was rudimentary at best. Except in the seaports of Boston, New York, Philadelphia, and Charleston there was no contact with the European artistic tradition. Furthermore, the conditions that fostered the fine arts in Europe did not exist in America. There was no monarchy to flatter and no national church to commission huge cathedrals and altarpieces; on the contrary, the Puritan tradition flatly rejected images and lavish display.

This does not mean there was no art in the broadest sense. Itinerant portrait painters called limners roved the country painting crude but lively likenesses; Yankee composers such as William Billings wrote hymns, psalms, and anthems for church and social uses. Mainly, however, artistic expression manifested itself in useful objects of a remarkably high order of craftsmanship: the silver tableware of Paul Revere; the furniture of Duncan Phyfe. Anonymous artisans—carpenters, sign painters, shipwrights—retained the craftsman's respect for their materials and for the functions of the objects they made.

In these circumstances it is remarkable that several painters did achieve reputations outside the country during the late Colonial era. A self-taught Boston limner, John Singleton Copley (1738–1815) surpassed the primitivism of his fellow portrait painters, expressing in his work a vivid sense of character and strong sculptural form (Plate 18). Emigrating to England in 1774, Copley attained considerable success. Benjamin West (1738–1820), a Pennsylvania Quaker, also moved to London, where his portraits and historical scenes brought him such renown that he became Court Painter to George III and President of the Royal Academy. Samuel F. B. Morse (1791–1872), who had been a successful portrait painter while living in England, received so few commissions on

Figure 25.1 The Oxbow *is the kind of nineteenth-century wilderness painting that prompted Easterners to abandon their crowded cities. Artist Thomas Cole and others of the Hudson River School spread their talents from New York State to the far west. (The Metropolitan Museum of Art, Gift of Mrs. Russel Sage, 1908)

his return home that he was forced to turn his attention to developing the telegraph.

By the 1820s and 1830s the United States had achieved commercial and industrial prosperity, while the rise of Jacksonian democracy had created a sense of nationalism. Westward expansion brought about a realization of the immense size and natural wonders of the continent, a view of nature reflected in James Fenimore Cooper's *Leatherstocking Tales* and Washington Irving's tales of the Hudson River region that celebrated the rustic life.

At the same time, a group of painters who came to be known as the Hudson River School began depicting the natural wonders of the wilderness. Starting with the Catskills and Adirondacks, they moved westward to paint the Rocky Mountains, the Grand Canyon, Yosemite, and other spectacles of nature. The painters of the Hudson River School—including Thomas Cole (1801–1848), Asher Durand (1796–1886), Frederic B. Church (1826–1900), and Albert Bierstadt (1830–1902)—combined a romantic outlook with a realistic technique. Their paintings were vastly popular, undoubtedly influencing many Easterners to trek to the wilderness.

Along with the new interest in the wilderness, there was a fascination with the lives of the people who settled it, giving rise to genre scenes of everyday life. These scenes reflect the predominantly rural society: square dances, turkey shoots, country fairs, the existence of farmers,

Figure 25.2 Genre paintings like George Caleb Bingham's The Jolly Flatboatmen in Port *depicted everyday life of the wilderness settlers. The great popularity of such paintings was at least partly due to their satisfying a nostalgia, among many city dwellers, for a simpler way of life. (The St. Louis Art Museum)*

Figure 25.3 Thomas Eakins' Portrait of Mrs. Edith Mahon *exemplifies the realism that infused American art late in the nineteenth century. Psychological insight and scientific objectivity were hallmarks of Eakins' portraits. (Smith College Museum of Art)*

Figure 25.4 Frank Lloyd Wright designed the Kaufman House at Bear Run, Pennsylvania, as an "organic" extension of nature's landscape. Such idealization of nature echoes the influence of the Hudson River School. (Hedrich Blessing)

trappers, hunters. Two of the finest American genre painters were William Sidney Mount (1807–1868) and George Caleb Bingham (1811–1879).

Even as the genre scenes were being painted, America was slowly changing from a rural to an urban society. Genre paintings and lithographs were in great demand, for they expressed a nostalgia for an idealized past. This art had a musical parallel in the songs of Stephen Collins Foster, a song like "Camptown Races" being the musical equivalent of a genre scene.

After the Civil War, the United States entered a period of expansion, not only in Western territory, population, commerce, and industry, but in growth of cultural institutions. During this period, increasing numbers of universities, museums, symphony orchestras, and art and music schools were founded. Wealthy collectors acquired European masterpieces but generally ignored "modern" art such as that of the French Impressionists. Nor were American artists themselves ready to assimilate such advanced styles.

By the 1880s the realism in painting, pioneered a generation earlier by Courbet in France, had begun to influence American painters. Combining realism with the American tradition of portraiture, Thomas Eakins (1844–1916) took as his subject matter the middle-class life of his native city, Philadelphia. Portraits by Eakins (who was also a mathematician, astronomer, and photographer) possess profound penetration; there is no attempt to beautify or flatter the sitters, who are viewed with the objectivity one would expect from a scientist.

Another tradition, the Romantic, is reflected in the work of Albert Pinkham Ryder (1847–1917), undoubtedly the most original American painter of the nineteenth century. Ryder drew on poetry and legend for his completely visionary landscapes and seascapes; the free manner in which form and color are used to convey feeling prefigures the Expressionist painting of twentieth-century France and Germany (Plate 19). As an experimental artist, Ryder was as far ahead of his time as the American composer Charles Ives, whose distinctively American works were neglected for nearly half a century.

Two highly accomplished American painters of the late nineteenth century lived so long in Europe that they may be considered international figures: James A. M. Whistler (1834–1903) and John Singer Sargent (1856–1925). Sargent was a virtuoso portrait painter whose work mirrors the elegance of the late Victorian and Edwardian eras. Whistler, a theorist, conceived of painting less as an imitation of nature than as a transformation of nature into visual design.

At the turn of the century the most significant American art was architecture. Musically, the United States was a province of Germany; painters and sculptors were influenced by the academic rather than the avant-garde artists of France. Architecture, too, was dominated by academics who turned schools, bank, railroad stations, museums, and office buildings into replicas of Roman temples. Two American architects broke this mold: Louis Sullivan (1856–1924) and Frank Lloyd Wright (1869–1959). The original American contribution to architecture, the skyscraper, was in danger of being turned into an ornate wedding cake. Sullivan first, then Wright, stripped away classical ornamentation and constructed their buildings in terms of materials and function. Sullivan's skyscrapers clearly echo the steel skeletons that hold them up. In the tradition of the Hudson River School, Wright idealized nature; his houses blend into the landscape instead of dominating it, whether they are built on low, flat ground or perched above a waterfall. As often happens with experimental American artists, Wright first gained a reputation in Europe before becoming recognized at home.

With few exceptions, American artists, until well into the twentieth century, were conservative; even the most accomplished (excepting Ryder and Whistler) worked in an academic tradition; some (such as Eakins) overcame the academic limitations through their own genius. Curiously, at the turn of the century, art did not reflect the growth and dynamism that created continent-spanning railroads, airplanes, automobiles, and bridges. When this dynamism began to be expressed in art, the impulse came from Europe.

In 1913 a large exhibition of modern European art, including works by Picasso, Matisse, and Duchamp, was held in New York—the famous Armory Show. It made clear to American artists how far advanced Europe was. The timing could not have been better. Only a year earlier, the last Western territory had become the forty-eighth contiguous state; the frontier was closed. The great waves of immigration from Central and Eastern Europe had swelled the population to a new high, especially in the cities. One year later World War I broke out, ending immigration and cutting off European artistic influence.

In this now "completed" and self-contained United States, the Cubist and Expressionist European paintings at the Armory Show acted as a catalyst. The public was fascinated and repelled by "modern" art; artists were challenged. Many artists who did not follow Cubism into total abstraction were nevertheless attracted by Cubism's concentration on form, geometric precision, and ability to show different aspects of objects simultaneously. Influenced by European art, they began depicting the subject matter of urban America (Plate 20). In a similar way, American composers such as Aaron Copland assimilated the subject matter of the United States into their music. The decade of the 1920s was a period of innovation and experimentation in American art, music, and literature.

The stock market crash of 1929 and the long depression that followed put a damper on experimentation. During the 1930s the tendency was to reflect the hard times through social realism that depicted the plight of the workingman, the farmer, or blacks. For the first time, the federal government began subsidizing artists by commissioning paintings, murals, and statues for public buildings, thus fostering a wide popular acceptance of art, much of it in a distinctly modern idiom. Then World War II brought refugees from Europe who helped bring American art into the international mainstream (Plate 21).

chapter 26

The history of music in America can be viewed as a series of alternations between two extremes. At one end is the complete imitation of European music; at the other is a totally independent, native American music.

American Music

The Seventeenth Century

The religious dissenters who settled New England in the early seventeenth century had come from a world rich in music and the other arts. The Pilgrims, for example, loved and practiced music, but had little time to spare for entertainment in their new land. Their music was functional, and used mostly for worship, in church and at home. Church congregations sang the psalms together in unison, without instrumental accompaniment. The tunes were taken from older hymns or folk songs that they had brought with them from England and Holland. In their homes the colonists sang and played the same psalm tunes in polyphonic settings.

The first book printed in the Colonies was a new translation of the psalms, called the *Bay Psalm Book* (1640), to which music was added in a 1698 edition. By the end of the century, however, the average congregation no longer could read notated music. A leader was chosen to sing the psalm or hymn, one line at a time, after which the group repeated it. The leader was free to vary the tune, or ornament it, and often each of his followers felt free to do the same. The effect probably was not a high order of musical excellence, but apparently it was enjoyable and was done with great enthusiasm, strengthening the social cohesion of the congregation.

The Eighteenth Century

This folk music style of congregational singing led many ministers to attempt to reform the musical elements of the worship service. In an effort to standardize the tunes, they encouraged everyone to learn to read music and sing in parts. Many churchmen wrote instruction books for the study of musical notation and sight-singing. Soon itinerant singing masters began to tour the country, giving classes and promoting the latest

Figure 26.1 William Billings, who headed the first, short-lived school of American composers, specialized in rugged, hymn-style music. This frontispiece for Billings' The New-England Psalm-Singer *was engraved by Paul Revere. (Library of Congress)*

collection of psalm and hymn tunes they had published. These singing schools were an important part of musical and social life in America around the middle of the eighteenth century.

Outside of New England, other religious groups also had continued their own musical traditions. Several communities had musical styles that were more polished and sophisticated than those of the New England region, but the others never became part of the mainstream of American culture. The most outstanding example was the music developed by the Moravian Brethren, a religious sect that settled in Pennsylvania and the Carolinas. The Moravians brought to America music by European composers such as Bach, Handel, Haydn, and Mozart. They performed with skill and composers from their own ranks wrote in the current European manner. But they remained isolated, and their flourishing musical establishment had no real effect on the rest of America.

(Frontispiece engraved by Paul Revere, from The New-England Psalm-Singer, composed by William Billings and printed by Edes and Gill, Boston, in 1770. Courtesy of The Library of Congress)

Thanksgiving

Serve The Lord with gladness! Come into His presence with singing! (Psalm 100: 2)

Secular music began to flourish in the Colonies during the eighteenth century, particularly in such major cities as New York, Boston, Philadelphia, and Charleston. Through shipping and trading, the people in these cities remained in close contact with the artistic life of Europe. As the cities prospered, the growing middle class acquired both the leisure and the money to support the arts.

Concerts in eighteenth-century America were not so serious or impressive as those in the major European cities. The most popular concert programs in America consisted of patriotic songs, opera airs, traditional folk songs, and dance tunes. Programmatic or absolute instrumental music were of secondary importance. Instead, music publishers catered to amateurs and produced works of modest proportions and demands.

Beginning in the 1730s, there were concerts, operas, and other musical events that featured immigrant musicians. These professionals worked both as performers and as "professors" of music. They taught music to gentlemen amateurs who, in turn, supported the rapid growth of music in America. The supporters included Thomas Jefferson, one of the outstanding patrons of music of his day, and Benjamin Franklin, who served capably as a performer, inventor of an instrument (the glass harmonica), and music critic. Another of the gentlemen amateurs, Francis Hopkinson (1737–1791), who wrote genteel songs, claimed to be the "first native of the United States who has produced a musical composition."

By 1770 there was a group of native American composers with enough in common to be considered a school. Led by William Billings (1746–1800), these composers produced music with a simple, rugged hymn style, angular, folklike melodies, and stark harmonies. Not feeling bound by the European traditions of composition, they created their own new style. One of the favorite devices of Billings and his contemporaries was the *"fuguing tune,"* a hymn or psalm tune with brief polyphonic sections that have imitative entrances. Billings and the others of this school felt that these pieces were "twenty times as powerful as the old slow tunes."

Unfortunately, however, this virile new style was soon abandoned, and native American music returned to a position of subservience to the European style. The original style created by the New England composers was considered crude by comparison with that of the European masters; and Americans were becoming self-conscious about their lack of sophistication and cultural heritage.

The Nineteenth Century

The musical culture of nineteenth-century America was marked by two significant phenomena. The first was the division between what we now call "classical" and "popular" music. Classical music was meant either for serious study and listening or for religious purposes, while popular music aimed only to entertain. Earlier music had served both functions. For example, the fuguing tunes of the eighteenth-century New Englanders were written for worship and enlightenment, but learning and singing them was also an enjoyable social function.

The second phenomenon of nineteenth-century music was the imitation of German music by American composers, a trend that became most evident after the Civil War. By that time the pattern of immigration to the United States had changed, as more people came from the European continent and fewer from Great Britain. The Europeans brought to America the ideas of the Romantic movement, which was strongest in Germany. Soon Romanticism influenced every area of American musical life.

American Composers before the Civil War

In the years preceding the Civil War, many songs with texts of extreme sentimentality were written and published primarily for use by amateurs in their homes. The great songwriter of the period did not follow in the European tradition, but wrote for the parlors and minstrel shows of America.

Stephen Collins Foster (1826–1864) wrote music that appealed to a large segment of the American population—those who were neither from the sophisticated Eastern cities nor the frontier. He articulated the uneasy feelings of dislocation and transition in a rapidly changing country.

Although his formal musical training was not extensive, he had an unmistakable gift for melody. Many of his songs are filled with nostalgic yearning, often for an unattainable love; both the text and music of his best-known songs, like *I Dream of Jeanie*, are gentle and tender. Foster also wrote many songs for the minstrel shows that were a popular form of entertainment in the North, both before and after the Civil War. The music of minstrel shows had a robust quality that was missing from the household songs of the period. Dance tunes and songs in Negro dialect were the basis of the shows, and Foster contributed many of the latter, including his well-known *Oh! Susanna* and *Camptown Races*.

While Stephen Foster wrote in a style that was uniquely American, composers of sacred music centered their attention on European styles. The Civil War and Reconstruction years were marked by a growing taste for hymns adapted from the music of the great European composers, from Palestrina to Mendelssohn. Lowell Mason (1792–1872) composed and adapted many such hymns. His efforts also brought music education into the public school curriculum for the first time.

Much American music—original compositions, arrangements of songs and dances, and sets of variations on well-known tunes—was written for the piano, the ideal instrument of the Romantic movement. American piano builders became some of the best in the world. One of the most colorful and talented figures in American music before the Civil War was a virtuoso pianist from New Orleans, Louis Moreau Gottschalk (1829–1869), who adopted many of the mannerisms of Liszt. He composed numerous works for both piano and orchestra, many of exaggerated sentimentality, and also made use of such exotic musical materials as Afro-Caribbean rhythms and Creole melodies.

Most of the music performed by American orchestras was by European composers, although the works of the American George Bristow

(1825–1898) were sometimes performed. Bristow wrote six symphonies in a style almost identical to Mendelssohn's. The New York Philharmonic, of which he was a member, was founded in 1842. A typical orchestral program in this period carefully mixed "heavy" music (single movements of symphonies, never complete ones) and lighter music (marches and overtures).

After the Civil War

From the end of the Civil War to World War I, German music had its greatest influence. Symphony orchestras were formed in many of the major cities, and large concert halls were built, including Carnegie Hall in New York (1891). Conservatories were established, and music departments appeared in colleges and universities.

A group of Romantic composers formed in Boston under John K. Paine (1839–1906), a conservative and serious workman who became the first professor of music at Harvard. Other talented members of the Boston group were Horatio Parker (1863–1919) of Yale and George Chadwick (1854–1931). These men composed instrumental and choral music: symphonies, sonatas, chamber music, and oratorios. Stylistically, they were closely allied with the early German Romantics, such as Schubert, Mendelssohn, and Schumann.

Edward MacDowell (1861–1908) represented another aspect of Romanticism in America. A tone poet, he wrote small evocative genre pieces. Although most of his works were piano solos and songs, often with programmatic titles, he also wrote for orchestra and chorus. His *Woodland Sketches,* containing "To a Wild Rose" and "To a Water Lily," and *New England Idyls* are among his best-known works.

Late in the century American musicians began to react against the domination of German ideals and attitudes. Some American composers decided to make use of American Indian and Negro themes—a challenge put forth by Czech composer Antonin Dvořák on his visit to America from 1892–1895. Arthur Farwell (1872–1951) was an American composer who accepted Dvořák's challenge and concentrated on using Indian themes in his works.

The reaction against German influence was also seen in an increased interest in the new musical ideas from France and Russia. Charles T. Griffes (1884–1920), whose creative talents were cut short by his premature death, showed, in his early works, the influence of Debussy, Ravel, and Stravinsky. He also developed an interest in Oriental music and his last works, especially the *Sonata for Piano* (1918, revised 1919) and the *Poem for Flute and Orchestra* (1919), contain the seeds of a synthesis of his various interests.

The Twentieth Century

One of America's most extraordinary composers, Charles Ives, wrote prolifically around the turn of the century, until ill health forced him to compose very little after 1921. He revolutionized American music with his open-minded approach to all musical sources, classical and popular; he rejected dogmatic ideas and created his own musical philosophy.

Ives (1874–1954)

The Bettmann Archive

Charles Ives was raised in the small town of Danbury, Connecticut, where his father was town bandleader, church organist, music teacher, and composer. His father had an unusual interest in musical experimentation, a fascination with sounds, which he transmitted to his son. This was undoubtedly one of the most important musical influences in Ives' life.

The young Ives studied music at Yale and then launched a successful career in life insurance. He deliberately chose to earn his living in an enterprise separate from his composing on the theory that both efforts would be the better for it, and he never regretted the decision. He composed furiously during evenings and weekends, storing his manuscripts in his barn. Ives' music was totally unknown until he published his *Concord Sonata*, a volume of songs, and a collection of essays in the early 1920s. Even then, his works were not readily accepted; only since World War II has his music become widely performed, published, and recorded. As his works became better known, Ives' influence on other composers increased, and today many people consider him the generator of a new, experimental trend in American music.

His work is considered to be so important among musicians and his popularity with the concert-going public is such that the one hundredth anniversary of his birth was widely celebrated in 1974.

The musical isolation in which Ives worked led him to develop an unusual philosophy of music. He had little regard for technical skill, either from the composer or from the performer. Rather, he was accustomed to, and indeed liked, the sounds made by amateur musicians, understanding the value of the spirit with which this music was played. This idea came from Ives' father, who was quoted as saying: "Don't pay too much attention to the sounds. If you do, you may miss the music."

His Work

Ives wrote several symphonies and a considerable amount of chamber music. Some of his chamber music was for traditional combinations, like the string quartet, but Ives also enjoyed creating new and unusual groupings of instruments. His *The Unanswered Question* (1906) is scored for trumpet, four flutes, and offstage strings. *Hallowee'n* (1907?) is for string quartet and piano, with optional bass drum, with each of the strings playing in a different key. Ives also wrote several violin sonatas, piano sonatas, and other solos, and almost 200 songs.

Many of Ives' works contain musical quotations from well-known patriotic songs, marches, and hymns. He borrowed themes by other composers ranging from Handel to Tchaikovsky. He felt that all these sources had validity. Some of his pieces are programmatic, in the sense that they describe particular events or places in his life; Ives often wrote comments in the margins of his scores explaining the subjects of his works. For example, the Sonata No. 1 for Piano (1909) is about "outdoor life in Connecticut villages in the '80s and '90s." This reminiscence includes a barn dance, a hymn tune, and the town band, with appropriate music quoted for each.

Sonata No. 2

Record 8/Side 1

One of Ives' greatest works, the Second Piano Sonata, was privately printed in 1919–1920 along with six *Essays Before a Sonata*. However, this immensely difficult work remained generally unnoticed until 1939, when the American pianist John Kirkpatrick presented it at Town Hall in New York City. This performance, highly acclaimed by critics and the public, perhaps more than anything else set off the long-delayed discovery of Ives' music.

Subtitled *Concord, Mass. 1840–60*, the sonata consists of four movements: "Emerson," "Hawthorne," "The Alcotts," and "Thoreau." In Ives' words:

The whole is an attempt to present one person's impression of the spirit of the transcendentalism that is associated in the minds of many with Concord, Mass., of over a half century ago. This is undertaken in impressionistic pictures of Emerson and Thoreau, a sketch of the Alcotts, and a scherzo *supposed to reflect a lighter quality which is often found in the fantastic side of Hawthorne. The first and last movements do not aim to give any programs of the life or of any particular work of either Emerson or Thoreau, but, rather, composite pictures or impressions.* *

As with so many of Ives' major works, much of the *Concord Sonata* evolved from earlier, often unfinished, pieces. One of his most ambitious projects was a series of *Men of Literature Overtures* for orchestra, which included works on Browning, Matthew Arnold, Emerson, and Hawthorne. The first two movements of the sonata are, in effect, a recomposition of the latter two overtures. The third movement is derived from the *Orchard House Overture*, another early symphonic work intended to evoke the home life of the Alcott family.

In a footnote near the end of the Epilogue to his *Essays Before a Sonata*, Ives describes his initial conception of each of the movements:

The first movement (Emerson) of the music which is the cause of all these words was first thought of (we believe) in terms of a large orchestra; the second (Hawthorne), in terms of a piano or a dozen pianos; the third (Alcotts), of an organ (or piano with voice or violin); and the last (Thoreau), in terms of strings, colored possibly with a flute or horn. †

*From Charles Ives, *Essays Before a Sonata and Other Writings*, Howard Boatwright, ed. (New York: Norton, 1961), p. 1.
†*Ibid.*, p. 84.

First Movement

"Emerson" comes closest to employing a traditional structure, using elements of a sonata-allegro scheme. Two motives are announced at the beginning: the first is lyrical in nature, sounding in the left hand

Example 26.1

and the second, more epic in spirit, is a direct quotation of the opening motives of Beethoven's Fifth Symphony. The original is notated

Example 26.2

Example 26.3

and Ives has it appear first in the right hand, then in the left:

The motive from Beethoven returns, in different settings, throughout the entire work, functioning as a unifying device.

The vast first movement unfolds as a series of contrasting "prose" and "verse" sections, to use Ives' own terminology. The two motives of the opening form the basis for the prose section (roughly analogous to the first-theme group of a sonata-allegro exposition), and a more extended, almost folklike melody initiates the verse (the second-theme group of an exposition):

Example 26.4

Like Beethoven, Ives begins developing his material as soon as it is stated. The epic and lyric motives pass through numerous transformations in rhythm, melodic contour, and harmonization. There is no key signature or definite tonal center, and the meter is highly irregular. The movement comes to a climax with the epic motive repeatedly enunciated at a fortissimo level against the lyric motive in the bass. Then the texture thins out, the pace slows, and the movement gradually fades out with echolike overtones sounding above a rocking figure in the bass.

Second Movement

"Hawthorne" again makes use of the epic motive, but also introduces several other quotations. The "half-childlike, half-fairylike phantasmal realms"* of Hawthorne's imagination are suggested by the rapid, swirling figuration of the opening. The texture, now expanding, now contracting, is full of brilliant virtuoso effects. The epic motive enters in the right hand, fortissimo, and then suddenly the rapid-fire pace slackens as the hymn tune *Martyn* ("Jesus Lover of My Soul") quietly enters. Cut off by the scherzo figurations, it begins anew, ever more intense.

Example 26.5

This brief, churchlike reverie is again broken off with the return of the scherzo figuration. A jaunty march tune that Ives borrowed from an earlier work takes over:

Example 26.6

The march, in turn, is superseded by the complex syncopations of a ragtime. The pace gets faster and faster, the rhythms ever more complex, and toward the end a few bars of "Columbia, the Gem of the Ocean" make their way into the free-for-all.

Third Movement

Example 26.7

The shortest and most simple of the movements, "The Alcotts," opens with a hymnlike version of the epic motive:

Op. cit., p. 42.

But as the motive continues to expand, it becomes apparent that the opening is also that of another hymn tune, "Missionary Chant":

Example 26.8

Ye Chris-tian he-ralds, go, pro-caim   Sal - va-tion through Im-man-uel's   name.

In the juxtaposition of Beethoven and revival song, one flowing into the other, the two motives seem to suggest a musical Sunday afternoon at the Alcotts around "the little old spinet-piano Sophia Thoreau gave to the Alcott children, on which Beth played the old Scotch airs, and played at the Fifth Symphony."* The "old Scotch airs" dominate the movement, building up in sonority to culminate in the return of Beethoven's Fifth.

Fourth Movement

"Thoreau" is the most contemplative and dreamlike of the four movements. Bits and pieces of material heard earlier in the work are recapitulated, and suddenly—at the very end—Ives adds a separate line for solo flute (there is an alternate version if no flute is available). An ostinato figure in the bass enters, continuing to the very end, and the work concludes with a final statement of the epic motive, gradually diminishing.

The Twenties

From the end of World War I to the beginning of the Depression in 1929, American music enjoyed a very optimistic and progressive period. As the country experienced unprecedented prosperity, young composers experimented with the new ideas and sounds that had been proposed by progressive European composers such as Stravinsky. The changes in American music that took place in the 1920s developed in several different directions. They included a search for a truly "American" musical idiom, experimental work with new sounds and instruments, and an attempt to fuse the popular and classical streams of American music.

One of the most influential and innovative composers of the 1920s was Edgard Varèse (1883–1965). Born in Paris, Varèse came to New York to live in 1915, and challenged America's musical traditions with a series of outstanding compositions. Varèse defined music as "organized sound," meaning *all* sounds, including some often classified as nonmusical noises. Large groups of percussion instruments are featured in many of his pieces. *Ionisation* (1930–1931), for forty-one percussion instruments and two sirens, is a fascinating study in rhythms and sonority, without conventional melody or harmony. Varèse dreamed of finding instruments capable of producing the sounds and rhythms he had in mind, a dream that came true with the advent of electronic music.

Important developments in the field of popular music also took place in the 1920s. One of the most successful songwriters of the decade was George Gershwin (1898–1937). He brought the musical idioms of jazz and Broadway into the concert hall, with his *Rhapsody in Blue* (1924), *Concerto in F* (1925), and *An American in Paris* (1928). His contributions to

*Op. cit., p. 47.

the Broadway stage, particularly the musical satire *Of Thee I Sing* (1931) and the folk opera *Porgy and Bess* (1935), were also outstanding. Gershwin played a significant role in the attempt to bridge the popular and classical streams of American music, which had been widely separated since the beginning of the nineteenth century.

Figure 26.3   Edgard Varèse challenged American musical tradition by incorporating the noise and harshness of modern, industrialized society in his compositions. His vivid, imaginative style blossomed fully with the advent of electronic music. (Eugene Cook)

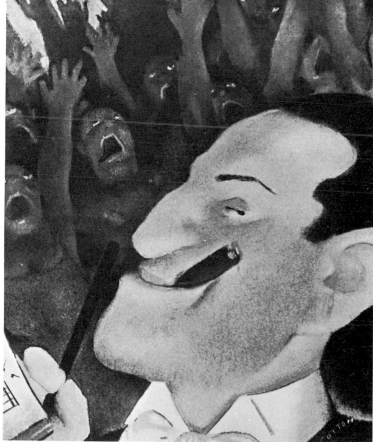

Figure 26.4   George Gershwin, here depicted conducting his Porgy and Bess, *helped reunite the popular and classical streams of American music. Master of song, stage, and orchestra, he introduced the musical idioms of jazz and Broadway to the concert hall. (Reprinted from* Vanity Fair, *Copyright © 1935 (renewed) 1963 by The Condé Nast Publications Inc.)*

Copland (b. 1900)

Eugene Cook

Aaron Copland was the first of a series of important young American composers to study with the remarkable Mlle. Nadia Boulanger (b. 1887) in Paris. She trained her pupils to develop their own personal styles, following Stravinsky as an example. Thus Copland's early works show Stravinsky's influence. At the same time, however, he was looking for a style that would be truly "American." As he later described it, "Our concern was not with the quotable hymn or spiritual: we wanted to find a music that would speak of universal things in a vernacular of American speech rhythms of contemporary dance music, such as the Charleston." This jazz influence can be seen clearly in his *Music for the Theatre* (1925), a suite for chamber orchestra.

During the late 1920s Copland gave up his reliance on dance music and developed a more abstract "American" style. One of his finest works is the *Piano Variations* (1930), in which he treats the piano as a percussion instrument.

Copland's music reflected an interest in regional America. His ballet scores *Billy the Kid* (1938) and *Rodeo* (1942) dealt with the American West, while *Appalachian Spring* (1944) depicted life in rural Pennsylvania.

Appalachian Spring

*Record 8/Side 1;
Side 2*

Appalachian Spring, the last of Copland's three ballets on American frontier themes, was written on commission for Martha Graham's modern dance company. The work, choreographed by Miss Graham, premiered in October, 1944.

Scored originally for a chamber orchestra of thirteen instruments, the ballet was later revised by Copland as a suite for symphony orchestra and is best known today in this form. The ballet itself is virtually plotless, having for its characters a young bride (originally danced by Miss Graham), her farmer husband-to-be, an older pioneering woman, and a preacher with his followers.

The music, evoking a simple, tender, and pastoral atmosphere, is distinctly American in its use of folklike themes suggesting barn dances, fiddle tunes, and revival hymns. Only one is actually a genuine folk tune: the Shaker song, "Simple Gifts," which forms the basis for a set of five variations. Not only his melodic material, but also Copland's compositional techniques suggest a native American musical style. The orchestral texture is, by and large, open and transparent, with the different instrumental choirs—string, woodwind, brass, and percussion (chiefly piano and harp)—scored as individual units and juxtaposed against one another. The vigorous, four-square rhythmic patterns, particularly in the music for the revivalist preacher and his followers, could not have originated anywhere but in the folk music of the American frontier.

Figure 26.6 Copland's Appalachian Spring *was commissioned for Martha Graham's modern dance company, shown here performing this distinctly American musical masterpiece. The orchestral version of* Appalachian Spring *is a favorite of today's concertgoers. (New York Public Library)*

The orchestral suite falls into eight distinct sections, set off from one another by changes in tempo and meter. The opening section, marked "very slowly," introduces the characters, one by one. Over a luminous string background, solo woodwind and brass instruments enter one by one—paralleling the balletic action—with slowly rising and falling figures that outline different major triads. It is not until the solo flute and violin enter that these triadic figures coalesce into any kind of definite "theme":

Example 26.9

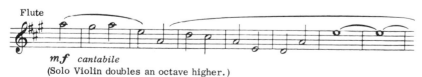

m.f *cantabile*
(Solo Violin doubles an octave higher.)

Example 26.10

The serene mood of the introduction is suddenly broken by a vigorous, strongly accented theme sounded in unison in the strings and piano.

The action of the ballet now gets under way. The theme—initially built on the notes of an A-major triad—is soon broken down into smaller motives with the rhythmic figure ♫ ♩ predominating.

Musical development intensifies as these motives are passed back and forth between different orchestral choirs and solo instruments. Constant changes in meter and shifts in rhythmic accents add to the increasing momentum of this section.

Then follows a *pas de deux* for the bride and her husband-to-be, and the mixed feelings of tenderness and passion are expressed in a lyrical melody originating in the clarinet.

Example 26.11

The melody gradually expands and takes a definitive shape through numerous changes in tempo, finally culminating in a statement divided between the oboe, clarinet, and flute.

The revivalist preacher and his followers take over, announced by a cheerful tune that seems to have come right out of a country fiddlers' convention. Though heard first in the oboe and then the flute, the tune is not fully given until the entry of the violins.

Example 26.12

As in the second section, the rhythmic aspects of the tune soon prove to be more important than the melodic ones. The pace becomes more frenetic, cross-accents and syncopations soon predominate, and the section ends in a very Stravinskian manner with alternating meters of $^2/_4$ and $^5/_8$.

An extended solo for the bride follows, in which she expresses extremes of joy and fear, and exaltation at her coming motherhood. A presto theme forms the basis for most of this section,

Example 26.13

but toward the end a lyrical theme—very much like that of the earlier *pas de deux*—enters in the solo violin and oboe, gradually leading into a short recapitulation of the introduction.

A solo clarinet presents the melody of the Shaker song, "Simple Gifts."

Example 26.14

The action of the ballet at this point, scenes of daily activity for the bride and her intended, seems perfectly reflected in the tune. The text of the song runs as follows:

'Tis the gift to be simple,
'Tis the gift to be free,
'Tis the gift to come down where we ought to be,
And when we find ourselves in the place just right,
'Twill be in the valley of love and delight.
When true simplicity is gain'd,
To bow and to bend we shan't be asham'd,
To turn, turn will be our delight
'Till by turning, turning, we come round right.

The five variations following the statement of the tune present the melody in a variety of contrasting textures and accompanimental figures, often with new lines of counterpoint. At the end, the full orchestra blazes forth in a broad choralelike setting of the tune.

In the final section, the bride takes her place among her neighbors, and they depart quietly, leaving the young couple alone. Once again the luminous sonorities of the introduction return, and the work concludes in the atmosphere of serenity with which it began.

Copland also wrote four film scores during this period. Several patriotic works, including the *Lincoln Portrait* (1942) and *Fanfare for the Common Man* (1942), were occasioned by the entry of the United States into World War II. Almost all these works used American subjects and were aimed at the wider audience provided by the new mass media. The style of writing was smoother and more relaxed, and many pieces used folklike or hymnlike themes.

The Thirties

The economic and social depression that followed the stock market crash of 1929 was fully reflected in the world of American music. The excited and optimistic movements of the 1920s gave way to a period of conservatism and isolationism during which the public showed little interest in modern music. Within this basically conservative philosophy, however, several new trends did appear. They included an interest in regional Americanisms and an attempt to communicate with a larger and less sophisticated audience.

Virgil Thomson (b. 1896), after studying with Nadia Boulanger in Paris, turned to American hymns as one of his sources. He wrote in a

Figure 26.7   Composers like Roy Harris flourished in the more conservative, egalitarian trends of post-Depression music. Harris' works ranged from violin and piano concertos to avowedly patriotic symphonies and choral settings. (The Bettman Archive)

melodic style, with humor and artful simplicity. His opera *Four Saints in Three Acts*, with a libretto by Gertrude Stein, is a charming work full of fantasy. It was first produced by the Friends and Enemies of Modern Music in Hartford, Connecticut, in 1934. Thomson also wrote music for several documentary films.

The music of Roy Harris (b. 1898), another Boulanger pupil, is characterized by chromatic but strongly lyric melodies, contrapuntal techniques, and an interest in Baroque procedures, such as fugue and ostinato. His Quintet for Piano and Strings (1936) and Symphony No. 3 (1938), both abstract instrumental pieces, are considered among his best compositions. Harris also has a strong interest in native American topics and musical materials, evidenced in his *Folksong Symphony* (1940), *Gettysburg Address Symphony* (1944), his choral settings of two texts by Walt Whitman, and many other pieces.

Other important composers of the 1930s held positions as professors of music at American universities. One such composer is Walter Piston (b. 1894) who spent his entire career at Harvard. His approach is Neo-Classical, using the traditional forms of instrumental music. His abstract but elegant style and high level of craftsmanship won him the respect of many of his fellow composers. Piston is also the author of several widely used college texts on harmony, counterpoint, and orchestration. Other composer-educators of the 1930s included Roger Sessions (b. 1896) at Princeton and Berkeley, Douglas Moore (b. 1893) at Columbia, and Howard Hanson (b. 1896) at the Eastman School of Music.

The older, established composers of the period from 1930 to 1945 were basically conservative, in that they did not experiment with new forms, sounds, or styles. Even the younger composers who became prominent in these years were conservative in the same way.

Samuel Barber (b. 1910) has maintained a neo-Romantic, lyric style throughout his career, as evidenced in his setting of *Dover Beach* (1933) for voice and string quartet, and *Knoxville: Summer of 1915* (1948). Even his more abstract instrumental music has an expressive, almost vocal quality.

Figure 26.8   A composer of the Romantic tradition, Samuel Barber is known for the expressive, lyric style which pervades even his more abstract instrumental music. (The Bettmann Archive)

Schuman (b. 1900)

Fabian Bachrach

William Schuman came to classical music with a background in performing and writing popular music. Evidence of this early affiliation appears in the energetic rhythms and bright orchestrations of his symphonies. Although abstract instrumental works form the core of Schuman's work, he also has produced pieces with American subjects and musical materials. *American Festival Overture* (1939), a cantata based on Walt Whitman's *A Free Song* (1943), and *New England Triptych* (1956) are among his best-known works.

New England Triptych

Record 8/Side 2

Like Copland, Harris, and other American composers prominent in the 1930s and 1940s, Schuman interested himself in musical Americana, producing a number of works that drew upon eighteenth- and nineteenth-century folklore and music. His *William Billings Overture* (1943) was based upon three singing-school pieces by the eighteenth-century Boston composer. And with his *New England Triptych* for symphony orchestra, Schuman again employed three pieces by Billings. In his program notes to the work, Schuman remarks:

The works of this dynamic composer capture the spirit of sinewy ruggedness, deep religiosity and patriotic fervor that we associate with the Revolutionary period. Despite the undeniable crudities and technical shortcomings of his music, its appeal, even today, is forceful and moving. I am not alone among American composers who feel an identity with Billings and it is this sense of identity which accounts for my use of his music as a point of departure. These pieces do not constitute a "fantasy" on themes of Billings, nor "variations" on his themes, but rather a fusion of styles and musical language.

The pieces forming the basis of each of the three movements of the *Triptych* are an anthem, "Be Glad Then, America," a round or canon, "When Jesus Wept," and a hymn tune, "Chester."

First Movement

The first movement—the most extended and varied of the three—draws its material from three short phrases of the original anthem. The final portion of the anthem's text runs as follows:

Yea, the Lord will answer
And say unto his people. Behold,
I will send you corn and wine and oil
And ye shall be satisfied therewith.

Be glad then, America,
Shout and rejoice.
Fear not O land,
Be glad and rejoice.
Hallelujah!, praise the Lord.

The phrases forming the basis of the movement are given below in
Billings' setting. The particular motives extracted by Schuman are indicated by brackets.

Example 26.15   1. (And ye shall be satisfied)

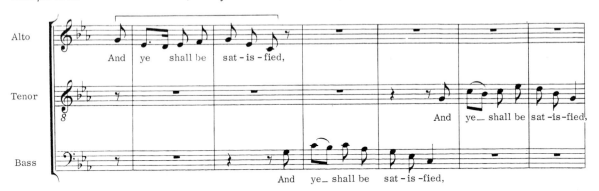

Example 26.16   2. (Be glad then, America, shout and rejoice)

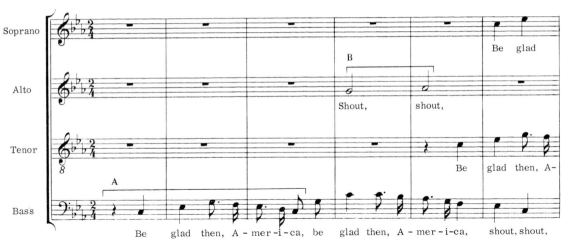

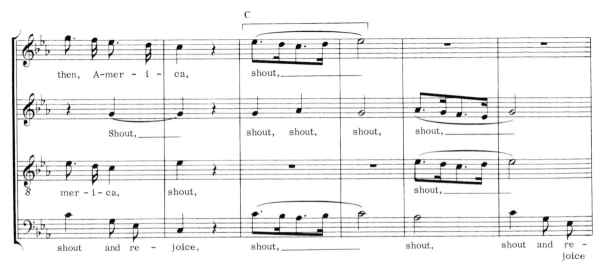

Example 26.17   3. (Hallelujah, praise the Lord)

Despite the composer's statement that the movements constitute neither a "fantasy" nor "variations" on these themes, both terms seem entirely appropriate to describe the compositional techniques employed in the work, particularly the first movement. It opens with a solo for timpani.

Example 26.18

The theme is suggestive, at least melodically if not so much rhythmically, of the "Hallelujah" section of the anthem. Over long pedal notes in the bass clarinet and bassoons, the cellos begin to develop the theme.

Example 26.19

Following the strings, the other sections of the orchestra make their entrances—low woodwinds, high woodwinds, horns—gradually building up to a hammering climax. Trumpets and trombones announce the main section of the movement with two short motives from the theme of "Be glad then, America."

Example 26.20

Attention quickly focuses on the rhythmic development of these motives, and paticularly of the figure ♪♪♩. The various instrumental families of the orchestra are played off against one another in contrapuntal fashion as they exploit this sharp, jagged rhythmic cell. As the texture becomes less thick, the short motive on the word "shout" enters in the trumpets and trombones. Soon only the horns and upper strings are left, and, paired with each other, they turn the "A" fragment into a two-part canon.

The timpani, again solo, leads to the middle section, which is based on the theme, "And ye shall be satisfied." Like Billings' original version, this section is primarily fugal. The motive is heard first in the cellos and violas.

Example 26.21

It is then taken up by all the members of the string family, and the texture again thickens as woodwinds and brass enter. Trumpets and trombones reintroduce the "shout" fragment, which gradually takes over the full orchestra. The "A" fragment, sounded in the brass, closes the middle section.

Piccolo and oboe together initiate the closing section with the "Hallelujah" theme.

Example 26.22

All four horns and then a solo trumpet take up the smoothly flowing figure. At the end, the figure ♩♫♩ so prominent in the first section of the movement, returns to form the basis for the final orchestral climax.

Second Movement

Record 8/Side 2

Billings' melancholy canon, "When Jesus Wept," is the basis for the quiet and lyrical second movement. Its form is a simple ABA structure, and the instrumentation is limited to tenor drum, bassoon, oboe, and string choir.

Example 26.23

The original canon runs as follows:

William Billings   from The New England Psalm Singer, 1770

When Je - sus wept, the fall - ing tear in mer - cy flowed be - yond all bound: When

Je - sus groaned a trem -bling fear Seized all ___ the guil - ty world ___ a - round.

The movement opens with the muffled sound of the tenor drum. A solo bassoon intones the melody, which is then taken up by the oboe an octave higher. A strangely dissonant counterpoint emerges as the bassoon continues to play, not the original melody in canon, as one might expect, but rather a freely invented line, which moves in descending phrases underneath the oboe.

Example 26.24

The dissonant sonorities of bassoon and oboe suddenly give way to luminous consonance as the strings take over the melody. The middle section, entirely given over to strings, constitutes a seamless, contrapuntal development of the melody. The thick string texture gradually subsides as bassoon and oboe return with the original melody.

Third Movement

The closing movement forms a bright, dazzling contrast to the subdued character of "When Jesus Wept." Billings' hymn tune "Chester" was adopted by the Continental Army as a marching song, and Schuman presents both the hymn and march aspects of the melody. The woodwind choir plays the tune as a straightforward hymn, the melody itself being given in the first flute and oboe.

Example 26.25

The tempo suddenly changes to *allegro vivo*, and over drumlike tone clusters in the brass and strings the high woodwinds play the tune at double its initial speed. Short rhythmic motives are freely tossed back and forth as the texture changes to all woodwind sonorities. Strings take up the rhythmic impulses, and the melody returns in the brass—now in extra-long note values. The movement builds to a brilliant close as brass and percussion are set against strings and woodwinds.

After World War II   In the years immediately preceding World War II many European composers immigrated to this country. By 1940 Hindemith, Bartók, Schoenberg, and others were teaching at American colleges. Their presence helped to break down the wall of musical isolationism that had been built during the 1930s; by the beginning of the postwar period there was no longer any real distinction between "American" and "European" styles. Several eminent European scholars of music history also arrived, who encouraged the acceptance of musicology as a legitimate field of academic study in this country.

The end of the war marked an end to the period of conservatism and isolationism in American music. The postwar years were characterized by tremendous activity, with new ideas and techniques evolving in all directions. The trends that appeared at this time were, for the most part, unrelated to each other. The audience for American music grew with the country's increased prosperity and the introduction of long-playing records in 1948.

The twelve-tone technique became accepted by many composers after the war. Earlier it had been considered the special property of Schoenberg and the people working with him. After the war almost all the young composers in Europe and America used it, and some older composers adopted it too, including Copland, Sessions, and Stravinsky. As Copland pointed out, twelve-tone writing is a technique, not a style; thus it can be used by composers with very different personal styles.

Summary   The religious dissenters who settled New England in the early seventeenth century came from a world rich in music. Their music was functional and used mostly for worship, in church and at home. Outside New England, other religious groups also continued their own musical tradition.

During the eighteenth century, secular music began to flourish, particularly in the cities along the Eastern seaboard. By 1770 there was a group of native American composers with enough in common to be considered a school. In the nineteenth century, particularly after the Civil War, American composers increasingly imitated German styles. Toward the end of the century, however, some American composers began to react against the German influence.

Charles Ives, who wrote at the turn of the century, revolutionized American music with his open-minded approach to all musical sources, rejecting dogmatic ideas and creating his own musical philosophy. His works contain excerpts from marches, hymns, and patriotic songs and themes by other composers from Handel to Tchaikovsky.

The 1920s were an important decade in American musical history. Aaron Copland sought to create a truly American style by incorporating the jazz rhythms of contemporary dance music into his compositions.

Edgard Varèse defined music as "organized sound," challenging conventional sonority with his use of nonmusical "noises." George Gershwin, a successful songwriter, brought the musical idioms of jazz and the Broadway stage into the concert hall.

During the 1930s composers became interested in regional Americanisms and began to make use of the musical materials of early

America. Virgil Thomson turned to American hymns as source material, and Roy Harris used native American subjects, such as folk songs and the Gettysburg Address, in his symphonies. William Schuman produced works that drew upon eighteenth- and nineteenth-century folklore. Another important group of composers, including Walter Piston, Douglas Moore, Roger Sessions, and Howard Hanson, held positions as professors of music at American universities.

In the years immediately preceding World War II, many famous European composers, including Hindemith, Bartók, and Schoenberg, immigrated to the United States. In the period after the war American music adopted new ideas and activities which developed in many directions, and during this period the twelve-tone technique of composition became widely accepted by almost all young composers.

chapter 27

The popular music of the United States includes a wide range of styles, many of which are native to this country. In addition to its folk music, American music includes jazz, rock, soul, and musical comedy.

Popular Music

Folk Music

The folk music of the United States has origins as diverse as those of its people. The earliest immigrants brought their music with them—music for worship and music for singing and dancing—and traces of these original elements survive today.

One of the most enduring folk syles is the ballad, a strophic song form that has been popular in England since Elizabethan times. It was brought to this country at the end of the eighteenth century by the Scotch-Irish, many of whom settled in the southern Appalachian mountains. Because they remained isolated until this century, the old English ballads are sung there now in pure eighteenth-century form. Modal melodies and harmonies, which were common before the major and minor keys became dominant in the Baroque era, are carried over in much of their folk music to the present day.

The old English ballads traveled west with the pioneers. New words were written for old tunes, and the tunes themselves gradually changed. New songs were written—many of them about particular occupations. Cowboys, sailors, lumberjacks, and railroad men all had songs about their jobs and their lives.

The most significant contribution to American folk music came from the black population. Blacks arrived in this country with an old and sophisticated musical tradition. The harmonic system of African music was similar to that of European music, but its rhythmic organization was much more complex, frequently involving the simultaneous use of several different patterns. When this African musical heritage was combined with the Anglo-American folk music of the South, a new music resulted.

The new secular music included blues songs and plantation songs. (The latter were preserved in the minstrel shows after the Civil War and later became the basis of ragtime and traditional jazz.) There were also religious songs: the spirituals and gospel hymns that grew out of the slaves' work songs. Many of the sacred songs follow a traditional African pattern of call and response, where the leader sings a line first, and the group repeats it. Another tradition in folk music, the improvisation of harmony, played an important part in the development of jazz.

Popular Music

Thus the English and African musical cultures have existed side by side in America. Material and ideas have been traded back and forth, until today it is difficult to find any folk songs that belong completely to either one group or the other.

In the period since World War I folk music has become increasingly popular. An outstanding generation of performers, including Huddie Ledbetter (Leadbelly), Woody Guthrie, and Pete Seeger, paved the way for the current, and commercially more successful, artists. The rise in popularity of folk music on college campuses in the early 1960s was due in part to the common concern with topics of social protest: first civil rights, and then the antiwar movement. Folk music has always reflected topics of importance to the country's activists, and contemporary leaders, such as Simon and Garfunkel and Joan Baez, continued that tradition.

A specialized style of contemporary folk music, called *country and western,* is centered in Nashville, Tennessee. It features the distinctive nasal twang of the hillbilly singer, often accompanied by country fiddlers. Country and western music descends from the old English ballads that survive in the southern mountains. One of the most popular and successful country and western singers is Johnny Cash.

Jazz

Born in New Orleans at the end of the nineteenth century, jazz is often considered to be America's greatest contribution to music. Owing its inspiration to the folk music of the American black culture, as well as to such diverse sources as African rhythms, Protestant hymns, and nineteenth-century European impressionism, jazz was a new musical language, drawing upon the old, but adding a special vitality and uniqueness of its own. Despite changing styles within the jazz movement, it is possible to define jazz generally as a series of *improvised* variations (melodic and rhythmic) on a theme.

Ragtime

One of the earliest and most popular forerunners of jazz was known as ragtime. Influenced by popular European dances, military marches, and the cakewalks of the minstrel shows, rags were unique to the realm of music because of their unprecedented emphasis on improvisation. Although they featured a strict two-part form and used conventional harmony, rag style relegated the pianist's left hand to maintaining a steady beat, but freed his right hand to decorate the tune in a variety of ways.

This technique of creating unusual rhythmic patterns by playing sometimes before and sometimes after the beat is known as syncopation. Though utilized in other styles of music, the device enjoyed its most consistent treatment in ragtime jazz. One of the most highly recognized composers of this style was Scott Joplin (1869–1917). His *Maple Leaf Rag* (1899) is considered a classic, and his compositions earned him the title "King of Ragtime." Only recently the music of Joplin has been enjoying a considerable revival both in concert halls, on records, and in films such as *The Sting*.

Blues

Another forerunner of jazz, known for its lamenting and melancholy style, is known as the blues. Derived from the folk music of the slaves, the blues originally possessed a structured style, featuring a distinct form for both the lyrics and the melodies. The standard pattern consisted of two rhyming lines of poetry with the first line repeated (AAB). The harmony was usually very simple, frequently utilizing simple chord progressions.

Despite this simplicity of structure, blues introduced a number of unique musical devices, often applied to complement the mood of the music. One technique was to alter the major scale by lowering the third and seventh notes somewhat less than a half-step. These "blue notes," as they were called, could also be manipulated by allowing the performer to slide into them, rather than by hitting them solidly. The result was "bent" or "glided" pitches that resulted in a highly distinctive sound.

Early blues was conceived as a vocal phenomenon, but instrumentalists soon adopted blues devices and techniques. One of the most famous vocal stylists and interpreters of this art was Bessie Smith (1895–1937), whose powerful emotional and poetic style is legend. The musicians who accompanied her used their instruments to wail, sob, and growl in imitation of the pathos of her blues technique. Occasionally, the blues were performed without a vocalist, creating the distinctive sound and mood solely through the manipulation of the instrument. "Jelly Roll" Morton was one of the widely recognized blues pianists, transferring the "blues style" from the vocal idiom to that of the keyboard.

New Orleans

Ragtime and blues began to evolve into the New Orleans Jazz style by about 1900. Black street bands became very popular, and the city soon boasted a large population of self-taught but very talented instrumentalists. These individuals sometimes gathered in small groups to improvise on blues tunes or other popular songs, and from this early kind of improvisation grew the first real jazz.

The band now expanded in size to include a "front line," made up of trumpet or cornet, trombone, and clarinet, and a rhythm section, consisting of guitar, piano, string bass, and drums. Improvising from a basic well-known tune with its underlying chord sequence, the musicians greeted each repetition with an increasingly elaborate treatment of the theme, until the original melody became almost completely unrecognizable. This kind of improvisation constituted the beginning of jazz, and through the efforts of such jazz immortals as Joe "King" Oliver, a master trumpeter, the style gained rapidly in popularity and spread beyond New Orleans.

Chicago

In the 1920s, jazz moved up the Mississippi to Chicago. The riverboats, making regular excursions between New Orleans and the northern towns, brought the fun and excitement of jazz to people at all the small-town levees on the river. As jazz achieved a wider geographical popularity, stylistic changes began to take place. The ensemble became somewhat larger, much more emphasis was given to the role of the soloist, and the saxophone became a major element in the "jazz sound." One of the first of these pioneering musical geniuses was Louis "Satchmo" Armstrong (1900–1971). Exploring the possibilities of solo freedom, he

Figure 27.1 The versatile soloist James "Trummy" Young and Louis "Satchmo" Armstrong end a number. Armstrong popularized individual soloist improvisation in the middle sections of each piece, leaving the beginning and end for ensemble performance. (Dain, Magnum)

utilized the integrated ensemble approach at the beginning and end of each piece, but reserved the middle sections for improvisations by soloists. Each front-line performer was given one chorus to improvise on either the theme or its harmonic structure while the other members of the band rested or played background parts.

As jazz gained in popularity during the twenties and spread beyond the confines of New Orleans, white musicians began to take part in its development. One of the first of these was Leon ''Bix'' Beiderbecke, whose virtuosity as a jazz cornettist was widely acclaimed.

Big Bands

By the 1930s, New York had replaced Chicago as the major jazz center, and jazz moved out of the saloon and into the ballroom. This was the era of the big band, consisting of a dozen or more musicians. The old New Orleans front line was increased from three instruments to include brass sections of trumpets and trombones and woodwind sections of clarinets and saxophones. These jazz orchestras also produced a new sound and their style was known as swing.

As swing moved into the dance halls, a new era of jazz emerged. Because of the large number of musicians, improvisation became impractical except under strict controls. So arrangements, with specified areas for soloist interpretation, were written out. Unexpectedly armed with mass appeal, jazz virtuoso performers rapidly became personalities of star quality and drew large numbers of enthusiastic fans. Such names as Duke Ellington (1899–1974) emerged. This band leader-pianist-composer-arranger brought out the best in his soloists with music so masterfully arranged as to create the effect if not the fact of improvisation.

Figure 27.2   The great Duke Ellington, pianist-composer-arranger for half a century. His works ranged from popular songs to sacred music. (Black Star)

There were many other famous personalities and outstanding musicians who gained widespread attention in the swing era. Count Basie, leader of another popular band, became prominent, along with a number of his great soloists, including saxophonist Lester Young. Another well-known band leader was Benny Goodman, the clarinetist from Chicago referred to as the "King of Swing."

Bop

The 1940s ushered in a new era in the dynamic and changing jazz idiom. This time it was in the form of radical experimentalism, and its result was the "modern age of jazz." The proponents of this style, called bebop or bop, were a group of musicians who sought to achieve a totally new sound by inserting an element of unpredictability into their music: wide leaps in melody, phrases of uneven lengths, and rhythmic variety. Abandoning the diatonic restrictions of big band harmony, these modern musicians, including Charlie Parker and trumpeter Dizzy Gillespie, turned instead to chromatic harmony, thereby expanding the musical range of harmonic possibilities. Another feature of the bop era was the introduction of the electric guitar, now sufficiently amplified by electric power to become a frontline instrument.

Cool Jazz

The techniques of this new chromatic style of jazz were explored at an amazing rate. By the 1950s, the chromatic formula for freedom was fast becoming the very constraint from which the modern soloist wished to free himself. Initiated in 1948, under the tutelage of Miles Davis, a new jazz idiom was evolving. Referred to as "cool" jazz, this new style was composed for small groups, using a combination of written arrangements and improvisations. In comparison with the earlier style, it was economical and understated.

Modern Jazz

By the end of the 1950s, the search for a more challenging and modern jazz style had gained momentum. Its goal was best expressed by alto saxophonist Ornette Coleman, who was pressing for a form that allowed the soloist to create any sound at any time without constraint. These abstract or free improvisers, as they called themselves, were determined to play without having to adhere to harmonic or tonal rules and without fixed tunes or fixed series of chords and steady beats. Their efforts were aimed at producing modal, dissonant, atonal, and even meterless jazz.

At the same time, other pioneers in modern jazz were seeking ways to integrate jazz with concert music. Many musicians pursued the goal of merging the work of the extemporaneous composer of jazz with the heritage and forms of Western orchestral music.

Rock

With roots in such diverse areas as the rural South and the urban North, the West Coast and the East, rock was the product of two independent and isolated musical styles. The first, known as rhythm and blues, was primarily black popular music of the decade after World War I. The second was country and western music, the local music of southern bluegrass districts, such as Nashville and Memphis. The merging of these two musical styles in the 1950s resulted in the creation of a national popular music, written for and purchased by a new teenage generation of Americans.

Rhythm and Blues

Rhythm and blues were an outgrowth of jazz and the black folk music of the South. Primarily restricted to black southern communities, the music migrated north with the black population in the 1940s and 1950s. Celebrating this music as part of their cultural identity, members of northern black communities nurtured its growth by supporting the talented black entertainers who explored this style and by eagerly consuming their recordings. Among the black musicians who were popular during this period were such memorable names as Muddy Waters, B. B. King, and John Lee Hooker. There was also Bo Diddley, whose dynamic sound, stage mannerisms, and lavish costuming were later to have an important influence on Elvis Presley; and Chuck Berry, whose twanging guitar style soon won him a large number of imitators.

Country and Western

Even preceding rhythm and blues in popularity was rock's other inspirational source, country and western music. Broadcast in Nashville over station WSM as early as 1925, the *Grand Ole Opry* program promoted the country and western sound, including the hits of Jimmie Rodgers, and Lester Flatt and Earl Scruggs. It was not long before city dwellers were attracted by this music, and its localism ended as it spread rapidly northward. Both rhythm and blues and country and western music were to be a major influence in the trends that the later rock sound would explore.

Rock 'n' Roll

By the early 1950s, the rhythm and blues style had found a new audience outside the black community—the young white teenagers whose search for self-expression found compatibility with the driving rhythms and earthiness of this music.

Responding to the taste of his listeners, disk jockey Alan Freed began to air some of the current rhythm and blues records on his radio show, *Moondog House*. Seeking a new label to give this music relevance to his burgeoning audience, he renamed the style rock 'n' roll, two words that appeared in most of the songs of the day. The new name caught on immediately, and Freed later adopted it as the name of his famous radio program, *Rock 'n' Roll Party*, carried on the New York station WINS.

By far the most popular name of the early 1950s was that of Elvis Presley, who began his singing career as a part-time vocalist in a touring country and western show and whose name later became a household word.

The Beatles

By 1960, it was evident that rock 'n' roll was in need of a new direction, but few expected that the revolutionary force would be a group of English boys called the Beatles. Paul McCartney, George Harrison, John Lennon, and Ringo Starr, a group of neatly dressed, well-scrubbed, long-haired, and appealing Beatles from Liverpool soon won the hearts of American teens.

Although their early songs were in the traditional rock format, the Beatles soon emerged from being just another successful recording group to being serious investigators of the musical potential of the rock style. They began by experimenting with more complex rock meters and by adding classical and foreign instruments and techniques to their compositions.

Figure 27.3   Four young Liverpudlians rocketed to fame as the Beatles and revolutionized rock music by experimenting with more sophisticated musical forms and instrumentation. (McCullin, Magnum)

Psychedelic Rock

Experimentation in rock was to break new ground in 1967, entering a phase of electronic innovation. Sometimes referred to as *psychedelic rock,* it called for the use of magnetic tape, echo chambers, feedback effects, and other electronic techniques. In the hands of the Beatles, this music relied on symbolic lyrics, symphonic elements, and complex orchestrations. It also sought material and ideas from other cultures, particularly India, and from older music. In this vein, the Beatles produced *Sgt. Pepper's Lonely Hearts Club Band,* an important album, and one of the first to be recorded as a continuous song cycle rather than as a collection of independent works.

Acid Rock

Rock as a complex musical form was taken a step further when a hard-rock group called The Rolling Stones developed another new style in the mid 1960s. Called *acid rock,* it had the same spirit and drive as traditional rock, but its structures and rhythmic elements were more sophisticated, and the texts took on a literal rather than a symbolic importance.

Folk Rock

While the strains of rhythm and blues were being carried to new heights in rock, the country and western style was also undergoing translation into the rock movement. Even before the Beatles came to America, another performer was examining the folk potential of the rock phenomenon. Born in Hibbing, Minnesota, and schooled in the folk tradition, Bob Dylan introduced a new, poetic quality to rock lyrics. His social criticism, phrased in folklike melodies, earned him national attention when his song *Blowin' in the Wind* was adopted as the theme of the rising civil rights movement.

As with the Beatles, the electronic possibilities of 1965 captured Dylan's imagination. Abandoning his folk guitar for an electric version, he became an important part of the emerging folk-rock trend. Two of his albums—*Highway 61 Revisited* and *Bringing It All Back Home*—set forth this style with great success, but the triumph of his new album *Blonde on Blonde* forced the rock world to pay strict attention to the young man from Minnesota. The Beatles, the Stones, the Mamas and the Papas, the Beach Boys, and others soon found themselves following his pace-setting innovations. But Dylan again disrupted the rock world in 1968, when he reversed his previous style to produce a tranquil and refreshingly simple album, *John Wesley Harding.*

Raga Rock

The folk-rock style continued to explore the unlikely combination of rock rhythms and the simple melodies and harmonies of folk music.

Figure 27.4 Bob Dylan, who brought a more lyrical quality to the rock movement, blended social criticism with folklike melodies. (Black Star)

One particular area of exploration was a form of folk-rock music with an Eastern influence, known as *raga rock*. Borrowed from the music of India, ragas are prescribed forms of note groupings, each possessing its own mood and character. The musicians are permitted to improvise within these forms, using such instruments as the sitar, the tamboura, and the tabla (a set of drums).

Recent Trends

Today, rock has branched out to explore new musical territory. Borrowing from classical music, a rock opera, *Tommy*, was written by a group called The Who, and several groups have written masses and other sacred music in the rock style. Many groups have based pieces on the music of classical composers, or they have included classical works in their song. The Baroque technique of using ostinato bass has also been adopted.

Electronics continues to be a source of experimentation in the rock field, and loud speakers, amplifiers, and electrified musical instruments have become part of the rock setting.

Musical Comedy

Musical comedy occupies a unique position in American culture, lying somewhere between the commercially popular song and serious art music. In many ways it may be considered a hybrid of the two styles. In the last century, more than 2000 productions have opened on Broadway in New York City. Because the cost of such ventures is very high, the producers do everything they can to secure a favorable audience reaction. This has led to a great deal of variety in musical shows and to the incorporation of many types of music into a production. Thus, solos, duets, dances, and jazz numbers are often present together in a single show. Even rock has been included; the first rock musical, *Hair*, opened in 1968.

Historically, musical comedy evolved from the *musical revue* and the *operetta*. A musical revue is basically a series of unrelated singing and dancing numbers, with no plot. An operetta, on the other hand, is a somewhat relaxed opera. The plot is usually light, often fanciful, with some spoken dialogue.

Beginning in the early years of this century, with the works of George M. Cohan and Irving Berlin, the two forms began to merge. Popular musical styles, especially ragtime and jazz, were included, and plots became more realistic and contemporary. In the early 1930s, political satire was a popular topic. Just before World War II, dance was introduced into musical comedy, as an integral element of the production and as part of the story line. Musical comedy became a total theatrical form, dependent on the interrelation of story, music, lyrics, dance, scenery, and costumes. One of the high points in the development of this style was *Oklahoma!* (1943), composed by Richard Rodgers, with lyrics by Oscar Hammerstein II.

Figure 27.5 Broadway's Oklahoma!, *by Rogers and Hammerstein, provided a high point in the development of musical comedy. An American creation, musical comedy weaves together plot, music, lyrics, ballet, scenery, and costumes. (New York Public Library)*

American musical comedy has a distinctive national flavor. More recent productions have often had plots of contemporary significance. Leonard Bernstein's *West Side Story* (1957), for example, dealt with gang warfare and racial tensions in New York City. The revival of Bernstein's *Candide* in 1974 caused a sensation both on and off Broadway.

Commercial Music

Radio, television, and electronic recording have revolutionized popular music in this century. As a result of these inventions, a large mass audience is able to purchase the latest hits on records or tapes, listen to them as they drive in their cars, or watch them performed in their living rooms. In recent years, rock music festivals have attracted weekend crowds of hundreds of thousands to the American countryside. Popular music has become big-money business, with stars such as the late Jimi Hendrix receiving as much as $50,000 for a single appearance.

Music is used for many purposes today, and not all of them involve entertainment. It is used in advertising to attract attention to promote products. Huge amounts of money are spent to create clever thirty-second "hits," which subliminally pressure consumers to make purchases. Music is also used as a pacifier; the music piped into elevators, supermarkets, airplanes, and shopping centers is designed to be ignored. It serves its purpose best when it is least obvious. This music encourages listeners to relax, slow down, and buy. Business firms provide background music for their workers, to blot out distracting noises and increase efficiency. Farmers supply the same "canned" music to their livestock to increase milk and egg production.

The unfortunate aspect of all this background music is that it has conditioned the listener to not listen. Almost in self-defense, one learns to block out such music automatically.

Summary

American folk music is the product of the folk styles of many nations. European immigrants and African slaves brought with them a rich musical heritage, to which they added new songs about the American experience.

Owing its principal inspiration to black folk music, a new musical language called jazz arose in the late 1800s. Distinguished by its emphasis on improvisation and syncopation (a deliberate disturbance of the expected beat), the origins of jazz were a piano style, known as ragtime, and a lamenting vocal art, known as the blues. The first real jazz, featuring collective improvisation on a basic theme, was born in New Orleans about 1900. Solo improvisation began in the 1920s, and the era of the Big Bands followed, as jazz took on mass appeal and moved into the dance hall. Today jazz is characterized by experimentation.

Rock developed from black rhythm and blues and country and western music in the 1950s. Renamed rock 'n' roll, its audience consisted largely of teenagers, and its early heroes were Little Richard, Bill Haley, and Elvis Presley. Characterized by a strict two-four beat, rock underwent a revolution with the arrival of the Beatles. Abandoning the older format, they began experimenting with new meters and instruments. Electronic innovation ushered in a period of psychedelic rock and acid rock styles. There was also a merging of folk and rock music, championed by Bob Dylan. Recent trends include a classical orientation, electrical explosion techniques, and new approaches to the concept of rhythm.

Part VII Suggested Listening

Barber, Samuel

Knoxville: Summer of 1915. One of Barber's most representative and beautiful works, this is a setting for soprano and orchestra of James Agee's autobiographical prose poem that prefaces his novel, *A Death in the Family.*

Copland, Aaron

El Salón Mexico. Inspired by a trip to Mexico, this highly popular and picturesque work—based on actual Mexican folk melodies—was a deliberate attempt to write "tourist music."

Gottschalk, Louis Moreau

Night in the Tropics. This large-scale tone poem by one of America's most popular nineteenth-century composers is a fascinating and exotic mélange of South American dance rhythms, folklike melodies, and colorful orchestration.

Ives, Charles Edward

Three Places in New England. Each of the three movements of this often-played work illustrates a different facet of the composer's highly individualistic technique: the first (The "St. Gaudens" in Boston Common) presents a subtle and complex use of traditional American melodies; the second (Putnam's Camp, Redding, Connecticut) depicts a lively Fourth of July celebration, complete with colliding brass bands, and is one of Ives' most famous examples of polytempo; and the last (The Housatonic at Stockbridge) is a wonderfully evocative tone poem portraying a quiet-flowing New England river.

Partch, Harry

Oedipus Rex. Well known for his development of new and exotic instruments, Partch set Yeat's translation of Sophocles' tragedy for speaking, chanting, and wailing voices, monophonic women's chorus, and an ensemble comprising both traditional and his own invented instruments.

Thomson, Virgil

Sonata da Chiesa. Literally "church sonata," this chamber work for clarinet, trumpet, viola, horn, and trombone is cast in a Neo-Classical style, with skillful and expressive use of dissonance.

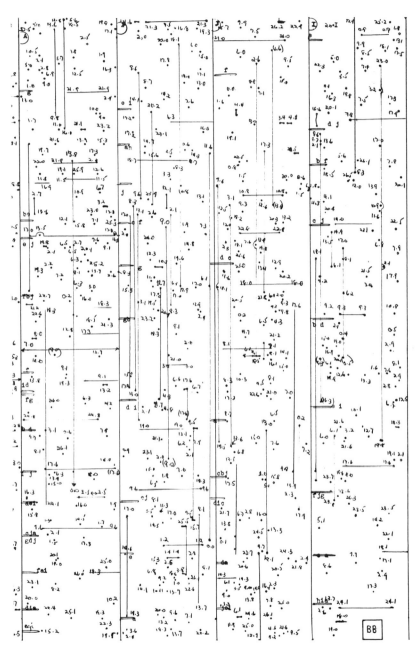

Jerry Hunt's score for Sur (Doctor) John Dee. *(Courtesy of* Source:
Music of the Avant Garde, *Sacramento, California)*

Plate 21. The expressive emotion, color, and free form of paintings like Willem de Kooning's Composition (1955) exerted tremendous influence on European postwar art. Often combining Expressionism and Surrealism, American artists soon made Abstract Expressionism an international style. (Willem de Kooning, Composition, 1955. THE SOLOMON R. GUGGENHEIM MUSEUM COLLECTION, New York.)

part VIII   Music after World War II

Late in the 1930s many great European artists came to America as refugees from fascism. Some of these, including Laszlo Moholy-Nagy, Josef Albers, Piet Mondrian, Hans Hofmann, and Fernand Léger, were in the vanguard of abstract painting. They greatly influenced a young generation of Americans who felt attracted to the Expressionist tradition of subjective emotion, emphasis on color, and freedom of form. We have already noted in Chapter 22 how Jackson Pollock combined the influence of Expressionism with the Surrealist tradition. Pollock and other Americans painting in

The Arts after World War II

a similar vein created a new school, Abstract Expressionism, that went beyond anything that had been done in Europe.

The work created in the 1940s and 1950s by such American artists as Arshile Gorky (1904–1948), Robert Motherwell (b. 1915), Clyfford Still (b. 1904), Mark Rothko (1903–1970), Barnett Newman (b. 1905), and Willem de Kooning (b. 1904) exerted a profound influence on European art as Abstract Expressionism became an international style (Plate 21).

As the twentieth century moves toward its fourth quarter, the only assertion about art that one can make with any confidence is that today's avant-garde becomes tomorrow's tradition. Already the art movements of the 1960s have entered the textbooks of art history:

OP ART. A form of pure abstraction that makes use of optical principles to produce visual sensations.

POP ART. A form based on the banal features of daily life—advertisements, comic strips, billboards, canned goods, plumbing fixtures, and other often-disregarded products of a materialist society.

MINIMAL ART. A reaction to the visual extravagances of op and pop that reduces painting and sculpture to elementary color and form. Examples of minimal art are canvases of single colors or a sculpture in the form of a simple square.

Moving outside their studios, some artists have taken as their medium the earth itself, digging miles-long trenches in the desert or swathing millions of square feet of coastline in wrapping paper. While such "earthworks" cannot be exhibited in a gallery or museum, they become effective statements of artists' opposition to the commercialization of art by treating it as any other commodity.

Figure 28.1   Claes Oldenburg's subject matter for his Giant Soft Fan *is typical of the banal, easily overlooked objects of modern society which typically serve as Pop Art models. (Claes Oldenburg.* Giant Soft Fan *(1966–67). Vinyl, wood, and foam rubber, 10'×10'4"×6'4." The Sydney and Harriet Janis Collection. Gift to The Museum of Modern Art, New York.)*

Figure 28.2   Rafael Ferrer's Untitled *reflects modern art's disenchantment with traditional media and methods, as well as its preoccupation with the cluttered landscape of our overproductive, throw-away society. (Nancy Hoffman Gallery)*

Also discontented with conventional media, many artists attempt to use the elements of twentieth-century technology, making artworks from electronic devices and machinery. The new media and techniques adopted by artists have given rise to multimedia "happenings" that combine light shows, drama, music, dance, and film. As a result of their mutual involvement, all of the arts have expanded their conventional boundaries. A painter, for instance, may also work in sculpture, cinema, and music. For example, film, the only visual art of the twentieth century that appeals equally to artists, critics, and the public, has been given a new impetus by the avant-garde movies made by Andy Warhol, a painter and sculptor.

Avant-garde composers have transformed music, taking it beyond the innovations developed by Schoenberg. Not only is music performed by computers that generate sound, but it is also "composed" by computers programmed to write it. Avant-garde composers such as John Cage have incorporated into their work the random noises of daily life and also that rarest element of urban life, silence.

More and more, art defies definition. In the words of Marcel Duchamp, the godfather of twentieth-century avant-gardism, "Art is what artists say it is." If so, the artist has become both creator and arbiter, usurping the traditional role of art critic.

Common to all these new forms of expression is their internationalism. No longer is a style developed in an art center like Paris or New York, from which it slowly spreads to other centers. Though avant-garde artists are unified by their exploitation of novelty, it is questionable whether the public is united in its acceptance of the artists' efforts. Yet the public has not been alienated. Never before has there been such a large audience for art as there is now. A new youthful audience comprehends intuitively the attempts of avant-garde artists to impose some sense of order on a chaotic world. It is no easier for artists than for anyone else to resolve the paradoxes of contemporary life, but by expressing them—even if their expression is chaotic—they reflect and comment upon the times in which they live.

chapter 29

The essential feature of the musical period between the two world wars was the struggle between the forces of the new tonality and those of serialism. In terms of sheer numbers the tonally oriented side was far ahead; virtually all American composers, as well as Stravinsky, Hindemith, Bartók,

Music after World War II

and others in Europe, were in its ranks. Serialism was considered the exclusive property of its inventor, Schoenberg, and his students. The division between these two ideas was thought to be irreparably wide. Within a few years of the end of World War II, the situation had changed completely: Neo-Classicism had dropped out of favor, and the twelve-tone technique of composition was dominant among young composers but was by no means accepted by the concert-going public.

Even Stravinsky, whose opera *The Rake's Progress* (1951) was the epitome of Neo-Classicism, performed an about-face that astounded the musical world; he began to study Schoenberg's music and to experiment with serial technique. Other well-established older composers followed suit, including Aaron Copland, Walter Piston, and Roger Sessions.

What were the reasons for this sudden change in the status of serial composition? There are essentially two reasons. One is really the same as Schoenberg's motivation for developing serialism in the first place—it permits the construction of larger forms. Traditional functional tonality had been the foundation of most formal structures prior to the twentieth century; without it another organizing force was required, and twelve-tone techniques could provide it. The other reason for the widespread adoption of serial procedures was the realization that they did not have a limiting or determining effect on style. Serialism provides techniques for handling musical material but does not eliminate a composer's personal stylistic characteristics.

Music has been moving in many directions during the last few decades. For example, serial procedures have been expanded and composers have introduced new sound sources and allowed chance to play a role in the compositional process. All of these diverse innovations are interconnected, and each has affected composers on both sides of the Atlantic. There is no longer anything to be gained by discussing European and American music separately

New Ideas in Modern Music

Although it is not possible to lump all modern music under any one of two stylistic classifications, there are certain ideas that are new in the postwar period and that are common to many contemporary composers:

1. There is an interest in the isolated, individual sound as a musical event, a willingness to consider the very basic building blocks of music as separate entities. This interest is largely an outgrowth of the new appreciation of Webern's music that began after the war.
2. Sounds from all possible sources are now considered legitimate material for composition. Many of the sounds used today would formerly have been dismissed as mere "noise"—natural sounds, electronically generated sounds, sounds from new instruments, new sounds from traditional instruments. Today the emphasis is on *how* the composer organizes his sounds, not on *where* he got them.
3. All aspects of the musical sound are considered to be equally important; pitch and duration are no more or less significant than timbre and volume.
4. There is a wide variation in the amount of control the composer exercises over the different aspects of his music. This control ranges all the way from very extensive, almost total control of pitch, dynamics, note lengths, and articulations to a very improvisatory freedom in which chance and the performers' interpretations affect the outcome of the piece.

Origins of the New Ideas

The new interests of today's composers have their roots in two different sources; the first is the early work of Stravinsky, Schoenberg, and Webern. These pioneers of twentieth-century music had gone through stages of rejecting old assumptions and finding new ideas. The younger composers were not necessarily willing to accept what the older men had done, but they looked to them for guidance in striking out on their own. For example, it was possible to adopt Schoenberg's serial techniques without embracing his personal style.

The other major source for the ideas that dominate contemporary composition is a group of experimental composers who never belonged to the mainstream of twentieth-century music. They worked in isolation and produced unusual and highly original results, which have had their effects on today's avant-garde composers. The foremost American composer in this experimental tradition was Charles Ives.

Another influential composer who spent most of his creative life in America was the French-born Edgard Varèse (1883–1965). He preferred to think of his work as "organized sound," and was particularly attracted to percussion instruments. His principal contribution to modern music was the relative importance he gave to rhythm, texture, and sonority; they were central in his music, much more important than melody and harmony. Varèse wrote for many combinations of instruments; among his best-known works are *Ionisation* (1931), for percussion ensemble, and *Density 21.5* (1936, revised 1946), for unaccompanied flute.

The two most isolated and experimental composers in Europe differed greatly from each other. The German Carl Orff (b. 1895) is usually considered a conservative, since his style is deliberately simple and popular sounding, in opposition to the complexities of his contemporaries Schoenberg and Hindemith. His *Carmina Burana* (1936), a pseudo-Medieval setting of thirteenth-century wandering monks' songs, has always been scorned by the avant-garde but is popular with audiences.

The opposite pole is reached by the French composer Oliver Messiaen (b. 1908), whose style is both esoteric and expressive. He has an unusually wide range of interests, including religious mysticism, nature (particularly birdsongs), and non-Western music, and they all have influenced his own compositions. Messiaen has been very important as a teacher of composition; his students include most of the prominent younger European composers.

One way to look at the musical developments from the end of the war to about the mid-1950s is to divide them into two categories: those that tend to give the composer greater control over his musical materials and those that give him less control. The first category would include extensions of serial technique and the development of electronic music; the second includes so-called chance music and improvisational techniques. All of these developments occurred almost simultaneously.

Extensions of Serialism

Schoenberg's original serial techniques applied only to pitch; all other aspects of music were left to the composer's discretion, although they were determined in relation to the use made of the tone row. After World War II, interest in serial procedures increased at least partially as the result of the music of Anton von Webern. Webern's music is lean, uncluttered, and compact. His use of twelve-tone techniques is even more systematic than Schoenberg's.

The first composer to try to adapt serial procedures to aspects of music other than pitch was an American, Milton Babbitt (b. 1916). In his *Three Compositions* (1948), for piano, he systematically organized not only pitches but also durations, tempos, dynamics, articulations, and timbre. This was a much more rigorous approach to composition than serialism's original developers had ever envisioned; Babbitt was aiming for total serial control over his musical materials.

At almost the same time, Messiaen was experimenting independently with the concept of total serialization. He regarded it as just one of many possible approaches, but one of his students, Karlheinz Stockhausen (b. 1928), became fascinated with the idea and continued to develop it. Stockhausen is considered by many to be the foremost European theorist and composer in the field of serial technique (Fig. 29.1).

Figure 29.1 Karlheinz Stock-hausen is considered one of Europe's foremost theorists and composers. Extending serial technique much further than Schoenberg ever anticipated, Stockhausen has experimented widely with the concept of total serialization. (German Information Center)

In the early days of expanded serialism a very narrow interpretation of the system was used. The composer would set up a series of twelve durations (note values) and one of twelve dynamic levels to correspond to his row of twelve pitches: the usual transformations could be applied to these rows—inversion, retrograde, and retrograde inversion. But this strict approach did not last very long. There are twelve pitches, and hence twelve tones in the pitch row. But there is no really good reason to feel compelled to use twelve of anything else. A series with a different number of durations, for example, can still be treated as a series.

As the theory behind the expanded serial system grew more and more exacting, it became increasingly difficult for performers to play the pieces accurately. Almost all serial composers, including Babbitt, Stockhausen, Luciano Berio (b. 1925), and, to a certain extent, Pierre Boulez (b. 1925), turned to the newly developing medium of electronic equipment for performance of this kind of music.

Figure 29.2   Pierre Boulez was one of many composers who depended on electronic equipment to produce his exacting serial compositions. The inaccuracy of live performers in this medium made precision electronics irresistibly attractive.
(Newsweek/Robert McElroy)

Electronic Music

The first step in the development of the phenomenon known as electronic music took place in 1948 in France, at the studios of the French National Radio. Sounds were tape-recorded, then altered mechanically or electronically, and finally combined into organized pieces. The technique is known as *musique concrète*. Most of the sounds used are not "musical" in the traditional sense; many, including street sounds, sounds from nature, and human speech, in addition to unusual sounds from musical instruments, would be considered noise by most people.

The alteration of the original taped sounds takes place in many ways: two or more tapes can be dubbed onto each other, tape can be cut and spliced, the speed can be changed, loops can be made (to repeat patterns endlessly), and filters can change the characteristics of the sounds. This is tedious work, but for many composers the finished product is worth it. The result is the actual piece itself, not a written version that a performer will interpret more or less accurately. Taped music represents the composer's precise intentions. He has total control over every aspect of the composition, including its performance.

The next step in the development of electronic music was to use electronically produced sounds. Rather than taping natural sounds, composers taped the sound output of tone-producing machines. With the machines, not only could familiar sounds be duplicated synthetically, but entirely new sounds could be "invented."

Some of the routine work involved in producing and combining electronic sounds can be relegated to a computer or to a synthesizer (a system of electronic equipment that is simpler to operate than its separate components would be). But the creative aspect of composition, the decision-making role, is still the composer's. No machine can make the choices necessary to produce a piece of music, unless it is a computer programmed by the composer to do so, in which case the ultimate responsibility still rests with the human programmer.

In addition to offering composers complete and accurate control over tone color and rhythm, electronic generation and modification of sounds

Figure 29.3 Complex electronic systems like this Moog synthesizer make the composer's goal of total control much less tedious to achieve. Although such machinery both produces and combines electronic sounds, the ultimate creative work — the decision making — is left to the artist. (RCA Records)

provides a whole new realm of pitches to work with. Although composers and theorists had speculated ever since the Renaissance on possible divisions of the octave into more than twelve semitones, very little was actually done. On most instruments *microtones* (intervals smaller than semitones) can be produced only with great difficulty, if at all. Most of the experimental instruments built for the purpose of playing microtonal music are impractical to use, such as keyboard instruments with forty-three or fifty-three microtones to the octave. Thus, although there was some effective use of quarter tones by such composers as Ives, Berg, and Bartók, microtonal music seemed to be essentially self-defeating.

Electronically generated sounds can be produced just as easily at one pitch as at another; in fact, there is literally an infinite number of pitches available, and no technical reason to prefer any particular ones. Of course, there are limits beyond which the human ear (or mind) cannot distinguish differences. There are also some composers who prefer to stick with our basic equal-tempered set of twelve pitches, but it is now a matter of choice rather than necessity, since any variety of microtonal music is now perfectly feasible because of the nature of the musical machinery available.

The first real explorations with electronically produced sounds took place in Cologne, Germany, in 1951, although preliminary experiments had taken place all over the Western world. The high degree of composer control that the method offered had great appeal to many contemporary composers, and soon there were electronic music studios in most countries. One of the first was set up in New York in 1952 at Columbia University by Otto Luening (b. 1900) and Vladimir Ussachevsky (b. 1911), and they soon joined forces with Babbitt at Princeton. The resulting Columbia-Princeton Electronic Music Center is the most

Figure 29.4   One of the first of its kind in the world, the prestigious Columbia-Princeton Electronic Music Center is a vital center for the modern music genre. Pictured in the Center are (l. to r.) Milton Babbitt, Mario Davidovsky, Vladimir Ussachevsky, Pril Delson, Alice Shields, and Otto Luening. (Vernon L. Smith, Scope Associates)

prestigious in the country. It is unique in possessing a huge RCA Synthesizer, which Babbitt has used extensively since the late 1950s.

Most composers of electronic music today work with a mixture of naturally and electronically generated sounds. Many also combine taped electronic music with live performers, a step away from the total control they had initially found so attractive. Luening, Ussachevsky, and Varèse were the first to explore the relationship between live and taped music. Varèse led the way with his *Deserts* (1953), for winds, percussion, and taped industrial noises; Luening and Ussachevsky followed with *Poem in Cycles and Bells* (1954) for tape recorder and orchestra.

Other composers joined the search for satisfactory ways to combine live and taped materials. Milton Babbitt's *Vision and Prayer* (1961) and *Philomel* (1963–1964) use a singer with prerecorded material. Younger composers in the United States, including Mario Davidovsky (b. 1934), with his set of six *Synchronisms* (1963–1970), and Charles Wuorinen (b. 1938), with *Symphonia Sacra* (1960–1961) and *Orchestral and Electronic Exchanges* (1965), and, in Europe, Stockhausen, with *Mikrophonie* (1964), have added to the repertoire for mixed performing media.

It is impossible to describe electronic music in any sort of general terms, since an enormous variety of material is available and being used by composers. The problem of finding musical forms that suit the medium is a serious one, and many of the works being written today are experimental in that regard. It is possible, however, to apply some of the older principles of musical organization to electronic music, as Babbitt and Stockhausen have shown by writing some electronic pieces in serial technique.

Chance Music

Although many composers felt they could realize their musical ideas only if they could control totally all aspects of composition and performance, others felt that this could only produce rigid, mechanical music. They moved in the opposite direction and tried systematically to avoid controlling their materials. Instead of making conscious choices, such composers would throw dice or consult the *I Ching* to determine various elements of their pieces.

The outstanding figure in the field of chance, or aleatory, music and one of the most controversial composers in the history of music is John Cage (b. 1912). Originally a Schoenberg pupil and then a follower in the Ives tradition, he has become more and more experimental and now rejects the idea of putting musical ideas together. Instead, he just lets them happen. Cage is very interested in the role of silence in music and in the unpredictable background noises that are always present. His classical piece of nonmusic, *4'33''* (1954), consists entirely of environmental sounds: a pianist sits quietly at an open piano for four minutes and thirty-three seconds and then leaves the stage.

Cage's pieces are all wildly different, but they have something in common; they are programmed activities with certain boundaries set by the composer. He has no actual control over the outcome of the piece, and no way of predicting it. The performers make decisions on the spur of the moment, and thus rational control is avoided.

Figure 29.5 The controversial John Cage stands near the open piano which is never played during 4'33,'' his four-and-one-half-minute classical, nonmusic tribute to silence and the ever-present, ever-changing sounds of the environment. (Culver Pictures)

Aleatory music makes use of sounds from all kinds of sources: traditional, electronic, environmental, and so on. In some works even the performing medium is deliberately left indeterminate, as in Cage's *Fontana Mix* (1958), which has been recorded in several different versions, some electronic and some live. The visual and theatrical aspects of this kind of music are quite important and have had considerable influence on all the arts.

It is interesting to note that to the average listener, the results of total control and random noncontrol are indistinguishable; both sound equally random. The indeterminate elements of a piece of aleatory music are not necessarily evident in a single hearing. Of course any "repetition" of such a piece is bound to be rather different, which would reveal its chance elements. For this reason a recorded version of an aleatory piece is almost a contradiction in terms, since it presents only one of an infinite number of possible versions of the piece.

Control and Freedom

Record 8/Side 2

In the early 1950s serial music and chance music were both highly experimental, and each seemed to be diametrically opposed to the other. But the recent past has shown that they can interact successfully, if not actually work together. The search for forms appropriate to the materials is common to both; composer control versus performer decision are subjects to be explored together. As we have seen in this book, all music is a study in unity and contrast, an attempt to make them available simultaneously. There is no longer any one accepted way to do this; each piece must have its own material, must take its own form, and must stand or fall entirely on its own merits.

The combination of live and recorded material is only one aspect of the new comprehensive outlook. Another feature common to much very recent music is a renewed interest in virtuosity. The individual performer is pushed to his limits, in both controlled and improvised situations. Many composers write specifically for certain virtuoso performers. The virtuoso aspect of the music is not superficial embellishment, however; it is an organic part of the music itself.

The works of Elliot Carter (b. 1908) have a thread of virtuosity running through them. He writes in a very chromatic but nontwelve-tone style, with formal structure provided by carefully organized textures, rhythmic groupings, melodic and harmonic materials, and articulations. The virtuosity of the individual parts is the common factor in his second String Quartet (1959). The same masterful control of opposing forces provides the basis for his Double Concerto (1961) for piano and harpsichord with orchestra, in which the independent parts are integrated in a very expressive way.

One technique for uniting the ideas of composer control and performer decision is to vary the degree of control within a single piece. Stockhausen has been a leader in this field, beginning with his wind quintet *Zeitmasse* (1956). Some sections of the piece are tightly controlled, while others are flexible, with directions to the performers like "play as slow as possible." In his most recent works he has attempted to serialize the degree of complexity and freedom at any given point in the piece. Another approach to linking freedom and control is to use the mathematical formulations of probability theory as the basis for random events.

In all of these approaches the basic principle of organization seems to be that music is no longer theme-oriented. Instead of using melodic and rhythmic ideas as the skeleton for a structure, the sounds themselves are the most important element. Rather than serving as vehicles for thematic ideas, the sounds are used for their own qualities. This has led to a much greater sensitivity to details of timbre, articulation, and mixtures of sonorities.

The Performer's Role

In some avant-garde music the performer plays the same role he always has: he does his best to interpret the composer's score accurately and with feeling. He is allowed to make minor variations in things like tempo and dynamics, but otherwise he does what he is told. In chance music, however, the composer has given up some of his normal prerogatives and the performer takes them over. He may be allowed to decide what to play or even whether to play.

The opposite extreme is reached in some electronic music; the role of the performer has been completely taken over by the composer and the machine. In pieces produced directly on tape, the composer has made all the decisions himself and there is no performer. This leads to an interesting and still unanswered question: Should purely electronic music be performed in a concert hall while the audience sits looking at a loudspeaker? Perhaps the setting should be changed, or perhaps records, not concerts, are the best means of presenting this music to the public.

Many pieces of electronic music require the collaboration of live musicians. The visible human element makes a more dramatic presentation. American composers have been particularly fond of joining live and taped sounds ever since the early days of electronic music, as in *Poem in Cycles and Bells* of Ussachevsky and Luening for taped sounds and orchestra. The live element can consist of an instrument or singer, or of a small ensemble. Mario Davidovsky's *Synchronisms* use several different combinations and illustrate a successful resolution of the problem of coordinating a constant-speed tape recording with slightly variable human musicians.

The Notation of Modern Music

Many of the new sounds and methods described in this chapter cannot be written down in the conventional system of music notation. The system used for traditional music has been standardized since about 1500, but before that it was in a constant state of flux. Now more changes will be needed, or else completely new systems must be invented. In fact, composers are practically forced to invent them as they compose.

Since the present system can distinguish only the twelve pitches of the chromatic scale, microtonal music must be written in a new way. Quarter tones can be indicated by the addition of little arrows or other marks, but smaller intervals require a totally new notational system. Chance music has solved most of its notational problems by giving written directions to the performer about the choices he must make or by simply telling him the length of time he has to improvise in. The new noises that are being made on traditional instruments require new notations too. The various squeaks, slides, and rumbles must all be indicated for the performer in some way.

The real stumbling block, as far as notation is concerned, comes with electronic music. But since an electronic piece is stored on tape, is a written score needed at all? No performer ever needs to "interpret" the composer's instructions; the composer has done it all himself. Actually there are several reasons for having a written score, but most of them have nothing to do with problems of performance. Composers who work with a synthesizer or computer must have their instructions to the machine completely mapped out beforehand. Since the machine will do only what it is told, the composer's instructions to it are a tape of written score, although in a completely different form. Even the composer who works in a tape studio must keep records of which machine was used for how long and what the dial settings were; this is also a score. Some form of written notation is needed to satisfy the requirements of the U.S. copyright laws. At the present time tapes and records cannot be copyrighted.

The use of electronic sounds with live performers also requires a written indication of the taped music. Without it the performers would have no idea of how their parts fit with the electronic sounds. The score serves as a cue sheet for the live musicians. The notation does not have to be so exact that someone could recreate the electronic part from it. It is often more pictorial in style than our standard notation. In this problematic area almost anything goes; each composer is free to invent a system that suits his particular needs.

The Future

Some observers of the contemporary music scene feel that the gap between composers and the public is widening steadily. The new music seems to be more complicated than ever and the average listener has little or no idea of composers' intentions. This analysis of the situation is partially true. Most contemporary composers earn their living as university teachers; they have no need to write music to please a patron or an audience. Most listeners, on the other hand, have little training in listening to music. School music curricula have not done very much to help the public appreciate new music.

But is a gap like the present one really a new phenomenon? Of course not; this same lack of communication between composers and listeners has occurred over and over again in the course of music history. Remember, for example, that Mozart's music was once thought to be too complicated. Furthermore, there have always been a few composers who deliberately wrote some esoteric music that only other composers could appreciate. Bach was one such composer, and Beethoven was another.

Of course, some of the avant-garde music we hear today is not good. We hear all of it now, the good and the bad. Time will eliminate the less effective pieces. Perhaps some sources of sounds and methods of organization will be dropped; we can be almost certain that new ones will be invented. Music is one of the creative arts, and creation, by definition, involves the production of something new. Music will continue to change.

Summary

Before the end of World War II serialism was the exclusive property of Schoenberg and his students. But within a few years after the end of the war, the situation had changed completely. Neo-Classicism dropped out of favor and the twelve-tone technique became dominant. In it composers found an underlying support for the construction of larger forms. They also found that while it provided techniques for handling musical material, it did not work against their personal stylistic characteristics.

Originally, serial techniques applied only to pitch. But in the late 1940s composers began systematically to organize durations, tempos, dynamics, articulations, and timbre as well. The foremost experimenters with this expansion of serial procedures were Milton Babbitt, Olivier Messiaen, and Karlheinz Stockhausen.

At the same time, composers began to look to electronic media for the organization and production of sound. At first sounds were tape-recorded, then altered mechanically or electronically, and finally combined into organized pieces. Later they began to tape the output of tone-producing machines. In this way they could not only duplicate familiar sounds synthetically, but also "invent" entirely new sounds. Some of the leading work in this field is done at the Columbia-Princeton Electronic Music Center in New York by Otto Luening, Vladimir Ussachevsky, and Milton Babbitt.

Although many composers feel they can realize their musical ideas only if they totally control all aspects of composition and performance, others move in the opposite direction and try systematically to avoid controlling their materials. The outstanding composer in the field of chance music is John Cage, who rejects the idea of putting musical ideas together, but instead allows the performer to make the decisions that control the outcome of his music.

The principle of organization in post-World War II music seems to be that music is no longer theme-oriented. Instead of using melodic and rhythmic ideas as the skeleton for a structure, the sounds themselves are the most important element. Rather than serving as vehicles for thematic ideas, the sounds are used for their own qualities.

**Part VIII
Suggested
Listening**

Babbitt, Milton

Vision and Prayer. A setting of Dylan Thomas' poem for voice and electronic accompaniment composed on the synthesizer; the vocal style ranges from *Sprechgesang* (speech-song) to recitative.

Boulez, Pierre

Le Marteau sans maitre (The Hammer Without a Master). Scored for soprano solo and chamber orchestra, with a wide variety of percussion instruments, this work consists of nine vocal settings set off by instrumental "commentaries." The vocal style owes much to Schoenberg's *Sprechgesang* (speech-song).

Cage, John

Fontana Mix. Designed for indeterminate performance with the score providing for a prerecorded voice-tape montage as well as for theatrical and other musical performances (versions have been made for electrically amplified piano, guitar, and percussion instruments).

Ligeti, György

Requiem. Scored for soprano and mezzo soloists, double choir, and orchestra, this stark, impressive setting of the Catholic Mass for the dead uses traditional forms and contrapuntal techniques within a context of highly avant-garde concepts of harmony, texture, and choral tone-color.

Messiaen, Olivier

Chronochromie. This immense and highly varied orchestral work demonstrates all of the significant characteristics of the composer's style, including melodic material derived from birdsongs, highly complex polyrhythmic patterns, huge percussive effects, and intricate, polyphonic textures.

Penderecki, Krzysztof

Threnody for the Victims of Hiroshima. Scored for fifty-two strings, this work is a study in experimental string sonorities; the thematic material consists of tone clusters and harmonic overtones combined within an essentially polyphonic structure.

Stockhausen, Karlheinz

Gesang der Junglinge (Song of the Youths). An outstanding "electro-acoustical" work, combining sung sounds with electronically produced sounds. The sung sounds—though often distorted in various ways—become comprehensible words from time to time. The text is based on the account of Shadrach, Meshach, and Abednego being cast into the fiery furnace (Daniel 3).

Suggested Reading

(An asterisk denotes books published in paperback.)

PART I

*Baines, Anthony, ed. *Musical Instruments Through the Ages*. Baltimore: Penguin Books, 1961.

A brief chronological survey of the development of instruments and their performance capabilities.

*Carse, Adam. *The History of Orchestration*. New York: Dover, 1964.

A standard historical survey of the orchestra and the art of orchestration from the sixteenth century through the late nineteenth century; the text is comprehensive (the development of individual instruments is clearly outlined) and largely nontechnical.

*Cooper, Grosvenor W. *Learning to Listen*. Chicago: University of Chicago Press, Phoenix Books, 1957.

A compact survey of musical elements and concepts, including chapters on rudiments of theory and notation, rhythm, harmony, form, and style.

*Copland, Aaron. *What to Listen for in Music*. New York: New American Library, Mentor Books, 1957.

A highly useful, introductory guide to the elements of music, including chapters on basic structural forms (fugue, variation, sonata-allegro).

*_____*Music and Imagination*. New York: New American Library, Mentor Books, 1959.

An anthology of lectures on various aspects of music. Of particular interest are the chapters on "The Gifted Listener," "The Sonorous Image," and "The Creative Mind and the Interpretive Mind."

*Erickson, Robert. *The Structure of Music: A Listener's Guide*. New York: Noonday Press, 1963.

Explores the nature of melody, harmony, and counterpoint from a nontechnical point of view. Emphasizes the manner in which rhythmic momentum and melodic direction operate within a musical work.

Malm, William P. *Music Cultures of the Pacific, the Near East, and Asia*. Englewood Cliffs, N. J.: Prentice-Hall, 1967.

Well illustrated with both drawings and musical selections, this volume explores the anthropolog-ical, historical, and musical aspects of the subject cultures. Conveys a precise and sensitive appreciation of the material covered. Part of the Prentice-Hall History of Music series.

Nettl, Bruno. *Folk and Traditional Music of the Western Continents*. Englewood Cliffs, N. J.: Prentice-Hall, 1965.

The editor of the journal *Ethnomusicology* describes in some detail representative folk music of Europe, America and, despite the title, Africa south of the Sahara. A somewhat technical treatment, which both explores the cultural context of the music discussed and guides the student toward a precise understanding of folk and ethnic musical idioms. The more general introductory chapters are especially valuable. Part of the Prentice-Hall History of Music series.

*Tovey, Donald Francis. *The Forms of Music*. Cleveland: World Publishing Company, Meridian Books, 1956.

A collection of articles originally written for the fourteenth edition of the *Encyclopedia Britannica*; all are clearly written, with topics ranging from musical genres (symphony, oratorio) to structural forms (sonata-allegro, rondo, fugue) to special topics (programmatic music, instrumentation, harmony).

Vlahos, Olivia. *New World Beginnings: Indian Cultures in the Americas*. New York: Viking, 1970.

An evocative and sensitively written account of the prehistory and history of American Indians, from Canada to Cape Horn. Primarily directed to younger readers, but of interest to readers of all ages. Illustrated with maps and well-researched drawings.

Warren, Dr. Fred, and Lee Warren. *Music of Africa: An Introduction*. Englewood Cliffs, N. J.: Prentice-Hall, 1970.

A rather impressionistic but lively account of African vocal and instrumental music. Not extensive enough to deal with the subject in depth, the book still serves as a general introduction to the subject. Illustrated with line drawings and photographs.

PART II

*Dart, Thurston. *The Interpretation of Music*. New York: Harper & Row, 1963; hardback edition, 1954.

A survey of performance practices in early music through the eighteenth century. Chapters on the

Middle Ages and the Renaissance discuss the use of early instruments, methods of performing vocal pieces, and the various religious, ceremonial, and social occasions for which music was composed.

*Lowinsky, Edward E. "Music in the Culture of the Renaissance." *Journal of the History of Ideas*. Vol. XV, No. 4 (1954). Reprinted in *Renaissance Essays*, Paul O. Kristeller and Philip P. Wiener, eds. New York: Harper & Row, 1968.
An excellent, nontechnical introduction to Renaissance music and its place in the culture of the period. The change in musical thought and the development of new musical forms after 1450 are emphasized.

*Robertson, Alec and Denis Stevens, eds. *The Pelican History of Music, Vol. 1: Ancient Forms to Polyphony*. Baltimore: Penguin Books, 1960.
A collection of essays on early non-Western and European musical developments up to the fifteenth century. European topics include Gregorian chant, the earliest types of polyphony, and the music of Machaut and his generation.

*————*The Pelican History of Music, Vol. 11: Renaissance and Baroque*. Baltimore: Penguin Books, 1963.
Also a collection of essays. The Renaissance section emphasizes the place of music in society. The discussion of musical performance in the sixteenth century is excellent.

PART III

GENERAL WORKS

Bukofzer, Manfred F. *Music in the Baroque Era*. New York: W. W. Norton, 1947.
A comprehensive history of the important musical developments in the Baroque period. Of particular interest are the chapters on "Renaissance versus Baroque Music," "Musical Thought of the Baroque Era," and "Sociology of Baroque Music."

*Hutchings, Arthur. *The Baroque Concerto*. New York: W. W. Norton, 1965; hardback edition, 1961.
A comprehensive study of the solo concerto and the *concerto grosso* from the late seventeenth to the late eighteenth century. Particular attention is given to the spread of the *concerto grosso* from Italy to Germany, France, and England.

*Jacobs, Arthur, ed. *Choral Music*. Baltimore: Penguin Books, 1963.
A collection of essays, five of which deal with choral music of the Baroque era.

BACH, JOHANN SEBASTIAN

Geiringer, Karl. *Johann Sebastian Bach: The Culmination of an Era*. New York: Oxford University Press, 1966.
The most up-to-date biography in English, incorporating the large amount of new research on Bach done since World War II.

HANDEL, GEORGE FREDERICH

Dean, Winton. *Handel's Dramatic Oratorios and Masques*. London: Oxford University Press, 1959.
A thoroughly researched study of a number of Handel's major vocal works.

Lang, Paul Henry. *George Frideric Handel*. New York: W. W. Norton, 1966.
Emphasizes the social and cultural background of the times and the musical antecedents upon which Handel built.

MONTEVERDI, CLAUDIO

Arnold, Denis. *Monteverdi*. New York: Farrar, Strauss, and Giroux, 1963.
A concise biography, including an extensive study of the composer's music.

PART IV

GENERAL WORKS

*Pauly, Reinhard G. *Music in the Classic Period*. Englewood Cliffs, N. J.: Prentice-Hall, 1965.
A concise survey of the period in two parts, the first tracing the evolution of the Classical style from the Rococo through Haydn and Mozart, the second discussing the principal forms and genres of the period.

WORKS ABOUT OPERA

Grout, Donald Jay. *A Short History of Opera*. New York: Columbia University Press, 1965.
The standard English-language history of opera, this work surveys the most significant works and the major developments in operatic style from its beginnings through the early twentieth century.

BEETHOVEN, LUDWIG VAN

*Thayer, Alexander Wheelock. *Life of Beethoven*. Princeton: Princeton University Press, 1964; paperback edition, 1970.
The standard biography of Beethoven; remarkably comprehensive and detailed.

HAYDN, FRANZ JOSEPH

*Geiringer, Karl. *Haydn: A Creative Life in Music.* Berkeley: University of California Press, 1968. An excellent survey covering the composer's life and his works.

MOZART, WOLFGANG AMADEUS

*Einstein, Alfred. *Mozart: His Character, His Work.* New York: Oxford University Press, 1965; hardback edition, 1945. A thoughtful, leisurely study of the composer; Part I is a study of his character, his education, and the influences on his development as a person; Part II surveys his musical development; and the other three parts review his instrumental, vocal, and operatic works.

PART V

Abraham, Gerald. *Slavonic and Romantic Music.* New York: St. Martin's Press, 1968. A series of essays providing informative data on nationalistic composers.

Berlioz, Hector. *Evenings in the Orchestra.* Translated by Jacques Barzun. New York: Alfred A. Knopf, 1956. Thoughts on contemporaneous musical ephemera. Delightful to read.

Einstein, Alfred. *Music in the Romantic Era.* New York: W. W. Norton, 1947. Basic for the student wanting to comprehend the generating and sustaining forces of the Romantic period.

*Goldman, Albert and Springhorn, Evert. *Wagner on Music and Drama.* Translated by H. Ashton Ellis. New York: E. P. Dutton, 1964. A compendium of Wagner's literary works containing first-hand information from the composer on his musical creations and essays on nonmusical themes.

Walker, Alan, ed. *Frederic Chopin. Profiles of the Man and the Musician.* London: Barrie and Rockliff, 1966. A valuable anthology of scholarly studies on Chopin, concentrating on his music. Excellent, concise tables are appended.

Werner, Eric. *Mendelssohn: A New Image of the Composer and His Age.* Glencoe: The Free Press, 1963. The comprehensive biography of Mendelssohn containing many excerpts from the composer's correspondences not commonly available. Dis-

cussion of his music complements biographical narrative.

The *Master Musicians Series* contains a biographical-musicological survey of composers. These have a similar format: biographical study, discussion of musical works, and various appendices. Published by Farrar, Straus, & Giroux, the series includes:

Beckett, Walter. *Liszt.*
Hutchings, Arthur. *Schubert.*
Latham, Peter. *Brahms.*

PART VI

Austin, William. *Music in the 20th Century. From Debussy Through Stravinsky.* New York: W. W. Norton, 1966. A detailed survey of modern music that is an essential reference source for comprehending the forces affecting it. Excellent directive to primary sources published before 1965.

*Lang, Paul Henry, ed. *Stravinsky. A New Appraisal of His Work.* New York: W. W. Norton, 1963. A group of essays by accepted authorities on twentieth-century music. Positive criticism of Stravinsky's music describing effects of his music on modern compositional styles.

*Lockspeiser, Edward. *Debussy. His Life and His Mind.* London: Cassell, 1962. The most definitive, up-to-date book on Debussy. Divided into two volumes arranged chronologically. Objective discussion of his music is interspersed with informative anecdotes about the composer and his peers. Attached appendices are indispensable to the student of Debussy's era.

Reich, Willi. *Alban Berg.* Translated by Cornelius Cardew. New York: Harcourt, Brace & World, 1963. An informative study of the life and works of Berg. The second of two parts is an exhaustive study of his works.

*Salzman, Eric. *Twentieth-Century Music. An Introduction.* Englewood Cliffs, New Jersey: Prentice-Hall, 1967. A comprehensive survey of contemporary music. The book discusses musical and nonmusical forces generating creativity, while using few musical illustrations to objectify concrete ideas.

*Stevens, Halsey. *The Life and Music of Bela Bartók.* New York: Oxford University Press, 1964. This most important work on Bartók in English is divided into two sections: a biographical study and a categorized, subjective analysis of his music. Extensive notes, a chronological list of works, and a revised bibliography are appended.

PART VII

*Amram, David. *Vibrations.* New York: Viking, 1971.

A composer and musicologist of wide-ranging interests, the author explores, through the medium of personal reminiscence, the meeting between jazz, street music, rock and classical music to produce a form unique to the 1960s and '70s. Absorbing in its evocation of period and personality, the book has been highly praised by major contemporary writers. Illustrated.

Chase, Gilbert. *America's Music.* New York: McGraw-Hill, 1966.

A comprehensive and widely ranging survey of American music from colonial times through the 1960s. Of particular interest in the extensive section on the twentieth century is the final chapter, "The Scene in the Sixties."

*Cohn, Nik. *Rock From the Beginning.* New York: Stein and Day, 1969.

One of the best histories written of rock music, this wide-ranging, fast-paced book covers the rock movement from its beginnings in the 1950s to 1969. Sensitive to personalities and technique, Cohn organizes a large mass of material into a coherent, readable narrative.

*Copland, Aaron. *The New Music: 1900–1960.* New York: W. W. Norton, 1969.

A collection of essays on important stylistic trends and composers in Europe and America. The American section, largely devoted to individual composers, includes chapters on Ives, Harris, and Thomson.

*Cowell, Henry and Sidney Cowell. *Charles Ives and His Music.* New York: Oxford University Press, 1955.

The standard biography of Ives to date, written by two close friends of the composer. Approximately half the book is devoted to a study of Ives' musical style and major works with many quotations from the composer that are not found elsewhere.

Dobrin, Arnold. *Aaron Copland: His Life and Times.* New York: Crowell, 1967.

A short biographical sketch, including general discussion of the composer's ideas and musical activities.

*Eisen, Jonathan, ed. *The Age of Rock: Sounds of the American Cultural Revolution.* New York: Vintage, 1969.

An anthology, dedicated to the late folk-rock composer Richard Fariña, of vivid and reflective writings on various aspects of the rock scene. Includes thirty-eight articles by, among others, Nat Hentoff, Ralph J. Gleason, and Tom Wolfe. Illustrated.

*Garland, Phyl. *The Sound of Soul: The History of Black Music.* New York: Pocket Books, 1971.

A detailed, sensitive study of the roots and forms of black music in America, by the New York editor of *Ebony* magazine. A masterfully stated discussion of the music of the early years serves as a prelude to a more extended treatment of the major "soul" singers of recent years. With thirty-two pages of photographs.

*Hitchcock, H. Wiley. *Music in the United States: A Historical Introduction.* Englewood Cliffs, N. J.: Prentice-Hall, 1969.

An excellent and concise survey of American music. Particularly fine are the chapters on nineteenth-century popular music and Charles Ives.

*Hodeir, André. *Jazz: Its Evolution and Essence.* New York: Grove Press, 1956.

A classic, scholarly, and idiosyncratic treatment of developments in jazz, by a celebrated French musicologist. Discusses in technical detail jazz traditions from African origins to the death of Charlie Parker.

*Ives, Charles. *Essays Before a Sonata, the Majority, and Other Writings.* Selected and edited by Howard Boatwright. New York: W. W. Norton, 1970.

A collection of Ives' writings on music, philosophy, and politics. The "Essays" were written to accompany his Second Piano Sonata, the "Concord."

Lowens, Irving. *Music and Musicians in Early America.* New York: W. W. Norton, 1964.

A delightfully written collection of short studies concentrating on the colonial and Federalist periods. Of particular interest are the essays "The Origins of the American Fuguing-Tune" and "Our First Matinee Idol: Louis Moreau Gottschalk.

Machlis, Joseph. *American Composers of Our Time.* New York: Crowell, 1963.

Short, interesting vignettes on the lives and musical activities of sixteen American composers, ranging from Edward MacDowell to Lukas Foss.

Mellers, Wilfrid. *Music in a New Found Land.* New York: Alfred A. Knopf, 1965.

A British music critic and historian explores various aspects of American music, dividing his attention between popular (jazz, blues, the Broadway musical) and art styles. Important composers discussed include Ives, Ruggles, Copland, Carter, Varèse, Cage, Barber, and Foss.

*Shapiro, Nat, and Nat Hentoff. *Hear Me Talkin' to Ya.* New York: Dover, 1966.

Reprint of a classic 1955 collection of first-person reminiscences by many major figures from the richest years of jazz history. Presents a vivid, kaleidoscopic picture, as seen from the inside, of America's most distinctive contribution to world music.

*Williams, Martin. *The Jazz Tradition.* New York: Mentor, 1971.

A clear and vivid narrative of developments in jazz from the early 1920s through the 1960s. Through sketches of leading jazz figures from Jelly Roll Morton through Ornette Coleman, the author discusses their techniques, idioms, and the musical and social worlds which shaped and in turn were shaped by them. A valuable short introduction places the subject in the context of Western musical culture.

PART VIII

The most important source of information on contemporary music is periodical literature. Two significant periodicals devoted to contemporary and avant-garde composition are *Perspectives of New Music* (published by Princeton University Press) and *Die Reihe* ("The Row," a German periodical, published in translation by Theodore Presser Co.). While many of the articles in these publications are highly technical, both periodicals act as forums for the presentation and discussion of the latest ideas in composition. Well-known composers are frequent contributors. Other periodicals devoting attention to the latest musical trends include *The Score* (London), the *Journal of Music Theory* (New Haven), and the *Musical Quarterly* (New York).

"The New Music—its Sources, its Sounds, its Creators." *High Fidelity,* Vol. XVIII, No. 9 (September, 1968).

A general survey of avant-garde trends in the early sixties, with comments by the composers themselves.

Babbitt, Milton. "Who Cares if You Listen?" *High Fidelity,* Vol. VIII, No. 2 (February, 1958).

A personal and unusual statement by one of America's most influential composers defending his concepts of an esoteric and "cerebral" style of composition.

———."The Revolution in Sound: Electronic Music." *University, A Princeton Magazine,* Vol. IV (April 22, 1960).

A clear discussion, in relatively nontechnical terms, of the use of the synthesizer in composing electronic music.

Cage, John. *Silence.* Cambridge, Mass.: M.I.T. Press, 1966.

A collection of writings on experimental music, techniques of composition, and other miscellaneous topics. It is an invaluable source for the author's ideas on music of chance. Among the most interesting essays are "Forerunners of Modern Music," and "History of Experimental Music in the United States."

*Lang, Paul Henry and Nathan Broder, eds. *Contemporary Music in Europe: A Comprehensive Survey.* New York: W. W. Norton, 1965.

Originally published as the fiftieth anniversary issue of the *Musical Quarterly,* Vol. LI, No. 1 (1965), this group of essays discusses postwar musical trends in each of the major European countries.

*Salzman, Eric. *Twentieth-Century Music: An Introduction.* Englewood Cliffs, New Jersey: Prentice-Hall, 1967.

This excellent and concise survey includes valuable chapters on avant-garde music through the early sixties.

GENERAL READING LIST

Cannon, Beekman C., Alvin H. Johnson, and William G. Waite. *The Art of Music, A Short History of Musical Styles and Ideas.* New York: Crowell, 1960.

A general introduction to the background of music for readers with little musical background.

Crocker, Richard L. *A History of Musical Style.* New York: McGraw-Hill, 1966.

Emphasis on the evolution of characteristic musical styles within major historical periods; contains many analyses of musical works, with concise discussions of forms and techniques of composition.

Einstein, Alfred. *A Short History of Music.* New York: Vintage Books, 1954.

Long recognized as one of the best concise histories of music, this work is a nontechnical chronological survey of important composers and musical genres from the Middle Ages through the nineteenth century. No musical analyses are included. (Also available in paperback.)

Grout, Donald Jay. *A History of Western Music.* New York: W. W. Norton, 1960.

An excellent college-level text, with thorough coverage of European music from the end of antiquity through the early twentieth century. The sections on Baroque and Classical music are particularly good.

Kinsky, Georg. *A History of Music in Pictures.* New York: Dover, 1951.

The standard one-volume pictorial history of music, arranged chronologically from antiquity to the early twentieth century. The pictures include musicians' portraits, music in art works, facsimiles of early music, and plates of early instruments.

Lange, Paul Henry. *Music in Western Civilization.* New York: W. W. Norton, 1941.

A highly influential work, the book discusses music in the context of political, cultural, and social trends in Western civilization from ancient Greece through the nineteenth century.

Glossary

A Capella Designating choral music without instrumental accompaniment.

Accidentals Signs used in musical notation to indicate or cancel out chromatic alterations. The sharp (♯) raises a pitch by one half step, the flat (♭) lowers it by one half-step, the natural (♮) cancels out any of the other signs.

Aleatory Music, Chance Music Music in which the composer introduces unpredictable elements into either the composition or the performance of a work. In composition, for example, pitches may be chosen by the throw of dice; in performance, players may be allowed to play or not play certain sections of a work at will.

Antiphonal Singing or playing in responsive or alternating parts. Originally the term applied to chant sung by alternating choruses; it is also applied to polyphonic music for two or more performing groups.

Aria A composition for solo voice and instrumental accompaniment. The da capo aria, developed in Italy during the late Baroque period, is in ternary form (A B A), with the repeat of A indicated by the designation da capo at the end of section B.

Arioso A vocal style that is midway between recitative and aria; its rhythm is determined by musical as well as textual considerations. Its meter is less flexible than that of recitative, but its form is much simpler and more flexible than that of the aria.

Arpeggio A broken chord. A chord whose tones are played one after another rather than simultaneously.

Atonality The absence of tonality. Atonal music does not have a recognizable tonal center, or tonic. The development of atonal music began in the late nineteenth century and is clearly seen in the works of Arnold Schoenberg prior to his development of the twelve-tone technique.

Basso Continuo, Continuo Continuous bass. A bass part performed by (1) a keyboard player who improvises harmony above the given bass notes, and (2) a string player—usually cello or viola da gamba—who reinforces the bass line. This accompanimental practice, first developed by composers of the monodic style (ca. 1600), was universally adopted for both vocal and instrumental music in the Baroque era. See also *figured bass*.

Basso Ostinato See *ground bass*.

Bel Canto "Beautiful song." Italian vocal technique of the eighteenth and early nineteenth centuries, developed primarily in opera; it emphasized beauty of tone over dramatic expression.

Binary Form A basic musical form consisting of two contrasting sections (A B), both sections often being repeated (A A B B); both sections are related in terms of key, A usually beginning in the tonic and modulating to the dominant, B beginning in the dominant and modulating back to the tonic. If the A section is repeated, in whole or in part, at the end of B, the form is called rounded binary.

Bridge In a musical composition, a section that connects two themes; it often effects a modulation. In sonata-allegro form, it is used to link the first and second themes or theme groups in the exposition.

Cadence A harmonic or melodic formula coming at the end of a musical phrase, section, movement, or entire composition, which brings about a pause or full stop in momentum.

Cadenza A section of indeterminant length, in the style of a virtuosic improvisation, usually placed near the end of a movement of a concerto. In it, the solo performer is expected to demonstrate his technical mastery of the instrument. The cadenza originally was to be provided by the performer; however, beginning with Beethoven, composers in the nineteenth century began writing their own.

Canon A contrapuntal technique in which an extended melody in one part is strictly imitated in its entirety by another voice or voices. The imitating voices may begin on the same pitch as the initial voice (canon at the unison) or on another pitch (canon at the fifth above, the fourth below, etc.).

Chamber Music Music written for a small group of instruments, with one player to a part.

Chord A combination of three or more tones sounded simultaneously. See also *arpeggio*.

Chromatic Scale See *scale*.

Church Modes A system, originating in the Medieval period, of eight scales, each built on the tones of the modern C-major scale (the white keys found on the piano), but beginning and ending on the notes d, e, f, or g. To each of these notes are attached two modes. These scales form the tonal foundation for Gregorian chant and for polyphony up to the Baroque era, when modern scales and tonality came into existence.

Clef A sign placed at the beginning of a staff to

indicate the exact pitch of the notes.

Coda The concluding section of a musical work or individual movement, often leading to a final climax and coupled with an increase in tempo. In sonata-allegro form, the closing section following the recapitulation.

Consonance An interval, chord, or harmony that imparts a sense of stability, repose, or finality.

Continuo See *basso continuo.*

Counterpoint A musical texture consisting of two or more equal and independent melodic lines sounding simultaneously. See also *polyphony.*

Da Capo "From the beginning." Indicates that a piece is to be repeated in its entirety or to a point marked *fine* ("end"). Used most frequently in the Baroque aria and, in Classical music, at the end of the trio to a minuet, indicating that the latter is to be repeated following the trio.

Development In a general sense, the elaboration of musical material through various procedures such as altering the melodic and rhythmic contours of a theme, shifting the underlying harmony through successive chord and key changes, or restating melodies with varying tone colors and accompanimental patterns.

Dissonance An interval, chord, or harmony that gives a sense of tension and movement; this lack of stability implies resolution to a consonance.

Dodecaphony See *twelve-tone technique.*

Dominant The fifth note of a given scale; it is the note that most actively "seeks" or creates the expectation of the tonic note. The chord built on the fifth degree of the scale is called the dominant chord and creates the expectation of movement to the tonic chord.

Dynamics, Dynamic Level Terms that designate degrees of volume. The most common dynamic marks (and abbreviations) are, from soft to loud, pianissimo (pp); piano (p); mezzo piano (mp); mezzo forte (mf); forte (f); fortissimo (ff).

Exposition In sonata-allegro form, the first section containing the statement of the principal themes. In a fugue, the first section in which the principal theme or subject is presented imitatively.

Figured Bass, Thorough Bass A shorthand method of notating an accompanimental part; under the bass notes are placed numerical and other figures to indicate the principal intervals and chords to be sounded above the bass notes. See also *basso continuo.*

Flat (♭) See *accidentals.*

Frequency, Frequency of Vibration The rate at which a sounding body vibrates. The pitch of a tone depends upon the frequency of the vibrations that produce it.

Fugue A type of imitative polyphony based on the development of a single theme or subject. The subject is stated at the beginning by one voice alone, then imitated by other voices; following this exposition of the subject, a contrapuntal development takes place.

Ground Bass, Basso Ostinato A short melodic phrase that is repeated continually as a bass line, above which one or more voices have contrasting material.

Homophony A musical texture in which one voice predominates melodically, the other parts blending into an accompaniment providing harmonic support; it is the opposite of polyphony, in which all parts are of equal significance. The term is also applied to music in which all parts move in the same rhythm; this texture is often designated as "chordal style" or "note-against-note" texture.

Imitation The repetition, in close succession, of a melody by another voice or voices within a contrapuntal texture. Imitation is most consistently employed in the canon.

Interval Designates the distance in pitch between any two tones; intervals are counted in steps, including both tones. For example, the interval between the notes c and d is a second, between c and e, a third,

Key Signature The group of sharps or flats placed at the beginning of each staff to indicate which notes are to be raised or lowered one-half step. Each particular combination of sharps or flats also indicates the key of a composition.

Ledger Lines Short horizontal lines added above or below the staff to indicate notes that are too high or too low to be placed within the staff.

Legato "Linked, tied"; indicates a smooth, even style or performance, with no noticeable interruption between the notes.

Leitmotiv "Leading motive." A compositional technique, primarily used in operas, in which particular characters, objects, ideas, and emotional states are represented by short musical motives. The technique was most extensively and consistently developed by Richard Wagner in his later operas.

Major Diatonic Scale See *scale.*

Meter The pattern of fixed, regularly recurring pulses, called beats, by which music is regulated in time. Groups of beats are indicated by bar lines that mark off measures. See also *time signature.*

Metronome A clockwork apparatus that sounds

regular clicks (beats) at adjustable speeds; it is used to set the exact tempo of a musical work.

Minor Diatonic Scale   See *scale.*

Mode   See *church modes.*

Modulation   Harmonic movement from one key to another within a composition.

Monodic Style   Designates a type of accompanied solo song that evolved in Italy around 1600 in reaction to the complex polyphonic style of the late Renaissance. Its principal characteristics are (1) a recitativelike vocal line, (2) an arioso with basso continuo accompaniment.

Monophony   A musical texture consisting of a single melodic line without accompanying material, as in Gregorian chant.

Motif, Motive   A short melodic or rhythmic figure that reappears frequently throughout a work or section of a work as a unifying device.

Musique Concrète   Concrete music. A musical style originating in France about 1948; its technique consists of recording natural or "concrete" sounds, altering the sounds by various electronic means, and then combining them into organized pieces.

Octave   The most basic and perfect musical interval; its perfection results from the fact that the upper tone gives the impression of duplicating the lower tone at a higher pitch level (octave quality).

Pedal Point   A long-held tone, usually in the bass, sounding through changing harmonies in other parts. Frequently used in organ music and as a device in fugal writing.

Phrase   A musical unit, consisting of several measures, which corresponds to a sentence in speech.

Pitch   The location of musical tones, in terms of "high" and "low." The pitch of a tone is determined by the frequency of vibration of the sounding body.

Pizzicato   A performance technique in which stringed instruments are plucked with the fingers instead of bowed.

Polyphony   Many voices. A texture combining two or more independent melodies heard simultaneously; generally synonymous with counterpoint. The term polyphony is used in contrast with monophony and homophony in classifying different types of textures.

Polyrhythm   Highly contrasted rhythmic patterns sounding simultaneously in different voice parts of a musical texture.

Program Music   Music that relies for its inspiration on a nonmusical idea, this idea often being stated in the title or in an explanatory program note. The "program" may be poetic, descriptive in a pictorial sense, expressive of human emotions, or may rely on imitation of natural sounds (bird calls, thunderstorms, flowing water).

Recapitulation   See *sonata-allegro form.*

Recitative   A form of "singing speech" in which the rhythm is dictated by the natural inflection of the words. Two main types evolved in the Baroque era: recitativo secco, in which the vocal part is sung to a basso continuo accompaniment only; and recitativo accompagnato or stromentato, in which the voice is accompanied by a larger instrumental ensemble.

Scale   The arrangement of adjacent tones in an order of ascending or descending pitches. The two basic scales employed in Western music are (1) the major diatonic scale, in which the octave is divided into five whole steps(W) and two half steps (H) arranged $W\ W\ H\ W\ W\ W\ H$; (2) the minor diatonic scale, in which the same number of whole and half steps is arranged $W\ H\ W\ W\ H\ W\ W$. Other scales commonly employed are the chromatic scale, in which the octave is divided into twelve consecutive half steps; the whole-tone scale, in which the octave is divided into six consecutive whole steps; the pentatonic scale, consisting of five tones.

Semitone, Half Step   One half of a whole step; the smallest interval in traditional Western music.

Sequence   The repetition, in the same voice part, of a musical motive or phrase at different pitch levels.

Serialism, Serial Music   Music organized on the basis of sets determining pitch, duration, dynamics, and timbre.

Sharp   See *accidentals.*

Simple Meter   See *meter.*

Singspiel   A form of comic opera, developed in eighteenth-century Germany, that employed spoken dialogue interspersed with musical movements.

Sonata-Allegro Form   A musical form consisting of three sections: exposition, development, and recapitulation—the last often followed by a coda. In the exposition, two themes or groups of themes are presented in contrasting keys, linked by a bridge passage, which modulates from one key to the other. In the development, these themes—or portions of them—are elaborated in various ways; in the recapitulation, the basic scheme of the exposition is repeated with certain modifications. In most early examples of this form, the exposition is stated twice.

Sounding Body, Elastic Body   The source of audio vibrations. A sounding body may be a solid, like a violin or guitar string, or a gas, like an air column in a trumpet or organ pipe. See also *frequency*.

Staccato "Detached"; indicates a highly articulated style of performance in which each note is played in a short, crisp manner.

Staff A graph, consisting of five lines and four intermediate spaces, on which music is notated.

Stretto A type of imitation in which repetitions of a theme occur in rapid time intervals, each successive voice entering before the phrase is completed in the previous voice; usually employed in fugues or fugal textures.

Stromentato See *recitative*.

Strophic Designating a song in which all verses of text are sung to the same music, in contrast to a through-composed song, in which new music is supplied for each successive verse.

Subject In a fugue, the principal theme, introduced first in a single voice and then imitated in other voices, returning frequently during the course of the composition.

Syncopation A deliberate disturbance of normal metrical pulse.

Tempo The rate of speed at which a composition is or should be played. It is indicated by tempo marks such as allegro, andante, presto, or by reference to metronome timings.

Ternary Form A basic musical form consisting of three sections, A B A, the final A section being a repetition or slight variation of the first.

Texture Designates the relationship between the horizontal or successive and vertical or simultaneous aspects of a piece of music. The principal classifications are monophony, homophony, and polyphony.

Theme A musical idea that serves as a starting point for development of a composition or section of a composition. See also *sonata-allegro form and variations*.

Thorough-Bass See *figured bass*.

Through-Composed Term applied to songs in which new music has been composed for each successive verse, in contrast to strophic songs, in which all verses are sung to the same melody.

Time Signature A numerical sign placed at the beginning of a composition to indicate the meter. The upper number designates the number of beats per measure; the lower number designates the unit of measurement equivalent to a beat (half note, quarter note).

Tonality The character of a musical composition as determined by the relationship of tones to a central tone called the keynote or the tonic.

Tone Color The characteristic quality, or "color," of a musical sound as produced on a specific instrument or combination of instruments.

Tone Poem, Symphonic Poem A type of orchestral music, developed in the nineteenth century, that is based upon an extramusical idea—often literary or descriptive in a pictorial sense. A highly developed species of program music, it is usually in one-movement form.

Tone Row See *twelve-tone technique*.

Tonic The tonal center. The tone which acts as a musical home base, or point of rest and finality in a piece of music.

Transpose To move a melodic pattern from one set of pitches to another, while keeping the interval relationships among the pitches unchanged.

Trill A rapid alternation between adjacent tones.

Twelve-Tone Technique, Dodecaphony A system of composition developed by Arnold Schoenberg. It consists of arranging the twelve pitches of the chromatic scale in a particular order (known as a tone row, or series, or set) chosen by the composer. The row may be transposed to any pitch level, used upside down (inversion), backward (retrograde), or upside down and backward (retrograde inversion); but no pitch may be repeated until the other eleven have appeared. The content of a musical work derives from variations of the row or portions of it.

Variations, Variation Form A musical form in which a theme is stated and then subjected to a number of modifications, each of these constituting a "variation." The most frequently employed of the numerous variation techniques are those (1) in which the melody itself is ornamented in different ways; (2) in which new harmonies are applied to the original melody; and (3) in which new melodies are invented to go with the original harmonic scheme.

Verismo An Italian operatic point of view, developed during the late nineteenth century, in which the idealistic or romantic plots of earlier operas were rejected in favor of realistic subjects taken from everyday, often lower-class, life.

Index

Index

3.30

ROMANTIC

MUSICAL EVENTS	DATES	COMPOSERS
Wagner's *Oper und Drama* (1851)	1850	Franz Liszt (1811–1886)
Wagner's *Tristan und Isolde* (1859)		Richard Wagner (1813–1883)
	1870	Giuseppe Verdi (1813–1901)
		Bedřich Smetana (1824–1884)
		Anton Bruckner (1824–1896)
		Stephen Foster (1826–1864)
First Wagner Festival held at Bayreuth (1876)	1875	Johannes Brahms (1833–1897)
Edison invents the phonograph (1877)		Alexander Borodin (1834–1887)
		Georges Bizet (1838–1875)
		Modest Moussorgsky (1839–1881)
		Peter Ilyich Tchaikovsky (1840–1893)
New York Metropolitan Opera founded (1883)		Antonín Dvořák (1841–1904)
Development of French Impressionistic music		Giacomo Puccini (1858–1924)
		Gustav Mahler (1860–1911)
		Edward MacDowell (1861–1908)
		Richard Strauss (1864–1949)

TWENTIETH CENTURY

MUSICAL EVENTS	DATES	COMPOSERS
	1900	Gabriel Fauré (1845–1924)
Debussy's *Prélude à l'après-midi d'un faune* (1876)		Claude Achille Debussy (1862–1918)
		Jean Sibelius (1865–1957)
		Erik Satie (1866–1925)
German Expressionism, represented chiefly by		Ralph Vaughan Williams (1872–1958)
Schönberg and Berg, developed before the First		Arnold Schönberg (1874–1951)
World War		Charles Ives (1874–1954)
		Maurice Ravel (1875–1937)
Stravinsky's *Rite of Spring* (1913)		Ottorino Respighi (1879–1936)
		Béla Bartók (1881–1945)
		Igor Stravinsky (1882–1971)
Schönberg announces his method of composing with		Zoltán Kodály (1882–1967)
twelve tones (1922)		Anton von Webern (1883–1945)
		Charles T. Griffes (1884–1920)
		Alban Berg (1885–1935)
American jazz heavily influences European composers	1925	Edgard Varèse (1885–1965)
in the 1920s		Sergei Prokofiev (1891–1953)
		Darius Milhaud (b. 1892)
		Paul Hindemith (1895–1963)
		Virgil Thomson (b. 1896)
		George Gershwin (1898–1937)
Many European composers emigrate to the United		Roy Harris (b. 1898)
States during the 1930s and early 1940s, including		Aaron Copland (b. 1900)
Schönberg, Stravinsky, Hindemith, and Bartók		Dimitri Shostakovich (b. 1906)
		Olivier Messiaen (b. 1908)
		Elliott Carter (b. 1908)
		Samuel Barber (b. 1910)
Early experiments in electronic music; development of		William Schuman (b. 1910)
musique concrète in Paris (1948)		John Cage (b. 1912)
		Benjamin Britten (b. 1913)
		Milton Babbitt (b. 1916)
American experiments in electronic music at Columbia	1950	Lukas Foss (b. 1922)
University (1952)		Pierre Boulez (b. 1925)
John Cage develops aleatory music in the 1950s		Gunther Schuller (b. 1925)
		Karlheinz Stockhausen (b. 1928)